Domestic Arrangements

Domestic Arrangements

A Novel by NORMA KLEIN

M. EVANS AND COMPANY, INC.
New York

Thanks are due to the following for permission to use the material included.

Epigraph: a selection from *Shine On, Bright and Dangerous Object* by Laurie Colwin. Copyright © 1975 by Laurie Colwin. Reprinted by permission of Viking Penguin Inc.

Selected lyrics from "Old Friend," © 1978 Fiddleback Music Publishing Company Inc. A Tommy Valando Publication. Music by Nancy Ford. Lyrics by Gretchen Cryer. From the show *I'm Getting My Act Together and Taking It on the Road.*

"She's Leaving Home" by John Lennon and Paul McCartney. Copyright © 1967 Northern Songs Limited. All rights for the U.S.A., Mexico, and the Philippines controlled by Maclen Music, Inc. c/o ATV Music Corporation. Used by permission. All rights reserved.

"now-times for people with now-dreams" by Jennifer Fleissner.

Library of Congress Cataloging in Publication Data

Klein, Norma, 1938-
  Domestic arrangements.

  SUMMARY: An unusual New York family deals with their
14-year-old daughter's success as a nymphet film actress
and with her first affair, their 16-year-old daughter's
wish to have one, and the breakup of the parents'
marriage.

  [1. Family life—Fiction]   I. Title.
PS3561.L35D6   [813'.54]   80-28476

ISBN 0-87131-343-X

M. Evans and Company, Inc.
216 East 49 Street
New York, New York 10017

Manufactured in the United States of America

9 8 7 6 5 4 3 2 1

In memory of Henry Robbins

What arrangements people construct in the name of love
are as formal and artful as any other product of human
devotion. You figured them out as you went along, with an
eye toward grace, as if you were writing a sonata, and
the sense that propelled you was the goodness of the thing.

Shine On, Bright and Dangerous Object
LAURIE COLWIN

Chapter One

Daddy was livid at breakfast.

I knew he would be. What I was hoping was that he'd sleep late, which he usually does. Mornings are usually kind of hectic around our house; everyone gets up at a different time. Delia and I go to different schools—I've been at Hunter since I was five, but poor Deel has shifted around lots of times. First she was at Columbia Grammar, but she didn't like it and didn't have that many friends so Mom put her in Bank Street, which was okay except it ended in 8th grade. Now she's at Riverdale, which she likes except she's failing Math and getting C's, which gets Daddy hysterical because he always had his heart set on Deel going to Harvard, like he did.

Mornings in our house usually go like this. I get up at 5:45. That sounds dumb and even crazy to a lot of people since I don't have to be in school till 9:00, but I like having time to myself in the morning. What I do is get up, have breakfast—a toasted bagel with butter and honey and a glass of milk—and then go back to bed. By then I'm dressed, but I just kind of lie there, thinking about things. If I don't have that, if I oversleep and have to rush off to school, I miss it. Meanwhile Deel is still in bed. She always tells me to wake her up at 7:00, but when

I do, when I go into her room and poke her, she starts mumbling and grumbling and pulls the covers over her head. Deel is strange that way. She often actually *sleeps* with the covers pulled completely over her head. Then, at 7:30, she suddenly bounds out of bed and starts screaming at me for not waking her up early enough! Her school is way uptown—it takes her 45 minutes to get there—and mine is just across the park. The only bad thing for me is when the bus is so crowded I can't even get on and have to walk through the park. That's only happened a couple of times, though.

Mom's schedule varies. Usually she sleeps late and I don't even *see* her in the morning. That's because she has an erratic schedule, depending on whether she has to go for a shooting or an audition or something. What she does for a living is act in television commercials. Deel thinks it's gross that Mom appears in all these really sexist commercials like the one where she's inside a huge roll of toilet paper with just her head and arms and legs poking out and a man comes along and squeezes her and says, "Hey, you're softer than the one I have at home." But Mom says she made enough off that one commercial alone to pay for one year of Deel's school and that once Deel is out in the real world she'll stop being such a snot nose and learn to compromise a little. Deel says she never will. Mom is quite sexy for a mother. She's really tall, five-ten—about two inches taller than Daddy, even more with heels—and she has bright red-blond hair. I guess I shouldn't reveal this, but that's not her real hair color. Her real hair color is brown, but when she was doing a Broadway musical in her twenties she had to play a role called Carrot Top, so she dyed it and everyone said how sexy it looked and she's done it ever since. Her main problem is that she has to dye her eyebrows too or she'll look weird. Mom's main assets as an actress are her legs, which are really long, and her smile. She has a kind of big mouth and her teeth are parted a little in the middle (just like mine) but directors like that. They think it looks engaging and natural so she's never had it corrected.

Daddy is usually just about getting up at 8:15, which is when I leave. He comes into the kitchen in his jogging suit—it's a leisure suit, really, which Mom's brother got him; he doesn't actually jog—and gets out his juice and Product 19. Poor Daddy has gotten a little bit plump—he's *always* on a diet. I know what he weighs—169—and what he wants to weigh is 155 like he used to. His problem is noshing. He's usually good until after dinner when he sometimes reads or watches TV and sneaks into the kitchen for little snacks. Daddy has an office he goes to—he's a filmmaker and does things like figure out projects and try to raise the money, and then, if he does, he directs them. They're usually documentaries about serious things. You might have seen the one he did about this man who was dying of cancer: "Death Rites." That was on TV five years ago and it won an Emmy. Daddy's quite a serious person in general. He takes everything very hard, which is probably why he got so hysterical last night when he found Joshua and me fucking in the bathroom at four in the morning.

"We have to talk about this," he started saying as I was going to get my knapsack.

"Daddy, I'll be late for school," I said. I started getting into my coat.

Mom had gotten up, which is unusual for her. Maybe Daddy had told her about what happened. She was wearing one of her sexy nightgowns, the tiger-skin one with the plunging neckline, and her hair was all rumpled the way it usually is in the morning. "Darling, *please*," she said, taking Daddy's arm. "There's plenty of time to talk about it this evening. Why make her late for school?"

Daddy whirled around. "You're treating this like some trivial, irrelevant incident," he yelled. "This is our *daughter!*"

"It is?" Mom said wryly. "Gee, you could've fooled me."

Daddy hates it when Mom horses around about things he thinks are serious. "Okay," he said, sighing heavily. "Nothing matters. Our children don't matter, the state of the world doesn't matter . . . it's all just one big, delightful joke."

"Sweetie," Mom drawled in her soothing voice (she comes from Kentucky and doesn't have a southern accent at all, except, as she says, "when it's helpful"), "I'm just saying why wreck everyone's day by making a huge scene at eight in the morning? Tat'll explain everything to us tonight, won't you, hon?"

I smiled at Mom. Mom's my ally, she's always on my side. I can count on her. "Sure," I said, swallowing. Actually, I'm not sure I *have* a very good explanation, but maybe I can think of one during the day.

"You come *right* home after school," Daddy yelled at me as I went out the door. "No fooling around. Straight home!"

Fooling around? What did he mean? Basically, they've been after Deel this year not to "fool around" after school, meaning go to some friend's house and smoke pot. Some of our friends' parents don't mind if they smoke pot at home. Some of our friends' parents don't mind *what* they do. Like Gina's parents. Her mother says that as long as they're going to do it, why not do it at home? That sounds so *sensible*. When I'm a parent, that's what I'm going to tell my children.

Joshua's not in my school. He goes to Stuyvesant. Actually, he used to go to Riverdale and was friendly with some kids Deel hung around with. That's how we first met. He came over with some of Deel's friends one afternoon, and we kind of hit it off. The boys in my class are just not that great. I mean, they're okay, but nothing to write home about. I guess 14-year-old boys just aren't that, well, polished or suave. Suave's sort of the wrong word—Joshua's not suave, exactly. But he's just more—you can talk to him about things. He's more laid back. You don't have to worry that he's going to just lunge at you all the time. Like with sex. He says he wants *me* to enjoy it too. I like it when boys are considerate that way. Joshua's such a nice *person*, which is why the whole thing with Daddy is so ironical. I mean, it wasn't even Joshua's *fault* he stayed so late last night. It was mine. *I* was the one who suggested it. That's why I really hope I haven't gotten him into trouble. I just pray Daddy doesn't call up his parents or do something unspeakably gross like that.

This is what happened. I might as well tell you so you'll know the facts because Daddy's version will make it sound all lurid and hideous and it wasn't at all.

The deal I have with Mom and Daddy is this: on weekdays I have a curfew of 10:00 and on vacations and weekends 1:00. Actually, it's Daddy more than Mom who sets the rules. He's more of a rule person, if you know what I mean. Mom always says you have to make up your own rules, which gets Daddy mad; I guess he thinks she's setting a bad example for us by saying things like that. Last night was a Sunday so usually

Mom and Daddy would have been home, but this particular Sunday Mom's college roommate, Angela Weitzman, had invited them to dinner. Daddy hates Angela Weitzman, partly because she lives way out in Connecticut someplace, which is an hour's drive both ways, and also because her husband is a gynecologist who breeds horses. Daddy says he's a Philistine and a bore, and he wishes Mom would meet Angela for lunch and not force him to go out there. Mom says it's only once a year and Angela would be hurt if she had the feeling Daddy didn't like her. "She loves you, Lionel," Mom'll say to Daddy. "She wishes Herman was like you, she's always saying that." "Well, she should have married me then," Daddy will say. "Why didn't she?" "Because *I* got to you first, sweetie, that's why," Mom'll say. Mom can usually get around Daddy and get him into a good mood, even if he wasn't in one to begin with.

I knew that if they were going to the Weitzmans' they'd never be back till way after midnight, so I guess I wasn't that worried about when Joshua would leave. He stayed for dinner and we had linguine with this really good pesto sauce that Mom bought last week at Pasta and Cheese. It's all green and garlicky, but I figured if we both had it, it wouldn't matter so much if I reeked of garlic. Then we studied a bit and then we fucked and then we fell asleep. We both just fell *sound* asleep. Mom and Daddy got home around two. I was still sleeping at that point, but Joshua had gotten up and gone to the bathroom. When he heard Mom and Daddy come home, he figured he'd better stay in there till they were safely asleep. So he waited around half an hour till everything was quiet.

At that point I woke up. I saw that Joshua wasn't in bed with me and didn't know what had happened. I went to the bathroom and there he was, poor thing, sitting in the bathtub all wrapped up in a big orange bath towel, reading *Lord of the Flies* (he has to do a book report on it for school). I got in the bathtub with him and we began to kind of horse around. I suddenly realized I hadn't even washed my hair, which I usually do Sunday night. Joshua said he'd help me wash it, so we took a shower together. Then we got out and began drying each other off and, well, one thing kind of led to another. We didn't want to go back to my room because we were a little scared about

Mom and Daddy so we did it in the bathtub, which wasn't that bad. We spread out a lot of towels and turned the portable heater on. It was really quite cozy and comfortable.

Right while we were, like, in the middle of doing it, suddenly the door rattled. "Who is it?" I called out.

"It's me," Daddy said. "What are you doing in there, Tati?"

"I'm just washing my hair, Daddy."

"Do you know what *time* it is? It's almost three in the morning! Don't you have school tomorrow?"

"Yeah," I said breathlessly. It was a little hard to talk with Joshua lying right on top of me. "I'll be out soon, I'm almost done."

Then Joshua got out of me. We figured the mood had been spoiled, sort of, and there'd be other times. I wrapped myself up in a towel and slowly unlocked the bathroom door. Joshua was still in the bathtub, huddled up in the towels, but the shower curtain was all around him like a tent. Daddy was standing in the hallway in his pajamas, looking angry.

"It was crucial that you wash your hair at three in the morning?" Daddy said.

"It just felt kind of itchy," I said. "You know. It was bothering me. I couldn't sleep." I smiled at him, hoping to change the subject. "Did you have a good time at your party?" I said cheerfully.

Just then Joshua sneezed. He'd had a cold about two weeks ago, but was over it mostly. But I guess lying there with all those damp towels must have started it up again. Daddy looked at me sternly. "What was that?"

I shrugged my shoulders like I had no idea and hadn't even heard anything.

Daddy went into the bathroom and pulled aside the shower curtain. There was poor Joshua, his hair all wet, cringing in the back of the bathtub. "All right," Daddy said. "This is it. I don't want to hear one word of explanation. I want you out of here in precisely ten minutes or I'm calling your parents right this minute."

Joshua rushed naked back into my room and got dressed in about one second. He tried saying, "It wasn't Rusty's fault, Mr. Engelberg. See, I had this term paper to do so we—"

"I said out and I mean out," Daddy said, pointing. "Go!"

"Daddy," I said after Joshua had gone. "We just fell asleep, that's all. Joshua had a really bad virus two weeks ago and he just lay down and—"

"As a first step," Daddy said, "I'm calling his parents tomorrow morning. Don't they know where their children *are* at night? Don't they *care?*"

"Daddy, *please* don't call his parents," I begged. "It'll never happen again. Really."

"Tat," Daddy said, looking at me gravely, "I've always trusted you. As you know I believe in trust between parents and children. I'm just saddened, more than anything else, not so much shocked as saddened, at the way you've taken advantage of that trust."

I looked up at him mournfully. "I'm sorry, Daddy. Really."

Usually if I look up at Daddy that way and kind of lean against him, he softens, but this time he just said stiffly, "We'll talk about this in the morning. I don't think you realize how serious—"

I lay in bed worrying about Daddy calling Joshua's parents. Would he do such a sick, awful thing? Daddy can be nice. He's really not a mean person, despite what I might have made him sound like here. I mean, he really wants what's best for us. It's just that things have changed so much since he was my age and he can't understand that. He says he tries to, but he just can't. Mom's always saying that Daddy's views about women are straight out of the 50s when women were supposed to be virgins and men were allowed to screw around and do whatever they wanted. "If those were the good old days, you can have them," she says. Actually, Joshua's father is not that different, though I don't especially think he and Daddy would get along. Joshua's parents live in this really fancy duplex on Park Avenue. That's because Joshua's father, whose name is Patrick Lasker, is a lawyer who makes a lot of money on divorce cases. That's how he met Joshua's mother, in fact. She was trying to get a divorce from the person she was married to, John someone, who drank, and she went to Joshua's father and I guess they liked each other so much, Joshua's father decided to get divorced too. So they got married and had Joshua and his two brothers.

Joshua hates his father; he calls him Patricia behind his back.

He says that he has girl friends and is seedy and gross in all sorts of ways. He's sort of tall with thick, long grayish hair and glasses and he always wears turtlenecks with this funny pendant around his neck. Joshua thinks he looks like a fag. Joshua's mother is this little sort of nervous-looking woman who works in charities and is worried because Joshua's oldest brother took a year off from college and is traveling around Europe, playing the guitar. She's afraid he'll never come back.

I know Mom and Daddy would *hate* Joshua's parents. Daddy has this thing about people who live on the East Side. He says they're all decadent and phony and he doesn't respect people who make a lot of money unless they do it by mistake, doing something worthwhile. Also, I know Mom would hate Joshua's parents' apartment. It's really elegant with lots of antiques and peach-colored carpets. It looks just like the apartments Mom sometimes points to in *House and Garden* and says, "God, don't you just want to *vomit!* How can people *live* like that?" I guess Mom thinks our apartment is nice and it is in a way. Mom doesn't "believe" in carpets so we just have bare wood floors and Indian rugs and lots of books. It's kind of messy. When I was sick in third grade after I had my tonsils out, my teacher came to visit me and she looked around as though she didn't know what to say. Finally she said, "My, this certainly looks very lived in."

All day at school I worried about Daddy calling Joshua's parents. What if they decide we can't see each other anymore? What if they set some horribly strict curfew like nine o'clock? What if Daddy says he thinks we're too young for sex?

I decided I better do what Daddy said and come straight home from school. So I didn't even go out for pizza with Shellie like I usually do. Deel has her math tutoring on Monday so she doesn't get home till six. Her tutor is this friendly old man who has around six cats and a huge tank of tropical fish. Deel likes animals a lot so they spend most of the time talking about animals. Maybe that's why she's still failing Math.

When I got home, the house was quiet. At first I thought no one was there. But when I went into the kitchen for a snack, there was Mom, sitting on a stool, reading a cookbook. "Oh, hi, sweets," she said, giving me a kiss. She was wearing her snakeskin jumpsuit. It's not really snakeskin, it's just velour patterned to look like that. Daddy doesn't like it, but he says he's learned to live with it. I love it. When I get tall enough, Mom says I can borrow it.

"Did he call Joshua's parents?" I said anxiously, taking down the Oreo cookies.

"Not yet."

"Is he going to?"

Mom sighed. "I'm afraid so."

"Oh Mom! I'm going to be so *humiliated* . . . couldn't you stop him?"

"Well, the second you were out the door, he was reaching for the phone, sputtering about statutory rape and that type of thing. I tried pointing out that it might be better if he called when he was a trifle calmer. *And* I also said that it was clear as day that whatever you were doing with Joshua, you were doing because you wanted to, so rape is scarcely a fitting—"

"*Then* what'd he say?"

"He said he'd wait and call Joshua's father at the office."

"Mom, Joshua is really a nice *person*."

"Darling, I *know!* I think he's a perfect sweetie . . . but that's really totally irrelevant."

"It is?"

"Basically . . . see, the thing is, what's bothering Lionel is that it's *you*, his little darling, having sex, and that totally freaks him out."

"Didn't he think I ever would?"

"Oh, he knew you would *eventually*, but he probably hoped you'd be like him and wait till college."

" 'When I was your age, my grandparents were still tucking me into bed'? That's a line from *Manhattan* that Woody Allen says to Mariel Hemingway; she's seventeen."

"Precisely."

"Would he feel just as bad if it were Deel?"

"Not quite, I don't think . . . Oh, it's *lots* of things, hon. It's complicated. There's one crucial fact that I think— An awful thing is about to happen to Lionel."

I felt scared. "What?"

"He'll be fifty in two weeks—five oh."

"So?"

"Well, to you fifty is fifty, nothing special. But to Lionel it's a whole big deal. It's half a *century*. It's, well, definitely middle age. It means time is running out."

"But what does that have to do with me and Joshua?"

"Well, here he sees you blooming, going forth into the world . . . and here *his* options are more and more limited. When you're young, you have a feeling you can conquer the world, anything can happen, and then it dribbles away bit by bit. It's been five *years* since he won the Emmy and nothing much has really worked out since then, so he's kind of in a general funk about everything. . . . He's gotten plump, poor thing."

"Yeah," I said, seeing what she meant.

"And then it's his whole relationship with you, Tat. He *adores* you. You're his little pet, his darling. Remember how the two of you used to go to photography shows on Saturdays or to screenings together? And to you it was such a big deal, such a wonderful surprise and treat. And now you wouldn't be seen dead with him."

I felt awful. "That's not true! That I wouldn't be seen *dead* with him!"

"Well, *you* know what I mean. Whenever he suggests something, you've made other plans. Before he was big, wonderful Daddy who knew everything and you looked up at him with those big, beautiful eyes and it made him feel terrific, and now . . . well, you're looking at Joshua that way."

"You mean he's jealous?"

"Sort of . . . Look, hon, the whole thing is as normal as blueberry pie, but when it strikes home, when it's *your* daughter, that's when it hurts."

"Poor Daddy." I sat down on a stool next to Mom and began eating some cookies.

"I know." Mom sighed. "Poor Lionel."

"Do you think there's something I could do to make him feel better . . . I mean, other than not seeing Joshua?"

Mom nodded. "You know, I was thinking, you remember how you and Deel used to give little parties for us when we had our birthdays? Well, I'm giving Lionel a surprise party when he turns fifty, but I thought if the two of you did it with me,

baked something nice, maybe made him some special present . . .
Remember how you used to make those collage calendars? Just
kind of make a fuss over him."

"Sure, I could do that."

"I mean, let's face it," Mom said. "Part of it there's nothing
you can do anything about. He just has to come to terms with it
himself. But I think if you kind of snuggled up to him, just a
touch, maybe—"

"Okay," I said. That sounded easy.

Just then the phone rang. Mom answered it. "Oh, hi! Yeah,
sure . . . what time *is* it again? Five thirty? Okay, well, what
should I do? Should I pick you up or what? Great, see you
then."

When Mom hung up the phone, she closed the cookbook.
"Hon, listen, I have to run, I'm going to have a drink with Simon.
I'll be back around six thirty, okay? See you!"

She ran off to get her coat.

Simon used to be Mom's director. It's really a sad story.
For four years Mom had this terrific job on a TV soap called
"The Way We Are Now." It was one of those gummy things
that are on from 2:00 to 3:00 every afternoon, but Mom's part
was really terrific. She was a kind of villain or villainess. That's
the kind of part Mom likes; she likes roles you can sink your teeth
into. She says she always hated ingenue roles, even when she
was young enough to play them, and now that she's thirty-nine,
she says she doesn't feel like trying to look ten years younger
than she is. Actually, Mom looks younger than she is anyway, but
I know what she means.

On TWWAN Mom played this woman named Myra who'd
had a really terrible childhood. Her uncle, her stepmother's
brother, seduced her when she was eleven, but she was too scared
to tell anyone, and that gave her all kinds of complexes about
men. Then, when she finally told her mother about it, when she
was eighteen, her mother threw her out of the house and she
got into the car and drove off. Only it was a rainy night and
her car crashed and she was horribly disfigured and had to have
facial surgery. The trouble was that the doctor who did surgery
on her, Dr. Morrison, fell in love with her and that led to all

kinds of complications because he was married and his wife got really mad. So Myra (Mom) left town and moved to Chicago where she met a really nice man named Fred, but he was leafing through some old letters one day and found out about her uncle and that very day he left her. She felt heartbroken and decided to go back to her hometown and be a nurse there. By a strange coincidence Dr. Morrison was in that same hospital as a patient (he had to have something done with his kidneys) and they fell in love *again* and his wife got mad *again*.

Anyway, the awful thing is they wrote Mom out of the show six months ago. They'd put these new writers on the show and they wanted to build up some other part, so they had Mom in a car crash where she died. Dr. Morrison has been a real mess ever since then; he seems to have lost the will to live and no one knows what to do with him. Even his wife says she wishes Myra were around to cheer him up. But it's too late. Once you've killed a character off, that's that. But the main thing is, poor *Mom!* Because she was doing a terrific job. You should see all the fan mail she used to get. Four men even proposed to her! One of them said she looked just like his childhood sweetheart and another said he lay in bed every night dreaming about her. Another one said he'd read her sign was Taurus in some TV magazine and that meant she was perfect for him because he was Aquarius. So that proves she was doing a great job, and she was earning all this money. Of course she can still do commercials, but it's not the same thing.

Anyhow, that's how Mom met Simon. He's only thirty-three, which Mom says is young for a director, but she said he's really good. Maybe he can help her get another job on another soap, but Mom says they're terribly hard to get just because they're so insanely lucrative. Mom loves earning money. She's totally different from Daddy in that respect. She says if she earns money, she can do splurgy things from time to time like buy those wine-red leather boots that she got for me last month. She told Daddy they cost $60, which he thought was decadent and horrible, but really they cost $150! She told me not to tell him. She said he'd die if he knew. Partly, it's that Daddy is a socialist, sort of, meaning he worries about how many poor people there are in the world and feels guilty that he isn't poor. Mom was sort of poor herself when she was little, and she says she doesn't feel guilty about it at all. Also, she says she likes getting nice things for me and Deel since she couldn't have them when she was little—nice sheepskin coats and cute sweaters and stuff. I'm glad she's like that because I like clothes too. Deel is a little more like Daddy. She mostly just wears jeans and her desert boots and a turtleneck.

Chapter Two

Deel got home around six. "Shit," she said.

"What?"

"I hate math! I *hate* it. I hate it so much I wish I knew the person who invented it and I'd go out and *kill* him." Deel's glasses were fogged over. She has dark frizzy hair and a big nose, like Daddy, and when she's mad, she gets this really fierce expression that used to scare me when I was little.

"Gee." It's funny. I really kind of like math. I mean, I wouldn't want to be a mathematician or anything like that, but I like math. "Isn't he helping any?"

"Dodson? Not really . . . we never do any math. He just tells me stories."

"But what'll you do? What if you fail again?"

Deel shrugged. "Where's Mom?"

"Out having a drink with Simon."

"So, did Daddy shoot anyone yet?"

I sighed. "Mom said he was going to call Joshua's father from the office." I started biting my nails, something I made myself stop doing six months ago.

"God, Rust, you are dumb! How come you let him stay so late?"

"We fell asleep."

"So, what happened? What were you doing in the bathroom?"

"Just kind of fooling around."

Deel looked at me suspiciously. "At three in the morning?"

"I remember I hadn't washed my hair so . . ."

Deel sniffed; she has a cold. "What happened with Daddy, though?"

"He began hammering on the door."

"While you were washing your hair?"

I felt sheepish. "No, we'd finished with my hair."

"What do you mean we?"

"Well, Joshua said he'd help me."

Deel's eyes widened. "Oh, wow! You mean you were—"

"Yeah."

She whistled. "And Daddy— You were, like, doing it, when—"

"Yeah."

"Oh boy, you *have* got problems."

"It *was* dumb," I agreed.

I feel kind of funny talking about sex with Deel, just for this reason: she's never fucked with anyone, even though she's a year and a half older than me. It isn't on moral grounds or anything. It's just no one has asked her. She says if no one does by February, when she's sixteen, she's just going to go out and find someone, in cold blood, sort of, and do it to get it over with. I guess she feels a little humiliated that I did it first. Deel has this theory, though, that younger sisters usually do things first in terms of marriage and sex. She says older sisters tend to do better academically and become doctors and lawyers. The trouble is, I do pretty well in school and it's Deel who's failing Math. It seems like all our lives people have said to Deel, "Well, are you still reading a mile a minute?" and to me, "Look at that hair! Look at those eyes! Aren't you as cute as a button?"

By the way, the reason we have such weird names is Daddy. He used to teach at the Yale Drama School—that's were he met Mom, who was in his class—and he wanted to name us after literary heroines. Deel's real name is Cordelia after someone in a play by Shakespeare called *King Lear*. It's worse for her because she hates "Cordy" and doesn't much like "Deel," but she doesn't want people to go around calling her "Cordelia" either. She says at school her teachers always call her "Deelyer" which she hates most of all. I'm named after this person in a Russian opera, *Eugene Onegin*. It's about this girl who falls in love with somebody who doesn't love her back, but then she gets married to somebody else and he changes his mind, only then it's too late. My friends call me Rusty because of my hair so that's not such a problem. Mom calls me Tat or Tati, but Daddy likes to call me Tatiana if he's feeling affectionate. He likes graceful, romantic names for women.

"Listen, Deel?" I followed her into her room.

"What?" Deel was sneezing and changing into another sweatshirt.

"Mom was saying—well, you know Daddy'll be fifty next month? And she's giving him a surprise party and she thought we might, like, do something special for it, like bake something?"

"Sure," Deel said.

"Do you want to do the Dobos Torte?"

"Yeah, that's yummy."

Deel and I make regular things like brownies and pound cake, but our specialty is Dobos Torte. It's this wonderful chocolate cake with around eight layers. It takes a long, long time to make, but it always tastes wonderful.

"Mom says Daddy's feeling sad and we should try to cheer him up."

"It's like in *Passages*," Deel said. She's reading that just for pleasure. Deel does a lot of reading, not for school, just because she feels like it. *Passages* is this book that tells about all the problems adults have. It sounds like a kind of depressing book. "He's a classic case."

"Yeah?"

"I'll read it to you later. I think—" Just then the door opened. We looked at each other.

"Daddy?" Deel called out.

"Hi," Daddy called from the hall. He came down with his coat still on. "Where's Amanda?"

"She's having a drink with Simon," I said. "She said she'd be back at six thirty."

"It *is* six thirty," Daddy said. He likes things to happen when they're supposed to.

"Maybe I'll set the table," I said, scurrying in there.

Daddy followed me. "Well, I called Mr. Lasker," he said. "We're having a drink with him and his wife at nine."

"Tonight?"

"Yes."

I put the silverware out. Daddy stood there, watching me. "He said he appreciated my concern," he said dryly.

I folded the napkins. I didn't know what to say.

"Tat, there are two issues here."

"Uh huh?"

"One is the simple matter of rules. Now, you know, we are very, very, I would even say inordinately, flexible about rules. So the few we have are just set up for your benefit. Having a curfew of eleven on a night before school is hardly Draconian by any standards, even the most liberal."

"We fell asleep," I said, looking at him pleadingly.

"Yes," he said. He kept staring at me. "There *is* another issue, however, which is . . . Well!" He cleared his throat. "You see, darling, sex is a very complicated thing. It's . . . it's a very intimate, important, thrilling thing that can happen between two people."

"Uh huh?"

"It's . . . well, it's an expression of feeling, it changes a relationship. . . . It's not something you rush into."

"But we didn't," I said.

He stopped and sighed. "The point I'm getting at is this . . . you're just *fourteen*, darling. You have all of life ahead of you. If you experience everything now, before you're ready, what will be left?"

"I'm not exactly sure what you mean," I said. I looked at him, frowning.

"I mean that I doubt you and Joshua are ready for this kind of intimacy. Did he pressure you in some way and make you feel—"

I shook my head. "No. Really, Daddy. Not at *all*."

"He didn't make you feel that unless you did it, he'd be angry or wouldn't see you again?"

"No . . . really, we're just doing it because we want to."

"Doing it?" Daddy looked startled.

Suddenly I wondered if we were talking about the same thing. "What we were doing last night when—"

"You've done it before?" He looked horrified.

"Well . . . yeah."

"How many times?"

I giggled, mainly from nervousness. "I don't know. I haven't been keeping track."

Daddy still had that horrified expression. "But, I mean, for how long? When did this start?"

"In June."

"June? That's four months ago!"

I nodded.

"You've been doing it for four *months?*"

"Yeah."

He seemed at a loss for words. "Who knew about this? Did Delia know? Did Amanda know?"

"I guess I thought everyone knew," I said sheepishly. Actually, I hadn't been sure, but I'd sort of assumed it.

"How old is Joshua?" Daddy said sternly.

"Well, he'll be sixteen at the end of October . . . His birthday is the same week as yours, Daddy. He's a Scorpio too."

"And, I mean, has he had many . . ." he waved his hands ". . . amorous involvements?"

"You mean with girls?"

"He's done it with boys, too?"

"No, I just wasn't sure what you meant."

"Does he go around fucking every pretty girl he can lay his hands on or what?"

"No!" What an awful thing to say! "Joshua's not *like* that, Daddy. Really. We're in *love* with each other."

"Love?" Daddy looked dismayed.

I looked at him, puzzled. "Well, didn't you think we were? That's why we do it, because we love each other."

"Darling." He heaved a huge sigh.

"What, Daddy?"

"You're fourteen years *old*."

"I *know* that, Daddy."

"Love and sex— You should be out flying kites, going to parties, having fun."

"I *am* having fun."

"This is your childhood. You'll never have it again. Once it's gone, it's gone."

"Daddy, fourteen isn't childhood."

"Well, it's too young for screwing around!" He looked angry.

I felt like I was going to cry. "It's *not* screwing around."

"That boy's parents should be taken to jail. 'Our son knows what he's doing.' Bullshit!" His face was getting red.

Just then the door opened and Mom came in. Her cheeks were all pink—she has very light skin. She looked pretty. "Oh, hi, darling. Sorry, I'm a little late. Thanks, Tat, for setting the table." She threw her coat on the front-hall table. "Oh God, wait till I tell you what Simon said about the show."

"Simon said," Daddy said grimly.

"The chicken'll only take a sec," Mom said placatingly. "It just has to be warmed up. Go call Deel, will you, hon?"

As we sat down, Mom said, "Listen, you're not going to believe this but—"

"I gather no one here is interested in what happened with the Laskers," Daddy said, interrupting her.

"The who's?" Mom said, ripping off a chunk of bread. Mom is like me. She can eat everything in sight and never get fat.

"The Laskers?" Daddy said patiently. "Joshua's parents?"

"Oh, right," Mom said. "Yeah, what happened?"

"We're meeting them for a drink at nine."

"Oh great," Mom said cheerfully. "I've always wanted to meet them. Isn't he a lawyer or some such thing?"

"Correct," Daddy said. "He—"

"What does *she* do, Tat?" Mom said. Mom is always more interested in what mothers do.

"Something with charities," I said, cutting my chicken. Mom had put wine in it and mushrooms, which I don't like. I began heaping them neatly to one side of my plate.

"Ugh," Mom said.

"Ugh?" said Daddy.

"I just *hate* people who do things with charities."

"Well, that's a nice charitable attitude to have," Daddy said dryly.

"Oh, *you* know what I mean, sweetie. All those ghastly people who lord it over you, doing good."

"Would you like them if they were doing bad?" Daddy said, pouring himself a second glass of wine.

"I think so," Mom said. "I mean, doing good is so *dreary*. At least doing bad is inventive."

"She's his second wife," I said.

"Who?" said Mom.

"Joshua's mother."

"Okay," Mom said. "I can't very well inveigh against second wives, being one myself."

"He divorced her," I said. "I mean, he got *her* a divorce, and then he got himself one and then they got married."

"And from which union did Joshua spring?" Daddy asked.

"She didn't have any kids from the first one. I think he had, like, a few, one or two or something."

"One tends to lose count," Daddy said.

"They're grown up," I said. "In college or even out of college. They have regular jobs and stuff like that."

"Now can I tell about the show?" Mom said.

"Yeah, what's happening?" Deel said.

"So, we're just going to drop the Laskers and the whole topic?" Daddy said. "Is that the idea? Everything's said that can be?"

Mom looked at him, her head to one side. "Sweetie."

"Sweetie *what?*" Daddy said.

"Well, I mean, do we have to *brood* about this all evening? We're going to meet them, we'll hash it all out. Why rant on endlessly?"

"Was that what I was doing?" Daddy said. "Ranting on? Pardon me."

"*Do* you have anything more to say?" Mom said. "Say it, then."

"Well, I don't want to interrupt some fascinating tidbit about your show," Daddy said.

Mom looked furious. She hates it when Daddy says condescending things about her show. She says just because he taught Chekhov and Shakespeare doesn't mean he has the right to look down his nose at her for taking work where she can get it. "Oh, fuck off, Lionel. Really!"

"I just want to know one thing," Daddy said. "I gather that Tatiana's involvement with this charming, well-connected young man has been common knowledge to everyone present . . . with the possible irrelevant exception of myself."

"Common knowledge?" Mom said.

"They've been fucking around for four months and no one has said a word about it!"

"We haven't been fucking around, Daddy," I said, hurt.

"These two young people have had carnal knowledge of each other since last spring," Daddy said. "Is that correct, Tatiana?"

"Lionel, Jesus!" Mom said.

"No, I'm just mildly *puzzled* that this state of affairs has been considered so trifling that no one thought to bring it to my attention."

"Some of us like to mind our own business," Mom said, pushing her plate aside.

"Oh?" Daddy said. "Well, no doubt there are other events of a similar nature about which I am likewise in the dark. What have *you* been up to, Delia? How many lovers do *you* have on the side? Your mathematics tutor? The doorman?"

Delia grinned. "Right, Daddy . . . I like older men."

"Lionel, don't you remember what it was like to be in love?" Mom said.

"Love?"

"Yes, love . . . remember? That's what this is all about."

"It is, is it?" Daddy said.

"Yes, it *is*, is it," Mom said. "And will you stop that dreadful ironic tone about everything. You're throwing a pall on our whole evening."

Daddy threw his hands up. "Which, of course, is the ultimate sin."

"What's happening with your show, Mom?" Delia said in a friendly way. She hates it when Mom and Daddy fight.

"Can I tell about it?" Mom said, casting a wry glance at Daddy. "Am I given permission?"

"Yeah, what's happening?" I said. I didn't want to keep talking about Joshua.

"Well, you'll never believe this . . . but I may go back to it."

"How? You died," Delia said.

"Here's what they're thinking of. It's still in the planning stage, so far. Poor Dwight has to go back to the hospital."

Dwight is Dr. Morrison, the man Myra (Mom) loves.

"His kidneys again?" Daddy said. I could tell he was trying to act nice to get back on Mom's good side.

"Yeah, they're acting up, something . . . Anyway, while he's there, he thinks he sees me."

"Only *they* think he's hallucinating," Daddy said. He began to mix the salad.

"Right . . . only he's not. Because there's a new nurse— that'll be me—who looks exactly like me, only has different hair, I'd wear a wig or something."

"*Is* she you?" Delia asked.

Mom shook her head. "My twin sister."

"I didn't know you had one," I said.

"Neither did I," Mom said. "Neither did anyone! The reason is, we were separated at birth and each adopted by another family, and neither of us knew we were twins. But Dwight sees the resemblance, and one day he notices a birthmark I evidently had on my thigh."

"How does he get a look at your thigh?" Daddy said. "I thought you were in the hospital."

"I'm wearing a short skirt," Mom said breezily. "Who knows?"

"And Myra had the same birthmark?" Daddy said.

"Right," Mom said.

"Well, that's exciting, darling," Daddy said. "When do you hear definitely?"

Mom gave him a fishy glance. "Do you really think it's exciting?"

"Of course I do." Mom always says Daddy is supportive of her career; one, because she makes money and they do things like take trips and, two, because it makes her happy to work and if she's not happy she gets in a rotten mood.

Daddy got up and went over and gave Mom a hug. I think they do love each other, even though they yell at each other a lot. Deel says love and hate are closely connected. I guess that's so, but I don't think I hate Joshua. Not yet. Right now I just love him.

Chapter Three

At nine Mom and Daddy got ready to go out and meet Joshua's parents. "Have a nice time," Deel said.

"We will." Mom gave me a hug. "Don't worry, hon."

I *was* a little worried. I went in and called Joshua. He works at a camping store till eight Tuesday and Friday, but he'd just gotten in.

"They just left," he said about his parents.

"Mine too . . . I'm scared."

"Don't be, Rust . . . it'll be okay."

"He thinks fourteen is too young," I said.

"It depends on the person," Joshua said. "You're very mature for your age."

"Do you think so?"

"Sure."

"He thinks it's just screwing around."

"He sounds as dumb as *my* father."

"He's just sort of . . . What if they say we can't see each other anymore?"

"We will, anyway."

"I'd hate to have to sneak around and—"

"It's going to be okay, Rust. Really."

"Yeah?"

"Sure."

"How's your cold?"

"Better. . . . Are you okay?"

"Sure. . . . I got an eighty-five on the French test."

"Terrific. . . . Hey, listen, the bathtub wasn't such a bad place, you know?"

"Well, with all the towels . . . You didn't feel uncomfortable?"

"Uh uh . . . it was nice."

"Yeah."

"You're nice."

"You too."

"I wish you were here right now," Joshua said intensely.

"Ummm."

"I'm going to pretend you are as soon as we hang up. I'm going to look at the photos."

Joshua once took some photos of me without any clothes on. That's how we got the idea of doing it the first time, actually. "Call me tomorrow," I said.

"Okay," Joshua said. He lowered his voice. "Sleep tight. I love you."

"I love you too."

There *is* one difference between Joshua and me about sex. I don't know if this is the difference between boys and girls or just the difference between us as people. It's that when we're apart, he says he thinks about fucking with me all the time. Even when he's working at the camping store. Or in school right in the middle of math class. Practically all the time, he says. Whereas I don't think about it except when we're doing it. I think about Joshua, but not so much about fucking with him.

I don't know if that means I'm not as interested in sex as he is. Maybe. He says it's something you have to get into gradually and that the more you do it, the more you get into it. Especially with girls. He says they don't always take to it right away, but after a while they do, most of them. I like fucking with Joshua, but I don't *love* it. Not yet. But maybe eventually I will.

In the morning Daddy slept late, but Mom was up. She had a call-back at nine for a commercial about coconut icing.

"How'd it go?" I asked her when we were both in the kitchen.

"Pretty good," Mom said. She poured some wheat germ into the blender. That's to make this drink she has in the morning, which has honey and a banana and milk in it to give her energy. "Lionel was actually fairly civilized. It really just all boiled down to minor things like curfews and how Joshua should be home by eleven. There was really no point of disagreement."

I swallowed. "How about sex?"

"Well, sex actually wasn't *directly* discussed," Mom said. "Lionel kept saying 'we don't know if you realize how young Tatiana is,' and Joshua's parents looked abashed and said they hadn't. Then there were lots of vague comments about modern-day teenagers and how things have changed and the differences between boys and girls, but no one quite came out and said . . . It's going to be okay, Tat, really. Lionel'll simmer down. He always does."

"Joshua and I do *lots* of other things besides fuck," I said. "It isn't like that's all we do when we're together."

"Of course you do," Mom said, pouring her drink from the blender.

"People always think teenagers are sex maniacs," I said. "Like, that's all they ever do."

"I know," Mom said. "And basically it's adults who . . ."

"Are sex maniacs?" I said, surprised.

"Well, women don't really get interested in sex till they're thirty," Mom said. "Or even forty."

"Really?" That was surprising. "How about men?"

"Oh, I suppose men vary," Mom said vaguely.

"Is Daddy interested in sex?"

"Lionel?" She looked uncomfortable. "Well, I'd say . . . sure, moderately. I mean, not *dis*interested. . . . Have you met Joshua's father, Tat?"

I made a face. "I don't like him that much. Neither does Joshua."

"Well, he is kind of . . . He kept kind of nudging up against me in the restaurant and raving on and on about what a wonderful actress he'd heard I was and now that he'd met me, he knew why I had such an exquisite daughter. I mean, his wife was sitting right there. Maybe she's used to it, though."

"What did she say?" I said nervously.

"Oh, she and Lionel had this intense discussion about teenage morals and the horrors of drugs and how the modern world was a dreadful place for the young. You know, that type of thing. . . . I think Lionel liked her. She has a kind of nervous intensity if you like mawkishly moralistic mouselike types."

"I didn't know Daddy did," I said.

"Lionel?" Mom looked pensive. "No, no that's true. His basic type is more—"

"Like you?"

"Isn't that funny, I'm not sure I *am* Lionel's basic type. I think his basic type is a bit more the lady intellectual thing. Some one he can snuggle up with and burble on about the downfall of Western civilization and weighty topics like that."

"Is Daddy *your* type?" This was a really interesting conversation to have.

Mom looked at the clock. "Hon, you know, you better get cracking. It's almost eight."

"Oh, wow, I didn't even wake Deel up yet."

I never found out if Daddy was Mom's type or not.

That evening Deel and I ate early because Daddy had to go out to dinner with someone he might do a film with who was just in from California for the day. He got back around 9:30. I was in my room, studying for the French test.

"Hi, Daddy."

"Hi, Tat." He didn't look so mad anymore.

"Did you have a nice time at dinner?"

"Yeah, I did actually." He started telling me a little about the movie he and this man might make. It didn't sound that interesting to me. It's about teenagers and drugs. I guess it's kind of ironical that Daddy would make a film like that since Deel is such a pothead. Well, not pothead, really. Actually, she only smokes Tuesdays and Thursdays, which are the days she has Math, and weekends. Real potheads are stoned all the time, like Richy Mulz.

"Did you have a good time with Joshua's parents?" I asked.

He sighed. "Yes, well . . . his mother seems like a very reasonable, concerned person. I felt we really saw eye to eye on everything."

"How about his father?"

"I didn't care for him. There's something fundamentally shifty and irresponsible-seeming about the man."

"Joshua says he has girl friends."

"I wouldn't be surprised." Daddy came over and sat on the edge of my bed. "See, Tat, I just don't want . . . I don't want you to get into anything you can't handle, that will end up causing you a lot of pain and anguish."

"I'm not."

"There's nothing wrong with easing into life and . . . One needn't jump in with both feet. I know that peer pressure affects everyone and—"

I bit my lip. "Can I still see him?"

"Well, yes, but . . . no more middle-of-the-night escapades. And if you ever want to talk to me about it, please feel free to. There's no need to hide anything from me, Tat. I'm not some ogre."

"I know." I looked up at him with what Mom calls my "big blue eyes" look (actually my eyes are gray). "Daddy, you know, I was thinking . . . Remember you said there was that show of photos by that woman photographer you knew? Well, I thought, like, maybe on Saturday, we could go to it?"

Daddy looked so pleased, I felt awful. "Well, that would be awfully nice, Tat. I'd love that . . . but aren't you and Joshua—"

"Well, I might see him in the evening, but during the day I'm free."

"I'm really glad you mentioned that," Daddy said, still with that happy expression. "I've been wanting to see that show and I just . . . Maybe Abigail will join us." Abigail is a film editor who helps Daddy on some of his films.

"Lionel!" Mom was calling.

"I'm in here," Daddy called back, "in Tat's room."

Mom came bursting in one second later. "Listen, it's Charlie on the phone," she said excitedly. "Guess what? They've done the final cutting and we can see the movie three weeks from now."

"Oh damn," Daddy said.

Mom and I stared at him.

"Oh damn what?" Mom said.

"That damn movie!" Daddy said.

"Lionel, what are you *talking* about?"

"Why did I let it happen? I let my own daughter be exploited, used."

"Sweetie, my goodness, you ought to be *proud!* Your own daughter has a lead in a major motion picture, quote un-quote, and is probably fantastic. Where does exploitation enter in? How absurd!"

Mom and I both looked at Daddy. He tried to smile. "I *am* proud," he said, not that convincingly.

"Look, he's on the phone. Do you want to speak to him or not?"

"Charlie? Okay, sure." Daddy rambled off.

"Isn't that exciting, Tat?" Mom said. "God, I can't wait to see it."

"Me too," I said.

Chapter Four

I should have mentioned the movie before this; it *is* kind of a big thing in my life. But then, in a way it isn't. Of course, it hasn't opened yet—not till December 19. My life hasn't changed because of it. I guess life is like that. Things you'd expect to make a big difference don't always and sometimes little things change everything. It was a real fluke I was in the movie at all. I've never acted, though I guess I've heard Mom and Daddy talk about it a lot since so many of their friends are in films or TV or stuff like that. Charlie is this friend of Daddy's from a long time ago. I think they were in the army together. Daddy says he's not a friend. He says, "He's more than an acquaintance and less than a friend." Anyway, he makes movies like Daddy does and one day he came over all excited because Columbia Pictures had just said they'd give him three million dollars to make his first feature film. It was from a script he'd written called *Domestic Arrangements*.

This is what the movie is about. It's about a 14-year-old girl named Samantha (that's me). Samantha has a crush on a boy named Warren who's sixteen. Their parents are friendly and they've spent every summer, since they were babies, on Fire Island. One summer they fuck, just by chance, sort of (they're

38

really more friends). The thing is, at the same time, Warren's father is having an affair with Samantha's mother, but Warren's mother and Samantha's father don't know about it. Then Warren's father and Samantha's mother get married. That's the beginning of the movie. The first scene is their wedding.

They move into this big, fancy, new apartment. Samantha's an only child, but Warren has an older sister who's away at college. Anyhow, Samantha's mother and Warren's father don't know Samantha and Warren are boyfriend and girl friend and they don't *want* them to know because now they're step-sister and brother. So they pretend to not even *like* each other. Samantha's mother keeps asking her to be nicer to Warren who's kind of shy. But when the parents are out, like in the evening, Samantha and Warren fuck and stuff like that.

That goes on for a year or so. But what happens is Samantha's mother and Warren's father start to fight and not get along. And at the end they get divorced. The last scene is Samantha and Warren driving out to California to visit his sister. No one ever finds out about what they were doing. In fact, Samantha's mother says something to her like, "Well, at least you and Warren finally got to be friends."

When Charlie was talking about the film, way before it was made, he began saying how the role of Samantha was crucial, how he wanted someone fresh and sensual in a totally unspoiled way. "I don't want some cutesy little actressy type," he said. "I want someone *totally* natural." And all of a sudden he looked at me and said, "Like Tatiana. I want someone exactly like Tatiana." Then he and Daddy looked at each other and Charlie said, "Tatiana, have you ever gone to an audition?" I shook my head. "Listen," he said to Daddy. "Bring her around next week, okay? I mean, what can we lose, right?" "She's never acted," Daddy said. "Perfect," Charlie said. "Look at that hair. God, I'd hire her for that hair right this second."

People always make a big thing about my hair. It's bright red. Mom says I get it from her mother, who used to be a redhead. Now that Mom dyes her hair red-blond, people think I get it from her, and when they say that, she just smiles. I have unusual coloring for a redhead, too. That is, I don't have freckles the way a lot of people with red hair do. I have very light skin.

The other unusual thing about me is my eyes, which are big and a funny light gray color. Joshua says I look like a werewolf because my eyes are so light. He says they shine in the dark, like a cat's. Charlie even wrote a scene in the movie about my hair. It's the scene Daddy hates most of all and is hoping they've cut. I don't think they will, though, because Charlie likes it so much.

It takes place this night that everyone is out except Samantha and Warren's father. Warren's father sort of likes Samantha. You know that because he gazes at her moodily from time to time. Anyway, in this scene Charlie had me sit naked (except for a pair of bikini underpants that say "Bloomie's" on them) in front of a full-length mirror blow-drying my hair. Daddy says he doesn't mind nudity in films if it's really an intrinsic part of what the movie is about. But he didn't think this was. Actually, you don't see all that much of me since my hair is so long. It kind of hangs over my breasts to some extent.

Anyway, in that scene I'm sitting there drying my hair when Warren's father, who's been out at a faculty meeting, comes home. He opens the door and there I am. He's a little embarrassed, but he stands there, talking to me. At that point, he and Samantha's mother aren't getting along that well. He says: Where's Warren?

I say: He's at the library studying.

He says: You've been a good influence on him, Sam. . . . His grades have really improved this year.

I put the blow dryer down and say: Thank you, Mr. Erikson.

He says: Bill.

I just smile at him.

He says: You have extraordinary hair.

I say: It's sort of a funny color.

He says: I've never seen hair like that. (He's supposed to be a little high.) It's right out of a story by Katherine Mansfield.

I say: Who's she?

He says: An English writer . . . I'll read it to you, okay?

I say: Okay.

He comes back with this book. He reads me this part that goes: "How tragic for a little governess to possess hair that made one think of tangerines and marigolds, of apricots and tortoise-shell cats and champagne."

I say: Gee, that's pretty, Mr. Erikson, I mean, Bill. Then I put on a T-shirt. Just then my mother comes home. She walks into the room.

She says: What's going on?

Warren's father says: We're reading Katherine Mansfield. (He's an English teacher.)

I don't think I got the part because of Charlie being Daddy's friend. I think one reason I might have gotten it was I wasn't at all nervous for the audition. Maybe that's because I don't think of myself as an actress. There were lots of girls auditioning who'd done a lot of stuff on TV, or had been models or went to Performing Arts, or took acting lessons. So to them it was really a big deal. Whereas I know I'm not going to be an actress when I grow up. I liked being in the movie, it was fun and maybe I'll be in some other ones, but that's not what I want to be. Everyone thinks being in a movie must be so exciting, but it isn't, really. Mostly you stand around, waiting, and they make you do the same scene over and over.

When I went for the audition, all the other girls were biting their nails and looking sick with nervousness. I guess I'm not so much the nervous type about things in general. Delia is the exact opposite of me in that respect. She hates it when she has to get up and read something in front of the class, or give a speech or anything. She ran for editor of the school newspaper and she had to get up in assembly and make a speech in front of the whole school. Even though she got totally stoned, and had the whole speech typed up, she said it was one of the worst experiences of her whole life. The other way in which Deel is totally different from me, is she hates being photographed. Whenever we have family photos, Deel is always sort of slouching to one side, squinting at the camera, looking like someone just kicked her in the shins.

I didn't even mind being photographed in the nude, actually. Well, maybe I would have if I was totally naked, but I didn't mind about my breasts so much. My breasts are sort of nice. Daddy said the thought of thousands of seedy middle-aged men drooling over his daughter's breasts made him violently ill. He had a really big fight with Charlie about it. Charlie said the scene was in perfect taste, that there was nothing salacious about it, that I looked like a Renoir, not like a *Playboy* centerfold, and that if *he* had a daughter of such exquisite beauty and radiant charm he would be the happiest man on earth. That's the way Charlie talks. He's a very exclamatory person. On the set he was always either terribly up and pleased with everything or really scowling and angry. In the beginning I used to feel awful when he was scowling and angry. A couple of times he made me cry. But then I realized it was just his personality.

I know Daddy thinks I wouldn't be fucking Joshua if I hadn't been in the movie. He thinks I never would have thought of doing it if I hadn't acted the part of a girl that does. Daddy has such weird, *naive* ideas about things. Doesn't he think I know about sex anyway? Maybe he means that being in the movie made me conceited, but I don't see what that has to do with Joshua either, and anyway, I *didn't* get conceited. People've always told me I'm pretty, that's nothing new, and I don't care about it. Anyway, Joshua doesn't think I *am* that pretty. He says he likes me because I have such a nice personality. He doesn't even like red hair!

Daddy has so many prejudices. I hope it doesn't get worse once the movie opens. I don't see how it *could* get worse, but you never know.

———————

Saturday Deel had to meet with this group she belongs to at school. They're going to go on a march against nuclear power next week and they're planning it now. Deel is very active politically, which pleases Daddy because he used to be too, especially when he was younger, in college. He used to belong to the Young Socialists Club and things like that. Mom had to go down to meet one of the writers for the show about the possibility of them putting her back in as her twin sister. Daddy and I had lunch by ourselves. Then we set out to meet Abigail.

Abigail is a little bit strange looking. She's really short, only 4 feet 10, and she only weighs around 90 pounds. She has very short black hair with bangs, and big black eyes. She looks like a little kid in a way, especially since she always wears jeans and sneakers and big floppy sweaters that are much too big on her. I used to wonder if she was gay, but she was married once. Now she's divorced and has this little kid named Kerim.

"She has a hard time," Daddy said on the way to the show. "It's really tough."

"In what way?"

"Well, she has to work very hard, yet she has Kerim who still needs a lot of attention and care."

"Can't her husband help her look after him?"

"He lives in Boston . . . he's not that involved with him. And he doesn't give her much money."

"Does she wish she didn't have him?"

"Oh, no, she's crazy about him . . . but it's tough."

When we got to the show, Abigail was there already. She was wearing this loden coat she has with a hood. When she has the hood on, she looks sort of like a monk. You just see her face with those big eyes peeking out at you. "Hi," she said.

Kerim was with her. He had the same coat, only in red. They look kind of alike. Kerim is little and thin with shiny black hair too, only he wears glasses. You always feel sorry when you see a really little kid, just five or six, who has to wear glasses.

"It's nice you could come," Abigail said. "Look, there's even a line. I'm so glad for Jenny."

"Do you know her?" I asked.

"I used to . . . before she got really well known."

"She's not *that* well known," Daddy said.

"She is, Li . . . you just don't move in those circles. She's having a book out in June, and Hallmark wants to use a whole bunch of her photo designs for wallpaper, all that."

Daddy raised his eyebrows, as though to say, "So what?"

"She's making money hand over fist," Abigail said, a little mournfully.

"*I* make money," Kerim said. He took a dollar out of his coat pocket to show me. "See."

"That's pretty good," Daddy said. "Did you earn that?"

"I trimmed her prints," he said, pointing to Abigail.

"He's a good worker," Abigail said. "I pay him two dollars an hour."

"What're you going to do with the money?" I asked Kerim. He was looking at his dollar.

"I'm going to save it," he said. "I have a bank account."

"Me too," I said. "I have one." I had a big fight with Daddy about my bank account. He wants to keep it in both our names, mine and his. I don't think that's fair. After all, it's *my* money, money *I* earned, so why should his name be on it? I know why he wants it that way. He's afraid now that I have a lot of money, I'll run out and spend it on dumb things. But the thing is, if I want to, that's my business, and who says I will? He says if the movie is a hit, and I make another one, I'll earn a lot. I only earned $1000 a week on *Domestic Arrangements*.

"So you're going to be a star, huh?" Abigail said, smiling at me.

"What do you mean?"

"Well, Lionel said the movie's opening in December."

"Yeah, we're going to see it next month. Charlie's giving a party. He's the director."

"Yes, I know Charlie. He's a friend of mine."

"Oh? I didn't know that."

"He's a friend of *mine*," Kerim said. "He paid me five dollars."

"For what?" I asked.

"For being quiet while he took a nap."

"That's pretty good rates," Daddy said. "*I'll* be quiet for five dollars an hour. How come he had to take a nap?"

"He was tired," Kerim said.

"He seems very up about the movie," Abigail said.

"I didn't know you still saw him that much," Daddy said.

"Just from time to time . . . God, did he tell you the latest with Beth?"

Daddy shook his head.

"Who's Beth?" I said.

"His third wife," Abigail said. "She wants to go to cooking school, and it costs—well, she wants him to pay forty thousand dollars alimony over a three-year period."

"For cooking school?" Daddy said.

"Evidently that's what it costs . . . it's a whole big deal. You have to learn restaurant management and how to make puff pastry for a hundred people."

"I thought she was just a little slip of a thing," Daddy said. "I thought her whole aim in life was to gaze at him dotingly."

"It was," Abigail said, "but I guess she got fed up with that . . . as even the most doting among us tend to." She smiled slyly.

Daddy smiled back. "Poor Charlie."

"Why poor Charlie?" I asked.

"Well, this is his third go-around . . . what comes next?"

"Who was he married to before?" I asked. I thought Charlie was a bachelor. He was always flirting with everyone on the set.

"Let's see, who *was* the first one?" Daddy said.

"Jessica," Abigail said.

"Oh, right . . . the prom queen from his hometown."

"Then there was, you know, the one with the braid," Abigail said.

"Suki . . . wasn't she the one with the cross-eyed kid?"

"Right . . . they corrected it with surgery, but . . . well, he *says* he's had it with marriage."

"I would think," Daddy said. "Three mistakes, after all."

Abigail looked at him indignantly. "Why mistakes? Just because they ended in divorce?"

"Well," Daddy said. "Yes."

"They were right at the time. He changed, they changed . . . that doesn't make them mistakes!"

Daddy looked taken aback. "Well, I didn't mean it in any pejorative sense. Just that . . . I don't think he knows what he wants from women."

"Men never do," Abigail said dismissively.

Daddy laughed. "Never?"

She shook her head. "No, they just follow whatever fantasy appeals to them and depending on their degree of gullibility, it lasts till the smoke clears."

"I can't allow my sex to be so maligned," Daddy said. "*I* have no such illusions about women. I look at them with total clarity."

Abigail smiled. "Sure."

"What do you mean, 'sure'?" Daddy said.

"Hey, let's look at the show, what do you say?" Abigail said. To Daddy she said, "Your illusion is that you have no illusions. That's the most dangerous illusion of all."

I think Abigail likes Daddy, even though she teases him.

The show was sort of interesting. It was big color photos of naked men. In some of them you couldn't tell they *were* naked men; they were such close-ups they could have been of anything. Like one just showed a nipple as big as a sunflower, practically. And in some, the man's body was all bent to one side so you couldn't see his head.

"That's a penis," Kerim said, pointing. Daddy was carrying him on his shoulders because he got tired.

"Is it?" Daddy said. "Yes, I guess it is."

"It's big," Kerim said, impressed.

"That's because it's a close-up, honey," Abigail said. "You know, I like her wild ponies better."

"I know what you mean," Daddy said. "She used to go to this island and photograph wild ponies," he explained to me.

"She says Willie has such an incredible body, it made her see the possibilities in male nudes. She said she could stare at him all day."

"Now so can a lot of other people."

"Who's Willie?" I asked. "Her boyfriend?"

"Kind of." She looked pensive. "He's only eighteen. Well, I guess she was mainly interested in great sex."

"Great sex with an eighteen-year-old?" Daddy said disdainfully.

"Aren't men at their peak then?" Abigail said. "That's what they say."

"Well, maybe biologically," Daddy said, "but in terms of finesse—"

Abigail looked thoughtful. "Oh, finesse . . . well I don't know. Maybe."

"I'm hungry," Kerim said.

"Let's go to the cafeteria," Abigail said. "I'm getting a little tired of penises. I think I've seen enough for one morning."

We had soup and sandwiches and Kerim had yogurt with fruit. Mostly, he just mushed it around his plate. He ate the fruit, though. When we went outside again, the sun had come out. Abigail took out her camera. She usually carries it with her. It's a Pentax.

"Be mad," she said to Kerim.

He jumped up on a park bench and started scowling and stamping his foot.

"Be happy."

He started waving, with a big grin on his face.

I jumped up beside him and started waving too.

"Be sad," Abigail said.

Kerim and I looked at each other. He sniffed. I let a tear roll down my face. I can do that.

"Oh, do that again, Tat," Abigail said.

She took a bunch more pictures of both of us. She wanted to take Daddy too, but he said he was too self-conscious.

"That hair," she said to me. "Wow."

"It's because of my grandma," I said.

"Kerim is great, though," Daddy said. "You should try to get him in something."

Abigail made a face. "The thing is, someone wants him for a commercial for some dumb toy, but I . . . I just *hate* commercials! I feel like it would be going against all my principles."

"I know what you mean," Daddy said.

"Mom does commercials," I said. "She says it's okay because it's real acting. She says it's what you bring to it that counts."

"But how about the whole exploitive aspect of it?" Abigail asked. "How does one justify that?"

"I don't think Amanda loses a lot of sleep over issues like that," Daddy said.

If Mom had been there, she'd have gotten mad at that remark. She always does when Daddy says things like that.

Abigail lives way down in the Village on Broome Street, or something, so Daddy and I didn't go home with her and Kerim. She said she thought he was tired and needed a nap.

"No, I don't," he said loudly. But his eyes were kind of drooping shut.

"*I* do," Abigail said. "Naps are one of the world's great inventions . . . whoever invented them deserves a medal."

She and Daddy kissed each other good-bye, and Daddy and

I took a cab home. Usually Daddy doesn't believe in cabs, at least as much as Mom does. Mom says she's addicted to cabs. If it's farther than three blocks away, she takes a cab to it. Daddy says that's one bad habit he doesn't want me to pick up from her. He says public transportation is a wonderful thing, and we should be glad we have it. But still, at the end of the day, when you're tired, it's nice to take a cab.

Chapter Five

Daddy likes to talk to cab drivers. He likes to just start talking to people he doesn't know, sort of joking around. When we got into the cab, the cab driver (his name was Juan Martinez) said, "You know, I was about to go off duty, but the little lady looked so cold and tired, I decided what the heck. That's my trouble—I'm too good-hearted."

"Oh, you can't be *too* good-hearted," Daddy said. "That's not possible."

"No, it *is* possible," Juan Martinez said. "Let me tell you. You're good-hearted and what good does it do you? Does anyone notice? Does anyone care?"

"I'm glad you stopped," I said shyly. "I *was* tired."

"It's October," Juan Martinez said. "October does it to me."

"What does it do?" Daddy said. "Why October?"

"Well, I'll tell you," he said. He was looking at us in his rearview mirror. "You really want to know?"

"I do," Daddy said. "I'm on the edge of my seat. Aren't you, Tat?"

Sometimes I think Daddy teases people a little, but they don't always seem to notice.

"Well, you may not believe this," Juan Martinez said, "but I used to be the soccer champion of Brazil."

49

"And then what happened?" Daddy asked.

"Then what happened? Then I had a family; then I had kids to support; then I came to this country and got a job driving a cab . . . and there you are."

"What is it about October, though?" I asked.

"Well, that's when I quit. I quit back in October 1967."

"Do you miss it?" Daddy asked.

Juan Martinez looked at him. "He wants to know if I miss it," he said. "What do you think, mister? Do *you* think I miss it?"

"I imagine you do," Daddy said.

"*You'd* rather be driving a cab in this crazy city than out there with crowds cheering when you make a goal? *You'd* rather be bucking traffic, getting held up, sworn at?"

"No, I don't think I would, now that you mention it," Daddy said.

"Listen, I'm not complaining," Juan Martinez said. "I had my moment of glory, right? I mean, lots of people, they spend their whole lives waiting. I had it. So they can't take that away from me, can they?"

"They certainly can't," Daddy said. "Tat, do you have a single? This corner is fine," he said. We were right at our house.

Juan Martinez took the change. "Everybody should have one moment of glory," he said.

"Definitely," Daddy said. "I couldn't agree with you more. At least one."

"Listen, mister," Juan Martinez called out the window. "I hope you won't be offended by my saying this, but you've got a gorgeous daughter, you know that?"

Daddy smiled at me. "Of course I know that."

"Thank you," I said.

"You look after her," Juan Martinez said. "You keep an eye on her."

"I'm trying to do just that," Daddy said as we walked into the lobby.

We looked at each other and smiled.

"You know, Tat," Daddy said in the elevator, "I think there's an object lesson in that exchange."

"There is?" I thought he was going to say something about how I shouldn't be conceited about my looks.

"What I'm thinking of," Daddy said, "is what he said about a moment of glory. He's right. We all have it, usually anyway, at one point or another, but it doesn't always lead anywhere. You think it's a high point and you'll go on and on, but you don't necessarily."

I wondered if he meant about his having won the Emmy five years ago, and not having won another one. I remember when the shooting started for *Domestic Arrangements,* Mom said that she was worried Daddy would be envious of Charlie since he'd always had vague thoughts of making a feature film. He optioned a book for about four years and then the author sold it to someone else for more money. I think that made him feel bad.

"Do you know what I mean?" Daddy said.

"About the Emmy?" I said.

"No, about you, darling. . . . You don't know, but when *Domestic Arrangements* opens, you may suddenly get a lot of attention and, well, it'll be a nice thing, but it'll be helpful if you try to take it in perspective, appreciate it, but—"

"Don't let it go to my head?" I finished.

"Right. . . . Lots of people will be crowding around you, telling you you're gorgeous and talented, which you are . . . but you've got a whole life ahead of you. It's something you have to . . . work on. Things won't always come that easily, just strolling in and getting a lead in a feature film without any acting experience. That's great, but don't expect life to be like that."

"I won't," I promised him.

Mom was at home, stretched out on the couch.

"How'd it go?" Daddy asked, giving her a kiss.

She gestured. "Not bad . . . God, those writers are *idiots!* You have to sit there, listening to such total junk, and pretend it's the most fascinating thing you ever heard. How was the show?"

"Fair," Daddy said. "A lot of male organs, larger than life."

"Huh . . . oh, honey, that reminds me, did you put those kidneys back? They were supposed to be for dinner. How's Abigail? Still as relentless as ever?"

"Never saw the kidneys," Daddy said. "Abigail's fine, not especially relentless that I could see."

"You should introduce her to Simon," I said, taking off my boots.

"What?" Mom and Daddy said together, in horror.

I was taken aback. "Well, you just said"—I meant Daddy—"she doesn't get that much money from her husband and you're always saying"—I meant Mom—"Simon ought to get married, so I thought—"

"Tat," Daddy said. "Abigail is a highly cultured, sensitive person. She loves ballet, she's studied Oriental art. What would she talk about with someone like *Simon?*" He looked disdainful.

"Well, that's hardly the point," Mom said, bristling. "Simon likes women with some kind of spark, or pizazz. Abigail would probably bore him senseless, reading him the latest issue of *Ms.* from cover to cover."

"What do you mean?" Daddy said.

"Well, darling, *you're* the one that always said what a party liner she was about feminist things," Mom said. "I'm only quoting you."

"That was years ago," Daddy said. "She's softened considerably. I thought *you* said Simon didn't know what he was doing as a director, that he just got the job because his father knew somebody."

"That's how he *got* the job," Mom said. "But he's earned his keep. The cast *loves* him now. He has them eating out of his hand."

"I'm glad to hear it," Daddy said. "I thought all that LSD he took might have softened his brain."

"Lionel! That's his generation. They all take stuff. So what? Big deal. His brain is in fine shape."

"Big deal?" Daddy said. "To be stoned for ten years?"

"He wasn't stoned for ten years." Mom looked at him indignantly. "He went through a brief period in which he experimented with drugs a little . . . God, you're such a *moralist!*"

"It's his chromosomes," Daddy said. "Let *him* worry about them."

"I'm going to take a shower," Mom said. "When are you going out, Tat?"

"I'm meeting Joshua at eight." They were both looking at me so I said, "I'll be back at one, okay?"

"Fine," they said together.

Mom and Daddy were having guests for dinner, and Joshua's parents were going out, so we'd decided to spend the evening over there. Joshua's father has a wide-screen TV and there was some movie on Joshua wanted to watch. Joshua is an old-movie buff. He likes to watch all the movies some director made, every single one. They have this thing where you can record movies that are on in the middle of the night or when you're away, and play them back any time you feel like it. Joshua says he wants to make movies when he grows up. But he wants to make really *good* movies, not like *Domestic Arrangements* and not like the things Daddy does. He wants to make great movies, like Ingmar Bergman, or Lubitsch. I think he probably will. He's a very determined person. He said the minute he saw me, he knew we'd go to bed together or he'd die. I didn't think anything special when I saw him.

Joshua's parents were just leaving when I arrived. Joshua's mother was wearing a white fur coat. She had her hair in a gray turban. "Oh, hi, Tatiana," she said, smiling stiffly. Maybe she felt funny after that talk with Mom and Daddy.

"Well, there's the girl," Joshua's father said. "We had a nice time with your parents the other night, Tatiana. I'm glad we met them finally." He had this sort of loud, booming voice.

"Yes, they were glad too," I said hesitantly.

"Now I know where you get your looks," he said. "Your mother is quite a looker."

"Patrick, I think we *really* should be going," Joshua's mother said.

"The two of you should be in something together," he went on, ignoring her. "You'd be sensational. I want to talk to my pal Dan about it. He's looking around for someone to—"

"It's past eight thirty," Joshua's mother said. "And I'm in a fur coat."

"Sweetheart," Joshua's father said. "Don't be so uptight. No one ever gets there on time."

"Yes, they do. *We* just never do."

He sighed, and rolled his eyes. "You see, the tyranny of women," he said to Joshua and me. "How we are yoked and chained, but we submit." He lowered his head like a bull. "I submit. Carry me off. Do with me what you will."

After they'd left, Joshua shook his head and sighed. "The original wise guy."

"Daddy didn't like him," I said.

"No one likes him."

"Doesn't your mother?"

"Are you kidding? How could anyone like him if they lived with him?"

"So, why doesn't she divorce him?"

"I guess she figures why bother. He's rich."

"That's gross, that she just stays with him for his money."

"Yeah, well . . . I guess women do."

"Joshua!" I looked at him indignantly. "Women do *not!* *My* mother doesn't."

"Your father isn't rich."

"He's not poor . . . he says we're comfortable."

Joshua smiled. "Listen, Mom didn't even want to go to the West Side to meet your parents. She was afraid they'd be mugged the second they went west of Fifth. She says she saw a cockroach walking up the wall of the restaurant."

"Daddy liked her."

"She liked *him*. She said he was very sincere."

"He is."

"Maybe we should fix them up," Joshua said.

"Oh come on!"

"Why not?"

"My parents are happily married," I said.

"Nobody's parents are happily married," Joshua said. "Some just put on a better front than others."

"That's really a cynical attitude."

"Realistic."

"Cynical."

I glared at him. He came over in back of me and put his arms around me and hugged me. Then he slid his hands up under my shirt. "Hey, what's this?" he said, touching my bra.

"I went out with Daddy this afternoon. He doesn't like it when I go without a bra."

"How does this work?" he said, trying to unhook it.

"It hooks in the front."

He unhooked it and began stroking my breasts. "That's more like it." I could feel through his jeans he was hard already.

"Listen, I thought we were going to watch that movie," I said, flushing.

"We can do both," he said, reaching down to unzip my jeans.

"Joshua!"

"Why? You can't do two things at once?"

"Not that." I felt awful, that he would even want to.

"Hey." He tilted my head up. "I was just teasing . . . it's not on till nine."

"Where do you want to go?"

"The study . . . my room's a mess."

Joshua's room is always an unbelievable mess. Even Deel's room, which Mom calls a "disaster area," looks neat by comparison. His father's study is really a big room with a fireplace and a big modular sofa that could seat around twenty people. I could tell that unless we fucked first Joshua wouldn't be able to concentrate on the movie. He's like that. If he gets horny, he can't concentrate on anything. At first he tried to go slow, stroking me all over and kissing me, but then all of a sudden he began moving back and forth fast. His mouth was open on mine, hot, and he had his hands under my ass. "Oh, Rust," he gasped. "Oh, oh—" Joshua really gets carried away when we fuck. Sometimes I almost feel scared, like he's in a trance or something.

The bad thing is that I can't get an orgasm when we fuck. I know you're supposed to, but I can't. Maybe I worry about it too much. But afterward when Joshua takes me in his arms and kisses me and strokes me, then I can do it. Maybe it's partly because then he's calm and loving, and I feel relaxed and good, whereas when we're actually fucking, it's like he's a different person almost. I don't make a lot of loud, groaning sounds like Joshua when I come. Joshua says I purr. He says I sound like their cat when you stroke her on her back a long time and she purrs and purrs.

Afterward he lay with his head propped up, leaning on his elbow, and stared at me with that intense expression he has.

"I'm scared," he said.

"What of?"

"The movie . . . it's opening in eight weeks."

"Yeah, so?"

"I'm going to lose you," he said dolefully.

"What do you mean?" I said softly. "No, you're not."

"You're going to be surrounded by all these guys; older guys, suave, rich guys who'll buy you champagne."

"Joshua, come on. . . . Think what a terrible person I'd be if that kind of thing mattered to me."

"They're going to feed you some line," he said, ignoring me. "They're going to tell you you're gorgeous. They'll have penthouse apartments, they'll have coke in silver snuff boxes, they'll have Japanese houseboys who'll serve you pheasant under glass with seedless green grapes—"

I giggled. "Joshua!"

"Here I'll be forlorn, mooning over your picture in the paper, going up to people at parties saying, 'I once knew her, I once fucked her, she was once lying right in my father's study staring at me with her big werewolf eyes.' "

"I'm going to love you forever," I told him, putting my hand on his neck.

He melted. "No, you're not, Rust."

"I am, Joshua . . . why don't you believe me?"

"Nobody loves anyone forever . . . especially at fourteen."

"Juliet did."

"No one in real life."

"You'll probably find some other girl. You'll probably get together with Pamela."

Joshua fucked with three people before he met me. Pamela was one. She's in boarding school now, but she writes him these long, single-spaced letters and sends him copies of her poems in first drafts. She's even had poems published in magazines. I saw her picture. She's really tall and has a big nose and bright blue eyes. She looks like a better-looking version of Deel. Her parents were friendly with Joshua's and they used to fuck in her parents' roof garden in Scarsdale with all these plants and tropical birds all around. Joshua said one of the toucans shat on him once while they were doing it, right on his back.

He also once fucked with some girl at a party. They did it

right there, at the party, under a big pile of coats. He didn't even know her name till afterward. Her name was Georgette and he said she had great breasts. She went to Brearley and she'd already fucked with ten people. Evidently she liked to do it at parties. Anyway, they never saw each other again so I don't feel so jealous of her.

Then there was Marjorie who was a mother's helper for a family Joshua's parents knew at East Hampton. Joshua's parents had a house there one summer and this girl, who was in college, used to come over and use Joshua's parents' pool. He said she was skinny, but very friendly, and one day the two little kids she was looking after fell asleep and she asked Joshua if he wanted to go inside and have iced tea. He said she gave him a can of iced tea, and then she took her clothes off. Right there in the kitchen! She just took them off and then she asked if he wanted to see her room. He said he did. After that they fucked every day till the end of August when his parents went back to the city. She went to college in Colorado and said she'd write to him, but she never did. He said she really liked sex. I feel jealous of her, too. I feel jealous of Pamela because they used to talk about poetry and philosophy a lot, and other serious things, and I feel jealous of Marjorie because it sounds like she was more into sex than me and maybe fucking with her was more fun. Joshua said she always used to pounce on him. She liked to do it on top of him and all sorts of ways. He said she was a fun-loving person. She had her own horse at that college she went to.

"You know the reason Mom was so uptight about the thing with you?" Joshua said. "Last weekend Tommy was in and she found all this stuff in his drawer, coke, letters from girls. She really hit the ceiling."

Tommy is Joshua's older brother, not the one who's traveling around Europe—that's Neil. Tommy goes to this fancy prep school that Joshua's father went to, Andover. He's extremely handsome, almost like a movie star. He has really long, thick, dark eyelashes, and full lips, and a kind of slouching, brooding expression that evidently drives girls wild. He deals in drugs. Whenever he comes home on vacation, he gives Joshua whatever he wants.

"What did the notes say?"

"Oh stuff like, 'My night with you was so wonderful,' 'I'll never meet anyone like you . . . you've broken my heart.' All that. How come *I* don't get notes like that?" he said wryly.

"Do you want to?"

"Sure."

"Should I write you one? I can if you want." I took a piece of paper from the drawer, and a red Flair pen. I began to write. "Dear Joshua . . ." I looked up at him, smiling. "Now what?"

" 'I'll never meet anyone like you,' " he said.

"That's certainly true," I said, writing.

" 'I love every inch of your sensational body,' " he dictated.

"Okay." I wrote that.

" 'It's incredible that such wit and charm could emanate from one person.' . . . Um, let's see. 'Without you, life wouldn't be worth living. I want to keep fucking with you forever.' "

I wrote it all down. Then I folded up the paper and gave it to him. I leaned over and kissed him. "It's all true," I said.

Joshua frowned. He bit his lip. "Rust, what I really want is—I want you to get older, but not different. I want you to grow, but not away from me."

"Anything else?" I said.

"I want everyone to want you, but I want you to only want me."

"Greedy."

He laughed. "Of course."

"You want everything."

"Definitely. Why bother wanting less than everything?"

"Do you still want to watch the movie?"

He looked at the clock. "Oh, Christ, I forgot . . ." He turned on the set. We lay in the nude, watching. They sent up tons of heat in Joshua's apartment. It's usually 85 degrees. I know because there's a thermometer in Joshua's mother's bedroom. We lay on our stomachs and every now and then Joshua would reach over and start stroking my ass, but he still kept watching the movie. Movies mean as much to Joshua as sex, which is saying quite a lot. I guess one difference between him and me is that he likes to analyze every movie he sees, to figure out why he liked it and what was wrong with it, and how he would have done it if he'd been the director. I tend just to like things or not. Joshua says I'm too easy to please. He says I like everything. That isn't true. I didn't like *Star Wars* and I didn't like *Carrie*. There're lots of things I don't like.

After the movie we heated up some leftover pizza they had in the freezer and ate it in the den. Joshua had beer and I had Diet Pepsi. I'm not fat, but I don't want to be, ever, so I weigh myself every day. We have a digital scale and you have to kick it before you weigh yourself. After you kick it, it says 000. Then you step on. You can step on fast or slowly. I haven't figured out which way makes you weigh less. I weigh myself six times. Usually I get around three different weights and I pick the one I like best. Since I'm five-five, I think 115 is the best.

Joshua's skinny. He'll never have to worry about getting too fat.

"Are you staring at me because I look too fat?" I looked down at my belly. It did look puffed out a little, maybe from the pizza.

"Uh uh."

"I gained two pounds," I said nervously, "but I think I can lose them again. I might fast Monday."

Joshua began squeezing me, my stomach, my breasts. "No, I like it. Those are two terrific pounds. . . . Tat, come here." He likes to fuck with me sitting in front of him. He likes me to wrap my legs around him. Then he goes into me and we rock back and forth, sitting up. He ran his hands up and down my back, my hair, my ass. "God, you feel so good," he murmured. "What's that perfume?"

"Honeysuckle . . . I got it from Mom."

"Umm . . . oh wow!" Suddenly we lost balance. We rolled over onto the floor. Joshua's penis came out of me. He pushed it back in again, hard, all the way.

"Wait . . . that hurts, Josh."

"I'm sorry. Is that okay?"

"Yeah." But in that position, where I'm lying on my back, he can't seem to go slow the way he does when we're rocking together, so it was over pretty quickly. When we were done, he flopped over onto his back and rolled his eyes back, like he was fainting. "Wow, that honeysuckle really did me in. Hey, did I really hurt you?"

"Only a little."

"Should I kiss it and make it better?"

"Okay." But as he started to, I said, "Josh?"

"Yeah?" He lay there, looking up at me like a cocker-spaniel puppy with his big brown eyes.

"The thing is, do you wish I was like Marjorie?"

"In what way?"

"About fucking. Being more . . . fun-loving."

"You're fun-loving, Rust."

"More wild or whatever."

"No, you're good, Rust." He looked at me earnestly. "You're the best."

"It's just I'm sorry that I can't come while we do it. I try, but I just can't."

"You will, don't worry."

"Will I?"

'Sure." He began kissing me between the legs.

"Do you mind about it, though?" I closed my eyes.

"No . . . except I want you to be happy. I want to make you deliriously happy."

I smiled drowsily.

"No, I mean it. I want you to be so happy that it's like nothing else ever was."

"Is it that way for you?"

He nodded.

That makes me feel so good, that I can do that for someone. I like making Joshua happy. It's the best feeling.

Chapter Six

Daddy's birthday is on Saturday, October 27. I made him a collage calendar just like I used to. I love making collages. What I do is trim things out of magazines and move them around till I get an idea. Then I paste them on and draw connections with black India ink, figures that hold the design together. I like using 11-by-14 smooth white heavy paper; it has a good feeling to it. On the corner of each page, I paste a little month from a calendar.

Daddy used to want me to be an artist. I guess it was because when I was little I loved to draw. He'd take me around to art galleries and say to the owners, "Someday my daughter's work will hang here." I guess he was half joking, but it made me uncomfortable, even then.

I like it that Daddy is so proud of me and thinks I'm so terrific, but sometimes I think he overdoes it. I feel that with my acting too. Daddy used to act some in college and summer stock, and when I first got the part in *Domestic Arrangements*, he was ecstatic. But then he wanted to go over my lines with me every night and tell me how *he* thought I should say them. The thing is, he wasn't the director and I didn't want two people telling me what to do. But also, I wanted to figure it out myself. Mom says it bugs her when Daddy lectures at her. She says he doesn't even realize he's doing it; he just likes to tell people what to do . . . that's why he became a director. I think it hurt Daddy's feelings when I told him I didn't want to go over my lines with him. I told him Charlie had said I shouldn't, but I think he knew it was partly me.

Daddy's first wife, Dora, was ten years younger than him, just like Mom is. Mom says Daddy has a Pygmalion thing with women. He wants to take them as shapeless lumps of clay and mold them into some ideal image. I think he wants to do that with me too, a little. But I don't want him to. I want to figure out how I want to be myself.

Deel said she'd make the Dobos Torte if I made the praline cheesecake. We both worked in the kitchen all Friday afternoon the day before the party. Luckily we have a big kitchen. The praline cheesecake recipe is from Mom. It's an old southern recipe. What's good about it is it has brown sugar, and anything with brown sugar is good. Plus it has pecans chopped up into it. When it's done you rub maple sugar over the top, sort of massage it lightly. Everybody always loves it, Daddy especially.

Mom fixed up our terrace with balloons that had "50" printed on them. She tied them to the railing, but one got loose and floated away. We don't have a great view from our terrace since we're on 87th and Riverside, but it's nice being up high. In the summer we eat out there and Daddy plants tomatoes.

Mom told Daddy about the party Saturday morning because she didn't think he'd like it if it was a total surprise.

"Happy birthday, Daddy," Deel said. We both came into their bedroom. Deel gave him her present first. It was a new book of Cartier Bresson's photos.

"This is really lovely, Delia," Daddy said. He was sitting up in bed, his hair a little rumpled. "It must have cost a fortune."

Delia smiled. She's very good about money. She saves a lot. Over the summer she worked at Fortunay's, a soda fountain near our house, and earned over four hundred dollars.

Then I gave him the calendar I'd made. Daddy looked at each page carefully. He smiled at a lot of them. "I love it, Tat," he said, hugging me. "It's wonderful."

I was glad Daddy didn't get more excited about my present than Delia's because I knew she'd be jealous then.

Mom gave Daddy a work shirt to wear on the terrace while he's gardening. It's navy-and-white striped and ties in front. Daddy tried it on. It looked funny, sort of like he was a nurse; it had big pockets. "I'll feel very Tolstoyan," he said. He kissed Mom. Mom always says she wants to zap up Daddy's wardrobe. She gives him violet turtlenecks and funny ties with eyes on them; he doesn't always wear them.

After breakfast Mom told Daddy about the party. She'd been afraid he might not like the idea. He's not so much the party type. He doesn't mind small parties with people he really likes, but he doesn't like big parties with swarms of strangers, the way Mom does. Mom says she always thinks she might meet someone who'll change her whole life. Daddy says but has she ever met such a person, and Mom says no, but that doesn't mean it'll never happen. Anyway, for Daddy's party Mom invited fifty people since that's how old he was, but they were mostly people they'd known a really long time.

Charlie sent Daddy a telegram, which arrived at noon. It said: "Come on in, the water's fine." Daddy said what he meant by that was that Charlie was fifty already and it wasn't so bad.

"You don't *look* fifty, Daddy," Deel said.

"Not a day over forty-nine, huh?" Daddy said, crunching on a stalk of celery.

"*I* think you look forty," she said.

"Forty?"

"Yeah, really . . . Lucia's father is forty-two and his hair is all gray, all of it."

Daddy's hair is only a little gray. "Well, that's hereditary."

"It's your personality that counts," she said. "You *act* young."

"I do?" Daddy said, surprised.

"I don't mean in a bad way," Deel said. "But you have a playful spirit."

"That's true, I do, don't I?" Daddy said. "Why are you smiling, Tatiana, sweets? You don't think I have a playful personality. You think I'm dour and mean."

"No," I said, laughing.

"She thinks I'm an ogre," he said. He made this sad face he used to make when we were little and he used to entertain us telling us stories.

I went over and kissed him. "I don't, Daddy, really."

Mom and I decided to wear our Laura Ashleys. Mom's is made of a material called lawn, which is a very fine cotton. It has a high neck and long sleeves ending in lace. Mine is dotted Swiss with puffed sleeves and a sash that ties in the back. Deel would never in nine million *years* wear a dress like that. Even on fancy occasions, like this, she just wears a newish pair of jeans and maybe her Indian silk shirt. That's as fancy as she ever wants to be.

When Mom and I came into the living room, Charlie had arrived. He's Irish and he dresses in a funny way—bright green ties and tweed slacks with lots of colors in them. "Visions of loveliness, coming at me from all directions!" he said, staggering backward. "I'm in a dream . . . is this West 87th Street?"

"Let me get you a drink, Charles," Mom said.

Charlie followed Mom into the kitchen. "She can talk, she can walk . . ." He winked at Daddy, who was wearing his Tolstoyan work shirt with a navy turtleneck underneath. "Cheer up, kid, fifty is young."

"That's what I've been telling him," Mom said.

"Life begins at whatever age you are . . . till you're dead," Charlie said. He grabbed me by the waist. "What do you *do* to this girl?" he said. "Look at her! She gets more radiant every *second!* It's not possible. You're giving her too many vitamins. . . . Tatiana, stop taking those vitamins!"

Mom came in with the punch bowl. Deel and I had cut up strawberries all morning to float on top. Daddy and Charlie clinked glasses.

"To you, Lionel," Charlie said.

They drank and then Mom raised her glass. "To us," she said.

Daddy looked at her, puzzled.

"It's our anniversary," Mom said.

"What?" Daddy frowned. "But our anniversary is in—"

"The anniversary of when we first slept together, to use the euphemism of that bygone age."

"It was on my birthday?" Daddy said, still looking surprised.

Mom nodded and sipped her punch. "You see what a big impression it made on him," she said to Charlie.

"How old was I?" Daddy said.

"Thirty-three."

Daddy groaned. "Was I ever that young?"

"Where was it?" Deel asked. She loves to hear stuff like that.

"In Lionel's office."

"Did I have a couch in my office?" Daddy said. "I thought it was a kind of—"

"No couch," Mom said.

"God, I *must* have been young."

"Daddy, how come you don't even remember?" Deel said.

"Well, I . . . What were the circumstances?" Daddy said. "Refresh my memory."

Mom was smiling. "I was interviewing you . . . for the school paper."

"Oh God, yes . . . of course."

"Why'd you want to interview him?" Charlie asked.

"Oh, I didn't . . . but I thought it would be a good ploy, you know, drawing him out, asking breathy questions."

"It worked, of course?" Charlie said, glancing at Daddy.

"Like a charm."

"Wait a minute," Daddy said. "*My* memory of this is totally different."

"What do *you* remember, Daddy?" Deel asked.

"Well, I remember Amanda in my class . . . she was an excellent student," he said to Charlie.

"I can imagine," Charlie said, smiling at Mom.

"She was quiet, slightly demure, even . . . asked provocative, intelligent questions, wrote excellent papers. You got an A, didn't you?"

"B," Mom said. "You were afraid if you gave me an A, people would think it was because we were—"

"You deserved an A," Daddy said. To Charlie he said, "She definitely deserved an A."

"I'm sure she did . . . A plus, if it were up to me."

"I thought you were married to Dora then, Daddy," Deel said.

Daddy looked uncomfortable. "Well, it was unraveling . . ."

"What was Dora like?" Deel persisted.

Daddy gazed off in the distance. "Beautiful . . . in the beginning." He looked at Charlie. "Didn't you think?"

Charlie cleared his throat. "Beautiful? No," he said flatly.

Daddy squinted. "Fragile, dreamy, delicate . . . a porcelain figurine."

"Maybe," Charlie said. "I see what you're getting at. A few cracks by the time I met her."

"Lionel idealizes women," Mom said.

"He does, doesn't he?" Charlie said. "Bless his heart."

"So, did Mom, like, seduce you when you were married to Dora?" Deel said. I could tell she was getting all excited, hearing all these details of their private life.

"Well, kind of, I guess," Mom said.

"I always thought *I* seduced *you*," Daddy said.

Mom smiled. "Men like to think that."

"When really," Charlie said, "they're just leading us docilely along, tugging gently at the rings in our noses."

"I love that image," Daddy said, wryly.

"Did Dora mind?" Deel persisted. "I mean was it like in 'The Way We Are Now' with Dr. Morrison and Myra?"

Daddy choked on his punch. "Well, I'd hate to think of my life being like a third-rate soap opera," he said.

"Lionel!" Mom stared at him.

"What?"

"A *third-rate* soap opera?" Mom's cheeks were all pink. She really looked mad.

Daddy looked like he knew he'd said something dumb. "No, third rate was . . . I just meant—"

Mom wheeled away. "We know what you mean. Just like you think *Domestic Arrangements* is a third-rate film. *Everything* is third rate to you."

"Darling, no." He tried to sound soothing.

"Well, tell Charlie," Mom said, still mad. "Tell me all you were saying about how Tat is going to be exploited. Tell him!"

"Exploited?" Charlie said, looking at Daddy. "In what sense?"

Daddy really looked embarrassed. "No, it's just . . . that scene, you know, the hair-dryer scene. I just thought—"

"Lionel," Charlie said. "That scene is devoid of even the *vaguest* trace of sensationalism. I'd bring my Aunt Minnie in from Iowa City to see it. That scene will make people weep."

"Weep?" Daddy said.

"Yes, weep," said Charlie. "That expression with which Tatiana looks up at Winston, that wide-eyed, soft, radiant expression . . . there's no dirt there. Anyone who can find anything salacious in that scene is a dirty old man."

"See!" Mom said triumphantly to Daddy. To Charlie she said, "He just thinks if it's not Chekhov, it's third rate."

"Look, you have two choices in life," Charlie said. "You can spend a vast amount of time and energy inveighing against the way things are, or you can learn to live in the real world and make the best of it. I'm of the latter school."

"Me too," Mom said. "Sure, I could have spent the last decade auditioning for wretched little earnest off-off-Broadway plays which would run three seconds, and get wonderful reviews in the *Voice*, but so what? What would that *prove?*"

"Of course," Charlie said. "Instead you've used your skills, you've kept them alive."

"Exactly," Mom said.

Daddy looked sheepish. "People, please! I am being falsely maligned. Of course one compromises, I'm not saying that. I'm only saying it's important to keep the flame burning."

"What flame?" Mom said.

"The flame of idealism, of art, of something wonderful." He gestured vaguely.

"Listen," Charlie said. "This movie *is* wonderful. This is a *wonderful* movie, and your daughter is a *wonderful* actress. Okay? This is *fact*. I don't say it because I made it, I don't say it because Tatiana is your daughter. I say that because I came out of that screening shaking."

"Okay," Daddy said. "No, we're eager to see it, Charlie."

"*I* am," Mom said. "I'm eager."

I looked around the room. Deel wasn't there anymore. I went

to look for her. The front bell had started to ring and a whole lot of people poured in. Deel was in her room, sitting on the edge of her bed, smoking a joint.

"How come you're in here?" I asked.

"You want me to get stoned in front of Daddy?"

"No, I just meant . . . how come for the party?"

"I *hate* parties!" Deel said. "I hate all their phony, dumb friends."

"Simon's coming," I said. "You like him." Simon always plays Scrabble with Deel. They're both very good. They play in French, even.

"He'll be busy. He won't want to talk to me if he can talk to someone his own age. Anyway, Mom'll probably be flirting with him like a maniac all afternoon." She handed me the joint. "Want some?"

"Okay." I inhaled a little. I'm very suggestible when it comes to pot. A few puffs and I'm off.

"That is so *sick* about Mom and Daddy," Deel said.

"What?"

"She took him away from his wife. What a seedy thing to do!"

"Well, but he said their marriage wasn't that good . . ."

"Yeah, sure . . . they fucked in his *office!* You heard her."

"Well, I guess she liked him a lot," I said mildly. It's hard to argue with Deel when she's in that kind of mood.

"Yeah? She probably just wanted to get his scalp for her belt," Deel said, puffing ferociously.

"Deel, you're going to be, like, totally zonked if you—"

Deel glared at me. "So I'm totally zonked? What's it to you?"

I swallowed. "Anyway, I don't think that's true, what you said about Mom. She fell in love with Daddy. She married him."

"What's so wonderful about that?"

"Well, first of all, if it hadn't happened, we wouldn't *be* here."

"So?"

"What do you mean, so? Do you wish you weren't even born?"

Deel just looked mournful. "Sometimes . . ." she said, frowning. "I hate the way Mom acts at parties."

"In what way?"

"The way she acts with men, flirting with everybody, laughing hysterically at their jokes. It's so sick. It's so sexist."

"Well, she's from the South," I said.

"So? Jane is from Alabama, and she'd rather be drawn and *quartered* than act like that." Jane is Deel's best friend. She weighs 160 pounds, and is even more active politically than Deel.

"Mom says flirting is an art form, it's like acting."

"Sure, she says a lot of dumb things. So what?"

"Deel, come on . . . Daddy'll be hurt if you sit in here all afternoon. Let's go out and help serve, okay? We don't have to talk to anyone."

I guess what I worried about was whether Deel feels bad about my being in the movie, and about how Charlie was saying how terrific I am. Deel would hate to act, it's not that, but, well, I don't know.

I was glad when, later in the party, I saw Simon standing next to Deel, helping her serve the punch. You can always pick out Simon in a crowd. He's six foot five, and kind of gangling. He reminds me a little of this actor Joshua likes, called Jacques Tati. He has a mustache, which he twirls sometimes when he's nervous. He really likes Deel a lot. He says she has a truly original mind. That's true, she really does. I think Deel might have sort of a crush on Simon. He knows all about drugs and isn't at all moralistic about it, so I guess she feels she can talk to him more openly than she can to Mom and Daddy.

Everyone said how pretty I looked, and admired my dress. Charlie went around telling everybody about the movie. I think he was getting a little smashed at the end. At one point, he grabbed my hand as I went by and suddenly said, almost like he was yelling, "Ladies and gentlemen . . . I want you to meet the new star of the eighties . . . Miss Tatiana Engelberg."

Everybody cheered. I think they were all sort of drunk by then. I felt really embarrassed; Charlie wouldn't let go of my hand.

"The new Brooke Shields, huh?" someone said.

"Brooke Shields?" Charlie looked aghast. "Forget Brooke Shields, forget Mariel Hemingway, forget Bo Derek . . . forget *everybody!* This little girl, who never acted before, is going to knock you off your feet. Absolutely."

I tried to get him to let go of my hand.

"She's beautiful," Charlie said. "Tatiana, don't be bashful. It's the truth. I am telling the absolute, unadulterated truth. Not one *word* of exaggeration, not one *breath.*"

I tried to smile. Everyone was looking at me.

Daddy came over. "Charlie, come on, calm down . . . eat some praline cheesecake, and shut up already."

But Charlie just reached out and took Daddy's hand. "May I present the man who, single-handed, created what you see before you. Without these two splendid people—" he gestured toward Mom who was off at the end of the terrace with her shoes off, leaning on the railing, "—this creature, this enchanting, rapturous creature, would not exist."

Daddy had a lump of cheesecake on a fork. He stuffed it in Charlie's mouth. He smiled at me. "Come on, Tat . . . come on inside."

"I feel embarrassed," I whispered.

"He's looped."

Deel and Simon were sitting in a corner. "What's up?" Simon said.

"Charlie was just kind of ranting on," I said, sitting down next to them.

"That's his manner," Daddy said. He walked off to talk to someone.

I could tell from looking at Deel that she was zonked. Her eyelids were drooping. "Oh boy, this party has gone on for eighty hours," she said.

"Play Scrabble with me," Simon said.

"You can't at a party," Deel said.

"Who says?"

"I'm stoned out of my mind."

"So am I."

Deel looked around nervously. "Don't you want to talk to, like, regular people?"

"I thought I was."

"No, I mean, them. People your own age."

"Not especially . . . Is there anyone my age here? I thought they were all—"

Deel looked around. "Abigail," she said.

I remembered what Mom and Daddy had said. "I don't think they'd get along," I said. "I mean, in terms of romance."

"Who's Abigail?" Simon asked.

Deel pointed to her. She was out on the terrace. Abigail never gets that dressed up, even for parties. She had on a red Mexican skirt and a T-shirt.

"Not bad," Simon said.

"Mom says she isn't your type," I told him.

He laughed. "How come? In what way?"

It's always easy talking to Simon, much more than to Mom and Daddy's friends in general. I guess that's because he likes to joke around and stuff. "Well, Mom thinks she's too . . . I guess serious for you. I mean, too women's libish."

"Huh . . . and here I am, a guy with such diverse, and catholic tastes," Simon said.

"Mom thinks everyone is women's libish who doesn't drool continually over every man in sight," Deel snarled.

"Cordelia," Simon said, smiling.

"Well, it's true . . . *look* at her!" Way far off, Mom was dancing in a circle with a fat man in a green checked shirt.

"She's dancing," I said. "What's so bad about that?"

"Amanda is a lively, dynamic person," Simon said. "I don't think that's so bad."

"That's just because she drools over *you* and you fall for it," Deel said. She looked angry, and walked off.

Simon looked at me with widened eyes. "Oh dear," he said, sighing.

"Deel doesn't like parties," I said.

"So it would seem."

I frowned. "Simon, I'm really worried."

"What about?"

"That maybe Deel will be jealous of me once the movie opens."

"Yeah." Simon looked understanding.

"Daddy thinks the movie's dumb, Deel'll hate me," I said. "I wish I'd never *made* the thing! I don't even want to *be* an actress."

"Rusty, listen to me," Simon said. "You did it, I bet you were terrific, and you don't have anything to regret. Life is an adventure. Things happen you never expect—good things, bad things."

"Yeah," I said uncertainly. "Joshua thinks I'll get conceited and go off with older men . . . *I* don't think I will. I don't *want* to change."

"You'll change," Simon said. "Everyone does . . . but you'll handle it, don't worry. You'll handle it beautifully."

"I will?"

"Definitely. I don't have a doubt in the world."

I looked at him gratefully. Mom came over, still barefoot. Her cheeks were pink, and her hair was all tousled. "Are you having fun?" she said to Simon.

Simon nodded.

"I've been making a *total* ass out of myself. . . . George Phillips said he'd teach me disco dancing."

"We saw," Simon said.

Mom made a face. "Oh God . . . did I look awful?"

"You looked great." They smiled at each other.

"You are a kind and generous person," Mom said, looking right at him.

Simon looked abashed. "Well, I try."

"Hey, where's Deel?" Mom said, looking around. "Have you seen her, Tat?"

"I think she felt sleepy," I said nervously.

"I'll go look for her," Simon said.

I helped Mom carry some stuff into the kitchen. People were leaving. Only around eight were left, and most of them were still out on the terrace. "Simon was nice to Deel," I said. "But she seemed in kind of a bad mood."

"He's such a darling," Mom said wistfully. "Isn't he?"

"Yeah, he's nice," I said.

After everyone had left, Daddy sat down on the couch and looked through my collage calendar again. "This is my best present," he said, looking up at me. "It's beautiful, Tat."

"I'm glad you like it, Daddy."

"It's such a pity you don't do any drawing anymore."

"I might, again."

"You have such a wonderful free line. It's so inventive, really remarkable."

Luckily Deel was sleeping in her room at that point. I went to help Mom clear everything up.

Chapter Seven

The day before the screening, I called Charlie and asked if I could bring Joshua.

"Is he the young man who used to come to the set occasionally?"

"Yes."

"The one who wants to make wonderful and earth-shaking movies that'll make the rest of us look like fools?"

"Uh huh."

"By all means, bring him."

I feel mixed about bringing Joshua. I almost wish Charlie had said I couldn't bring him. I'm so afraid he'll hate it. Joshua has such high standards. Even movies that *everyone* likes, that get good reviews *everywhere*, like *Kramer Vs. Kramer*, he doesn't like that much. And I'm afraid he'll say I'm awful. I don't think he thinks I can act at all. And he's not the type that pretends and says nice things to make you feel better.

The screening was first. Then we were supposed to go to Charlie's house for a party. I sat between Joshua and Deel. Joshua never holds my hand or tries to make out in the movies the way some boys do. He says movies are important and deserve your undivided attention, just like sex. He sits straight in his seat and doesn't even eat popcorn.

I don't know. I guess I can't be objective about the movie either way. I didn't think I was bad. That was what I was really afraid of, that I'd seem just awful, like I didn't know what I was doing. There were some scenes where I was really good. One was a scene we did over and over and I remember I felt so tired at the end, but Charlie said that was good. He said when I was tired, I let my defenses down and just let emotion sweep over me. But there were some scenes where I think I looked self-conscious and funny, like I knew I was in a movie. I think it was a funny movie. People in the audience laughed. At some points they really roared, like the scene where my mother comes home unexpectedly and I dive under the covers and flatten out so she won't know I'm in bed with Warren. I kept sneaking looks at Joshua, but he didn't laugh that much. He just looked intent. Mom laughed out loud.

I guess the thing is you just can't judge a movie you're in, the way you can one you're not in. Like, if I see a regular movie, I don't even notice how the audience is reacting at all, whereas here I kept listening to see if they'd laugh, or I'd be surprised when they'd laugh at things I didn't think were so funny. Also, I guess, whenever I wasn't on, I kept waiting nervously for the times I would be again, so I didn't pay as much attention as I should have to the other actors. And when I was on, I felt so self-conscious, not just because of it being me, but because of everyone in my family, plus Joshua, being there, and wondering and worrying what they were all thinking. It was like an exam that's really important. The time went fast and slow. I felt exhausted when the lights finally came on. My heart was thumping a mile a minute. I looked over at Daddy.

"Well," he said, smiling.

"I loved it, Tat," Mom said. "I can't get over it . . . where did you learn all that?"

"It's in the genes," Daddy said.

"Did you really like it?" I said. I know that was a stupid thing to say, since she just said she did.

"You were sensational," Mom said. "No, I mean it. I've been

acting for decades and you did things I couldn't even . . . didn't you think, Lionel?"

We decided to sit there till everyone had cleared out, so we wouldn't be caught in the rush. I was glad because I didn't want anyone coming up to me.

"Yes, it was an interesting . . . the way—" Daddy started to say.

"And I thought the nude scene was handled in *perfect* taste," Mom rushed on. "Weren't you relieved, darling?"

"Well, I—" Daddy began.

"I thought it was gross," Deel said.

"The nude scene or the whole movie?" Daddy said.

Deel hesitated. "The nude scene."

"What did *you* think, Joshua?" Mom said. "Aren't you proud of Tat?"

Joshua had been sitting there quietly. Of course, with people he doesn't know that well, he can be quiet. "I thought it was good," he said.

I looked at him expectantly, thinking he'd say something more, about how he thought I was, but he didn't.

"I think we can chance it now," Daddy said, getting up. "All set?"

As we walked out, a woman rushed up to me and said, "Are you the little girl in the movie?"

"Of course she is," her friend said. "Look at her hair."

She squeezed my hand. "I thought you were just wonderful, dear. Just wonderful."

"Thank you," I said.

Mom and Daddy beamed, Deel scowled, and Joshua looked like some large water bug had just crawled up in front of him.

Outside, Charlie was talking with some friends. Abigail was next to him. "Here she is, everybody!" he said when he saw me. "My daughter of the spirit." To Daddy he said, "You don't mind, do you, Lionel? I need a daughter of the spirit. Here I am, born to be the father of daughters, and I have three sons. Where is the justice in life?"

"I'll go get a cab," Daddy said, and walked off.

"It's a good movie," Abigail said quietly, almost in surprise. "How was it seeing yourself, Tat?"

I frowned. "Funny . . . my voice sounded weird."

"It's hard seeing yourself for the first time . . . and you were on screen almost steadily. I really liked that part at the end where you're in the car with Warren, about to drive to California, and you suddenly say, 'I forgot Fred,' and run to get your teddy bear. That was nice."

Joshua and Deel were just standing around, looking awkward. I wished Joshua would at least say *something!* I wondered if he'd really hated it, or thought I was awful. But he could at least be polite! Just then, the boy who played Warren, Felix Propper, came over. He's really twenty-four, not seventeen the way he's supposed to be in the movie, but he looks young. He says now he doesn't mind, but he always has to show his driver's license before people'll give him a drink. He's gay and his friend, Marvin, who's also an actor, used to visit him a lot on the set.

"So, how's it going, Rust?" he said.

"Hi, Felix."

"You were in the movie," Deel said.

"Right." He smiled at her. "I was terrific, right? You want my autograph? You want an autographed photo of me to hang over your bed at night, and gaze at soulfully on long winter afternoons."

Deel smiled. "Yeah, well, you were good."

"I was sensational," Felix said. "You know, I was *so* scared I'd be awful. I was petrified! I've been on the toilet all day. I was ready to float away, Librium coursing through every vein . . . and then, as soon as I appeared on the screen, I thought: damn it, I'm good!" He grinned happily.

"What school do you go to?" Deel asked.

Felix smiled. "Well, the thing is, don't let this spread too far, but I'm actually a grandfather, I just look young."

"A grandfather?" Deel looked uncertain.

"No, I'm twenty-four, but I . . . it's my boyish impetuosity. I'm Peter Pan. I never grew up."

"Where's Marvin?" I said. "Did he come?"

"Can you believe this? He was too nervous. *I'm* the one in the movie, and *he's* too nervous. I'm going to call him. He said he'd come to the party. Listen, it was nice meeting you." To

Joshua he said, "Your sister's a great kid," he said. "Very sexy. She's going to knock 'em dead in a couple of years."

After he left, Joshua said, "What is he, a fag, or something?"

"He's gay," I said. Fag is a gross word. I hate it when Joshua says things like that.

Daddy was waving at us from the corner. "Where's Amanda?" he said.

"She went in a cab with Charlie," Deel said.

We all piled in. Daddy sat in front next to the driver.

"Did you think it was a good movie?" I said finally to Joshua.

"Well, the pacing was a little slow in the beginning," he said. "I think I would have done it differently. Serena Jowitt is really terrific."

Serena Jowitt plays my mother. She's been in lots of movies, usually in smaller parts. She's not that pretty, not as pretty as Mom, but she has an interesting face. She looks sort of like a ballet dancer. Her hair is black, parted in the middle. She told me she's part American Indian, I forget which part. She has really high cheekbones, and eyes that tilt up. Even though she's thirty-six, she's never been married. She says she's scared of kids.

"Will she be at the party?" Joshua said, like that was the only thing he cared about.

I felt mad. "I don't know . . . probably."

I think I hate Joshua. I think he's a mean person. If *he* was in a movie, a feature film, and had even a *little* part, even a walk-on part, I'd tell him he was wonderful whether I thought it or not. I'd make a big fuss, and shower him with praise. And all he's said so far is the pacing was slow, and Serena Jowitt was terrific.

I decided to get drunk at the party. They had champagne, which is the only drink I like that you can get drunk on. Charlie lives on the 30th floor with this really beautiful view of Central Park. His living room is gigantic, but it doesn't have much furniture in it. What I like is he has a chair shaped like a person. I wish I had a chair like that.

Mom was already at the party, talking to the man who played my father. Not Warren's father, who married my mother, but my real father who I see just a couple of times. Actually, they cut the scene where I visit him. Maybe they didn't think it was necessary. It's a scene where I go down to the Village, where he's living by himself. His name in real life is Horace Marone, and Daddy thinks he's a really fine actor. He's the kind of actor Daddy likes, who mainly acts in plays, and doesn't make much money. He's somewhat fat. We used to play chess sometimes on the set.

"What took you so long?" Mom said.

"Daddy couldn't get a cab," I said.

Just then Daddy came over and said to Horace, "Horace, you were wonderful."

"You noticed me?" Horace said. "You must have good eyesight."

"Why did he cut that scene with you and Tatiana?" Daddy said. We'd seen it in the rushes. "That was such a beautiful scene."

"Don't ask *me*," Horace said sadly.

"I loved that moment where Tat tells you her mother and Warren's father aren't getting along. Your expression! What economy of gesture. You can tell people who have acted, acted in the true sense, from movie people ten miles away."

Mom raised her eyebrows. "Lionel, heavens, do you mean to say just because people act in movies, they aren't real actors?"

"I don't mean that," Daddy said hastily. "I mean, with someone like Horace, you can sense that hours and hours of thinking have gone into every line, every move. It's rich, it's satisfying."

Horace was beaming. "Well, I'm glad someone notices."

"Anyone of discernment and taste will notice," Daddy said emphatically.

Mom walked off.

"And how about your daughter?" Horace said. "Not bad for a kid, huh?"

"A kid?" Daddy said. "This is no kid . . ." He put his arm around me. "No, I have to say I was impressed. She really held her own, didn't she?"

"I'll say," Horace said, rolling his eyes. "When she's on, you don't notice anything else."

"Though I do think," Daddy said, clearing his throat, "that

Charlie might have . . . I think maybe he was too easy on her in some ways."

"Too *easy?*" I could feel the champagne bubbling up my nose. "He made me do some scenes ten times!"

"Well, it's a matter of emphasis," Daddy said. "I think *I* would have . . .."

I went over to get another glass of champagne. The glasses were just standing there, in a row, already filled. Then I looked around for Joshua. He was in a corner, talking to Serena Jowitt. She was wearing this really dramatic dress, all black, with long, tight sleeves and no back. It had a slit that went way up one side. Joshua was staring at her like someone had hypnotized him.

"Hi," I said. I knew I was drunk. Everything seemed fuzzy and bright.

"There you are, Tatiana," Serena said. "Joshua, have you met the star of the movie?"

"Yeah, we know each other," Joshua said uncomfortably.

That was nice of him, to admit he knew me.

"Oh," Serena said, smiling. She has a dazzling smile with perfect white teeth. "From school?"

"Sort of," I said.

Then suddenly Joshua blurted out, "She's my girl friend."

Serena said to me, "That's lovely! I didn't know you had a boyfriend, dear." Then to Joshua she said, "You must be proud as all get-out. I mean, Tatiana must have men after her in *droves.*"

"Yeah, I guess she probably will," Joshua said, clenching his jaw, "after the movie opens."

"It's fun," Serena said vaguely. I think maybe she was drunk too.

"What's fun?" I asked.

"Having men dropping at your feet. . . . But it's . . . it's not *real.*"

"Yeah?" I said, not sure what she meant.

"They see you up there and they don't see *you.* You're a symbol, a *thing.* You're smart, Tatiana. You'll take it all with a grain of salt."

A man came up in back of her and put his arms around

her. She turned around. "Oh hi, Max . . . Have you met Tatiana and Joshua?"

Max had blond hair and sort of chunky, square features and a beard. "Tatiana, I feel like I know you," he said, gripping my hand. "You were magnificent."

"Thank you," I said.

"I'm not just saying this because you're gorgeous. I mean you *are* gorgeous, you know that, don't you?"

I shrugged.

"Max, stop embarrassing her," Serena said.

"You have a very special gift," he said, talking slowly and looking right at me. "Don't lose it, okay? Don't spoil it. It's pure and fresh and wonderful. . . . *And* you've got *incredible* tits."

"Max!" Serena nudged him. "Will you stop it? This is Tatiana's boyfriend, Joshua."

"You're a lucky guy, Joshua," Max said. "Hold the fort, okay?"

Joshua looked at him with loathing.

"Hang on to her," he said as Serena dragged him off.

Joshua and I stood staring at each other.

"Your chin is wet," I said grimly.

"Huh?"

"From drooling all over her."

He just looked at me.

"Well, I guess you're having a good time," I said.

"You look like *you* are," he countered.

"What do you mean?" I asked defensively.

"Well, you look like you're getting pretty plastered."

"So, why shouldn't I?"

"No reason."

"You're a real shit, Joshua, you know that? Trying to spoil the whole party for me."

I walked off and left him. Well, I'm glad I found out what an awful person Joshua Lasker is. I must have been really dumb not to have noticed it before. He's not only mean and selfish, he's insensitive and cruel and he's not even right about my being drunk. I only had maybe three glasses of champagne! I bet he had more than that.

At midnight Daddy said he thought we should go home. Deel had fallen asleep in the chair shaped like a person. Daddy had a hard time waking her up.

"What happened to Joshua?" she said, yawning as we went down in the elevator.

"He left early," Mom said.

Everyone looked at me.

"I don't think he likes parties that much," I said, trying to explain.

Nobody talked much on the way home. I felt lousy, sort of sick, but not sick enough to throw up. When I got home, I went right to bed. I didn't even take my makeup off or anything, I was so tired.

Chapter Eight

When I woke up in the morning, I felt strange. I felt like I hadn't brushed my teeth for a week and my tongue seemed all puffy. I lay in bed, dozing, for an hour or so and then got up. It was almost one. I took a shower and washed my hair. Then I went into the kitchen and had a big glass of orange juice. I felt better. Not wonderful, but better. There was a message Scotch-taped to the refrigerator. "Tat—Abigail called. Call her."

It turned out Abigail wanted me to baby-sit for her that night, if I could. She said it would be from seven to whenever she got home, maybe midnight or one. I said okay. Usually I see Joshua Saturday night. But after last night, I don't think I want to see him ever again. I feel badly about it. I mean, I loved Joshua, and I don't mean just sex. I really loved him and I thought he was a nice person. Lots of guys are mean and try to manipulate you in lots of ways, but Joshua never seemed like that. But it may show I don't have such good judgment in men.

I didn't do much during the day. I went out in the afternoon and walked along Broadway. There's a thrift shop that has terrific clothes sometimes. I bought an old sailor jacket there last month. Some of the things are real bargains, wonderful straw hats with

83

flowers and real embroidered stockings. I bought a pair of white crocheted stockings for only fifteen cents.

Daddy was home when I got back. He was looking at this menu that we have from Empire Szechuan, a Chinese restaurant we sometimes order from; they deliver. "How about sweet-and-sour pork?" he said. "How does that sound?"

"I can't, Daddy . . . I have to be at Abigail's at seven."

He looked surprised. "What for?"

"She wants me to baby-sit."

"Huh . . . well, it's pretty far. Better take a cab home."

"Okay, I will."

I sat down opposite him in the comfortable chair. He looked at me fondly. "So, how's the star?"

"Daddy, don't, okay?"

He frowned. "What's wrong?"

"No, I just don't like it when people make such a fuss over me. I mean, I'm still the same person."

"True . . . Are you feeling down, sweets?"

I nodded.

"Do you want to talk about it?"

I shrugged.

Daddy was looking at me with a kindly expression. He patted the couch next to him. "Come sit over here, okay?"

I went over and sat there, leaning against him.

"What is it, puss?" Daddy said softly. "Tell me."

"It's Joshua," I said and suddenly I began to sob into his arms. "He was so *awful!* He didn't even say he liked the movie. He didn't even say anything to me about how I was. He just spent all evening drooling over Serena Jowitt. I never want to see him again, ever!"

I sobbed and sobbed while Daddy put his arms around me and said, "Don't, darling, don't." Finally, when I was down to the sniffing stage, he said in a quiet voice, "Sweetie, look, obviously I don't know Joshua that well . . . But I think it might be— You see, he has this special relationship with you which obviously means a lot to him, and it's threatening and scary to him that now he'll have to . . . share you with the rest of the world. I can understand that."

"But he's not sharing me," I said. "He thinks I'm going to have stupid affairs with dumb men who are rich . . . but I'm not, Daddy! I don't even want to."

Daddy smiled. "Well . . . anyway, you know maybe this proves what I was trying to say the other day, Tat, that you're a little too young for such an intense, exclusive relationship. You need to go out in the world with many different kinds of men or boys so that when you do make your final choice, it'll be something lasting."

"Why can't I meet the right person now? Then I'd save all that trouble."

Daddy was silent a minute. He kept stroking my hair. "Well, you could, darling, but the chances are that any choice you'd make now wouldn't be something you could live with later on . . . just because you're changing. You're changing right this second. Six months from now you'll be a different person and two years from now different again."

"Because of the movie?"

"Partly, but not just that. Many things. Life is change. Nothing stays the same, neither things we want to nor things we don't." He sounded sad. I thought of the lyrics for this song in a musical I went to with Deel and Mom called *I'm Getting My Act Together and Taking It on the Road:*

Love is rare, life is strange
Nothing lasts, people change.

"I don't know," I said.

"Your life will have so many exciting, wonderful things in it, Tat," Daddy said. "It's all opening out in front of you. It's not a sad thing, it's a—"

"But doesn't that bother you, things changing that way?"

Daddy twisted a strand of my hair around his finger. "Well, of course, there's a part of me that wants to hang on to the past, naturally, that hates to see you grow up and change. But it's also an exciting, wonderful thing for me to watch it happen. I felt so proud watching you yesterday."

"Did you really?" I said, surprised.

"Of course. . . . All those things you did."

I smiled at him. "I'm glad, Daddy. I thought you were ashamed . . . especially with the nude scene."

"No. Ashamed? How could I be? I feel like Joshua must— torn. I don't want to share you. But I also feel like a proud parent wanting to go up to everyone and say: that's my Tatiana."

That made me feel so good. We sat there a few more minutes, not saying anything. "I feel better now," I said. I looked at my watch. "I guess I better get going."

I washed my face, got my knapsack and headed off for Abigail's.

I'd never seen her apartment before. It turned out to be a walk-up. You had to walk up four flights of stairs. I was out of breath when I got to the top. There was some chamber music on in the background, the kind Daddy likes to listen to. It was just one big room, the living room, and then a smaller room in back for Kerim and a little garden off to one side, with an iron table and three chairs. It was kind of bare. Like in the living room there was mostly just a couch with a lot of pillows and one sort of old-looking chair. On the wall were lots and lots of photos.

"Hi," Abigail said, letting me in. She was almost whispering. "Listen, you may be in terrific luck. He just fell asleep. He's been going full steam all day and he just kind of dropped, literally, in the middle of the floor. I covered him with a blanket."

"Will he wake up?" I asked, taking off my coat.

"Maybe. Sometimes he does and sometimes he doesn't. If he does, play with him awhile, read, whatever he feels like. He might want some milk or something." She put on her coat with the hood. "Tat, you were really impressive in the movie . . . I wanted to tell you. Lionel must be bursting with pride."

"Thanks," I said.

"I think it's a good movie," she said, judiciously. "Not a big money-maker, maybe, but I think it'll go places."

After she'd left, I sat down on the couch and took out this book I have to read for school, *Rebecca*. I read a little bit of it and then put it down. I kept thinking of everything Daddy said, especially the part about Joshua. I still don't see why he couldn't have been nice, I really don't. It still makes me feel bad, no matter what the reason was. It's not like I'm one of these people who has to have a boyfriend all the time and feels bad if she doesn't. But, well, I thought there was more to our relationship than that. I lay down and covered myself with a blanket and started to fall asleep.

Suddenly the phone rang. It was in the kitchen. I went in to answer it. "Hello?"

"Oh, hi, Rust . . . Is that you?" It was Joshua.

"How'd you know I was here?"

"I called your house."

"Oh."

"Listen, Rust, I feel bad about last night."

I felt like saying: you should! "Well . . ."

"Could I, like, come down there?"

"It's in the Village. It'll take you forty minutes."

"That's okay. I really want to. There's a lot I want to say, about the movie and everything."

I hesitated. "If all you want to do is fuck, we can't because Kerim is here and he might wake up and I don't want to anyway."

"That's not why I want to see you."

"Okay." I gave him the address.

I was afraid I might stop being mad at Joshua if he came down and acted nice so I sat there the whole forty minutes remembering how awful he was. When he rang the bell, I let him in but I didn't smile or anything.

"Hi," he said, obviously trying to be friendly.

I glared at him. "So, what'd you want to say?" I said, sitting back down on the couch.

Joshua cleared his throat. "Well, first, I wanted to say what I thought about the movie."

"You thought it stank."

"I didn't . . . I think it's quite a good movie. It's funny, parts of it are well written, and I think you were really good."

"Joshua, you know you make me so *mad!*" I turned away.

"Why?"

"Because you don't think *any* of that. It's a big lie. You just want to get back on my good side again. You're just a total liar."

"Rust, I would never lie to you about a movie."

"You wouldn't?"

"Never . . . what would be the point? Listen, I'll tell you the truth. I expected it to be lousy, I expected you wouldn't know your ass from your elbow. I was, well, pretty amazed."

I stared at him. "Do you swear that's true?"

He put up his hand. "I swear."

"You *really* thought I was good?"

"Here's what I thought." Joshua frowned. "I think you can act. I mean you know how. You become the person. You didn't act yourself. She was different from you."

"How?"

"Well, you're completely natural, she was kind of a tease. She played around with men—Warren, his father. She was the kind of girl who knew every second she was gorgeous and used it. She was a user. You're not."

I nodded. That was true. "That's what I didn't like about her."

"But you see, that's what was impressive. You could have just acted yourself, but it would have spoiled the movie. It was good that in the movie you feel ambivalent about her. She's kind of a little brat in some ways. I feel sorry for Warren."

"Yeah." Joshua is so smart! I think he's smarter than Deel or Daddy even, the way he can analyze everything.

"You didn't try to make the audience like you. You didn't play on their sympathies. You did a lot of really good stuff."

"Thank you," I said formally.

"Now you did some bad stuff, too," he said.

"I did?"

"Yeah, well, maybe not *bad*, but . . . You didn't always play to the other actors. Like Serena, whether she was talking or not, she was acting. You, when you weren't talking, just kind of stood there like you were thinking: I wonder if I got eighty-five on my math test. You, like, weren't there."

"Oh." I felt bad. Charlie said that to me a few times.

"Some of the actors fed you stuff and you didn't pick up on it. Like Marone. He tried to set stuff up with you and you kind of glided past him, like he wasn't there."

"Yeah, well." I looked sideways at him. "What'd you think of the nude scene? Did you think it was in good taste?"

Joshua looked solemn. "It had socially redeeming value," he said.

I looked at him to see if he was joking.

"Rust, your ass definitely has socially redeeming value. It does. It's an uplifting sight. It gives one the courage to go on."

I socked him. "Joshua!"

"And your tits . . . Well, one sight of them and anyone in their right mind is ready to go out and lead the revolution."

Joshua can always make me laugh. The trouble is, then I can't stay mad at him. "So, why'd you act like such a jerk at the party?"

He held up a finger. "One, because I always feel uncomfortable at parties; two, because I didn't feel like I could sit down and have a real talk with you like we're doing now; and three, because I felt sick when that handsome guy came over and began coming on to you."

"He *wasn't* handsome. He was gross."

"He was handsome. . . . And I thought of all the thousands of men like that who are going to start coming on to you once it opens and, well—"

I leaned over and put my arms around him. "I love *you*," I said.

"I'm a scruffy sixteen-year-old kid."

"You're not scruffy."

"I can't even give you an orgasm. I just pounce on you—"

"You don't, Joshua. You do everything right. You're terrific. It's me. I'm just uptight or something."

"I bet that guy would have had you coming all over the place in three seconds."

"Well, he'll never have the chance." I was silent a second. "But, Josh, would you tell me something?"

"Sure."

"If we didn't have sex, would you still see me?"

He looked at me, puzzled. "Why, don't you want to anymore?"

"No, it's not that, but I don't want to think you see me just to, you know, fuck."

"I don't, Rust . . . really. Whatever gave you that idea?" But he was smiling.

"Well, it seems like it's on your mind fairly often."

"Look, Rust, I mean, you're beautiful and sexy and I'm at my hormonal peak and all that, so it's hard for me not to think about it when I'm with you. But we don't have to do it so much if you don't want." He looked sad at the prospect.

"I just don't want to think that's the only thing you like about me."

"It isn't . . . Listen, I think you're a sensitive, terrific person."

"Really?"

"Definitely."

"But I can't write poetry like Pam."

"True . . . Well I can't ride a horse like Robert Redford."

I laughed. "I think *you're* a sensitive, terrific person," I said, lying down in his arms.

He shrugged, snuggling up next to me. "Well, I am. What can I say. It's immodest to admit, but—"

I began kissing him. "I guess I wouldn't have liked it if *you'd* been in a movie and been in a nude scene."

"The women in the audience would have been screaming," Joshua said, slipping his hand under my shirt to my breasts. "They would have gone wild."

"Josh . . . I'm afraid Kerim will wake up."

"No, he's out cold for the night."

"How do you know?" I was beginning to feel fuzzy.

"I'm psychic."

"Umm, oh, Rust." Joshua was making that crooning sound he does when he strokes my body. He stood up and took his clothes off. I wasn't worried about Abigail coming back so soon; it was only ten thirty. I took his penis in my mouth and sucked on it for a while. He really likes it when I do that. I'm never sure if I do it the right way, but whatever way I do it, he likes it a lot. I don't think I'd like it if he came in my mouth, though. He says he won't.

Fucking with him was nice. He really tried to go slow and he was really tender and caring. I love Joshua. I do. I don't care if I'm too young. The point is, what if you meet the most terrific person in the world and you happen to be fourteen? Does that mean you should give them up and look around at other people? That doesn't make sense to me.

When we were done, we got dressed, just in case, and then snuggled up under the blanket again. "Rust?"

"Yeah?"

"Did you ask them yet?"

"Ask who what?"

"Well, you said you were going to ask your parents to get you a diaphragm for Christmas."

"Oh right . . . I will."

"Do you think they'll get it for you?"

"Well, they should . . . they got one for Deel."

"But she was older . . . and they knew she'd never use it."

"She may use it eventually."

"I think it would be really good," Joshua said. "Tommy said his girl friend has one and he says it makes a big difference."

"Which one? I thought he has around nine million girl friends."

"That blond one, the one who's a waitress in New Haven who had a kid when she was sixteen."

"Oh right. . . . Well, I guess she doesn't want that to happen again."

"It can't."

"How come?"

"She's eighteen now."

"What does he say is so good about it?"

"Well, he says it just feels better. I mean, you don't feel it. You just put it in and forget about it."

"I'd be afraid I wasn't putting it in right."

"I'll help you."

"I wish it was easier. I wish fucking and getting pregnant weren't connected in any way."

"Yeah, well . . ."

"I wonder who thought of connecting them?"

"God . . . No, I don't know. It wasn't like a person sat down and thought of it."

"But do you see what I mean? How it would be better if they didn't have anything to do with each other so you wouldn't have to worry."

"If you get a diaphragm, you won't have to worry."

"I mean, I'd like to have children *eventually*," I said, "but like not for ten years maybe."

"I think we should have four kids," Joshua said. "Two will be redheads and two will be dark."

"But will you help me with everything, like giving them bottles and changing diapers? You won't just go off and leave me with all that?"

"Never . . . what do you take me for?"

"You might be off making movies."

"You might too."

I shook my head. "I think I'm going to be an obstetrician, actually."

"Really? How come?"

"I don't know. I just think I might like it."

"You'd have to go to medical school and all that."

"So?"

"You'd have to dissect corpses."

"I know."

Joshua is extremely squeamish about things like that. He told me he almost fainted in Biology when they had to dissect a frog. His partner did most of it. I guess he's just a very sensitive person. I think I'm sensitive too, but doing things like dissecting frogs doesn't bother me so much.

"You'd have to deliver babies," he said.

I smiled. "I know. That's the part I think I'd really like."

Joshua looked a little sick. "But they come out all slimy with stuff all over them, blood and—"

"Yeah, but they almost always survive and everybody is so happy. It must be a terrific feeling to make people happy that way."

"I guess." He didn't look convinced.

"That's why you want to make movies, isn't it?" I said, rubbing his belly button with my nose. "To make people happy?"

Joshua shook his head. "No . . . Why should I want to make people happy?"

"Well, you don't want to make them *sad*, do you?"

"Sure. I want to make them sad, I want to make them *think* about things they never thought of."

"Yeah." I think I sort of know what he means.

After that we had hot cocoa and navel oranges and listened to music on Abigail's radio. She came home at one thirty. Charlie was with her. I was surprised. I didn't know they went out on dates together.

"Greetings, fair Tatiana!" Charlie said. He turned to Abigail. "See, she's even radiant at one in the morning."

"I know," Abigail said. "It's not fair."

"And this, if I'm not mistaken," Charlie said, seeing Joshua, "is the splendid young man who is going to make monkeys of us all."

Joshua looked at him, puzzled.

"Aren't you the future Ingmar Bergman?" Charlie said. "I thought—"

"Tat, what do I owe you?" Abigail said.

I figured it out. "Better take a cab," she said, handing me the money. "It's starting to snow."

Charlie was already lying back, lounging on the couch. Joshua and I had fixed it up. I don't think you could tell we'd been fucking on it. "Farewell, my beauty," he said, waving at me languidly. "See you on the fifteenth."

Outside on the street we looked around for a cab. It was snowing lightly. "Do you think he's a good director?" I asked Joshua.

"Fair . . ."

"As good as Daddy?"

"Well, your father's never done a feature."

"Do you think he'd be good if he did?"

"It's hard to tell. . . . Does he want to?"

"Yeah, I think so. He almost did once, but it fell through."

I was so sleepy on the way home I fell asleep, leaning against Joshua. He took the cab the rest of the way to his house because he lives farther uptown. I don't feel mad at him at all anymore.

Chapter Nine

The next morning, Sunday, Daddy was up when I got up.
He was jumping rope on the terrace. That's supposed to be
good for his heart, as well as for losing weight. When he saw me,
he stopped and came in.

"You're up early," he said.

"It's ten," I pointed out. I guess Deel and Mom were still
asleep. "Daddy, I'm not mad at Joshua anymore," I said, going
into the kitchen. "He said he was sorry."

"When did you see him?" Daddy asked, puzzled. "I thought
you were baby-sitting last night."

"You gave him my number at Abigail's."

"No, I didn't. It must have been Amanda."

"Oh . . . well, anyway we talked about everything and I
feel good now."

Daddy was pouring some coffee beans into a cup. "Good," he
said, but in a slightly insincere way.

"Charlie was there," I said, pouring myself some grapefruit
juice.

"Where?" Daddy turned on the coffee grinder.

"At Abigail's. I didn't know she went out with him, like on
dates."

94

"Oh, she doesn't," Daddy said, raising his voice so I could hear him over the coffee grinder. "They're just friends."

"Oh."

He flicked the coffee grinder off. "What made you think otherwise?"

"What?"

"What made you think they were out on a date?"

"Well, just that he came back with her at one thirty and was still there when we left."

Daddy frowned. "Well, to the best of my knowledge . . . my understanding was that . . . the main thing is, I don't think Charlie is the kind of man that Abigail would be interested in."

"Why not?"

"Well, divorced three times. He's something of a womanizer. I just feel she would want someone more . . . serious, with more depth."

"Don't you think Charlie has depth?" I said.

"Not really. . . . Oh, he's charming, there's no doubt of that. But he skims over the surface of things."

I poured myself a glass of milk and added a big dose of coffee syrup to it. I like that on Sunday, with a sticky honey bun all covered with raisins. "I used to think Abigail was gay," I said, taking a bite of the honey bun.

Daddy smiled. "Why? Goodness, how curious."

"I guess she seemed sort of . . . Well, she never wears makeup or anything. She doesn't seem that feminine."

"Well, but darling, surely you realize all that is just a hype of our culture—makeup, perfume. . . . They want you to believe those things are necessary, so they'll sell their product. Not all women fall for that."

"Well, Mom wears makeup," I said, "and it looks nice on her."

"True . . . No, I'm not saying . . . I'm just saying when you're young like Abigail or you, why muck yourself up with all that junk? If your skin is nice, and your hair . . ." He looked thoughtful.

I know what Daddy means, but I like makeup. I like eye makeup the most. The thing is, it really makes a difference. I don't wear it a lot, just when I go out sometimes, but when I put lots of makeup on, my eyelashes really do look extremely long and it makes me look much older and more sexy than I do without it.

"Daddy?"

"Umm?" He was still looking bemused.

"You know how you said I should start thinking about what I want for Christmas?"

"Yes?"

"Well, the thing is, there is something I want and I thought I'd ask you about it before you got me something else."

"Umm hmm?"

"The thing is, it's a little bit expensive."

"How much?"

"I think about thirty-five dollars."

"That doesn't sound too exorbitant. What is it?"

I cleared my throat. "A diaphragm."

Daddy stared at me.

"You know, like what you got Delia?"

"Well, but Delia was older," Daddy said.

"So?"

Daddy looked at me, a funny smile on his face. "Darling."

"What?"

"Could you tell me one thing?"

"Sure."

"Whose idea was this? Was it Joshua's?"

"Well, sort of, but . . . I think it's a good idea. You don't want me to get pregnant, do you?"

"No, but surely there are other methods which—"

"The pill's supposed to not be that good for you, Joshua said."

Daddy poured himself some more coffee into his favorite mug. Mom got it for him. It has his sign on it. "Darling, now look, this is the point. I have the very distinct feeling that Joshua is pushing this side of your relationship when you're simply not ready for it."

"Daddy, that's not true! He just says it's more comfortable with a diaphragm."

"How does he know?"

"His brother's girl friend has one."

"I just don't feel comfortable with the idea," Daddy said. "You're fourteen, sweetheart. That's still extremely young."

"It *isn't*," I said angrily. "It used to be, but it isn't anymore."

"Tat, life has certain basic stages that everyone has to go through. If a child were to walk at two months, or talk at four, it wouldn't even be good. Nature has set things up so we ease into these things, so we take the next step when we're really ready for it, biologically, emotionally, physically."

"But, Daddy, we'll be doing it anyway . . . so what difference does it make? I'll just go get one on my own." I glared at him. "I thought you wanted me to be open about things. You sound just like everybody else's parents."

Daddy looked hurt. "I *do* want you to be open," he said.

"No, you don't!" My cheeks were flaming. "You just want to hear things you *like*. You don't want to hear the truth."

Just then Deel walked in. "About what?"

"I just said I want a diaphragm for Christmas," I said. "Like you."

"Well, but I'm older," Deel said, "and more mature."

Can you imagine? I was sure Deel would be on my side. "So? I'm mature for my age," I said huffily.

"You?" Deel looked incredulous. "That's a good one."

"Well, I have a boyfriend and you don't," I said.

"Big deal . . . I wouldn't want Joshua Poshua if he washed up on a desert island and I hadn't seen a boy in eighteen months."

Deel always calls Joshua "Joshua Poshua" when she wants to get my goat.

"Girls," Daddy said.

"Well, he wouldn't want *you*," I said. "You're just jealous because no one's even asked you."

"What do you mean?" Deel said, turning red. "*Lots* of people have asked me."

"Who? Name one."

"Percival Becker."

"Who's he? I bet he's not even real."

"He is *so* real, and he's a lot nicer than pimply old Joshua, I can tell you that."

Deel should talk about pimples! She washes her face around ten times a day and she still has them, even though Mom took her to some fancy skin doctor on Park Avenue who gave her all these special lotions and soaps.

"Girls," Daddy said. "Now wait . . . we're getting off the track."

"I don't see why you *don't* get it for her," Deel said savagely, opening the refrigerator. "She'll probably be fucking with everybody in sight once the movie opens."

"That's not true," I wailed. "I love Joshua. I don't want to fuck with anybody but him."

"Cordelia, that was uncalled for," Daddy said.

"So, why don't you want to give it to her? You're just scared."

"I'm not scared," Daddy said. "I was just questioning."

"She'll just get it anyway," Deel said, "the way she got those boots and those earrings. You're so dumb, you don't even know!"

I couldn't believe Deel would do such a mean, terrible thing, to tell Daddy something I told her in utmost confidence. I'm never going to trust her about anything again, ever.

"Cordelia, I consider my judgment in these matter sufficiently sound so that . . ."

"You don't even care!" Deel said. "Well, *I* feel ashamed to have a sister who goes around sticking her boobs in people's faces in 3D just because she gets paid for it. It makes *me* want to throw up!"

"You don't even have any to show anyone," I said. That wasn't nice, but it's true. Deel has less breasts than Daddy.

"Girls, I mean it," Daddy said. "This is ugly and I want you to stop it immediately. Tat, we'll talk it over further later. I want to discuss it with Amanda, and see—"

"Oh, she'll give her anything," Deel said.

"You're really a mean person, Cordelia Engelberg," I said. "You're a mean, terrible person."

"And you're a spoiled little brat," Deel fired back.

I slammed the door of my room, and locked it. Then I lay on my bed for half an hour, fuming. Deel can be nasty at times, but she's never been in a mood like *that*, ever. She must really be jealous of my being in the movie. Well, are any of those things my fault? *I* can't help it if I'm pretty and nice, and boys like me. Is that something wrong? *She's* the one who said she was just going to go out and fuck with the first person she saw, if no one asked her by February. I wouldn't do that. I wouldn't do it with anyone except someone I truly loved, who truly loved me.

When I came out later, Daddy was sitting listening to the opera. I just looked at him.

"Delia went out," he said.

I shrugged.

"Tat, listen, this is all very hard for her. You can understand that, can't you?"

"What?"

"All the attention you're getting, will get . . . it's very painful. Even if she wasn't older than you, it would be, but as it is . . . You know she's very thin-skinned. That's just her nature."

"I don't say bad things about *her*."

"You don't have to . . . you're not jealous of her."

"She's just mean," I muttered.

"No . . . she's not mean. She's just going through a difficult time. It would be hard, even without the movie. Anyway! Look, I've been thinking it over. The point is, what *I* say or think, or feel obviously, isn't going to change the reality of the situation. And, well, I do think being responsible about these matters is a good thing. I just have a terrible fear that, despite everything you say, none of this would be happening if Joshua hadn't . . . that you . . . you're not doing it for *your* pleasure, but for *his*."

I shook my head.

"You know, there've been studies," Daddy said, "that show that a full eighty percent of teenage girls having sex don't have orgasms."

"So?" I said nervously.

"Well, the point is—that indicates they're not getting any pleasure out of it."

"Do you think that's the only pleasure in sex, having orgasms?" I said.

"Maybe not the only, but . . ."

I felt defensive. "There's lots of nice things besides that."

Daddy looked embarrassed. "Yes, well . . ."

"Maybe it takes girls longer to catch on," I said. From Daddy's expression, I had the feeling he didn't feel comfortable talking about it. "It gives you something to look forward to."

Daddy didn't say anything.

"Didn't you like girls when you were a teenager?" I said.

"Well, of course I did," Daddy said.

"But, I mean, like someone special."

He reflected, "Well, it's true, there was . . . oh dear, what was her name? She had brown hair parted on the side, and she—"

"Did you go out with her?"

"Tat, in the high school I went to, no one went out especially. It just—I don't know—it wasn't done."

"So what'd you do about sex?"

He smiled sheepishly. "Dreamed."

"That's all?"

"Basically."

From what Mom has said, it was completely different in her school. She went out with lots of people, and did just about everything with quite a few. She says that in small southern towns there isn't much else to do besides make out on warm summer nights.

Later, when Mom got up, I told her about what had happened. She said she thought the whole thing was a tempest in a teapot and that Daddy was acting like a father in a Dickens novel, and that she'd make an appointment for me with her gynecologist next week. "I mean, my goodness," she said, "I think every woman over the age of eight should bow down to Mecca ten times a *day* for living in an era where there's reasonably safe, effective birth control. When I think of the hysteria *we* went through with missed periods!"

"Did you ever get pregnant?" I asked.

"I was one of the lucky ones . . . but just because my periods were irregular. Poor Sallie Keane actually had to *marry* Bob Conroy, and got stuck with *twins!*"

"What happened to her?" I asked.

"Oh, she dug her way out eventually . . . but it took fifteen years of total hell and diapers, and hideous dinners with his— whatever you call them. He worked at some garage. I mean, men in greasy overalls drinking beer! The kind of thing you see on TV, but don't think really exists in real life. Men who call women 'broads' and that kind of thing."

"I guess you were lucky meeting Daddy," I said.

Mom smiled. "*He* was lucky."

"Was Dora his type? Like you said—the woman intellectual type?"

"Dora?" Mom looked aghast. "Intellectual? Hon, the poor woman had trouble signing her *name*. No, that's not fair, but see, the basic thing with Jewish men of Lionel's generation is they all, to a man, married dim-witted, pretty, non-Jewish girls, Irish Catholic nurses, Mormons, you name it . . . and then even they got bored to stupefaction and moved on. I was just a variation on a theme."

Mom is pretty, and not Jewish. "But you're not dim-witted," I said.

"True, but, well, I'm not bookish, I'm more . . . street smart, if anything. No, I *was* definitely a step up, no doubt of that. . . . So listen, hon, you'll see Dr. Hubbard, okay? She's a sweetie, don't be nervous. I personally hate diaphragms, but I guess it's just as well."

"Why do you hate them?"

"Oh, it's just a drag, having to remember them, and making sure they're in place. They're a wave of the past, but, well—"

Mom has an IUD, I think.

When I told Joshua, he was really pleased.

The opening of *Domestic Arrangements* was on December 19. Daddy asked if it was okay if he and Deel didn't go. He said he felt it would be hard for Deel, that she'd seen it anyway, and he had to get up early the next day to go to Boston for a week to do this movie on lung disease. "Tat, if it means a lot to you, I'll go," he said. "But I thought in the interests of family harmony . . ."

"No, that's okay," I said. In some ways, I'll almost feel better if they don't come. Having your family around is a drag in certain ways. Mom said she wouldn't miss it for the world. She said Simon would go with us since he hadn't seen it yet.

Joshua didn't want to go either. "Do you mind, Rust? I mean, I just think it's not my kind of thing, an opening."

I laughed.

"What's funny?"

"Well, *you're* not going, *Daddy's* not going, *Deel* isn't going."

"Who'll you go with?"

"Mom and Simon . . . listen, it's okay."

"Are you nervous?"

"Sort of . . . you mean about the reviews?"

"Yeah."

"Daddy heard *Newsweek* is going to pan it."

"Well, those are the breaks. They might like you, but not the movie."

"I don't think they like me, either, but I think someone else did."

"Look, no matter what happens, you did a good job, and you know it. They can't take that away from you."

"Did I?"

"Yeah, you did, Rust. So don't let any of those snot-nose critics get to you. What do *they* know?"

That's nice of Joshua to say because I happen to know there are some critics he thinks are really good, like the one for *New York* magazine and Andrew Sarris in the *Voice*. He likes Pauline Kael, too. He says he doesn't always agree with her, but he respects the way her mind works. I bet all of them will hate it, and some dope that he thinks doesn't know anything will say I'm great!

I decided to wear my purple dress. Mom says there are two approaches one can have to having red hair. One is to wear gray and olive green and sort of drab colors like that. The other is to wear purple and shocking pink and orange and knock them right between the eyes. Mom says she's of the latter school. This purple dress, which we got together at Bendel's, is a really bright purple silk with a slit up one side. I wore it with these dark red boots, the ones Mom told Daddy cost less than they really did. Because Joshua wasn't going, I wore tons of eye makeup. He likes me best without any makeup, but I decided I should at least try to look glamorous. I washed my hair that morning and it looked really nice.

Mom wore a white dress she has with clumps of flowers strewn all over it. Simon wore a suit! I never saw him in one before. Usually he wears denim shirts and jeans. "Are you nervous?" he asked.

"No, not so much," I said. Mom was inside dressing. Dad and Deel had gone out to eat together.

"I'm really looking forward to it. Mandy says it's great."

The second time, seeing the movie, I liked it more. I mean, I enjoyed it more just as a movie. I wasn't so worried because I knew what to expect. And since no one was there that I knew personally, I didn't have to keep looking to see what their reactions were. Simon sat between me and Mom. There was one funny thing—he held Mom's hand. I just noticed it when I was leaning forward to pick up my glove.

When it was over, we walked out into the lobby. Suddenly a bunch of kids rushed over to me. One of them said, "That's her!" Another one said, "Can I have your autograph?" I looked at Mom and Simon. They just smiled and stood to one side. I signed my name around thirty times. One girl gave me a slip of paper. One boy asked if I'd sign his sneaker! Another one asked if I'd write my name on his hand. He had a ball-point pen. When I did, he said, "I won't wash it off—ever." I stared at him. I guess there are a lot of weird people in the world.

Felix was there, signing autographs, too. Toward the end, when people were moving out, he waved at me and walked over. "My poor hand," he said, holding it up limply. "It's getting so tired."

"Is it really?" I said. "Mine isn't."

He lowered his voice. "I'm just trying to sound properly world weary, like I do this all the time. Did you get any indecent proposals?"

I laughed. "No!"

He looked chagrined. "Me neither. What's wrong? Here we are—the sex symbols of the eighties and no one seems to notice."

"One boy wanted me to sign his hand," I said. I looked around. "Where's Marvin?"

Felix looked funny. "He—he didn't want to come. I don't know. This is all kind of rough for him, I mean, watching me—"

"I know," I said before he even finished. "It's the same with my boyfriend, and my sister. And even my father."

"Isn't it crazy?" he said. "Why don't they trust us? They think our heads are going to be turned just because thousands of besotted people think we're God's gift to the universe. Isn't that absurd?"

"It's crazy," I said. "I'm the same person I ever was."

"Me too . . . listen, the weird thing is I'm actually *more* humble now. Before I was going around feisty, arrogant, ready to charge at everyone. Now I've attained inner peace." He looked thoughtful. "You know, I think that's what's bugging Marvin. Here he's sitting around, mumbling his mantra and all that vegetarian shit, and *I've* attained inner peace."

I looked right at him. "You do look peaceful."

"I mean, let's face it, if the *Times* pans me, and loves everyone else, my inner peace will undoubtedly go down the drain in one second. . . . I hear the *Voice* likes us."

"Daddy heard that . . . but *Newsweek*—"

"Look, we did a good job, right? That's something we know, that's fact. So who cares what a bunch of cruddy little critics say?"

"That's what Joshua says."

"Who's he?"

"My boyfriend."

"The one who used to visit you? The shaggy one?"

"Uh huh."

"He's cute."

I nodded.

"He looked like a baby, though . . . how old is he?"

"Sixteen."

"That's a baby."

"*I'm* just fourteen."

"Yeah, but women are older. A fourteen-year-old girl is, like, thirty-five at least. Women are born knowing everything. Right from birth. They just open their big eyes and take one look around and, bingo, they know it all. Jesus, it's discouraging."

"*I* don't know it all," I said.

"Well, you will, kid, any minute now."

Mom and Simon said we could either go to the party, or just go out to eat. I said I'd just as soon just go out to eat, and maybe go to the party for a little while afterward. We went to an Italian place in the East 50s that Mom likes.

Simon said he'd liked the movie. "It's so amazing," he said to Mom, "how Rusty looks exactly like you in those close-ups."

Mom looked pleased. "Did you think so?"

"Exactly. It's uncanny. Remember those high-school photos you showed me once?"

"My hair was darker," Mom pointed out.

"But your eyebrows, the way they go up at the ends, that expression . . ."

"Well," Mom said sadly, "at least Tat made it, even if I never did."

Simon looked at her. "What do you mean? 'Even if I never did'?"

"Well, I mean, this is it. She's done something big. She hasn't futzed away her life on commercials and soap operas."

"Amanda," Simon said. "Come off it."

"It's true."

I was really surprised. Mom never talks like this.

"That's complete *shit*," Simon said. "You're a terrific actress and you know it. So you didn't get the breaks. You will, and anyone who sees you knows they're seeing the real thing."

Mom put her head on his shoulder. "I don't know."

"*I* think you're a good actress, Mom," I said.

"Do you, hon?"

"Yeah, I think you could've acted the part Serena Jowitt did. Don't you, Simon?"

"Of course!" Simon said. "You could act circles around her."

"Simon."

"Will you listen to me? There is one fact about me which you don't seem to appreciate. I do not throw the bull around about acting. Never."

"Yes, but—" Mom began.

"Where do you think Rusty *got* all that stuff?" Simon said. "By watching you. It's all you, filtered through her."

I don't know if that's true exactly, but it seemed to make Mom feel better. But I felt kind of funny. It seems like everyone in my whole family feels basically lousy, just because I made this movie. I wish there was one person at least who was just plain happy and proud, the way they're supposed to be.

At the party, this woman who's married to Peter Norton, who produced the movie, came up to Mom and said to her, "Didn't *you* once do some acting, Amanda?"

Simon wasn't around. Mom said, laughing, "Oh yes . . . I still do. I'm on 'The Way We Are Now.'"

"Oh?"

"It's a soap," Mom said.

"Oh yes . . . I've heard a great many people actually watch those," Mrs. Norton said, in a kind of snotty way.

"Yes, a great many people actually do," Mom said.

"And of course you take what you can get," she went on. "It's foolish to have too much pride. After all, one thing may lead to another!"

Mom was looking like she wanted to murder her. "What do you do?" she said, sort of aggressively.

"Oh, I'm a housewife, basically," the woman said. "Well, four children keep you busy. But I'm also a lyricist."

"Oh, what shows have you written for?" Mom said.

The woman blushed. "Well, no *shows* exactly, not yet, but . . ."

"It keeps you busy," Mom said, smiling.

When we'd moved on, Mom whispered to me, "God, I was a bitch, wasn't I."

I nodded.

Mom groaned. "Oh, women like that make me want to commit some indecent act. How can they stand there in cold blood, and say 'I'm a housewife' with those hideous simpering smiles on their faces? Why aren't they ashamed? Lyricist, my ass!"

Simon dropped us off in a cab. He kissed Mom and said, "See you tomorrow."

"Right . . . thanks, Si."

"It was fun." He kissed me on the cheek. "Congratulations, Rust."

"Thank you."

In the elevator, Mom just stared dreamily at the numbers.

"Simon is the first person who's said just plain congratulations to me," I said, almost to myself.

"The thing with Simon," Mom said intensely, "is that he doesn't have one tiny, malicious, back-biting, envious bone in his whole body. Not *one*. He is just a kind, warm, loving person . . . and that is incredibly rare. Don't ask me why."

"Yeah," I said. "He *is* nice."

"He's more than nice," Mom said. "Lots of people are nice. He's special."

Chapter Ten

The *Times* review was really good. That was the first one
I saw. It said:

In an otherwise dull holiday season, "Domestic Arrangements" comes along just in time to provide a sprightly, witty
two hours of entertainment. Like "A Little Romance," and
"Rich Kids," it focuses alternately on the lives of a pair of
unusually bright upper-middle-class teenagers and their
somewhat confused elders. By the time the movie is over,
we have come to respect and like Samantha and Warren,
who manage to preserve their own sexual relationship and
friendship while their parents and step-parents merge and
unmerge. What sets "Domestic Arrangements" apart from the
recent films of this type is the unusual frankness of the scenes
between the young protagonists. Director Charles O'Hara,
known previously for his documentary, "After the Cuckoo's
Nest," a profile of former mental patients, has focused with
insight and skill on newcomers Tatiana Engelberg and Felix
Propper. Ms. Engelberg is winsome and engaging as the
nymphet who innocently wreaks havoc in her mother's new
marriage. Propper, more subdued, is touching and sensitive as
the withdrawn, introspective Warren. What one remembers
from "Domestic Arrangements" are the scenes between

Samantha and Warren—playing chess after making love, quietly watching their parents go at each other before a large statusy cocktail party, horsing around on the same beach where their two parents have been trysting for the past decade. Would that the screenwriter, Joclyn Weber, had done equal justice to the lines she has placed in the mouths of the benighted adults. Serena Jowitt, looking startlingly like a young Maria Tallchief, snarls and lashes her way through a part which seems inadequately explained. As her temporary mate, Winston Lane gives the impression of sleepwalking through his part. His only moments of real life come in his brief scenes with the enchanting Ms. Engelberg, who gets through her first nude scene with a maximum of poise and grace. The pacing of "Domestic Arrangements" is uneven. The early scenes have a vitality and humor, which gradually erodes once the parents' new marriage is on the rocks. A saving grace is the camera work of veteran Sven Lundquist. Long shots of the young couple sprawled together in and out of bed seem like scenes from a Balthus painting, evoking a gentle sensuality which contrasts effectively with the rasping relationship of the older couple.

"Domestic Arrangements" has an R rating, due to a few partially nude scenes in which Ms. Engelberg can be glimpsed through masses of long red hair. The language is discreet with the exception of two four-letter words.

I remember Charlie talking about the R rating. He was afraid that if a movie about kids had an R rating, no kids could go to see it. On the other hand, he wanted to do something different, more realistic. It was kind of strange seeing my name in print, right there in the paper. This might sound odd to say, but it suddenly made the whole thing seem real. I guess up till now, it was like the movie was just something I did for fun, but I didn't so much think of it as something people would see and react to, not just people I know, but people I'd never even meet.

"Charlie must be delighted," Mom said. "Are you, hon? I think that's terrific. 'Enchanting,' 'winsome.'"

"They don't say anything about her acting," Deel pointed out. We were all having breakfast together.

"What do you mean?" Mom said. "Enchanting and winsome are about her acting."

"I guess," Deel said.

"Look, first they didn't say anything bad," Mom said, "which they could've. They even liked the nude scene."

"I wish people wouldn't keep talking about that," I said. "It's like three minutes of the whole picture, and you hardly even see me."

"*I* could see you," Deel said.

"That's our society," Mom said. "They make a big deal out of nudity, when in France, women don't wear tops on the beaches and no one notices or cares."

Daddy called from Boston and said he'd seen the *Times* review and was really pleased. "How about the *Voice?*" he asked.

"It hasn't come out yet," Mom said. "Sweetie, you can't imagine! The phone has been ringing nonstop since nine this morning. I feel like just yanking it out of the wall! Everybody we've ever known has come creeping out of the woodwork."

"Take it off the hook," Daddy said. "Still, it's exciting."

"How's your project going, Daddy?" I asked.

"Pretty good. We may get done a day or two earlier. I think I might be back Tuesday. Can you hold the fort till then?"

"Oh sure," Mom said. "We're fine."

After we'd hung up, I went over to her. "Mom?"

"Umm?" She looked distracted.

"Could Joshua, like, stay over tonight? I mean the whole night? Because it's Christmas vacation and, well, Daddy's not here, and . . ."

Mom looked thoughtful. "Till when?" she said.

I hadn't thought beyond just one night. "You mean, he could stay more than one night?"

"Look, hon, frankly I don't care if he stays every night. The whole curfew thing seems silly to me on nonschool nights . . . but we don't want to give Lionel a heart attack."

"I know."

"So, why don't you just do whatever you want, but we

won't mention it to him when he gets back. Does that sound okay?"

"Sure." I couldn't *believe* it. When I told Joshua, he couldn't either. First of all, it will really give us a chance to try out the diaphragm. I finally got it last week, and I think I understand about how to put it in. It's so ugly, though, and such a funny idea. I think when I'm older I'll go on the pill. But also it'll be nice having Joshua stay over not just for sex, but so we don't have to worry about falling asleep and him having to get up in the middle of the night when it's cold and windy, and go looking for a cab on Riverside. That's quite dangerous, really.

Some of my friends from school called, having seen the review of the movie in the *Times*. Mom went out and got the *Post* and the *News*, too. The *Post* didn't like it half so much. They said the pacing was "turgid" and said I acted like I was "in a trance." Actually, that's what Charlie wanted me to do. He said Samantha was a very dreamy person and I should look like I was thinking private, mysterious thoughts all the time. I didn't know how to do that exactly, so I would just stare straight ahead, and he'd say, "Great, I love it." The *News* gave it three stars. They called it a "sparkling farce with a myriad of witty, delightful scenes." It's odd how *they* thought Serena Jowitt was great, the best in the movie. They didn't like Felix that much. They said he "hardly seemed a fitting companion or lover for the dazzlingly lovely Ms. Engelberg." I hope he doesn't mind that.

I decided to clean up my room, partly in honor of the movie, but mostly in honor of Joshua sleeping over. I weeded through all my papers from last year and threw out about four wastebasketfuls of stuff. I went through my clothes and found three blouses and two pairs of jeans that I never wear. I gave them to Mom; she gives stuff that I don't like anymore to this family called the Spears who have six daughters and not that much money. They're always writing thank-you notes to me. Then I cleared absolutely everything off my desk, every single thing. I like completely clean surfaces, but it's hard when you have to keep doing papers for school. While I was sorting through stuff, I found the photos Joshua took of me naked last spring.

God, I'd forgotten all about that. That was how we . . . well, not met exactly, but how we knew we liked each other.

What happened was one afternoon Joshua came over, thinking Deel would be there. They were in the orchestra together—he plays the clarinet, and she plays the violin. Only she wasn't. I was there. I'd just washed my hair. Thinking it would be Deel or Mom, I answered the door just in my Japanese kimono, with my hair up in a turban. Joshua looked a little embarrassed when he saw me, but then he came in and sat in the living room while I dried my hair. At one point he asked if I'd mind if he took some photos of me drying my hair. He said he was doing a series for some project for this photography class he was taking at night. He said he had some new kind of color film he wanted to try out. I don't mind when people take my photo, so I just kept on drying my hair and he kept kind of circling around me, taking photos. Eventually, my hair got dry, so we went into the kitchen and had some cocoa. Then we went into my room and started to talk. I still had my kimono on, and while we were talking, I noticed Joshua kept looking at me in this sort of funny, intense way. I did this really bold thing; it's hard to imagine I even did it. I said, "I guess I better get dressed," and I went over to my closet and took my robe off and stood there with my back to him without anything on except my underpants, which I'd had on under my robe. Then I put on a shirt and a pair of jeans. When I turned around, Joshua was still sitting there with his camera, kind of staring at me with this totally glazed expression. Finally he said, "Rusty, I don't want you to get the wrong idea, but I wondered if you'd mind if I took some photos of you just . . . naked. I have, like, three or four shots left on this roll."

"Okay," I said. It was weird. I mean, I'd never acted like that with a boy before. I just took my clothes off and lay down on the bed and he took three or four photos of me. It only took a second. Then I put my clothes back on again and we just sat there looking at each other. Nothing happened that day at all except I think we both knew we liked each other. While he was waiting for the elevator, Joshua just stood at the door and finally blurted out, "You're beautiful," and dashed into the elevator. I guess he's shy with girls. That's what he says. He doesn't seem shy to me anymore, but maybe that's because we know each other.

When he came over later in the afternoon, I showed him the photos.

He looked at them. "Hey, I could sell these to *Playboy* now," he said.

"Joshua!"

"They're not bad, actually."

"I thought they were art photos."

"They are." He hugged me. "So, star, how's it going?"

"Joshua, please . . . I'm *not* a star."

"You're twinkling."

"I'm not . . . Don't make fun of me."

He put his arm around me. "I'm not, Rust . . . I feel proud of you."

"Do you? I thought you thought the *Times* critic was dumb."

"Well . . . Look, they only have a column or two. It's not exactly in-depth film criticism."

"The *Post* thought I acted like I was in a trance."

"Well, you do have a kind of trancy look at times."

I looked at him. I knew he was teasing. "Wasn't that nice of Mom? Saying you could stay as late as you want?"

"Wonderful . . . Your mother's a great person. I wish *my* mother was like her."

"She said you could stay every night till Daddy comes home . . . only I'm not supposed to tell him."

"How about Deel?"

"Yeah, I thought of that. . . . She's sleeping at a friend's tonight, though, so we don't have to worry."

We had a really nice, relaxed evening. Mom went out and we just heated up some pizza and watched TV for a while. We don't have any special room for the TV like Joshua's parents. It's just in the living room, but since no one was home, it was kind of private. Then we went into my room. Joshua helped me put the diaphragm in. I think we did it right. You have to make sure to use lots of jelly, so even if you didn't put it in right, the jelly will kill the sperm. They give you a booklet that ex-

plains everything. For me it didn't seem that different, but Joshua
said it really was much nicer for him. I guess having something
over your penis while you're fucking is like swimming with your
clothes on. Not that I can imagine what that's like exactly, since
I don't have one (penis, that is). But really, the nicest part of
all was just being able to lie together naked without having to
worry about waking up. Also, having the house quiet, with Daddy
and Deel away, was good, too. My bedroom is off the kitchen,
pretty far away from Mom and Daddy's, but still Daddy is a
very light sleeper and I always feel nervous when he's there. Mom
says cannons could go off when she's asleep and she wouldn't hear
anything. She has this odd sleep sound machine that she got at
Hammacher Schlemmer, which makes a roaring sound. She got it
when we were babies and used to get up at five and go screaming
around the apartment. Now she says she's addicted to it.

In the middle of the night we woke up. That is, Joshua
woke up and I heard him getting out of bed.

"Where're you going?" I whispered.

"To the bathroom."

"Oh." I hate having to get out of bed in the winter. I never
can find my slippers and the floor is always so cold. I snuggled
further under the covers. About one second later Joshua came
back.

"That was quick," I said.

"I didn't go," he said.

"How come?"

Joshua didn't say anything.

"How come you didn't go?" I said.

"Rust."

"Yeah?" He was acting really strange.

"You know that tall skinny guy with the mustache?"

"Simon?"

"Yeah . . . Well he was walking down the hall to the
bathroom."

"So?"

"Well, he was, like, naked."

"*What?*"

"I'm sorry, Rust. He was."

"What are you sorry about?"

"I don't know."

I thought a second. "Why was he naked?"

"Search me. I guess he was doing something he didn't need clothes for."

"What?"

"Well, maybe he and your mother . . ."

"Mom and *Simon?*"

"It could be. It certainly looks like it."

"Mom and Simon?"

"Why not? They're friends, aren't they?"

"Yeah, but . . . not in that way. Do you really think—"

"Look, Rust, I mean he may have just taken off his clothes because he felt hot for some reason."

"Like what?"

"I don't know."

By this time I was wide awake. "Poor Daddy," I said.

"Oh, poor Daddy's probably making it with some chick in Boston right this second," Joshua said, getting under the covers.

I sat right up. "Joshua, what a *horrible* thing to say! Daddy? He's not like that. He's not like your father."

"They all do it."

"They do *not!* Just because your father does seedy things with secretaries doesn't mean *everyone's* father does! Daddy thinks sex is a thrilling, important, meaningful experience."

"So?"

"So, he wouldn't do it with just anyone. He'd only do it with someone he really loved."

Joshua sighed. "Listen, you might be right, Rust, I don't know. . . . How about your mother? Is it a thrilling, important, meaningful experience for her too?"

"Will you quit making fun of my parents?"

"I'm not. I like your mother."

I thought about it a minute. "Maybe she's in love with Simon."

Joshua didn't say anything.

"I guess she must be."

"What makes you think that?"

"Well, she really loves Daddy, so if she did it with some-one else, it would mean she loved that person more . . . for some reason."

"Maybe she's just horny."

"Joshua! She's thirty-nine years old."

"Don't thirty-nine-year-olds get horny?"

"No, not in that way. Anyway Daddy's only been away two days. Oh, I hope they don't get divorced."

Joshua held me close. "They won't, Rust, don't worry."

"But if she loves Simon a lot, more than she loves Daddy . . ."

"You don't know that . . . Anyway, usually they like to stay together because of the kids."

"Yeah . . . Only I'd hate to think that was the only reason." I couldn't think which I wanted to be true. I'd hate to think Mom was fucking with Simon for some dumb, silly reason, but on the other hand, I hope she isn't in love with him the way I'm in love with Joshua. I don't think people that age fall in love. I think it's more that they're more compatible with one person than with another.

"Do you want to try again?" I said.

"Sure," Joshua said. His hand was between my legs.

"No. I meant go to the bathroom. Maybe Simon's back in the other room now."

"Later," Joshua murmured, parting the hair. I guess he wanted to see if I was wet.

"Josh?"

"Umm."

"I don't know if you can use it twice without taking it out and cleaning it."

"If you take it out, that does away with the whole point," he said.

"Is it safe?"

"Sure."

"Did the booklet say that? Are you positive?"

Joshua was already in me. "Positive," he crooned. I could tell he wasn't even thinking about the booklet.

He better not be lying.

Chapter Eleven

In the morning Simon wasn't there. Mom was lying on the couch, reading the Sunday paper. Joshua was in the shower.

"Hi," I said.

"Oh hi, hon . . . Listen, I made some batter for French toast if you and Josh want some. It's right near the stove."

"Okay." I love French toast. I felt really funny with Mom after the thing last night. Maybe Joshua imagined it. People do have hallucinations, especially when they're sleepy.

"Did you go out last night?" Mom said.

"Uh uh . . . we just watched TV."

"Simon and I passed the Coronet. There was a huge line."

I sighed. "I guess I'm glad it's over," I said.

"What?"

"The movie . . . the reviews and everything."

Mom smiled. "Hon, it's not over by a long shot. It's just beginning."

"What do you mean?"

"Well, you'll have to do publicity, interviews . . . all that. I got a dozen calls yesterday at least."

I frowned. "Well, but I don't *have* to do it if I don't want."

"You ought to do some. It's good to get used to all that—answering questions, TV. If you're going to stay in this business, that's all part of it."

"Well, I don't think I necessarily *do* want to stay in it," I said, biting my lip. "I mean, I don't really want to be an actress."

"No?" Mom looked surprised. "Why not?"

"I don't know. . . . You never know if you're going to get parts. And it seems like people who are good don't necessarily do well—all that."

Mom looked thoughtful. "Yeah, well, hon, it's true maybe you've seen the hard side of it since Lionel and I are in it, but there's so much—" she gestured "—joy in it, too."

"In acting?"

"Yeah . . . I mean, you look at people with nine-to-five jobs and they're plodding back and forth every day. Okay, sure, they have job security and all that, but they're bored out of their minds and they collapse in a heap at the end of the day or drink half a bottle of Scotch. But with acting, at least when you're doing it, you feel so alive. It's such a high, like you're floating."

I thought of that. "Yeah, but maybe there are other things that could make you feel that way."

"*I* never found any," Mom said. "Oh, maybe sex . . . but nothing I'd want to turn into a profession." She grinned.

"Delivering babies," I said.

Mom looked horrified. "Why would you want to do *that?*"

"I would think it would be exciting."

"But that's like an operation, women screaming and what have you. And what if they die?"

Boy, she's worse than Joshua. "They don't die, Mom . . . and not everyone screams."

"I did," Mom said. "I screamed my damn head off. See, the thing with acting which is so great is that it's not *real*. You have all the feelings of real life, but it's not real. No one really dies. It's all . . . magical."

I nodded. "Well, anyway, I don't have to decide now."

"No, of course not . . . But I don't think you should make this a one-shot thing either—I mean, just do the one movie and then bow out. Take it where it leads."

"How about school?"

"Well, school . . . You know everything by now, don't you? Pretty much?"

I laughed. "I don't know everything."

"Listen, lots of the greatest writers and actors and painters never went to school at all. Life is a school. You just walk down the street and you learn as much as you ever will in a classroom."

"You don't learn math."

"Math." Mom looked disdainful. "But who needs math? You can hire some little man to do your taxes for you. Count on your fingers. Math is a waste."

"That's not what Daddy says," I pointed out.

"True." That didn't seem to bother her much.

At that point Joshua came out of the shower so we couldn't talk anymore. I felt worried, sort of. First, I know Daddy's opinions about all of this are totally different from Mom's. He thinks school is extremely important and he wants Deel and me to do well and go to good colleges and all that. Not that that means he's right and Mom's wrong, but it just shows you can think two totally different ways about it. I think I'm somewhere in the middle. I don't think I'd want to just drop out of school and make movies now, even if I could. I think it's a weird kind of life. Felix went to Professional Children's School and he never led a regular life, being with regular people. All he knows are actors and actresses. I wouldn't like that. A lot of them are really phony, I think. I mean, they'll talk in this really dumb way about acting and expressing themselves and all that. I want to know lots of different people, not just actors. And even though part of school is dull, some of it is really interesting and I don't think I could learn about it just walking down the street. I wouldn't learn about chemistry just walking down the street, or philosophy.

Later in the morning, as Joshua and I were just finishing breakfast, Deel came home with Simon. She'd evidently run into him in the lobby. Simon and Mom greeted each other as though they hadn't seen each other in a long time. I looked sideways at Joshua and he looked at me. But I felt really weird. I wish in real life you could just ask people what you want to know. I wish I could take Mom aside and say, "Are you fucking with Simon and do you love him and do you want to marry him?" But you can't, especially with your own parents.

The other bad thing is that normally the person I'd most want to talk to about it is Deel, because she's the only one who'd care about it as much as I do. But now I don't know if I should. I'm scared she might tell Daddy, or think it was disgusting. I know she likes Simon a lot, but maybe she'd be jealous because of that. If it was someone she didn't like at all, like Charlie, she'd *really* be disgusted. I think maybe I'll kind of hint around about it and see how she reacts.

"When's Daddy coming home?" Deel asked.

"Tomorrow, I think," Mom said. "No, wait, I think he said Tuesday or Wednesday."

In the kitchen, when we were alone, Deel said, "How come Joshua's having breakfast here?"

I hesitated. "Because he stayed over."

"Does Mom know?"

"Yeah . . . she said it was all right."

"Did you try out your new acquisition?" She gave me a sidelong glance.

"Yeah."

"How was it?"

"It was good." It would really be helpful if Deel knew something about sex other than from books. She's read about nine million books on the subject, but I wish she'd actually *done* something. In fourth grade, she and Peter Town used to go into the bathroom and take their clothes off, but that was a long time ago.

"Do you want to hear something really sick?" she said.

"What?"

"You know Greg Calabrese?"

"Yeah?"

"He is actually doing it with Fiona Stone's *mother!*"

"How do you know?"

"Fiona came over to Jane's and told us. I mean, they actually go out on *dates* and he sleeps *over* and everything."

"She's divorced, isn't she?"

"Yeah, but she's, like, Mom's age. She's in her thirties! You know what Fiona said? She said Greg came over one time and her mother had this man friend of hers over, and Greg started to cry."

"I guess he likes her a lot," I said.

"She's thirty-*eight* and he's *seventeen.* That is really sick."

"Well, if they like each other, I don't see that it matters how old they are."

"You don't?"

"No . . . Daddy's ten years older than Mom."

"That's different. Anyhow, I thought it was pretty gross."

In the afternoon, Simon and Deel got into this long Scrabble game. I watched them play for a while. Joshua said he had to go home, but that he'd come back later. I felt a little funny, his staying over with Deel there. I wondered if Simon would be staying over again.

Later in the afternoon, at around five, Mom and Simon went out. Deel was lying on the couch. She'd lost the Scrabble game, not by much, but that sometimes puts her in a bad mood.

Finally I said, "I think Simon really likes Mom."

Deel shrugged. "I guess."

"I mean really a lot."

"Simon?"

"Yeah."

"Well, but he's so much younger than her."

"Just six years."

"But at that age, that's a lot."

"It's less than Daddy and Mom."

"Men like women to be younger than them, though, mostly."

"How about Greg and Fiona's mother?"

"That's an aberration. Anyway, Simon would probably like someone more in her twenties, someone more like a real actress."

"I think Mom's pretty."

Deel made a face. "If you can see her face through all that junk she wears. When she smiles, she has all those lines around her eyes."

"She says that gives her character."

"If she let her hair get gray, and stopped dyeing it, she'd probably look like ninety years old."

"Deel, come on! She would not!"

"You're the one that brought it up. I just think Simon has better taste than that. I mean, he may like her as a friend, someone to talk to about his problems."

I was quiet for a while. "How would you feel if he did like her that other way?"

"You mean, like—"

"Yeah."

"He never would. It's too dumb to even think of."

"But if he did. Just try to imagine it."

"I'd think he was a dope," Deel said savagely.

"What would you think about her?"

"Well, she'd be lucky if someone like Simon liked her. But it's all so sick. Why imagine sick things?"

"True." Well, so much for talking about it with Deel.

"You've got sex on the brain because of Joshua. People Mom's age are into other things."

"And Daddy's age too? How about *Passages?* You said—"

"Oh, those are like businessmen and housewives and people like that. People who've led dull, dopey lives, and suddenly realize it when they're middle-aged. The thing with Mom is just that she's in a profession where all that matters is how you look, so she's obsessed with that."

"I don't think she's obsessed with it. She just likes to look nice."

"Just because you're like her."

"Sure, I like to look nice. That doesn't mean I'm *obsessed* with it." Deel didn't answer. "What do you think you'll be? Do you ever think about it?"

"When I grow up?" she said sarcastically. "I think I'm going to be the first Jewish woman president."

"I mean really."

"I am. Don't you think I'd be good?"

I thought about it a minute. "Yeah, I do. I'll vote for you."

"Well, there's one vote. Now if I can just get a couple more—"

"You'd have to go to law school," I pointed out.

"Yeah, and I'd run for some other things first. Maybe Congress."

"Like Carol Bellamy."

"Or Elizabeth Holtzman. . . . I guess I'll run for Congress first, and then the Senate."

"That's good, that you have it all planned out," I said wistfully.

"Well, you have your life all planned out."

"No, I don't. What do you mean?"

"Aren't you going to be an actress?"

"I don't think so. I'm not sure." Suddenly I felt really sleepy. "Listen, Deel, I'm going to take a nap. Don't wake me up if anyone calls, okay? Just write it down on the pad."

I felt exhausted, not just from not getting that much sleep, but from everything. The movie opening. Worrying if it would change things, like in school, if people would treat me differently, expect different things from me. And then hoping I can handle it all, doing TV, and all that. I don't want to get phony and conceited and that kind of thing. I once saw Brooke Shields on TV and she acted like a real ass. She was wriggling and squirming and smiling all the time, and she talked in this whispery, kind of baby voice. I don't want to be like that. And I hope Mom knows what she's doing. I hope Deel doesn't find out and tell Daddy. I hope Daddy doesn't find out and get mad. He'd feel awful. Imagine! Poor Daddy.

I fell really sound asleep for two hours. I guess maybe sleeping with Joshua all night isn't the best way to get a good night's sleep either. Not just the sex. But it's funny sleeping in the same bed with someone, if you're not used to it. Sex is tiring. I think basically I'd like to do it just before I went to bed, and then just sleep during the night, but that might hurt Joshua's feelings. It's not that I don't like him, it's that I don't know if I really want to do it three times a night every night. It just seems like you want to kind of do it, and then think about it, and sort of savor it. He says that the more we do it, the more he wants to do it.

When he came over later, I tried to tell him how I felt.

He looked a little hurt. "We don't have to do it if you don't want, Rust. Why don't you tell me when you don't feel like doing it?"

"Well, the thing is, by the time I think about it, we're, like, in the middle of doing it, and I didn't think you'd like to stop in the middle."

"True . . . maybe I should ask you in a more formal way, not just leap on you, huh?"

"You don't exactly *leap* on me."

"Well, I do, sort of . . . I guess it's that one thing kind of leads to another. It's not even as though I know I'm in the mood myself."

"Sure, I understand."

"And I guess now that you have the diaphragm, well, it feels so terrific."

I smiled.

"Does it feel different for you?" He looked hopeful.

"Not that much, so far. But I think it will, eventually."

That night, it was odd in various ways. Simon didn't stay over, so Joshua, Deel, Mom and me were all in the house together. Mom and Deel watched *Notorious*, which was on from eleven to one. Joshua and I watched part of it, but then I started yawning. I felt tired, even though I'd had a nap. Finally Joshua said, "Do you feel like going to sleep, Rust?"

I nodded. "Yeah, I don't know why I'm so sleepy, I just . . ."

I could see Deel giving us this suspicious glance, like what he'd meant was, "Do you feel like fucking?" It was awkward. "Well, good night," I said. "See you in the morning."

"Night, Tat, Joshua," Mom said, still watching the TV. She acted like it was a perfectly normal thing, having Joshua sleep over.

"Good night, Delia," Joshua said, a little ironically.

"Good night, Joshua . . . sleep well," Delia said.

I was really relieved when we got in my room. "Whew," I said. I put on the new nightgown Mom got me. It's a Lanz. It's pink flannel with little red hearts all over it, and a high neck and long sleeves.

"You look like something out of Little House in the Big Woods," Joshua said.

"Well, I like that style," I said apologetically. I can't imagine wearing those sexy kinds of nightgowns you see in magazines, black lace and everything. I don't think I'm the type. "I'm sorry it's not that sexy," I said.

"It is," Joshua said.

I couldn't tell if he was teasing. "I feel funny with everyone here." We got into bed together. "I guess Simon isn't sleeping over."

"Well, I wouldn't think so . . . with your sister here. Anyway, they probably did it just on an impulse."

"Do you think so?" That made me feel much bettter. "Do you think basically they're just friends?"

"Yeah."

"Then how come they did it?"

"Well, friends fuck sometimes. . . . Pam and I are friends, basically."

"Even when you were doing it together?"

"Yeah, we *liked* each other, but—"

"How about Marjorie?"

"What about her?"

"Were you basically just friends with her?"

"Are you kidding? We barely exchanged five words."

"But you were doing it for a whole month!"

"So?"

"You mean you never even talked about anything?"

"Uh uh."

"How strange! Weren't you even curious?"

"About what?"

"Well, like, about how many brothers or sisters she had, or what movies she liked, or things like that."

"Not really."

"Then why'd you want to fuck with her?"

"Because she had a great body and she was terrific in bed."

"Oh." I felt really awful. What an awful conversation! I wish we hadn't ever started it. I didn't know what to say. I felt like crying.

"Rust?"

"Yeah?"

"Are you okay?"

"Sure."

"You sound funny. Is it because of Marjorie?"

"Yeah."

"It was just sex, that's all."

"But I don't like to think of you as that kind of person."

"Which kind?"

"The kind that would just do it like that, with someone you didn't even talk to."

"Well, we talked a *little* bit," Joshua said. "We talked about her horse. She had a horse named Linda. It was a palomino."

"What else did you talk about?"

Joshua sighed. "Rust, it wasn't . . . she wasn't that kind of *person*. She didn't have anything interesting to say."

"How did you know if you didn't try?"

"I could just tell . . . she had a very short concentration span. If I said anything that took more than two sentences, she looked glazed."

"She sounds awful."

"Well—"

"I mean, it just seems so awful to do it with someone you don't even *like*. *I* wouldn't."

"Maybe girls are different."

"That's a really sexist thing to say."

"I don't know what to say, Rust. It was just something I did. I don't regret it, really. I don't think she did either. It was like summer fun, that's all."

I turned over. Joshua put his hand on my shoulder. "I wouldn't do it now," he said.

"Well, you couldn't," I muttered. "She's in Colorado."

"No, I mean I wouldn't do it with someone like her, even if . . . say, you went away for a month."

"Even if you met some extremely sexy person, like Bo Derek?"

"Right."

"Even if they begged and pleaded with you?"

"Even if they got out on the terrace of our apartment and said they'd jump if I didn't." I could tell he was smiling, even though it was dark. "Anyway, think of all the guys you'll do it with," he said.

"What do you mean?"

"I mean in your life."

"I'll never do it with anyone but you."

"Sure you will."

"I won't . . . I don't want to."

Joshua began kissing my neck. "Hey, Rust . . . turn around, okay?"

I did. "You just don't believe me about anything."

"I do. Does this nightgown go over your head?"

"Why do you want to know?" I still felt mad a little bit, but not as much as before.

"I was just generally curious."

"You have to undo those buttons in the front."

He did. "Rust, do you feel like—"

"We have to be extremely quiet."

"Okay." He pulled the nightgown over my head. "Marjorie was a dope," he said, tossing it on the floor. "She wasn't half as pretty as you. She didn't even like movies." For Joshua, that's the worst thing he can say about anyone. "She didn't have nice round, soft nipples, like you," he said, kissing them.

"What'd she have?"

"Just little wrinkly ones."

"I thought her body was so great."

"It was fair . . . it seemed great at the time. She had a great tan."

Whenever Joshua starts kissing me all over, I can't think about anything else. My mind gets all fuzzy. "I love you," I said.

"I love you."

We rolled around, kissing, hugging. It was really good. I guess this is why people get married, so they can do it every night if they want, or even more.

Chapter Twelve

Monday afternoon, Mom took me over to *Seventeen*. They'd said they wanted me to pose for some summer fashions. I don't really want to model in general, but Mom said she thought it wasn't a bad idea. They said they want to interview me next week.

Luckily it was pretty warm in the studio. Otherwise I'd have frozen, wearing dresses with no sleeves, and sandals. Outside it was 20, and they said with the windchill factor, it was like minus 10. I hate it when they give you the windchill factor. What good is it to know? It just makes you feel even colder.

They had a backdrop like a farm, with real trees. In one photo I had to swing in a real swing with my shoes off.

"Wiggle your toes, hon," the photographer said. "That's the girl. Nice."

They had me sit under a tree with a big basket, eating cherries. They had real cherries. In December! They were really great. The big, juicy, dark red kind. The trouble was, I ate some and got cherry juice on the dress. They told me then that I wasn't supposed to really eat them, just pretend, that I could eat them when they were done shooting.

Some of the dresses were pretty, but some weren't my type

that much. There was this one with a tank top that was really tight, and had a short striped skirt. "I think we better try a bra with that one," the photographer said.

I would never wear a bra with that kind of dress, but I guess for a magazine they don't want it to look too sexy. I don't know. Basically, it was tiring and not that much fun, having to smile and smile all afternoon.

Mom was good. She stayed with me the whole time, and went out and got me a grilled cheese sandwich with bacon and a hot chocolate for lunch.

"Did you ever think of modeling?" this woman asked Mom. She was helping set up the shots.

"I used to, years ago," Mom said. "But I got bored with it. Acting's more challenging."

"I think so too," I said. "I wouldn't want to be a model."

"You'd be sensational," the woman said, "With that hair . . . Listen, I loved your movie, honey. You were just great! Where did you learn all that?"

"She's a natural," the photographer said. He came over and took a sip of my hot chocolate.

People always say that, but it's not true. They think I'm like the girl in the movie, and I'm not at all.

When we were done, the woman started getting into her jacket to go downtown. Mom said, "I love your jacket. Is it fox?"

The woman nodded. "I got it right around the corner here. There's this great store, Esther's. They're all marked down. You ought to go over and take a look."

"Is it warm?"

"Fantastic . . . it has a hood, see?"

Mom turned to me. "Tat, you'd look gorgeous in that color. Could she try it on one second?"

I put it on. It was very soft, fluffy fur in a sort of red-brown color.

"Sensational," the photographer said. "With her coloring."

"Run over there and get one," the woman said, "before they're gone."

I never had a fur coat. "Mom, I don't know. It might look too fancy, for school and everything."

"Not for school. But for other things, going out on weekends. Listen, fur is a great value, Tat. It lasts years. There's nothing warmer, and you look so darling in it. Let's get one for you."

We went to the store. They had two left with that color and style.

I have to admit it did look extremely nice and felt really warm. There were these special things in the lining that gripped your wrists so the wind couldn't blow up the sleeves, and the hood tied tight. But when I walked in the door, wearing it, Deel, who let us in, said, "What did you do—go out and skin a cat?"

"Hush," Mom said.

"It's fox," I said, taking it off and hanging it up.

"Sick. You mean some poor fox, a whole *family* of foxes, gave their *lives* for that jacket? That is really sick."

Mom sighed and went into the kitchen. "Delia, modify your ideological zeal, okay? Give us a break."

"*You* have a sheepskin," I pointed out.

"Sheep are different."

"How? Don't sheep have feelings just like anyone else? Poor, fluffy, defenseless sheep."

"They're dumb."

"So? Are foxes that smart? And who says it's only bad to shoot smart animals?"

"Sheep are old. They probably don't do it to them until they're about to die."

"So? You just want to think anything *you* feel like doing is okay, and anything *I* do is bad."

"Okay, well when someone decides to skin *you* just because they want a coat with long red hair, then see how you like it."

The trouble is, I sort of know what Deel means. But wouldn't you have to be consistent for it to make sense, like not wearing leather boots, or anything? "It's only for weekends," I said, sitting down.

"Tell that to the fox. He doesn't care."

"Cordelia," Mom said. "Are you willing to eat ham and macaroni and cheese for dinner?"

"Okay."

"How about the poor pig?" I said. "How about the poor macaroni that they strangled and stuffed into a cardboard box?"

Deel looked thoughtful. "Actually, it's true. We don't know what has a soul, and what doesn't."

"If everything has a soul, you'd have to starve to death," I pointed out.

"I know," she said sadly. "Oh listen, whatshisname called."

She knows Joshua's name! "What'd he want?"

"I don't know. What he usually wants, I guess. To know when you feel like fucking with him."

"Deel, will you stop that? Mom, make her stop!"

"Delia, what *is* this?" Mom said, peering out from the kitchen. "You sound spiteful and wretched."

Deel looked up at her sullenly. "At least I don't go out on dates when my husband is out of town for five days."

There was a pause. "I didn't know you had a husband," Mom said dryly. "Congratulations."

"At least I don't go flirting with men who are nine million years younger than me, drooling over them," Deel went on.

Mom walked into the room and stood in front of her. "What is all this, huh? What *are* you, the moralist of the century? Grow up a little, kid."

"Why don't *you?*" Deel said, and stomped into her room.

She wouldn't even come out to have supper. Mom and I ate alone.

"God, I thought fourteen was bad, but this takes it," Mom said, giving me the crusty part of the macaroni that I like the best.

"She might be in a better mood if she had a boyfriend," I suggested.

"Listen, *I* might be in a better mood if I had a million dollars. I mean, we could all use some divine intervention to make our lives fine and dandy, but we don't all go around snarling like little beasts if it's not forthcoming."

I ate awhile. "Do you think it's because of the movie?" I said.

Mom sighed. "Well, I doubt that that helped . . . I don't know. She's just . . . she takes everything so—"

"She wants everything to be perfect," I said.

Mom smiled. "Don't we all?" She sat there, gazing sadly into space. "Hon?"

"Yeah?"

"You don't mind about my going out with Simon while Lionel's away, do you?"

I shook my head, but my heart started beating faster. I didn't know if she was about to tell me about his staying over.

"We're just good friends," Mom exclaimed suddenly. "It's so ridiculous, the way people feel a man and a woman can't be friends. We're in the same business, he's supportive of me in my work, we have a lot to talk about. I mean, what's wrong with that?"

"Nothing," I said.

"He reminds me of my brother, Danny, actually," Mom said. "He's just a sweet, kind, smart person . . . and he likes being with me. So he's a couple of years younger? So what! That's so sexist, saying men can be with women who are a zillion years younger, but when women—"

"Anyway, you're not marrying him," I said.

Mom looked at me a second. "Right, I'm not marrying him at *all*. We just—"

"She has a dirty mind," I said, getting up to get the milk. "She thinks all people do is fuck."

Mom didn't say anything.

"She thinks, like, the only reason Joshua wants to see me is for sex . . . and it isn't! We talk about lots of things."

"I know you do, hon," Mom said.

"He's my *friend*," I said. "I mean, he's more than that, but he's also my friend."

Mom brought in the dishes. "Well, life is complicated," she said.

"What do you mean?"

"I don't know . . . Listen, would she join us for dessert, do you think? I got pralines and cream, her favorite. Try knocking on her door, okay?"

Deel said she'd have pralines and cream. She took a big bowl of it into the living room and turned the TV on. I went in to call Joshua.

The day before Daddy came back, Mom and I taped this interview together for TV. Mom said she and Daddy have to discuss how much of that kind of thing I should do, but she thought this would be fun and not such a big deal. It's an interview show where the interviews are done by this woman named Cheryl Munson who used to be an actress, like Mom. It's on every Monday at 7:30 but only people with cable TV can get it. The program is called "Talk," and it's half an hour long.

Mom said I didn't have to get that dressed up, so I just wore my shocking pink Gloria Vanderbilt jeans with a velour top to match, that I got this fall. I thought for TV something bright would be good. Mom wore a beige turtleneck dress and boots. She likes to be understated sometimes, she says.

"Well, Tatiana, this must be a very exciting time for you," Cheryl said, smiling at me. The cameras were on, but about ten feet away from us. "Tell me, how have your family and friends reacted to your being in *Domestic Arrangements?* Are they pleased, jealous or what?" She was a short woman with very thick curly black hair, almost like a wig.

"I think they're pleased," I said. "Mostly."

"Mostly?"

"Well, I haven't been back in school since the movie opened, so I don't know how that will be."

"Are you feeling nervous about the reactions of your friends?"

"No, not that much."

"How about—I know you're going to get asked about this a great deal—the reaction to the nude scene? Are you afraid that boys may ask you out just because they have certain expectations of the kind of girl you appeared to be in the movie?"

"Well, I have a boyfriend, so I don't go out with other boys," I said.

"And how does *he* feel about that scene?"

I hesitated. "I think he thought it was good . . . he thought I acted well."

"Was it a hard scene for you to do?"

"No, not that much. . . . Well, the thing is, at home we go around without clothes a lot, so . . . well, not a lot, but it isn't such a big thing."

She smiled and turned to Mom. "And how about you, Amanda? Did you have any feelings about Tatiana's appearing in a nude scene at her age? How about the accusations of kiddie porn? Did that disturb you?"

"Not in the least," Mom said coolly. "Everything is in the eye of the beholder. I think the scene is in *perfect* taste, nothing salacious in it at all. It's five *minutes* of a two-hour film, after all. I think it says more about our society and its hypocritical values about sex that so much attention is drawn to a scene that's so short."

"I was wondering," Cheryl said, "did this ever come up for *you* in the course of *your* career? You've done some acting on stage and TV. Were you ever required to do a nude scene?"

Mom cleared her throat. "Not exactly. I did have to soak in a bathtub with baking soda for six hours once . . . but I was wearing a body stocking. It was for a commercial."

"And I remember the one you did back in the early sixties where you're undressing behind a screen and one sees your clothing being tossed out."

Mom laughed. "But not me . . . Well, for commercials nudity would scarcely—"

"So evidently the issue never arose. But if it had, you would have had no compunctions about appearing in a scene similar to the one in which Tatiana appeared?"

"None at all," Mom said. "If you have a good body, what's the big deal? I mean, if that's *all* you have to offer, that's one thing. But if it's part of interpreting a role, I think it's fine."

Cheryl turned to me. "I gather you took several months out from school to make *Domestic Arrangements*, Tatiana. Was that hard for you? Did you find it hard to keep up with your school-work?"

"I had a tutor," I said, "so it wasn't so bad."

"And how about the future? Are you planning any other movies?"

I looked at Mom.

"We haven't decided exactly to what extent Tat will immerse herself in acting," Mom said. "She has a lot of other interests. And I don't know if full-time acting is what would be best for her right now."

"How do *you* feel about that, Tatiana?" Cheryl asked.

"Well, I guess I wouldn't want to do it *all* the time," I said. "Maybe in the summer and stuff like that."

"Do you see yourself going into it eventually as a career?"

"No. I'm going to be a doctor."

"You are! How fascinating. What kind?"

"The kind that delivers babies."

"Oh . . . well, that's certainly a far cry from acting. How do you feel about that, Amanda? Do you think Tatiana will make a good obstetrician?"

Mom smiled at me. "I think Tatiana will be terrific at whatever she does. She has *very* steady nerves."

"I don't get nervous," I admitted. "I don't know why."

"Not even when all the cameras were focused on you and you knew several millions dollars were at stake?"

"I guess I never thought of it that way . . . about the money part. I mean there were lots of other people besides me in the movie."

"True, but you certainly had to be visible a good proportion of the time. . . . Let me ask you, Tatiana . . . I don't have children myself. Would you say that Samantha was a typical fourteen-year-old, like your friends or yourself? I'm sure many parents are going to feel a certain anxiety after seeing the movie. Are their daughters in fact engaging in sexual activity to that extent?"

"Well, I don't know if she's *typical* exactly," I said. "I guess she seemed sort of naive to me . . . about some things."

"About what?"

"Well, like not knowing anything about birth control . . . thinking if you took the pill a couple of times, you wouldn't get pregnant. That seemed kind of dumb."

"You think most of your friends would . . . have a more complete grasp of the available contraceptive devices?"

"Yeah . . . I mean, they'd have, like, diaphragms or stuff . . . like I do."

"You do?"

"Yeah, I got one last week. My parents gave it to me for Christmas."

Cheryl looked at Mom. "Well, that's certainly an unusual gift . . . Then I gather from that that you and Tatiana are fairly open about discussing sex and other related matters?"

Mom nodded. "*I* think we are . . . we *try* to be. The thing is, my parents were so totally closed about everything, maybe I've tried almost too hard to be the opposite. But I think it's healthy. If they're doing it, they're doing it. Some girls are ready at thirteen, some at sixteen. I don't think it's an area where you can make hard-and-fast rules."

"I didn't like Samantha that much," I said. "In general, I mean. I didn't like the way she acted with her boyfriend. I wouldn't act like that."

"What did she do that you didn't approve of?" Cheryl said.

"She was just kind of phony," I said. "Sort of flirting with everyone."

"You feel you and your friends prefer to be more natural with boys?"

"Yeah."

"Well, also . . . of course the relationship between Samantha and her mother seemed very combative and tense . . . unlike the two of you."

"Yes, that gets me so *mad!*" Mom broke in. "I feel that's so much the way men directors look at relationships between women. It's so false! They see only the competitive, sexually competitive, aspect and ignore all the rest—the friendship, the camaraderie."

"You would have liked it if the mother had been a different kind of person then?"

"Well, I suppose Charlie, the director, felt . . . I didn't read the book it was based on, but yes, I thought the mother . . . I thought Serena did a fantastic job. But why yet another mother who has nothing to do all day but shop and make herself up? No one's like that anymore! We all work, we all have kids, we all do everything or want to. Why aren't *we* portrayed on the screen? Modern women."

"Yes," Cheryl said. "Perhaps now that women are taking more of a role in the actual producing and directing of movies, we'll see a change there. Well, I want to thank you both very much for appearing with me tonight. And I'm sure we'll be seeing a lot more of you, Tatiana, before you put on your white coat and disappear into a hospital."

After the show was taped, they said we could watch ourselves. I was sort of tired by then and would have liked just to go home, but Mom said she wanted to watch. "Oh, no," she said, as soon as it started. "Look at my hair! Oh, Christ, why did I wear that dress?"

"You look nice, Mom," I said.

"Oh my God, can we do it over?" she said to Cheryl. "Look at me."

"You look fine," Cheryl said. "And doesn't Tatiana look darling? The camera just eats her up. Where do you get skin like that, honey?"

"She's never had a pimple," Mom said. "Can you imagine?"

I thought I was okay in the interview, except it seemed like we didn't really talk that much about the movie, more about other things like sex. I wonder if I should have said that about having a diaphragm on TV. I don't see anything wrong with it, but still maybe it was too personal.

"I'm going to go home and shoot myself," Mom said as we walked out. "My God, I looked eight hundred years old."

"No, you didn't, Mom," I said. "You looked nice."

"Oh, and I seemed so . . . I shouldn't have run on that way about women's roles in movies. . . . Except, well, she asked and I—"

"Was it okay what I said about having a diaphragm?"

"It's okay with *me*," Mom said. After a minute she said, "I don't know how Lionel is going to react to the whole thing."

"Maybe he won't see it."

"Oh, I think he should see it," Mom said. "After all . . . Well, what's done is done. No, it's good, hon. You just have to get used to it, all those prying questions. Cheryl is one of the good ones. Lots of them don't give a damn about acting or anything serious."

"She seemed like a nice person," I said.

"Yeah." Mom looked pensive. "We were in *Oklahoma* together years and *years* ago. She was Ado Annie. Well, she's certainly put on a bit of weight since then."

Daddy came home that night, in time for dinner. After he'd kissed us, he said excitedly, "Hey, did you see the *Voice?*"

"Sure," Mom said. "How did you like it?"

"I couldn't believe it," Daddy said. "I mean . . ."

I forgot to mention the review of *Domestic Arrangements* that appeared in the *Village Voice*. It was sort of embarrassing, almost. This is how it started:

> I surrender. Carry me off and I will submit peacefully. Chagrined as I am to admit it, I have totally lost my heart and soul to a fourteen-year-old girl with a seemingly natural grace, sensuality, and charm that are, to say the very least, unforgettable. Tatiana Engelberg, of the incredibly translucent skin, glorious red hair and delicately nubile body, has burst forth on our screens in a new movie, which, with any other actress in the center role, might have aroused justifiable questions of taste. But the incomparable Ms. Engelberg manages to suffuse the role of Samantha with an integrity and directness that makes any salacious overtones of this startlingly frank teenage love story irrelevant. There are scenes in this movie that I personally will remember all my life: Engelberg peering up through a cloud of red hair at her besotted step-father as he drunkenly recites a lyrical passage from Katherine Mansfield; Engelberg sunken into the leather couch of her mother's new living room watching her boyfriend walking past in the hall outside; Engelberg peeking, flushed, out from under the covers whence she has been hiding from her mother and step-father. Frankly, I have no idea if Ms. Engelberg can act. It may well be that her performance is one of those acts of nature that come along every one in a while, and cannot be repeated. I hope from the bottom of my heart that this is not the case.

There was more about the movie, but he made it seem like I was the main thing in it practically. The last line was: "If you miss Tatiana Engelberg in *Domestic Arrangements*, you will have missed both an aesthetic experience and a possibly unique chance to understand what being young today is all about. I don't know if we older folk will find more to horrify us or to be pleased about in this clear-eyed view of adolescent sexuality, but I think we come away having seen a grippingly honest view of the world as it appears to the generation that will inherit it from us."

"God, he really flipped," Daddy said.

"Did you see *Newsweek?*" Mom asked.

The man in *Newsweek* had said, "I tremble for the men in America when the slender, silver-eyed Ms. Engelberg reaches full puberty. It is an event we can await with a certain fear as well as eager anticipation." The dumb thing is I don't even *have* silver eyes.

Daddy sighed. "I don't know."

"You better get back to Helen soon. She's been calling every *second* since you left." Helen is my agent. She's a friend of Daddy's.

"Let me catch my breath," Daddy said. He poured himself some sherry.

"How was Boston?" Deel asked. "Did your movie go well, Daddy?"

He looked pleased. "Yes, I think it did. I may have to go back next month, but we got most of the shooting done. So, Cordelia, how has life in the past week been treating *you?*"

"Nothing special," Deel said. "Nothing like what's been happening to old Silver Eyes."

"I don't even have silver eyes," I said. "One person said they were blue, one person said they were green. They're gray! Just plain gray."

Daddy came over and looked at me. "I think maybe they *are* silver, come to think of it."

"Daddy, they're *not*. They're gray. . . . We were on TV," I said. "Mom and me."

"Oh?" Dad looked at Mom. "You didn't mention that."

Mom looked flustered. "It was just— Remember Cheryl Munson? She has that interview show, 'Talk'? I thought it might be fun."

"How'd it go?"

"Good," I said just as Mom said "Awful."

Daddy smiled. "Which was it?"

"I looked like a wreck," Mom said. "Tat was terrific."

"When'll it be on?" Daddy asked.

"Next week."

That night, just before I went to sleep, Daddy came into my room. "So how does it feel, Tat, to be a—"

"Don't say star!"

"I have to . . . that's what you are."

"It's not! I just acted in one movie."

"No, well, look, darling, I think it's good, not letting it go to your head. But you ought to feel proud, too, that—"

"Should I?"

"Sure."

"Maybe it'll wreck my whole life."

"No . . . how could it?"

"Maybe I'll become one of those dumb awful people who acts phony with everyone, like Tatum O'Neal."

"Darling, you'll become whatever you want to become. The world isn't just something that happens to you. You happen to it."

"But, Daddy, I did one really bad thing already."

"What was that?"

"I got a fur coat. It's real fur. It's made out of foxes."

Daddy smiled. "Well, that doesn't seem—"

"What if the kids at school think I'm stuck up? I'm afraid everyone's going to tease me."

"Your real friends won't."

I sighed and looked up at him. I thought of Simon and Mom. I wonder if it's because Daddy's gotten plump that she . . . "Are you going to call Helen?"

"First thing tomorrow."

"Mom said Helen said lots of people want me to be in other movies."

"Well, that's to be expected."

"I just don't know *what* I want to do." I was beginning to feel really sleepy. "Do you think I should?"

"Why don't we wait and see what the roles are?" Daddy took my hand. "Just remember you don't have to do anything you don't want. No one's forcing you either way."

"I guess the trouble is I don't know *what* I want."

"Well, that's only natural. It's a complicated thing."

"Yeah." I yawned. "It's nice that you're back, Daddy."

"It's nice to *be* back."

But after Daddy left, I just lay there, worrying about everything. I don't even know if I was good in the movie. That's the trouble, I wish I really truly thought I was. But a lot of the time I didn't know what I was doing. Sometimes I wasn't even concentrating in the scenes some critics liked. And I hate the way all the reviewers talk about the way I look, as though that was such an important thing about me. What difference does it make what color my eyes are, or my hair?

Chapter Thirteen

The first day back at school was hard. Some of the boys began saying, "Hey, Silver Eyes" and this one boy I can't stand, named Mickey Rogers, started singing every time I walked past, "As I looked into her silver eyes . . ." Shellie said I should ignore them. She'd seen the movie after she got back from Texas where she was visiting her father.

"Did you like it?" I asked. I really respect Shellie's opinion.

"Well, I thought *you* were really good," she said after a minute.

"Really? Did you?"

"Yeah . . . Only wasn't it hard doing that scene?"

I frowned. "It wasn't, that much. I don't know. Charlie made everybody leave but the cameraman, and he just directed it like it was a regular scene, like I had my clothes on. And the man who played my stepfather was nice. Winston Lane."

Shellie grinned. "He was really good-looking. Did he make a pass at you?"

"Winston? Uh uh! He's really happily married to this extremely nice woman named Jo. She used to visit him and bring lunch to the set. They have twins."

"Huh . . . too bad."

I laughed. "Why? He's, like, thirty-eight or something."

"Yeah, but well I thought if you were in movies, movie stars would fall in love with you and that kind of thing."

"I don't think so. . . . Anyhow, nobody did with me."

"Didn't they even act interested?" She opened her can of tomato juice.

"Well, this one cameraman used to kid around with me a little, but that was all."

"I bet now that the movie's opened, they will."

"That's what Joshua says . . . but it won't be like that, Shellie. I'm not going to change. I might not even ever *be* in another movie."

"But think how rich you could be!" Shellie bit into her tuna-fish sandwich.

"Yeah, that's true. But Daddy won't let me have the money to spend, anyway. He says I have to save it. Like for college and stuff like that."

Shellie looked sympathetic. Her parents aren't that well off financially. They live in Forest Hills and she has to share a room with her little sister Zoe, who's eight.

"You know, one good thing about that movie," Shellie said. We were just about finished with lunch. "They showed how really shitty it is to have stepparents."

Shellie's parents are divorced and remarried to other people. "Like how?" I asked, finishing my Tab.

"Oh, the way they never really like you as much as they like their own children. They pretend to in the beginning, but once they move in, they act really nasty or bored. And then you have stepsisters and stepbrothers, which is really a drag."

"Yeah, well I guess that *is* hard," I said. Suddenly I thought of Mom and Simon. I bit my thumbnail.

She made a face. "Listen, why worry about it if you don't have to? Your parents get along, don't they?"

I nodded. I tell Shellie everything, but I didn't feel ready to tell her about the thing with Mom and Simon. "They both travel a lot with their work."

"Gives them less chance to fight."

I never thought of it like that. "Yeah. . . . God, Deel's been awful about everything."

"She's probably just jealous."

"Yeah, she—"

Just then a girl in our class named Teresa Shapiro came over.

"Oh, uh, Rusty? I was wondering . . . could I interview you for *What's What* sometime, about your being in the movie and all?"

"Sure."

She smiled. "That's really exciting. I saw it over vacation. You were great."

"Thanks."

After she left, Shellie smiled at me. "You'll have Rusty Engelberg fan clubs after you."

"Shellie, don't, okay?"

"What?" She looked surprised.

"I just . . . I don't want to make a big deal of it. It's like Daddy calling me star. I'm the same person. I haven't changed."

"Sure." Shellie looked sympathetic.

"If I start acting awful, will you promise to tell me?"

"Awful how?"

"Just, you know, stuck up or conceited."

"Okay."

One really good thing about Shellie is she isn't the least *bit* jealous of my being in the movie. That's because she wants to be a poet when she's older. In fact, she's already had four poems published. Not just in the literary magazine at school, but in a real magazine. And her father, who's an editor, showed some of them to someone at the *New Yorker* and he said she was "extraordinarily gifted." She's one of these people who's really shy and quiet till you get to know her, but when you're alone with her, she's not at all.

One weird thing happened at the end of the day. A girl named Lucia Tucker came up to me and said, "I'm not going to even see your movie," and walked off. She's not even someone I'm that friendly with. But the worst of all was when I was waiting to get the bus to go home. These three boys from my class, Roger, Nicky, and Evan, were standing at the bus stop. Evan is sort of nice, when he's alone, but when he's with Nicky and Roger he acts almost as dumb as they are.

"Hey, Rusty, you going to act some of the scenes from your movie at school?"

I shook my head.

He started waving one hand. "How tragic for a little governess to have hair that reminds one of—"

"Orange juice," Nicky said.

"Not orange juice, dope! Marmalade!"

Evan said, "Hey, we're embarrassing her. She's trying to pretend she doesn't know us," as I started moving to the corner to get on the bus.

"What do you expect?" Roger said. "She's a movie star." Then he started yelling in this loud voice, "Hey, folks, see that girl with the red hair? She's a movie star!"

Some people turned around to look at him.

"It's called *Domestic Perversions* and it's about this really horny girl who—"

Luckily at that point I got on the bus and couldn't hear any more. I felt so awful. God, boys are so dumb! Is this going to happen every day? I kept having the feeling people were looking at me on the bus, that they'd all seen the movie and hated it. Probably they hadn't, but I couldn't wait to get off. Maybe I should dye my hair black so nobody will recognize me. Maybe I should go to another school under a different name. I could go to a boarding school. Maybe a boarding school in another country where no one would have ever seen the movie. . . . I wish it had opened in June, just after school ended so by the time fall came, everyone would have forgotten. I feel so humiliated and awful.

"Hey! What's wrong?" It was Deel. I hadn't even seen her when I got home.

"Oh, hi."

"Did something happen at school?"

I shrugged. "Nothing special." I was afraid she'd just make fun of me, too. I went right into my room and fell asleep till supper. I know that's a bad thing to do, just sleep to escape from your problems, but when I wake up, I usually feel better.

I did feel pretty good through dinner. Then we all sat down to watch "Talk," the show with Mom and me on it. I didn't think it was that bad. None of us said anything till the end when Mom said, "You know, I didn't look so bad. Isn't that funny? When I saw the playback last week, I thought I looked like a total mess, but here . . . I just shouldn't have worn beige. It tends to look so drab. What did you think, sweetie?"

Daddy had a funny expression on his face. He kept staring at me. "What did you mean, Tati, saying we all go around without our clothes on?"

"What?" I didn't know what he meant.

"You said we never wear clothes."

"No, she didn't Lionel. What do you mean?" Mom said. "She didn't say anything *like* that. You're imagining the whole thing."

"Darling," Daddy said, "I just sat here and heard her say we never wear clothes."

"She didn't! She didn't say one word like that."

"Yeah, she did," Deel said. "She said, 'It wasn't a big deal to act in the nude because at home we go around without clothes a lot.' "

"Right!" Daddy said. "What did you mean?"

I tried to think. "Well, I just meant . . . Well, more Mom maybe . . . You used to more when we were little. I just meant some kids' parents never ever let them see them naked, like it was some big mystery . . . and you're not like that."

Daddy got up and then began pacing back and forth. "Darling, we have to talk about this. You see, TV programs are watched by *millions* of people. And there may be things that you feel, or which have some truth in them, but when you say them right out like that—"

I felt bad, after everyone making fun of me at school. "I just wanted to show that you practice what you preach," I said.

Daddy frowned. "What I preach? What do I preach?"

"Well, like about clothes . . . Like, Shellie went in by mistake to the bathroom and her father was in the shower and he started screaming at her to get out and wrapping towels around himself, like if she saw his penis or something, she might drop dead. You're not like that." Actually I haven't seen Daddy naked since I was little, but he used to not mind if you came in when he was getting dressed.

"It's the impression you're giving," Daddy said. "People

are going to think of us as a family that spends most of their time sitting around stark naked!"

"Lionel!" Mom looked at him in amazement. "You're being so literal. No one is going to think anything of the kind."

"I thought you might mind about my saying I had a diaphragm," I said. "I didn't even think about the clothes thing."

"Well, I was getting to that . . . Sweetheart, you know, one's sexual life is, or should be, a private thing, an intimate thing."

"Yeah?"

"To talk to your closest friends, to tell them certain things, is one thing, but to announce, right on TV, that—"

"Lionel, I am absolutely flabbergasted," Mom said.

"About what?" Daddy said, confused.

"I thought Rusty did a *marvelous* job. At her age, being so open and relaxed. . . . What is wrong with you? You should be proud!"

"I'm proud that she's relaxed," Daddy said. "I'm proud she's a fine actress. I just don't think she realizes the impression she's giving of our family when she says these things."

"But I said things that were true, Daddy," I said.

"That's not the point," Daddy said. "It doesn't matter if they are true or not."

"It doesn't?" I didn't understand.

"What concerns me," Daddy said, "is the way this is going to appear to the people listening to the show. To the average American a family that buys their fourteen-year-old daughter a diaphragm for Christmas, who go around stark naked all the time—"

"I just can't believe my *ears*," Mom said. "Since when are you so concerned about the average American? I thought you thought they were all total fools."

"I never said that," Daddy said, taken aback.

"You said everyone has to have their own standards and values apart from the common herd," I reminded him.

"That's true," Daddy said unhappily, "but—"

"I don't see why you're making such a big deal about it, Daddy," Deel said. "So the whole world knows she has a diaphragm? She'll just get a lot of guys wanting to—"

"I will *not*," I said.

"How about me?" Mom said archly. "Did *I* say anything to disgrace the family name?"

Daddy hesitated a second. "No, I thought you were . . . very composed."

"Except for all that feminist shit," Deel muttered.

Mom looked at her in surprise. "Why shit? I thought you—"

"Well, I wouldn't think someone who goes around playing housewives who get all hysterical if their wash isn't clean can exactly call herself a feminist."

"Cordelia, you are such at snot nose at times," Mom said. "Wait till you go out in the world! Wait till *you* have to earn a living."

"Well, I can tell you *one* thing," Deel said haughtily. "I'm not going to demean myself by doing TV commercials. I'm going to do something which will make the world a better place to live in."

"Bravo," Daddy said nervously.

"Oh, fuck it," Mom said. "And I'm making the world a *worse* place to live in, I suppose? My earning money so you can go to the best schools."

"Best!" Deel said. "It's full of creeps."

"What's wrong with doing TV commercials?" I said. "I don't see what's so bad about it."

"*You* wouldn't," Deel said. "You'd do *anything* just to—"

Daddy sighed. "I don't know. I have a terrible headache. I think I'm going to lie down."

"I think I'm going to lie down too," Mom said. She put her arm around him and rested her head on his shoulder. They both left the room.

"That was mean," I said. "You made Mom feel bad. She can't help how she earns a living."

"He's such a jerk," she said.

"Daddy?" I was amazed since Deel always seemed to admire Daddy so much. "What do you mean?"

"He comes back and all of a sudden she's drooling all over him, and when he's *not* here, she's—"

I felt nervous. "Ssh," I said.

"Ssh what?"

"They might hear," I whispered.

"So?"

"Come on in my room, okay?"

We went into my room. "What do you mean," I said, "about when he's not here?"

"Just her fucking around with Simon and God knows who else."

"How do you know?" I said anxiously.

"Well, what do you *think* they're doing?"

"I think they're just friends," I said.

"Sure."

"Men and women can be friends."

Deel looked at me. She hesitated. "Well, I wasn't going to tell you this, but one afternoon last week I came back early, like at one?"

"Yeah?"

"And Mom and Simon were on the living room couch and—"

"Did they see you?"

"Uh uh . . . I went out. So, this isn't just idle conjecture. It's hard fact."

My heart was thumping so fast I felt sick. "Are you going to tell Daddy?"

"No! Why should I?"

"They still could be basically friends," I said thoughtfully. I felt a little queasy.

"What's that supposed to mean?"

"Well, maybe just that one time, they—"

"Oh come on! *You* know how she acts with him. 'Simon is such a warm, kind, intelligent person,' " she mimicked in Mom's southern accent.

"I thought you liked him."

"He's okay."

We sat there in silence.

"Do you think they're going to get divorced?" I said anxiously.

Deel shrugged.

"Don't you care?"

"Yeah, I guess."

"Who would you want to live with," I asked, "if you had a choice?"

"Daddy. . . . Who would you?"

"Mom."

Deel looked at me. "You'd like to live with *her?*"

"Yeah."

"Ugh."

"I guess I don't feel the same way about her you do."

"Guess not. . . . Well, anyway, it probably won't happen. She's just at that age when women start getting nervous. Like in a few years they'll be old hags and no one'll want them so they have to—"

"Mom won't be an old hag. She's one of the prettiest women I've ever seen."

Deel went back to her room. I felt so lousy. First, school being so awful, then Daddy criticizing me for how I was on the show, then Deel saying that about Mom and Simon. I'm so glad she's not going to tell Daddy. That's one good thing. I mean, what good would it do? Daddy would just feel terrible. It's not *his* fault he's fat. When he was away, he bought this Scarsdale Diet book. Maybe if he sticks to it and loses fifteen pounds Mom will love him again the way she used to when they fucked in his office. Maybe she still loves him, but Simon is more . . . peppy. I'm glad they went in the bedroom together. I hope they do still love each other.

Chapter Fourteen

Joshua isn't sentimental about things, so I didn't even know if he was going to get me a valentine. But I got him one. It's cute. It's a Snoopy one of Lucy saying, "You're everything I want . . . and I want a lot." When I got home Valentine's Day, there was a letter addressed to me: T. Engelberg. I ripped it open. It showed a little creature balancing on a ball. Inside it said: "Be my Valentine. I'm difficult but adorable."

I called him up right away. "Josh? Listen, thanks for the valentine."

"Oh, I'm sorry, Rust. I didn't even think of it."

"I thought it was cute."

"What was cute?"

"Your valentine."

"What valentine?"

"The one you sent me."

"I didn't send you a valentine."

"You didn't?"

"Uh huh . . . I forgot."

"I wonder who it was from, then."

"Woody Allen?"

"Sure."

"I feel bad, Rust . . . I'm going to get you something. Can I bring it over later?"

"Okay."

"Yours was nice . . . I liked it."

When Deel came home, I showed her the valentine. "Joshua says he didn't send it. I don't know who did."

"Someone at school?"

"Maybe. I don't know." I looked at the envelope again. "Does this look like a *T* to you?"

Deel squinted. "I think it's an *L*."

"But it has that tail on top."

"Some people do their *L*'s like that. It's an *L*. Definitely."

"So maybe it's for Daddy."

"Daddy?"

"Well, he's an *L*."

"Yeah. But who'd want to send him a valentine?"

"I don't know."

Mom came in around six. She's started rehearsing for "TWWAN" again and she's been pretty busy. "Hi, hon."

I showed her the valentine.

"Cute . . . did Josh send it?"

"No . . . that's what we can't figure out. . . ." I showed her the envelope. "Does that look like a *T* or an *L* to you?"

Mom looked at it. "Well, an *L*. . . . Where do you get *T*?"

"That line on top."

"Yeah, but a *T* would go straight across. It's an *L* all right."

I made a face. "I guess I shouldn't have opened it then. It must have been for Daddy."

"For Lionel?"

"Well, he's L. Engelberg."

Mom looked thoughtful. "Goodness . . . I wonder who sent it to him." When Daddy came home, she said, "You have a secret admirer?"

Daddy looked at it, blushed, and said, "What's this?"

"It came in the mail, addressed to you . . . Tat opened it by mistake."

"I thought it was a *T*, Daddy, I'm sorry."

"Let's see the envelope," Daddy said. He looked at it. "It *is* a *T*," he said. "No doubt about it."

"It's an *L*," Mom said. "Where do you see *T*?"

"I've never seen an *L* that looked like that," Daddy said.

"I have," Mom said. "Many times."

"Joshua didn't send it," I said.

"Well, but I'm sure you have many other boys who—"

"I thought you'd be pleased, sweetie, to have a secret admirer," Mom said.

"I'd be pleased if I did," Daddy said. "But I don't."

She hugged him. "I'm sure you do."

He just smiled sheepishly. "Well, it's news to me."

"Don't you know anyone who's difficult, but adorable?" Mom said. She lowered the fire under the chops.

"Everyone I know is difficult," Daddy said. "But adorable? I don't know."

"Mom, did you send it?" I said. "I bet you did."

"No, absolutely not . . . mine is inside on your desk, Lionel."

Daddy went in and opened Mom's valentine. He came back and kissed her. "That's lovely darling . . . I'm afraid I forgot to—"

"Josh forgot too," I said.

I felt sorry for Deel, with no one to send a valentine to, *or* get one from. "I wonder who Daddy's admirer is?" she said thoughtfully. We were in her room.

"Do you really think he has one?"

"Sure, why not? He's cute."

I never thought of Daddy as being cute that much. "How about his being fat?"

"No, he's not fat, just pleasantly plump."

"I wish he'd stay on that Scarsdale Diet and lose fifteen pounds. Then Mom might—"

"I think he looks nice the way he is now."

"Do you think he's as handsome as Simon?"

"Simon's not so handsome."

"Well, but—"

"Daddy's kind of . . . I bet lots of women would like him a lot."

"Really?"

"Yeah, because he's really smart, he knows so much about lots of things—art, politics. He has high ideals about things."

I thought about that. "He's not that sexy though."

"So? Look at Joshua . . . and you like him."

I felt mad. "Joshua's *very* sexy."

She looked like I had said the most ridiculous thing in the world. "*Joshua* is very sexy?"

"Yes . . . he has a good figure, and he has nice hair, and beautiful eyes."

"Well, it's good someone thinks so."

"What's wrong with him?"

"Well, if you don't mind terrible posture, and lousy skin, and crooked teeth—"

"He doesn't! He doesn't have *any* of those things."

Just then the doorbell rang. It was Joshua. I'm glad he didn't hear any of those things Deel was saying about him. They're not even true! I mean, sure he could stand up straighter—he just forgets. Sometimes his skin breaks out, but mostly it's okay if he remembers to wash his face. And it's true, he has one crooked tooth, but it's way off to the side. You don't even see it unless he laughs and not even then, not unless you know it's there and you're really looking for it. Anyway, sexiness isn't just teeth and skin. It's the way you are as a person.

Joshua brought me a bunch of pussy willows and a bag of marzipan candies shaped like fruit. Those are both things I like a lot. I kissed him. Then I put the pussy willows in a jar and brought them into the living room.

"Hi, Joshua," Mom said.

"Hello, Mrs. Engelberg," Joshua said. "Hello, Mr. Engelberg."

"Those are lovely," Mom said. "I adore pussy willows. How thoughtful."

"Do you want some marzipan?" I said, offering some to Mom and Daddy. Mom took one, but Daddy said he'd better not, because it wasn't on his diet.

"I'm sure your secret admirer doesn't want you to be plump," Mom said, smiling at him.

"Darling," Daddy said. He reached out and touched her hand.

"Why shouldn't you have one?" Mom said. "I think it's terrific. You're a very attractive man."

Daddy sighed. "I think Joshua really sent that valentine . . . did you?"

Joshua shook his head. "I wish I had," he said. "I forgot."

"You can't get out of it that easily," Mom said to Daddy, smiling slyly. "No idea who it could be from? No one giving you sidelong glances?"

"Not a one."

Joshua went into my room with me. "Who do you think the card was from?" I said, taking out the marzipan and spreading it on the bed. I decided to eat the apple one first. I love the almondy taste of marzipan.

"His secretary, probably," Joshua said, eating the pear one. "They always have something going with their secretary."

"Joshua!" He gets me so mad at times. "Daddy's secretary happens to be about fifty years old and she weighs about two hundred pounds."

"How come he has a secretary like *that?*" He ate another piece of marzipan.

"Because he wants someone who's a good secretary. She's been with him for years."

"He should get one who's good at both."

"Both what?"

"Sex and typing. My father says those are the two main requirements in a secretary."

"Just because your father is the most gross person that ever lived, doesn't mean every father is."

Joshua grinned sheepishly. "He *is* kind of gross, you're right . . . but he has a cute secretary."

"Have you ever met her?"

"Sure . . . whenever I go to his office. He's only had her about a year. The other one left to get married. I guess she got fed up with him. This one is, like . . . well, not too quick on the uptake, to put it mildly."

"She might just be poor."

"What does that have to do with it?"

"Well, maybe she'd go to college if she had the money. She might be supporting her aging mother, or something."

"This one never got past sixth grade . . . maybe seventh if she had a kind teacher."

"You're prejudiced."

"True . . . well, anyone who's making it with Patricia has got to be mightily demented or slightly—"

"Your mother's not demented."

He looked thoughtful. "Yeah, she's more . . . worn out. I think if she had to do it over, she wouldn't marry anyone. That's what she says. She says she wouldn't get married, and she wouldn't have children."

"Huh . . . that's really sad. I mean, since she doesn't have it to do over."

"Yeah."

"I think Mom is glad she had us."

"Well, but your mother did something with herself, she looks good, it's totally different."

"True." I looked at him. Sometimes we just start staring at each other and can't stop. I kept thinking how Deel had said those awful things about how Joshua looks. It's true maybe he's not handsome in a movie-star way, but I think he's really nice looking. He has beautiful eyes. They can look all sorts of different ways, even without his saying anything.

"How's it been at school?" he asked.

"Not that great." Joshua's the only one I've told about all the teasing I've been getting at school, and I don't even tell him everything. Like today in Sex-Ed class, our teacher, Ms. Jetty, was talking about different forms of birth control and when she came to diaphragms and started passing one around so we could see it, Ethan said, "Why doesn't Rusty show us hers?"

Ms. Jetty didn't hear him, and the class was almost over anyway. Some of the boys started acting really dumb for a change, and began throwing the diaphragm around the room like a Frisbee. Roger threw it at me. I caught it and brought it over to Ms. Jetty's desk.

"Hey, Rust, how do you like yours?" Evan said. "Is it working out well?"

"Why don't you bug off?" Shellie said. "You're so immature."

"I bet her boyfriend likes it," Roger said to Evan.

"The boys in my class are really awful," I said, feeling bad just remembering it. "Maybe I should switch to another school."

"You could switch to Stuyvesant," Joshua suggested.

"But maybe people there would've seen the movie."

"Well, but by next fall everybody would've forgotten about it pretty much."

"But if I make another movie, then—"

Joshua frowned. "I thought you weren't going to."

"Well, I don't know. I guess when I go out to L.A., I might just talk to these people."

"What people? What're you talking about? Out where?"

I looked down. "Well, the thing is, I have to do this publicity for *Domestic Arrangements*, just a week or so. It's right when we have winter vacation. So I thought while I was out there, I could meet with these people who called Helen about the musical."

"Hey, wait a minute," Joshua said, putting up his hand. "You're going out to Hollywood? Since when?"

"It's just for a week."

"How come you didn't even mention it?"

"I just found out today."

He began bending a paper clip back and forth. "I thought you said you didn't want to get involved in all that shit."

"I don't . . . listen, it's just for a *week!* I *have* to, Josh. I can't just *not* do it. They'd get really mad."

"So?"

I couldn't believe he didn't understand. "Well, I mean, they've invested all this time and money . . . and I'll just have to be on some TV shows and do some interviews. Mom says it's good experience."

"For what?"

"For, like, if I do other shows. Learning how to answer questions and all."

"Just tell them to shove off." He looked angry. "The movie's doing okay."

"That's the whole point." I leaned forward. "They didn't expect it to do that well. So they want to, you know, capitalize on it."

"And you're just letting them use you—"

"Why're you making it sound so seedy? They're *not* using me."

Joshua was staring at me in this really cold, detached way. "So, what's this musical they want you to audition for?"

"I don't know that much about it. Anyway, I can't even sing! But they said not to worry about that. It's based on this book that was already made into a movie, *Lolita?* I don't know much about it. I never saw it."

"Oh shit!" Joshua said, sounding totally disgusted.

"What's wrong?" I was surprised. "It's supposed to be a really good book. Daddy said so. He said it's by this famous Russian writer . . . Pushkin, I think."

"Nabokov."

"Yeah, that's right. Daddy said he was one of the finest stylists of the English language . . . even though he was Russian."

"A musical version of *Lolita?*" Joshua said, as though it were the most disgusting thing he ever heard of.

"Yeah . . . I don't get why you're getting so upset."

"Do you know what the book is about?"

I shook my head.

"It's about this girl—you're too old anyhow—who makes it with men who are, like fifty years *old!* She does it with men that make my father look like Abraham Lincoln."

"Daddy says it's a witty satire on contemporary life."

Joshua shook his head. "I just can't *believe* your father would let you even consider something like that."

"Josh, first of all, I probably won't get the part. Secondly, I don't have to do it even if I do, and third of all, do you know what they'd pay me?"

"What?"

I lowered my voice in case Deel was listening outside the door. "A hundred thousand dollars."

"That is *sick*," Joshua said angrily. "God, I can't believe this."

"You don't know anything about it! You don't know who's directing it, or producing it, or writing the screenplay . . ."

Joshua got up. "I'm going to go home," he said. "I don't feel well."

"Just because of this?"

"Yeah, everything . . . I don't know." He stared right at me. "You said you'd make one movie and that was it. Now you're going out to Hollywood to make an ass of yourself in front of some—"

"Why do you assume I'll make an ass of myself?"

"Because that's what they want. They want some simpering, flirty little ass. They'll make you dye your hair blond."

"What do you mean, *make* me? I don't have to do anything I don't want."

"Oh, you'll do whatever they tell you to," he said bitterly.

I felt like crying. "What do you mean?"

"They'll probably make you audition in the nude and you'll say—" he mimicked my voice, " 'Well, Daddy said it was a great book, Daddy said . . .'!"

I just stared at him. "If you think I'm such an awful person, why do you want to even see me?"

"I don't know," he said, his lips tight. "I don't know why."

"All you want to do is fuck with me! That's all."

"Sure, that's why I picked you," he said sarcastically. "Because you're so great at sex."

"Well, I'm not going to do it anymore—with you or anyone." I went to the drawer and took out my diaphragm. I grabbed the scissors and jabbed a big hole in it, right in the middle. Then I hurled it in the wastebasket. "So, you can find someone else, if that's what you want," I said, my heart thumping.

Joshua was staring at me like I had gone crazy. "Rust, listen, I didn't—" he started to say, but I pushed him out of the room.

"Get *out* of here," I said. "And take your stupid marzipan. I don't even *want* it." I shoved the bag at him. There weren't too many left.

I locked the door behind him. I could tell he was standing there, right behind the door, but I didn't move or go to open it or anything. I just sat there not making a sound until I heard him walk away, toward the front door.

After he'd left, I pulled the cover over my head and cried and cried. I never felt so awful in my life. How can Joshua be so mean? I can't *believe* it. How could I have liked such a mean, terrible, selfish person? If it was him, and he got some offer to do something because people thought he was good at it, I'd be pleased. I'd say it was terrific.

I guess I shouldn't have told him how much money they'd

offered me. It is horrible in a way, when people are starving, that's true. But it isn't *my* fault. I mean, someone's going to get the money if I don't. The main thing is, I don't even think I want to do it and I never did. I'm not even sure I'll bother auditioning for it. If I got it I'd have to learn to sing and, well, it would just be sort of a big deal. I'd have to live out there, maybe, for a few months. The good thing with *Domestic Arrangements* was it was filmed in New York, so I didn't have to travel or anything.

Daddy says he questions whether it would be a good idea for me to be so involved in acting right now, before I've even finished high school. Mom says strike while the iron is hot, meaning I guess that maybe in a few years no one'll want me.

It's confusing. I don't want to do something stupid, or something I'll regret. But I wouldn't! I wouldn't act in something I thought was dumb. Joshua doesn't even know! Maybe it's a terrific script, really funny and everything. How can he tell if he never even read it? He's so prejudiced! And the point is, doing just one week of publicity isn't such a big thing. Everybody does that. It's good for your image. Then they'll all see what I'm really like and they won't have any misconception of me as being like the girl in the movie.

I went over to the wastebasket and took out my diaphragm. What an awful thing to do! It cost thirty-five dollars and had to be specially fitted and everything. But I'm glad I did it. I don't think I want to fuck with anyone for a long time. What's the point? Then that's all you do and you don't get to really know the person. Maybe if Joshua and I hadn't spent so much time fucking, I would have realized what he was really like.

In the middle of the night Joshua called. "Rust, are you still mad at me?" he said. His voice was very low, almost a whisper.

"Yes!" I said, and hung up.

Of course I'm still mad at him! He thinks if he comes over like he did to Abigail's, and says nice things and that he didn't mean it, I'll forget everything he said. Well, I won't. Not if I live to be a hundred.

Chapter Fifteen

That evening, I asked Daddy if he thought I would like the book *Lolita.*

"I don't think so, darling," Daddy said after a minute. "It's not really . . . you see, his style is rather complex, and . . . it's really about adults who have certain problems that you might . . . I don't think you'd find too much to empathize with, really."

"Then how come you think I should try out for the movie?"

"Well, I don't think you definitely should. I think we should wait and hear more about it. So much depends on what the script is like."

I bit my lip. "Is the girl in it stupid?"

"No, not stupid. . . . You see, hon, it's a satire, which means the people in it are being seen from a certain angle, a comic angle. It's not a novel about real life in the simple way *Domestic Arrangements* was."

"Do you think that was about real life?"

"Well, yes, by and large."

"But the people in it did such odd things!"

"Well, yes, odd, but not . . . outside the pale. They were still things one could imagine happening."

"They were?"

"Yes, I would say so . . . didn't you think so?"

I shook my head. "I couldn't imagine you having an affair with Joshua's mother!"

Daddy looked thoughtful. "Well, it's true. I don't know Joshua's mother that well. I've only met her once."

"I mean, with anyone's mother."

"Yes, well . . ."

"I can't imagine you and Mom being like the parents in the movie," I rushed on, "saying things like that to each other, such mean things."

Daddy stared at me for a long time. "No," he said finally. "We're different. Of course we married later than most people."

"What do you mean, later?"

"Well, I was thirty-four, and at that age you . . . you're more careful, you know more what you really want, and need."

"You mean, because Dora wasn't that good?"

"It wasn't that she wasn't *good*," Daddy said cautiously. "It was . . . we came from such different backgrounds."

"But you and Mom come from different backgrounds, too."

"True."

I looked at him intently. He was staring into space. "Daddy, what do you like best about Mom?"

Daddy laughed. "Why all these questions, Tat?"

"I'm just curious."

"Well, I think Amanda is a very energetic, intense person. She . . . throws herself into everything she does with a great deal of . . . She's very alive, she doesn't equivocate."

"What does 'equivocate' mean?"

"I mean, she doesn't . . . she says what she feels. She's very direct about things."

"So, do you think you're happily married?" I hoped he wouldn't mind my asking such personal things, but I really wanted to know.

"Of course I do." He frowned. "Don't *you* think we are?"

"Sure, but kids don't always know the real truth."

Daddy was looking off out the window of the living room. "You see, marriage is a very complicated thing, darling. It involves a lot of compromise, a lot of rearranging of one's own interests and needs in relation to another person."

"Like how?"

"Well, like living in New York. I'm not sure Amanda would have chosen to live here if it weren't that I had so many ties here. She might have been happier somewhere else."

"Like where?"

He shrugged. "I don't know . . . California, maybe. But the point is, one person gives in in one way, another in another."

I sighed. "I guess it's that so many people's parents seem to get divorced."

"Well, yes. It's certainly a prevalent thing nowadays," Daddy said. "But you don't have to worry."

I hugged him. "Good." I hesitated a minute. "I'm not going to see Joshua anymore," I said, walking over to the window.

"Oh? Why not?"

"I don't think I . . . I don't think he's such a nice person. I think he's selfish."

Daddy cleared his throat. "Well, I wasn't going to say anything, Tat, but the fact is, boys his age, teenage boys, just do tend to be essentially exploitive in their relationships with girls. I'm afraid that's a fact."

"You mean, like, being mostly interested in sex?"

"That, and . . . well—"

"I don't know about sex," I said suddenly, turning around to look at him.

"What don't you know?" he said in an affectionate voice.

"I don't know if I like it!" I blurted out desperately. "I don't know if I'm good at it."

"Darling." He smiled at me. "Come here."

I went over and stood in front of him. "What?"

"There's no such *thing* as being good at it."

"There isn't?"

"It's not a performance, it's . . . loving someone and expressing that love in a certain way."

"Uh huh?" I liked that, that sounded nice. Daddy expresses himself so well about things.

"Joshua comes from a certain kind of background," Daddy said. "It's not his fault. If he uses his father as a role model—"

"I don't think he does," I said hastily. "He doesn't like him."

"Still . . . something may have rubbed off. And—"

Just then Deel came home. "Hi, gang," she said cheerfully.
"Hi," I said.

"Hey, guess what? Lover boy's brother was in school today."

"Who?"

"Neil. He got back from Asia. The great one's older
brother," she explained to Daddy.

"Deel, quit it, okay?"

"The amazing thing is, he's really an interesting *person*. He
was in India, he met all kinds of people involved in politics in
East Germany. He said to me, 'Most people think I'm radical . . .
but compared to you, I'm like a member of Hitler Youth.' " She
laughed appreciatively. "He's a real iconoclast." To Deel, that's
about the highest compliment you can pay anybody.

I was glad Daddy and I had that talk about sex and marriage
and everything. Daddy is a very comforting person to talk to
sometimes. He's very solid. Sometimes that can bug you, but
mostly it's good.

Joshua began sending me these cards. They were little
funny cards that said, "Do you forgive me?" or "Life seems bleak
without you," stuff like that. I just threw them away. I'm just
going to work hard at school and keep up, so if I have to do this
publicity trip and other things, I won't fall behind. This awful
thing happened in one of my classes. It was Science, where I
usually do fairly well, but this year I haven't done so well.
We're doing physics and Mr. Gerston, our teacher, doesn't explain
it clearly at all. During one class I just couldn't understand one
concept he was explaining so I raised my hand and said, "I don't
understand, Mr. Gerston, about kinetic energy?"

He looked at me, and then said in this really sarcastic voice,
"I'm sorry you're having trouble understanding, Ms. Engelberg.
Why don't you hire a tutor to help you?" When I didn't say
anything he went on, "Why don't you hire a whole faculty?
Or a whole school for that matter? The whole city? I'm sure you
could afford it at this point."

Everyone was laughing and I tried to laugh too, as though I
thought it was funny, but I felt terrible.

"He's awful!" Shellie said afterward. She's been so good

about everything. I'm glad I have one really good friend I can count on. Even the thing about the diaphragm. I felt so ashamed about doing such a crazy, awful thing that I'd decided not to tell anyone. I wrapped it up in tissue paper and put it in a Ziploc bag, and threw it out in the garbage can on the corner of our block. But when I told Shellie about it, about the whole thing, the fights, and everything, ending with that, she started to laugh. Shellie has this really all-out laugh. She doubled over, gasping, and said, "You? With a nail scissors? I can't believe it!"

Somehow it suddenly struck me as funny too, and I began to laugh, remembering Joshua's startled face when I hurled it in the wastebasket.

"What if you'd thrown it out the window?" Shellie said, wiping her eyes. "Imagine people walking down the street, minding their own business, when this *thing* comes winging down from outer space."

"They'd probably have thought it was a flying saucer," I said, giggling.

"It's a bird, it's a plane, it's Rusty's diaphragm!"

When we stopped laughing, I said, "But seriously, I'm giving up on sex."

"Don't look at me. I haven't even started yet!" Shellie has this boy she likes whom she met at camp, but he's very intellectual and shy. They go to movies like *Hamlet* together and sometimes he holds her hand, but that's about as far as it goes.

"Teenage boys are just sex maniacs," I said. We were at our apartment.

"They are? Not Kenny."

"He sounds nice," I said wistfully.

"Well, I wouldn't mind if he was a *little* more . . ."

"Yeah, but this way you know he really *likes* you. It isn't like he's seeing you just to have someone to fuck."

"Was Joshua like that? I thought you said he wasn't."

I swallowed. Sometimes when I think about Joshua I feel just terrible, when I remember all the nice times we had together. "I don't know. I can't—" I broke off.

Shellie patted my shoulder. "I think he really liked you," she said.

"But why did he *act* that way? I didn't say I was going to

act in that movie. I just said I might try out for it if the script was really good."

Shellie thought a minute. "Maybe he's insecure. He might think if you get that rich and famous, you won't have time for him."

"But I told him that wasn't *true*."

"Are you really going to be on the 'Today Show'?"

I made a face. "Maybe . . . isn't that weird?"

"God, won't you be scared?"

"It's only for about fifteen minutes. It might not be so bad."

There's one thing I haven't even told Shellie about. It's that *People* wants to do an interview with me. They're sending someone around the week after next. The reason I haven't told her is I used to sometimes buy *People* or *Us* after school and Shellie would always say, "How can you read that junk?" She'd always buy *Rolling Stone* or *Omni,* this science magazine she likes. But the thing is, I don't like *all* of *People,* but they do have interviews with interesting people sometimes, like Donna Summer. And they find out all those little things that you're curious about but most magazines might think weren't that important.

Deel, of course, thought the thing with *People* was gross beyond belief, even when Mom pointed out that they'd interviewed Isaac Bashevis Singer and Mary McCarthy and lots of good, smart people. "Sure, for every person like that, they interview nine hundred total *blobs*," she sneered. Well, what do you expect from Deel? I was surprised that she didn't take Joshua's attitude about *Lolita*. "Yeah, it's the kind of thing you'd be good in," she said. "It's your kind of thing."

The weirdest thing of all is that Deel actually went out on a date with Joshua's brother Neil. He's the one they thought might be gay, the one who meditates. Deel says he's not gay, he's just sensitive. I don't know if that means he's made a pass at her or what. It's sort of a touchy subject with Deel because she always starts to like boys and gets crushes on them, and then they tell her they really like her a lot, but just as a friend.

While I was sitting there talking with Shellie, Deel came racing in from Daddy's study where she'd been reading. "You'll never believe this!" she said.

"What?" both of us said together. "What happened?"

"There's an obscene caller on the phone!"

"Which one?"

Mom and Daddy have two phones, one with the same number as Daddy's office phone, and one for their friends. "Daddy's . . . come quick."

"What's he saying?"

"It's a she."

"A woman?"

"Yeah . . . she was leaving a message on his answering service."

"A dirty message?"

We all ran in and Deel turned it on. I'm always uncertain about how it works. "Wait," Deel said. She pressed a button and turned it back. Then she turned it on again. First Daddy's voice came on, saying, "This is Lionel Engelberg. I'm not in right now, but if you wish to leave a message, you can do so after the beep." Then there was the beep, a quiet one, and then this woman's voice said, very slowly in this low, smooth voice, "Mr. Engelberg . . . I want to suck your long Jewish cock." That was all. We all stared at each other in amazement.

"I never *heard* of that!" Shellie said. "A *woman* making an obscene call?"

"Me neither," I said.

"Who do you think it is?" Deel said.

"I don't know . . . it doesn't *sound* like anyone special. Play it again."

We played it again.

"God, you know who it sounds like?" Shellie said, putting her hand over her mouth.

"Who?"

"Ms. Dean."

"Ms. Dean?" She's the counselor in our school, the person you go to if you have any special problems. "It couldn't be." We played it back. "I don't think it really does, not really."

"Just the beginning part."

"Maybe it's just some weirdo that has a thing about Jews," Deel said.

"That's *really* far out," Shellie said.

"Wait till Daddy comes home," I said. "Maybe he'll recognize the voice."

When Mom came home, we played it for her. "That has got to be the strangest thing I've *ever* heard," she said, shaking her head. "Goodness! Maybe it's the one who sent him the valentine."

I'd forgotten about that.

"Does it sound like anyone you know?" Shellie asked.

"I don't think so. . . . At first I thought maybe . . . just a tiny bit like Paula Henz, but not really. I think it's just she's always saying how sexy Jewish men are. . . . Play it again, Deel."

I reached over to press the button, but Deel shouted, "That's the wrong button. Oh, dope, you erased it!"

I felt awful. "How do you know?"

"You don't press *that* button. You press this one." She pressed it again. "See, it's gone."

"Well, we all heard it anyway," I said.

"But now Daddy won't be able to hear it and find out who it was."

"Maybe he knows," Mom said.

We looked at her. "How could that be?"

"Well, maybe it's a friend of his."

"A friend wouldn't leave a message like that!" Deel said.

"A crazy friend, maybe," Shellie said.

"A secret admirer," Mom said. "It's all very mysterious."

When Daddy came home, we all ran out and began telling him at once. "Wait a minute," Daddy said. "When did this take place?"

"This afternoon," Deel said, "but el dopo here erased it by mistake."

"Who was it, Daddy?" I said eagerly. "Who do you think?"

Daddy looked bewildered. "It was a woman?"

"Darling, did you think it was a *man?*" Mom said.

"Well, perhaps some gay man . . ."

"It was a lady all right," Deel said. "A crazy lady."

"Huh," Daddy said. "Well, there are a lot of peculiar people in the city. . . . What's for dinner, darling?"

"What's for dinner, darling?" Mom said. "Come on, kid! What's the story behind this?"

"The story?" Daddy's eyes widened. "There *is* no story. None that I know of."

"Is it the person who sent you the valentine?" I asked.

"How should *I* know?"

"But Daddy, *think*," Deel insisted. "Who do you *think* it could be?"

"Can I eat dinner and think at the same time?" Daddy asked.

"You'd better come up with something good," Mom said.

"Sweetie, I have no more idea than you do . . . especially since the tape was erased. Who did it sound like?"

"No one *I* know," Mom said. "A *tiny* bit like Paula Henz."

Daddy burst out laughing. "Paula? Terrific. I love it. I'm going to call her up after dinner and—"

"I said a *tiny* bit," Mom said. "It couldn't be Paula."

"Why not?" Daddy smiled. "I bet it's Paula."

"Lionel, seriously."

"All these years, I never suspected . . ."

"Lionel."

Daddy took a long sip of wine. "God, I hope it wasn't Margaret." Margaret is Daddy's secretary, the one who's fat and not at all sexy.

"Why in *God's* name would you think of Margaret?" Mom said.

"She just seems like the type somehow," Daddy said, thoughtfully.

"*Margaret* seems like the type to make an obscene phone call?" Mom said. "In what way?"

"Well, I guess I'm thinking of this girl who used to make calls like that to me at college," Daddy said. "She looked a lot like Margaret."

"What girl?" Mom said. "You never mentioned her."

"It's a sad story," Daddy said.

"Who was it, Daddy?" Deel said.

"Well, this girl used to call me. I guess she found my name in the phone book, and we'd talk about personal things—"

"Obscene things?" I asked.

"No, it was just . . . I'd never met her. We'd talk about sex, loneliness, you know . . . It went on for months. Then finally we arranged to meet. I went to this hotel and looked around but I couldn't see her. I saw this one girl, but I knew it couldn't be her because she was fat, funny looking, forlorn."

"But it *was* her?" Deel said.

"It *was* her," Daddy said sadly.

"God, I hope you had sex with her," Mom said.

"Darling, her *hair* was falling out. She had legs like—"

"This is the saddest story I have *ever* heard," Mom said.

"Did she keep calling you after that?" Deel asked.

"A few times," Daddy said, reaching for a raw carrot. "But the bloom was gone."

"So, wait a minute," Mom said. "The conclusion you draw from this is that forlorn, overweight women make obscene phone calls?"

"Well . . ."

Mom wailed. "Lionel, *shame* on you! Margaret? After all those years of loyalty and devotion?"

Daddy looked sheepish. "Okay . . . forget Margaret."

I felt so mad at myself for erasing the tape. Now we'll never know who it was. Unless that person calls back and leaves another message. I hope they do!

I kept thinking how, if I were still seeing Joshua, we'd joke about the obscene caller. I miss him at times like this. I miss him a lot, actually, though I haven't said that to anyone. Sometimes just walking down the street I'll think of him, or if I see some movie playing that he likes, or if I pass the Thalia or the Regency where we used to go to see old movies. I felt funny when his brother Neil came over one day with Deel. Deel and Neil. It sounds funny together.

I'd never met Neil since he was traveling around Europe when I started seeing Joshua. He's not really handsome like Tommy, Joshua's other brother. He looks a little bit like Joshua except he's taller and thinner and has darker hair. He has a black beard and sort of longish hair in a pony tail. What he does is he plays the lute. He even makes lutes and things like that. He learned how from a man in Italy and now he's thinking of doing that for a living. I didn't know that many people wanted lutes, but evidently they do. He kept looking at me, but sort of shyly, as though he didn't know what to say.

"I hear you're a very good actress," he said finally. Deel was in the kitchen making tea for both of them.

"Not really," I said. I wondered where he'd heard that.

"Joshua said you were." He kept staring at me. I wondered what else Joshua had said about me. That I was dumb and terrible at fucking? "I want to see your movie."

"It's not mine, exactly."

"It must be hard, being famous." He had very sympathetic dark eyes.

"I don't think I'm famous," I said.

Deel brought in the tea. "Sure you are," she said. "I was in the library today and someone pointed to me and said, 'Oh, that's what's-her-name's sister.' Great, I thought. I'll go down in history as what's-her-name's sister."

"I thought you were going to go down in history as the first Jewish woman president," I said.

"That sounds more like it," Neil said, lifting his tea glass. "*I'll* vote for you, Cordelia."

"I will too," I said.

"Is that what they call a constituency?" Deel said.

"You've got to start somewhere," Neil said.

"She's going to be in *People*," Deel said.

I shrugged. "Yeah, well . . ."

"What I'd think would be hard," Neil said, "is living the same life as before, but feeling changed."

"I *don't* feel changed!" I blurted out. "I don't! Everyone *thinks* I am, but I'm not." I thought of Joshua and felt a pang. "I'm the exact same person."

"Sure, except now nine hundred thousand people have seen you naked," Deel said.

"I wasn't naked," I said, hurt. I felt like she was just trying to humiliate me in front of Neil.

"What do you mean you weren't naked?"

"I had underpants on."

"Big deal . . . underpants!"

I sat there, feeling angry. When I looked up, Neil was gazing at me pensively. "Did you bring your lute?" I asked, just to change the subject.

"Yes, it's right in the hall," he said, smiling. "Would you like me to play something for you?"

He went and got his lute and played some really beautiful songs. Listening to the lute is soothing, it made me feel better. After he left, I lay there on the couch, half dozing.

"Listen you!" Deel said, shoving me.

I opened my eyes. "What?"

"Keep your grubby hands off him, okay?"

"Huh?"

" 'Did you bring your lute?' " she mimicked. "Cut that out. I *mean* it."

"What's wrong with asking if he brought his lute?"

"And sitting there batting your big silver eyes, quote unquote, at him. You're as bad as Mom!"

"Do you want me not to even talk to him?"

"You can talk to him, but don't *flirt* with him."

"I wasn't!"

"You were so."

I think Deel is really unfair. How is it flirting if you ask someone if they brought their lute? "I don't even like him that way," I muttered, closing my eyes again. "And I'm not interested in sex anymore."

"Sure," Deel said.

"I'm not . . . I threw my diaphragm away."

"You what?"

"Yeah, I don't want to do it with anyone."

"After all that fuss about getting it? You only had it a month."

"I know . . ." I opened my eyes. "Listen, don't tell Mom or Daddy, Deel, okay? Promise?"

She was frowning. "How come you threw it out? You could've just put it away for a couple of years."

"I just felt like it."

"Weird."

I wish I knew what Joshua had said about me to his brother, if he said he still liked me or what. Maybe he's started seeing someone else already. Maybe Marjorie came back from Colorado, or he went up to Andover to visit Pam. She was always writing him saying he should visit her. Anyway, Deel doesn't have to worry. I'm not going to steal her boyfriend, if that's what he is, *especially* if he's Joshua's brother. What does she think I am?

"Sweetie, where is Joshua these days?" Mom finally asked me when she came home. "He hasn't been around much lately."

"I'm never going to see him again."

"Oh? Did you have a fight about something?"

I hesitated. "Sort of."

"What about? Or don't you want to talk about it?"

"He was just interested in sex," I said. "He didn't really like me."

"Darling, I *know* that's not true."

"How do you know?"

"Well, the way he looked at you, acted with you. . . . It was clear he was terribly fond of you."

"No, he just pretended."

Mom shook her head. "You can't pretend about that kind of thing."

I didn't really feel like talking about it anymore. I went back to my room to wait for dinner.

Chapter Sixteen

The people from *People* said they'd come on Friday afternoon when I got home from school. They said they'd come with a photographer, and they might have to come back a second time.

"Darling, is that good for you?" Daddy asked Mom at breakfast.

"Is what good for me?"

"Well, they're coming at three. Will you be home by then?"

"Lionel! Of course I won't be home at three! We have rehearsal."

"Cancel it . . . you've *got* to be here."

Mom looked at him indignantly. "You've *got* to be kidding! Cancel a rehearsal? What for? It's Tat's interview. Why is *my* presence necessary?"

Daddy sighed heavily. "Your presence is crucial. We've been over this."

"In what way? What have we been over?"

"The point is this, this article will be read by thousands of people and it's terribly important that Tatiana not say anything that—"

"Daddy, I can handle it," I said. "Don't be silly."

"Precisely!" Mom exclaimed. "Silly isn't the word! Tat isn't a baby. She's an exceedingly self-possessed young woman who's perfectly capable of doing an interview with *People* or anyone else for that matter. I'm not going to be some stage mother sitting holding her hand and nudging her every time she opens her mouth."

"But look," Daddy said. "*People* is basically a sensational magazine, a scandal sheet of sorts. They are looking, *actively* looking for ways to make people look like fools."

"That's a total prejudice," Mom said. "In what way? What did they say about Isaac Singer that made *him* look like a fool?"

"Tatiana is fourteen years old. She is not a world-renowned writer who won the Nobel Prize."

"What don't you want me to say, Daddy?" I was really curious.

"It's no single thing," Daddy said. He was silent. Then he turned to Mom. "It's just one rehearsal. Just this one time, couldn't you—"

"Couldn't *I*? Couldn't *you*? Where are we? Back in the thirteenth century? If you want someone to be there monitoring her every word, *you* do it! *You* come home at three."

"How can I?" Daddy said. "We're shooting in New Haven."

"Darling, that is *your* problem. But my rehearsal is every whit as important as *your* damn movie."

"That's not the point."

"It is . . . You expect me to drop everything just because to you my work is utterly trivial and of no consequence, whereas what *you* do is world shaking. Well, I think that's totally sexist and shitty and I don't want to hear one more word about it!" She slammed out of the room.

Daddy looked at me. "Well!" he said.

"It'll be okay, Daddy," I said.

"Maybe I will try to rearrange things," Daddy said. "I might be able to make it by four."

"I won't say the thing about your not wearing clothes," I said. "Is that what you're worried about?"

Daddy looked unhappy. "I just—"

I looked at him soulfully. "Don't you trust me?"

"I do, Tat. . . . It's just . . . You're so open about things.

You just say whatever you feel and that's lovely in many ways, but these are journalists and—"

"Don't you like journalists?"

"Oh, they may be perfectly nice people in their personal lives . . . but in this case their main function is to get a good story."

"Deel will be here," I pointed out.

"True." He just sat there staring at the wall. "I wish Amanda wouldn't fly off the handle quite so easily. Why doesn't she understand?"

I didn't say anything.

"Women are very hard to understand," Daddy said. "Women, wives, marriage . . . it's all supremely confusing." He stood up. "Look at me, Tat! Do I look thinner? I've lost ten pounds!"

I hugged him. "That's great, Daddy. Is it hard? Do you feel hungry?"

"Starving. It's painful beyond belief. I have pornographic dreams about hot-fudge sundaes."

"How much more do you have to lose?"

"Ten pounds."

It's good that Daddy has so much willpower. I feel proud of him. I wonder if it's okay if I tell *People* that he's on the Scarsdale Diet?

The reporter from *People* was named Mike Nadler. He came with his wife who was the photographer. Her name was Trudy. I decided not to change into anything special, just to wear what I'd been wearing at school—jeans, my Disneyland T-shirt and a red long-sleeved shirt over it.

"Gee, I love this apartment," Trudy said, looking around. She went over to the window. "So much light! Have you lived here long, Tatiana?"

"All my life . . . but Mom and Daddy used to live in New Haven before they had us."

"Was that a long time?"

"No, because they . . . I think Mom was pregnant before they got married. See, Daddy was married before. To someone named Dora. Only Mom was in his class at Yale and they fell in love and—"

"One thing led to another," Mike said, smiling.

"Yeah." I was glad he understood. Maybe that's how he met his wife.

"Your mother's done quite a bit of acting herself, hasn't she?" he said. "TV commercials and so on?"

"Yeah, and they're writing her back into the script of 'The Way We Are Now.' " I told them all about what had happened with Myra and Dr. Morrison and about her twin sister.

"So, you've certainly grown up hearing a lot about the world of acting and film. Does your father—"

"Well, he was a child actor . . . but he stopped. He said he heard himself once on a tape and it was so awful, he never did it again."

"Daddy must be rather self-critical," Trudy commented.

"Yes," I said. "He's a very serious person." I didn't want to tell them what he said about *People* because that might hurt their feelings since they work for it.

"Maybe you'd like to show us around the apartment, Tatiana," Trudy said. "Your room and so on. I'll just keep snapping away. Does it bother you?"

"Uh uh."

"The natural light is marvelous."

I showed them my room, my records, everything.

"What a lovely dollhouse!" Trudy said, kneeling down to look into it. "Do you still play with it?"

"Sometimes . . . not as much as I used to. The lights go on, see?" Daddy put them in that way when I was ten. It looks so pretty at night. Even the fireplace goes on.

"This looks like a pretty average teenager's room, I'd say," Mike said, looking around at the Miss Piggy poster over my desk. "Would you say your life is pretty average too, Tatiana? Or can I call you Rusty? I gather that's the name your friends use."

"Rusty's okay," I said. I smiled at him. I had the feeling he thought I was pretty.

"You think of yourself as an average New York teenager?" he said.

"Pretty much," I said. Then I added, "In what way?"

"Well, just to veer off onto a topic you're probably sick of . . . But as you probably realize, there were certain scenes in

Domestic Arrangements which caused a certain . . . stir, some alarm, one might say, among parents. I think those of us with children in their early teens all wondered, *is* this what's really going on? Do *you* think it is?"

I thought of what Daddy had said. I don't know what he'd want me to say. "Um . . . what do you mean?"

He looked a little uncomfortable. "What I mean is . . . would you say the degree of sexual expertise, if I can use that phrase, of Samantha is typical of you and your friends?"

"No."

"In what way isn't it? Could you clarify that?"

I cleared my throat. "Well, most of my friends aren't actually . . ." I wasn't sure if you could say fucking ". . . doing it."

"Having sex?"

"Yeah."

"You say your friends aren't?"

"Right."

"And you?"

I licked my lips. I kept thinking of Daddy. "I used to have a boyfriend, but I don't anymore."

"Who was your boyfriend?"

"Well he's not anymore . . . and he wouldn't like me to mention his name."

"This was someone your own age or—"

"Yeah."

"Your own age?"

"Well, he's sixteen."

He nodded. "And, uh, would you characterize your relationship with him as, well, fairly intense?"

"What do you mean?"

"You saw each other a lot?"

I nodded.

"And I assume sex played a certain role in your relationship?"

"Uh huh."

"A major role?"

I felt wary. "Sort of . . . But I'm not interested in sex anymore. I decided I'm too young."

Trudy smiled. She was taking photos of me while I was talking. "You're fourteen now?"

"I want to work more and . . . maybe act. . . . Anyway I don't believe in sex unless you really love somebody."

"Do you think that at your age love is really possible?" Trudy said. "I'm just asking out of curiosity, really. Our daughter seemed to feel—"

I nodded. "Yes, I do," I said. I thought of snuggling with Joshua under the quilt at Abigail's apartment and how he used to look at me after we fucked and how we'd lie and talk in his father's study. "Definitely."

"Were you in love with your boyfriend?"

"Yes." I didn't care. It's true, so why shouldn't I say it?

"Well, I'm sure you'll be in love many times before you settle down with one man," Mike said. "And needless to say, I'm sure many men will find you extremely captivating."

"I don't know," I said.

He smiled. "What don't you know?"

"Well." I felt uncomfortable. "My father doesn't want me to talk about personal things that much," I blurted out. "He's afraid I'll say something dumb."

"I don't think he has to worry about that," Mike said. "You haven't said anything dumb so far."

I felt really relieved.

"Well, the thing is, I was on this show, 'Talk,' with my mother. And I said something about how my parents used to sometimes go around without clothes on. I didn't mean a *lot* . . . But Daddy was afraid people would think of us as this family that goes around naked all the *time!* So could you say that we don't? I just meant that when I was little, if I happened to go in the room when he was getting dressed, he didn't, like, scream bloody murder the way some fathers might."

"Would you describe your relationship to your parents as close?" Mike asked. He was writing down what I said, in shorthand.

"Yeah, I would . . . I mean, I talk to them about different things."

"In what way?"

"Well, Mom talks to me about acting a lot, how she does it and stuff like that. Daddy likes to talk about more serious things—like politics? And art and literature and things like that."

"Your parents have been married how long, Rusty?"

I thought. "Um . . . I'm not sure. I think it's, like, well, Deel is sixteen, so maybe seventeen years?"

Would you describe them as happily married?"

I nodded. "Umm hmm."

"That's rare nowadays, as I guess you must realize."

I swallowed. "Well, the thing is, they married late. I mean late for Daddy . . . he was thirty-four. Mom was just twenty-three—so he, like, knew what he wanted because his first wife, Dora, wasn't that smart. But don't put that in, okay, because she might read it?"

"I won't," Mike said, smiling.

"And they believe in stuff like having friends and traveling and—"

"Open marriage?"

"What's that?"

"That's where both husband and wife recognize that they're separate individuals who have separate interests. They allow each other freedom to pursue those interests. . . . Like Trudy and me." He glanced over at her.

"Yeah, that sounds like them."

"Well, I don't know if we're such a good example," Trudy said.

"In what way aren't we?" Mike said, curious.

"Well, we work together so much."

"Uh, right."

"And then, doesn't open marriage mean both people having affairs?" Trudy said.

"Not necessarily," he said. No one spoke for a minute. "Anyway!"

"My father got an obscene phone call last week," I said, just to say something. "But we don't know who it was from."

They exchanged glances. "What did it say?" Trudy asked.

"Maybe you better not put this in," I said. "But it was really weird! It was on his answering service. It was a woman. She said something dirty and then hung up. I erased the tape by mistake, so Daddy couldn't hear who it was. Mom thought maybe it was the same person who sent him the valentine."

"The plot thickens," Trudy said, smiling.

"Let's see," Mike said, looking down at his notes. "I gather you have an older sister, Rusty? Would you like to say something about her? How you get along? Has there been any jealousy on her part about your sudden emergence as a public figure?"

"Um, well, she's going to go into politics. She doesn't care that much about acting," I said. "She thinks it's dumb. She thinks it was gross that I did a nude scene."

"You weren't totally nude," Trudy said.

"I know! But she thinks so anyway."

"How do you feel about that?" Mike said. "Was that scene difficult for you to do?"

I shook my head.

"How about the fact that, well, men meeting you are going to have seen you that way. . . . Are you afraid they might start assuming, thinking of you in those terms?"

"I'm not sure what you mean," I said. He was staring at me in a funny way.

"Let's see . . . what I mean is, they might think of you sexually, whereas without that scene, maybe not."

I never thought of that. "You mean because they saw me without anything on?"

"Right."

"I don't *think* so," I said. I thought a minute. "Some boys in my class tease me sometimes. That's about all."

"What do they tease you about?"

I blushed. I didn't know if this was something Daddy wouldn't want me to talk about. "The thing is, I had this diaphragm. Maybe you saw that show where I talked about it?"

He nodded. "It was a present?"

"Yeah, well, actually I don't have it anymore."

"What happened to it?"

"I threw it out . . . but could you not put that in? Because it cost thirty-five dollars and my parents might get mad that I wasted all that money, especially after I made a big fuss about wanting to get it and all."

"Why did you throw it out?" Trudy said, curious.

"Deel says I should've just kept it. It's just I had this fight with my boyfriend and I just . . . well, this sounds dumb but I cut a big hole in it with a nail scissors. I just . . . I don't know."

There was a silence, then Mike said, "Well, sex is a complicated thing . . . at any age."

"Yeah . . . that's what Daddy says."

"Rusty?" Trudy said. "I wonder if I could get some shots of you out on the terrace while the light's still good? Would you mind?"

"Uh uh." I put on my fox jacket and went outside. I showed them Daddy's tomato plants.

"I love your jacket," Trudy said. "Is it new?"

"Yeah. Could you say it's fake fur? Because I don't really believe in fur coats."

"Well if it's not an endangered species. . . . Move just a little to the right. Could you look over your shoulder a sec? Great . . ."

I saw Deel in the living room. "That's my sister," I said. "Cordelia."

"Oh yes . . . the future politician," Mike said. He opened the terrace door. "Hi," he said. "You're Cordelia?"

"None other." Deel looked at them warily.

"Would you like to join us, Cordelia?" Trudy said. "I'd love a few shots of you."

"I hate being photographed," Deel said.

"I know how you feel," she said. "Well, suit yourself."

"Those are real foxes," Deel said.

"We know," Mike said. "How does all this strike you, Cordelia?"

"All what?"

"All this attention your sister is getting as a result of her performance in *Domestic Arrangements*? What reaction do you have to it?"

Deel looked at him with narrowed eyes. "Well, the thing is, Rusty's more like Mom. She just wants to entertain people. I'm like Daddy. I want to make the world a better place to live in."

"That's not true," I said. "I want to make the world a better place to live in, too."

"You do?" Deel looked amazed.

"Yeah, by delivering babies and stuff like that."

Mike said, "I'll tell you what . . . why don't we step back into the living room? It's getting a little chilly out here. Trud, do you have enough?"

"Sure."

We all went back into the living room. Deel sat down on the sofa. I sat in the leather chair.

"Rusty says you have political ambitions?" Mike said, turning a leaf of his notebook.

"My problem," Deel said, "is, I'm an idealist. I don't want to just be a slimy politician, the kind that makes deals. I want to help poor people and blacks and do things for women's rights. Like, I think marijuana laws ought to be changed."

"In what way?"

"Well." Deel was acting very poised; I was surprised. She usually isn't with strangers. "The point is, everyone smokes pot, everyone! So what's the point in having laws that everybody is going to break?"

Just then the door opened and Daddy came rushing in. He looked sweaty and nervous. "Oh, hi!" he said.

"Mr. Engelberg? I'm Mike Nadler and this is my wife, Trudy."

Daddy took off his coat. "I see things are . . . under way."

"Yes. You have two very lovely and sophisticated daughters, if I may be permitted to say so," Mike said.

"Thank you," Daddy said, sitting down. "*I* think so."

"Did your movie go okay, Daddy?" I asked.

"Well, the shooting won't actually start until tomorrow," Daddy said. "It's a film for the American Cancer Society," he told them. "About smoking."

"Cordelia was just telling us that she feels marijuana laws should be changed," Mike said. "How do you feel about that?"

"Well." Daddy licked his lips. "Before we go into that, could I offer the two of you a drink? Some sherry? Scotch?" He got them drinks. "Cordelia and I don't see eye to eye totally on this issue," he said. "I think there's a lot of potential harm in irresponsible use of drugs, especially among teenagers."

"Oh, Daddy!" Deel said.

"Around here I'm considered an old fogey," Daddy said. "In the world at large I'm considered fairly liberal."

"Then how, if I might ask, did you feel about *Domestic Arrangements*? Particularly some of the scenes in which Tatiana, Rusty . . ."

Daddy looked at me. "Well, I felt . . . I felt they were handled with a great deal of taste. I don't know if I would have directed the movie *quite* that way if it had been *my* movie, but—"

"And the much-discussed hair-dryer scene? Did that disturb you in any way?"

Daddy took a sip of his drink. "My feeling is that nudity, when it's an intrinsic part of the story, is perfectly acceptable. It can even enhance a story."

"And you felt that scene was intrinsic?"

"Yes, I did," Daddy said after a moment. "I would say that."

"I thought you didn't think it was, Daddy," I said. "I thought you didn't like it."

Daddy smiled. "Well . . . it's true at first. If it's your own daughter, of course . . . but I've come to see it differently. I think I see it more in perspective now."

"How about the future?" Mike said. "Rusty's future in films, that is? I assume she's getting a good many offers. Someone at Fox told us they're very excited about the possibility of her being in a musical version of *Lolita*."

"We're being extremely careful," Daddy said. "It's important that Tatiana finish high school and go to an excellent college. I don't want her to throw away these formative years doing nothing but act in movies. But if an occasional part comes along that seems intelligent and tasteful, well, then we'll think about it."

"How do *you* feel about *Lolita*?" Mike said, turning to me. "Have you read the book, Rusty?"

I shook my head. "But Daddy says it's good."

"We're waiting for the script," Daddy said.

"I can't sing," I said. "But they said they don't care."

"Of course we don't want Tatiana to be exploited in any way," Daddy said. "That's of the utmost importance to all of us."

"Sure," Deel muttered.

Mike laughed. "Are you worried about any possible exploitation of your sister, Cordelia?"

Deel shrugged. "Well, if she goes around playing teeny boppers and nymphets with their boobs hanging out all over the place, she won't exactly . . ."

"As a matter of fact," Daddy intervened swiftly, "I may be directing a performance of *The Tempest* over the summer and I've been thinking of using Tatiana as Ariel."

He never told me that! "Isn't Shakespeare hard?" Trudy asked.

"She can do it," Daddy said. "She has a remarkable natural talent, absolutely staggering. Just picks things up like that!" He snapped his fingers.

I was getting nervous that Deel would feel jealous the way she usually does when Daddy talks about me that way.

Trudy said, "How about a shot of you with Rusty, Mr. Engelberg."

"Where would you like us to be?"

"Well, Rusty, why don't you go over and sit right on the edge of your father's chair?"

Daddy looked up at me. Then I slipped and fell into his lap. I jumped up again. "She's getting to be quite an armful," Daddy said, embarrassed.

"Yes, she certainly is," Mike said, looking at my breasts. I never like it when men do that. Maybe he was getting drunk because Daddy gave him so much Scotch.

While Daddy was talking, Mom came home. She waved from the front hall. "Hello, everybody!" She came in. She was wearing bright yellow jeans and a purple silk shirt knotted at the waist. "I'm delighted to meet you," she said, shaking Mike's hand. "I'm Amanda."

"You're her *mother?*" he said. "Unbelievable. Were you a child bride?"

"Thanks." She smiled at him in that way Deel can't stand. "So? How's it going?"

"Very, very nicely," Mike said. "Your husband has just been telling us about how he met you."

"Oh?" Mom smiled mischievously. "I hope not everything." She looked at Daddy. "What are you telling them, sweetie?"

Daddy reddened. "No, I was just mentioning the production of *The Tempest* you were in and how I'd thought of Tat playing Ariel this summer."

"And what a fall was there," Mom said. She took a sip of Daddy's drink. "I mean, now, TV commercials, soaps—Tat's the only member of the family who'll even *speak* to me."

"Darling," Daddy said.

"No, that's a slight exaggeration," Mom said. "But the fact is, well, you get work where you can . . . and Pinter isn't exactly crawling to me on bended knees to play the lead in his latest."

"If he did, would you want to do that kind of acting?"

"Sure!" Mom sat down and crossed her legs. I could tell she was sort of flirting with Mike Nadler. "Listen, I'll do anything once. So you make a fool of yourself? Big deal. My best experiences in life have been doing things I thought I couldn't."

"I've found that too," Mike said.

"Have you?" Mom said. "In what way?"

He looked taken aback. "Well, lots of ways. . . . Mrs. Engelberg, how about telling us a little of your own background, how you got started in acting, and so on."

"First of all, Amanda, okay? I use my maiden name in my work. Mrs. Engelberg is in Florida right now, playing bridge with her friends, something you will never catch me dead doing at any age. Well, gee, you really want to interview me? Have you talked to Tat enough?"

"Yes, I think we've gotten quite a lot of material," Mike said, "and since Rusty clearly gets a lot of her interest and enthusiasm for acting from you, I think our readers would be curious. But if you'd rather not—"

"Oh, no! Listen, I *adore* talking about myself. I love it. I just didn't want to hog the stage when it was Tat's interview. Do you want, like from birth on? How it all began, and so forth?"

"Sure," Mike said, smiling. I could tell he really liked Mom. Trudy looked like she was falling asleep in her chair. "Would you say Rusty's talent at this age compares to yours? Were you into acting already at fourteen?"

"There's no comparison what*ever!*" Mom said. She turned to Daddy who also had a slightly glazed expression. "Darling, could you get me some white wine? I think there's some open in the refrigerator? No, well, Rusty is just nine *million* times more poised and put together and *everything* than I was. At fourteen I was a scrawny, six-foot-tall freckled kid who couldn't get a date to save myself. I mean, with falsies I was flat-chested. That kind of thing. *Member of the Wedding* is the story of my life. Rusty's grown up with intelligent, cultivated, artistic people. I come from a town in Kentucky with a population of, at best, three hundred people. It's too small to be called a town! It's a village . . . so it was absolutely the end of the line culturally. I mean, *the* end. No movie, no theater. So I was a complete freak, a rebel, a weirdo. They wished they'd strangled me at birth . . . it was all Peyton Place. You know? Three churches in a one-block radius and the deacon making it with the doctor's wife and poor bedraggled women with umpteen mongoloid children whose biggest kick was stealing candy bars from the local hardware store."

"I come from a town like that," Mike Nadler said.

"Do you?" Mom looked like that was the most interesting thing she ever heard. She reached up and took the glass of wine Daddy handed her. "How fascinating! Where?"

"Scipioville."

"I can't believe it . . . we were neighbors! Goodness! That is just an *amazing* coincidence. Lionel, did you hear that? Mike comes from Scipioville, just ten miles from Union. Was it the same for you?"

"Absolutely," Mike said.

"That's just amazing . . . but you don't have much of an accent."

"When I get mad, I do."

"Me too." She smiled and reached down to unzip her boots. He was watching her, but then glanced, first at his wife, and then at his watch. "You know, I'm afraid we're going to have to split now . . . but could we come back sometime and finish this?"

"Sure. Anytime!" Mom said gaily.

"I'll call you . . . sometime next week, perhaps?"

Mom frowned. "Well, next week I'll be in, of all places, Puerto Rico. We're filming a Duncan Hines coconut cake commercial, and I have the hideous feeling I'm going to have to climb a tree and sit there for hours, hanging on to some coconuts. . . . Still, it'll be warm."

"When you get back then?"

"Absolutely." She glanced over at Trudy. "I think your wife's asleep."

He smiled. "She's had a long day."

"How marvelous that you work together! I think that's the best thing for a marriage."

"It has its good side . . . and its bad," Mike said, getting up.

Mom sighed. "What doesn't?" she said.

When they'd left, Mom went into the kitchen where Daddy was mucking around trying to get dinner started. "Now, sweetie, aren't you ashamed, deeply and *horribly* ashamed of yourself?"

"What for?" Daddy said.

"Well, after all those dreadful comments about how awful journalists were—can you *imagine* two sweeter, nicer people?"

"Well, I—"

"Imagine his being from Scipioville. What a small world! And I was so touched, he wants to know all about me, Mother of Star."

"Mother of Star, what exactly are we having for dinner?"

"Well, Father of Star, if you see fit to light the oven, I think I'll just chuck in that chicken thing from Monday, unless you have any better suggestions. Oh, I—" She slipped and knocked her head against the cupboard. "Oh, Lord. I'm slushed, sloshed? What's the word? Hon, how did it go, did you think? Were they nice with you?"

"Very," I said. "They took a lot of pictures. Daddy, I told them we didn't go around naked that much so he won't get the wrong idea."

"Uh huh?" Daddy looked wary. "What else did you talk about?"

I tried to remember. "Just, regular things . . . school and boys and stuff."

"Did they take any nude photos?" Deel said, coming in.

"No," I said. "You saw! They just took them of me in my jacket out on the terrace . . . and some regular ones of me in my room. Oh Daddy, I did tell them you were on the Scarsdale Diet, is that okay? Is that too personal?"

"That's okay," Daddy said.

"She took millions of pictures," I said.

"Well, they never use more than a couple," said Mom. "I'm glad she fell asleep before she got any of me. I mean, the point is," she said, turning to Daddy who was getting something out of the freezer, "people have to earn a living."

"Yes?"

"So, here's this perfectly bright, charming guy who needs a job and maybe he can't get one on the *New York Times*, so he gets one at *People*. Does that make him someone to sneer at?"

"He kept staring at my breasts," I said. "But I think that was because he'd had all that Scotch."

"Yes, I thought he was a little—" Daddy began.

"Darling, *all* men stare at women's breasts," Mom said. "There'd be something wrong with them if they *didn't*. Why shouldn't they, for heaven's sake? They're pretty . . . goodness, I don't even have anything to stare at."

"Yes, you do," Daddy said.

"Well, but not compared to Tat."

"Well, how come he kept staring at you, then?" Deel said.

Mom looked taken aback. "Was he? I guess he was just dazzled by my wit and charm and all that."

"Sure," Deel said.

"Cordelia," Mom said. "I have had a long, hard day. Could we dispense with the Sermon on the Mount for this particular evening?"

"Well, if Daddy doesn't mind," Deel said, "why should I?"

"What shouldn't I mind?" Daddy said.

"That you're married to someone who salivates from every pore whenever there's a man in the room."

Mom burst out laughing. "Salivates from every pore! I love it! What a great image."

"Amanda is interested in people," Daddy said diplomatically. "She enjoys drawing them out."

"Sure," Deel said.

"Sweetie," Mom said, slicing the bread. "You know, for a girl with a dazzling IQ like yours, it seems to me the word 'sure' is a trifle overused, wouldn't you say?"

"There's a big difference in being *interested* in people, and sucking up to everyone of the opposite sex you happen to meet," Deel muttered.

"Okay, Delia," Daddy said firmly. "I think we get the point. There are different ways of looking at this, as there are with most subjects. Shall we agree to disagree?"

Deel just wheeled out of the room.

Mom raised her eyebrows. "I thought she'd be in a bad mood, but this!"

"You mean, because they were interviewing me?" I said.

"Yeah . . . here I thought she'd seemed fairly cheery, for her, since she's been seeing that forlorn specimen with the beard."

"He's not a forlorn specimen, Mom," I said. "He's Joshua's brother."

"Is he? Goodness, I didn't know . . ."

"He makes lutes."

"Does he? Well, if that's all he can find to—"

"Amanda!" Daddy said.

"I'm sorry," Mom said, giggling. She looked at Daddy soulfully. "Why did you give me such a huge tumbler of wine, you idiot? *You* know how I am."

"They're coming back," I said. "They want to meet me at school next week."

"Well," Daddy said, "I suppose we've been through the worst of it."

"And I'll be clinging to a coconut tree in sunny Puerto Rico," Mom said. "Will you all miss me horribly?"

"Of course we will," Daddy said. "Could you doubt it for a minute?"

Mom kissed him.

Chapter Seventeen

Mike Nadler and Trudy met me after school. I'd told them I didn't want them to come into my class or anything, but that I wouldn't mind if they met Shellie and went to the Pizza Place with us. They did. Trudy took some shots of us eating pizza.

"Are you Rusty's best friend?" Mike asked Shellie.

Shellie looked at me and smiled. "I guess . . . I *think* I am."

"She is," I said.

"How'd you like *Domestic Arrangements*?"

"I thought it was terrific," Shellie said. "And Rusty, too."

"You think she can really act? That she wasn't just playing herself?"

Shellie looked horrified. "Oh no! Rusty's not *all* like that girl. The exact opposite, in fact."

"The exact opposite?"

"Yeah . . . I mean that girl—Samantha, was that her name? —she was the kind who'd steal your boyfriend away and stuff like that. And who came on with older men and people's fathers. Rusty would *never* do that."

Mike smiled at me. "Would you never do that, Rusty?"

I shook my head.

"By the way," he said, "I meant to mention . . . That's some mother you have."

"Yeah?" I said.

"She's really dynamic," he said enthusiastically.

I nodded. "She's a really good actress, too. You should see her on 'The Way We Are Now'."

"I have . . . I watched the show this week. The two of you ought to be in something together."

"Maybe we will," I said.

"I guess that's where you get your red hair," he said.

"Sort of," I said. I didn't want to mention about Mom dyeing hers.

"What do you mean sort of?"

"Well, my grandmother had red hair too."

Shellie couldn't come home with me. I walked her to the subway and then Mike Nadler drove me home. At least I avoided Evan and Roger at the bus stop.

———————

The next day was Saturday. Mom had left the day before for Puerto Rico. Daddy asked if I wanted to go to a screening with him and Abigail. I said yes. Ever since I broke up with Joshua, I don't have that much to do on weekends unless there's a party that sounds really good. Basically, I haven't felt that sociable lately. I don't feel like meeting some other boy, so what's the point?

The movie was good after the first half hour, which showed this woman having a cesarean section. I hate gory things like that in movies. I kept my hand over my eyes until Daddy nudged me and said, "You can come out now."

"The Czechs are doing some interesting things lately," Abigail said when we got out. Then she looked at her watch. "Oh, help! Listen, I told the sitter I'd be back on the nose of four."

"We'll go with you," Daddy said.

We went back to Abigail's apartment. She paid the sitter. "I guess that's that," she said looking sadly at Daddy.

"Why? Bring him along. Do you like Chinese food, Kerim?"

Kerim began jumping up and down.

"See?" Daddy said. "Let's go."

We ate out at a Chinese place near our house. Daddy and Abigail began talking a lot about this film he's been doing, which she's editing. I sort of half listened and half didn't. We decided to walk home since it was still light.

"Oh, Daddy, can we go in there?"

"What is it, Tat?"

It was an art store that had these great hats. I've been meaning to get one for the longest time. They have horns on them and they're made of cotton. The store had a whole pile of them.

I tried on a lot of them. They came in all different colors. There were three kinds—one with horns like a goat, one with curled horns, and one with little silver wings. Abigail began trying them on too.

"Hey, you look great," Daddy said when she had on this red one with silver wings.

"Do I?" She looked pleased. "Doesn't it look silly?"

"*I* want one," Kerim said, pulling at her.

"Okay, sweetie, we'll get this for both of us." Abigail snuck up behind Daddy and plunked a hat on his head. "Ta da!"

"Oh, Daddy, you look so cute," I said.

"Me?" Daddy said, blushing.

"Li, you look darling," Abigail exclaimed. "I love it. Oh get it . . . really."

"Do they have a mirror here?" Daddy said. He went over and glanced at himself. He was wearing a blue hat with curled horns. Abigail came and stood next to him. She was still wearing the red hat with silver wings.

"See," she said, "it's really perfect."

Daddy smiled. "Well, since everyone seems to . . . But where will I wear it?"

"Everywhere!" Abigail said.

I got a green one with regular horns.

We all walked out, wearing our hats. People on the street stopped to stare at us. "I do feel slightly conspicuous," Daddy murmured.

"No. Don't be silly," Abigail said. "It's your new image . . . to go with losing all that weight."

Daddy is actually down to 150 pounds! Can you imagine? He says he hasn't weighed that since college. He does look a little different, actually. I mean, I liked him the other way. He was more kind of round and cuddly.

"Li, don't get *too* thin," Abigail said as we were going up in the elevator.

"Nonsense. Do I *look* too thin?"

"No, but . . . you do look a little . . . drawn almost." She reached out and patted him. "I mean, you have bones!"

"I always had bones," Daddy said. "They were just buried under mounds of fat, that's all."

"You were never fat," she said, "just—"

"Pleasantly plump," I said.

"Cheerfully chubby," Abigail said.

"Robustly round?" Daddy said wryly.

Upstairs no one was home. Deel was out with Neil.

"Looks like he's still going strong," Daddy said, looking at Kerim who was running around our living room.

"I'm afraid so," Abigail said, wistfully.

"Should I read to him?" I said. "Would he like that?"

"Would you?" Abigail looked delighted. She looked at Daddy. "Maybe we can just go over that one section."

I took Kerim into my room. I still have lots of picture books left over from when I was little, *Goodnight Moon, Where the Wild Things Are, George and Martha.* I read him about six of them. Toward the end he began leaning against me, sucking his thumb. It made a loud rubbery sound. Then I looked down and saw he'd fallen asleep.

I went back into the living room. "He's asleep," I said.

Daddy carried Kerim into the living room and covered him with an afghan. "Think he'll be okay?" he said to Abigail.

"Oh sure," she said. "He sleeps anywhere . . . like a log."

I went in to get into my nightgown. When I came back, Daddy came over to me. "Uh, Tat? I was wondering if I could ask you a tremendous favor?"

"Sure."

"Well, do you think you could possibly sleep in Delia's room tonight? Abigail and I still have quite a lot of work to do, and I thought since Kerim's fallen asleep, the two of them might stay in your room tonight."

"Sure, that's okay." I went into Deel's room. Deel happens

to be one of the great slobs of all time; I don't see how she can stand it. You can hardly even enter her room. She has two beds, one against each wall. When we were little, we both used to stay in this room, but when she got to be thirteen, Mom fixed up the back room for me because she thought Deel needed more privacy. At first I didn't like it at all. I used to sneak back into Deel's room sometimes because I felt so lonely by myself. But now I really like it, having my own room.

All of a sudden, someone gave me a shove. It was Deel. I guess I must have fallen asleep.

"What are you doing in here?" she said angrily.

I squinted up at her. "What?"

"Get back in your own room!"

"I can't," I said, yawning. "Abigail's in there."

"Oh, shit." She turned to Neil who was standing right behind her.

"Delia, come with me, okay?" he said softly.

"Where?"

"Just come."

I was really only half awake, and fell back asleep about one second later. When I woke up next, the room was still dark but Deel was sleeping in the other bed. I squinted at the digital clock; it said 3:20. I felt really thirsty, I don't know why. Quietly, I got out of bed and tiptoed down the hall, through the living room and dining room and into the kitchen. I poured myself a glass of grapefruit juice. Then I started feeling a little bit hungry so I got out this cannister of unsalted cashew nuts that Daddy buys from a special store on Broadway. They're good. I sat down on one of the stools and began eating them and reading some recipes Mom had Scotch-taped up on the kitchen wall. You may not know this, but one very soothing thing to do at night, if you can't sleep, is to read recipes. They're very organized, and reading about things like cups of honey and heavy cream really makes you feel sleepy. I gave a big yawn.

Then suddenly the door to my room opened, and Daddy came out. He was wearing this red flannel nightshirt that Mom got him for Christmas. When he saw me, he looked startled.

"Tat, what are you doing up?"

"I felt thirsty."

He stood there, looking worried. "Uh . . . what time is it?"

"Three thirty."

"I—Abigail and I had a lot of work to do," he said.

"Uh huh?" I looked up at him with my big-blue-eyes look. I remember Charlie asking me to look that way in one scene, sort of innocent and sweet.

"How long have you been up?" he asked, reaching for some nuts.

"About ten minutes."

"I see." He stood there, looking very uncomfortable. "Kerim was sleeping so soundly, we thought we'd leave him in the living room."

"Uh huh."

"Well, I'll see you in the morning, then." He tried to smile cheerfully.

"Yeah . . . sleep tight, Daddy."

"You too, darling." He padded off to his and Mom's room.

I went back to bed about five minutes later. At first my feet were cold from not having worn slippers, but I put a pair of Deel's wool knee socks on and pretty soon I fell asleep again.

When I woke up again, it was morning, almost eleven. Deel was lying in bed, her eyes open, looking at the ceiling.

"Hi," I said. "Listen, I'm sorry about last night."

"That's okay." She smiled at me. "We did it, Rust."

"Where?" She looked really excited and pleased.

"In the living room."

"I thought Kerim was there."

"He slept through it. We put this blanket over us in case he woke up . . . Oh Tat, he's so nice! I think I love him. And he loves me. He said up till now he never met a girl he could really, like, talk to about things. They were all just interested in screwing with him. He told me his mantra."

"He must really like you."

"And it isn't like he's desperate or anything. He's had lots of girl friends, but no one really special. He's making me a lute . . . he's going to give me lessons."

Deel used to play the guitar, but she gave up after about five lessons.

I stretched. "That's great, Deel." I felt a little sad, thinking of Joshua. Now I know how Deel must have felt.

"Rust? You know, Neil says Joshua misses you a lot."

"Yeah, well . . ."

"He says he talks about you all the time. He feels really bad about what happened."

I got out of bed. I didn't that much feel like talking about it.

Abigail and Kerim were in the kitchen making French toast. "Hon, easy on the vanilla," she said, grabbing his arm. "It's just for flavor. . . . Hi, Rusty."

"Hi," I said. "Um, that smells good."

"Want some? There's enough batter for lots of slices."

"Sure . . . where's Daddy?"

"I guess he's still sleeping." She seemed very casual, like nothing special had happened. Maybe it didn't. Last night was peculiar.

"Did Kerim sleep all right?"

"Yes, your bed's very comfortable."

"But I thought—" I looked down at him. "I guess kids sleep well most places."

"He does."

When Daddy got up, he went down and got the Sunday paper. We all sat around reading it and eating French toast. Daddy let himself have one slice.

"You're practically the thinnest person in the family," Deel said admiringly. "You don't have to worry anymore."

"I don't know about that," Daddy said. "It's a lifetime thing . . . but it's interesting, people do look at you differently. It's like coming back as a different person."

"How differently?" Abigail said.

"I think people feel safe with a fat person, unthreatened. . . . You're a kind of father figure for everybody."

"Well, but you *are* a father," I pointed out.

"True."

Daddy and Abigail went out around two. I looked over at Deel who was reading the Book Review section. "She's nice, don't you think?" I said.

"Who? Abigail? Yeah."

I wanted to tell Deel about last night, but this didn't seem like the right time, with her so absorbed in the thing about Neil. I thought some more about what she said about Joshua. I'd like to think that's true, that he misses me and thinks about me since I miss him and think about him, but I don't know. I guess I could even call him, but I just don't feel like it. I feel he really did hurt my feelings, implying that I'd act in just anything, and make a fool of myself, when he didn't know anything about the movie.

Anyway, how about the things I turned down? How about the TV movie about the Mormon girl who's raped by her father, but can't say anything because her family would be ostracized from the community? And how about the TV series where I would have been the teenage daughter of a woman judge who's married to a man who stays home and runs a day-care center? They would have paid me five thousand dollars an *episode* for that! And there was some movie that was going to be shot in Israel about a Jewish girl who doesn't look Jewish and goes hitch-hiking through the desert. There were lots of things! So if Joshua thinks I'm just the kind of person who'll do anything for money, he's wrong! I'm not at *all* that kind of person.

The script of *Lolita* arrived, and Mom and Daddy read it. They both liked it, Mom more than Daddy. It's by someone who did some other movie they thought was good, I forget what it was called. I thought it was a slightly weird story. I mean, the girl in it is really peculiar! Everyone in it is weird, especially the mother and that man who likes her. I don't exactly know what Daddy meant when he said it's a witty satire on American life. In what way? I don't know anybody like those people at *all!*

Shellie said the movie of *Lolita* was playing Sunday night at the Thalia and did I want to go with her and Kenny. I said I would. I thought that was really nice of her, to include me on her date. Shellie is that kind of person. She'd make a terrific mother. She's always thinking of other people and trying to do things to make you feel better.

One strange thing happened, though. As we were standing on line to go into the movie, I suddenly saw Joshua walking out of it. I turned my head away, but he saw me and looked over at me. He sort of stopped, as though he was trying to decide whether

to come over and say something, but then we got our tickets and
went in. My heart was beating so fast I felt sick. I sat in the
theater and didn't even pay attention to the first part of the movie.
I wonder if he went because of me, because I'd mentioned I might
be in it, or if he thought I might be there.

Mom came back Wednesday. She had a great tan and looked
terrific. Her skin isn't as light as mine. I can't stay in the
sun at all or I'll look like a lobster. "I was up in that tree for three
days," she said. "Can you imagine? We shot the whole thing and
then they lost the film! We had to do the whole thing over. My
God!" She noticed the new hat Daddy had bought for himself
when he was out with me and Abigail. "Sweetie, whatever
possessed you?" she said.

Daddy smiled. "I don't know. I just thought—"

Mom tried it on. Since she's so tall, she looked sort of like
Wonder Woman. Then she put it on Daddy. "Look at you!"
she said, laughing. "I can't believe it."

"It's his new image," I said.

"Will wonders never cease," Mom said.

Chapter Eighteen

It's definite about my going to California. I'll leave on a Monday and return the following Sunday. Helen has it all arranged with the publicity people. Felix is flying out too. I guess we'll be on most of the shows together. Helen said not to worry, that it would be fine, just answering the same kinds of questions I've been answering already. At first Mom thought she might come along since she loves California and has some friends there, but then she realized she'd miss rehearsals and couldn't.

"Will you be okay all by yourself?" she asked as I was packing.

"Oh sure . . . I don't mind," I said.

We'd gotten down some of my summer things since Mom said it might be quite warm. "I wish I could go," she said wistfully. "Give Janet a call when you get there, okay?"

"Sure." Janet is one of Mom's friends out there. "I don't know if I'll have time to see her, though."

"Oh, I know. . . . Listen, do you have enough pantyhose?"

"I don't usually wear them if it's warm."

"But for TV, hon, I think it looks smoother. Take a couple of pairs anyway."

The day I was due to leave, I had to go to the airport by myself. Mom and Daddy were both working. "Oh, hon, I feel so awful, not at least driving you to the airport," Mom said.

"Mom, really," I said. "It doesn't matter."

"Are you sure? Can you handle everything?"

"Positive."

In some ways, actually, I like going by myself. I'm glad Mom can't come with me. This way it's like it's just me. I don't have to worry about how Mom or Daddy or Deel is reacting to how I do. That can really be a drag. I wore this pretty new dress. It's short sleeved with red and pink stripes and a lace collar. I just wore my wool coat since it's supposed to be warm out there. Evidently the publicity people who'll be going around with us are out there already. They're supposed to meet me at the Los Angeles airport.

I bought some magazines and candy and went over to the ticket counter to weigh in my bag. I was really early, but I like to be early. It was two o'clock and the plane left at four. While I was standing there, watching the man punch the computer thing, I glanced around. There was Joshua, standing on the line next to me. I stared at him. He smiled. "Hi, Rust."

I took my ticket from the man. "What are you doing here?"

"I'm flying to Los Angeles."

"What?"

"Just wait one sec, okay?" I stood there while he waited for his ticket. "Well, I just thought why not take a brief vacation."

"Joshua! You mean you didn't know I was going to be on this plane?"

He looked sheepish. "Well, actually, I did know."

"How? From who?"

"From Neil."

"But . . ."

"I thought it would be good to talk a little. And since it's a five-hour trip . . ."

"And your parents don't mind? It's so expensive!"

"Well, actually . . . they don't know yet. Neil's covering for me. He's telling them I'm in Andover visiting Pam."

"So, how did you get the money?"

"I charged it to Dad's American Express card on the phone."

"You're going to get into terrible trouble."

"No. He can afford it. It's just a drop in the bucket for him."

"But we could have talked in New York!"

"I know . . . but I like planes."

"But, Josh, I'm going to be really busy out there. I can't do things with you or anything."

"Oh, I'm not staying there. I'm flying right back as soon as I get there."

"What?"

"Yeah. You know, the journey not the arrival matters?"

"Joshua, you're *crazy*."

"Sure."

"Why on a plane?"

"Why not on a plane? I figured there you'd be trapped. You couldn't run away from me."

I smiled at him. "I'm not going to run away from you!"

"You're not?"

"No." I looked at him for a long time. "I've missed you . . . a lot."

"I've missed you."

We stood there, staring at each other. "Did you like the movie?" I said, just to say something. I had a tingling feeling all over, the way I always get when Joshua looks right at me.

"What movie?"

"*Lolita*."

"Oh, well, I'd seen it before. . . . I was just trying to imagine you in the part."

"Can you?"

He hesitated. "Are you going to audition for it?"

"I might just go in and talk to them."

"In other words, yes."

"Daddy and Mom think it's a good script." I stared at him, wanting him to understand.

He smiled at me. Then he leaned over and kissed me. "You'll be terrific," he said wistfully.

"I may not even get the part."

"You'll get it."

"I may not even do it if I do."

On the plane we had seats in the middle. We talked a lot

about everything. Joshua was right. You do have a chance to really talk on a plane since you can't do much else. He said he'd thought everything over and he realized he had to trust my judgment, that I had a strong character and wouldn't let myself be corrupted the way he might under the same circumstances. It's funny—I don't think of Joshua as the sort of person who'd be corrupted at all! I think of him as really strong. He said that's not true, that he thinks he's eminently corruptible.

While we were sitting there, side by side, I began feeling really attracted to him again. Our shoulders were touching and it seemed like warm vibrations kept passing back and forth between us. We kept staring at each other and smiling.

"You have goose pimples," he said, touching my arm.

"I feel cold. . . . Could you get me down a blanket?"

He got a blanket down and spread it over my lap. We held hands under the blanket. Joshua began rubbing my hand back and forth slowly with his thumb. He glanced over at the person sitting next to me. It was a middle-aged woman; she was sleeping. He pulled the blanket up so it covered both of us up to our chins. Then he reached down and touched my breasts. I wasn't wearing a bra since it was the kind of dress that looks better without one.

"I thought it might be warm in California," I said, to explain why I'd worn that kind of dress.

"It's warm right here," Joshua said.

We were leaning against each other. I closed my eyes while he stroked my breasts, slowly going around each nipple. Then I turned around and put my arms around his neck. We looked at each other and smiled. Our eyes were half an inch apart; I could feel his eyelashes on my cheek and his breath, which smelled of the Wild Strawberry Bubbilicious gum we'd been chewing during takeoff to keep our ears from popping.

"I guess there are some things an airplane isn't good for," Joshua said wryly.

I nodded. I felt so nice and relaxed. "I feel sleepy," I said. "Is it all right if I go to sleep?"

"Go right ahead." It seemed awful to sleep when I wouldn't even see Joshua for a week, but I couldn't help it. I leaned against him, letting my head rest on his shoulder. At first I imagined we were together in a place in the woods with a log cabin like in *The Wilderness Family*. There was no one there but us and some friendly animals and birds. We went swimming and lay around in the sun and Joshua caught some fish and we made a fire. Then I guess I must've fallen asleep because the next thing I knew he was nudging me.

"We're here, Rust."

I blinked. "Already?"

"You must have had a good dream. You were smiling."

Suddenly my eyes opened wide. "I wasted all that time sleeping. Now I won't even see you for a week!"

"I'll come back to the hotel with you. My plane doesn't leave for a couple of hours."

We held each other close. I could hear Joshua's heart thumping. The stewardess came by and smiled at us. "I'm afraid all seats have to be moved to an upright position," she said.

We pressed our buttons to do that and sat holding hands while the plane landed. When I got off the plane, I looked around for Kelly Neff, the publicity person who was supposed to meet me. She came over to us. She was about twenty and looked a little like one of the airline stewardesses, with short blond hair and a slim figure.

"How was your trip, Tatiana?" she said.

"Oh, it was good," I said. "I had a really good trip." I could see she was looking questioningly at Joshua who was standing next to me. "Uh . . . this is my younger brother, Joshua. He's out here to look at colleges."

"Hi, Joshua," Kelly Neff said.

"Hi," said Joshua.

"I remember you as having a sister," she said, puzzled.

I cleared my throat. "Yeah, well, I have a sister, too."

"How nice that the two of you could come out together," Kelly Neff said. "Which colleges are you thinking of?"

"UCLA," Joshua said. "Berkeley . . ."

"He's going to be a famous director when he grows up," I said.

Kelly Neff smiled up at Joshua. "He looks pretty grown up already," she said.

I blushed.

"I suppose with your father in the same business," she went on to Joshua, "that's only natural."

Joshua looked blank.

"But, of course, he's done mainly documentaries, hasn't he?"

"Yeah," I said. "But he might do a feature film some day."

She looked from me to Joshua. "I can't say I see a *strong* family resemblance," she said, "but then, that's often the case, isn't it? My sister and I are twins and people never think we look alike at *all*."

"I'm the only person in my family with red hair," I said quickly. That's true, anyway. "Except my grandmother and she's dead."

"Well!" Kelly Neff said. "We have a pretty busy schedule lined up for you, Tatiana. I'm afraid you'll just have an hour to go to your hotel to freshen up and then we have an interview scheduled for three o'clock."

At the hotel Kelly Neff stayed there while I signed in. "I'll just help her unpack," Joshua said when I was done. "I've got a pretty busy schedule myself."

"Have a good stay in L.A.," Kelly Neff said to him. "Nice to have met you."

In the elevator Joshua and I smiled at each other.

"Why your younger brother?" Joshua said.

"I couldn't think of what else to say!"

"No, I mean why younger?"

"I don't know! Look, it's not real, so why does it matter?"

"She must think I'm pretty precocious, going off to college at thirteen."

"I just said you were looking at them. I didn't say you were going."

"I guess she didn't care."

I looked at him, scared. "Do you think she'll go back and look it up and find out you don't exist?"

"I don't exist?"

"You know, that you're not really my brother."

He smiled. "She'll think I'm the skeleton in the closet."

They'd gotten me a really gigantic room in the hotel. The

bathroom was twice the size of my bedroom at home. In it was a big bouquet of flowers. I opened the note lying on the table. It said, "Welcome to L.A. We can't wait to meet you. Love, Greg and Jim."

"Who're they?" Joshua said, reading over my shoulder.

"Those people . . . about *Lolita*."

"They sign it 'love' and they've never even met you?" He threw it down on the table.

"People are like that out here," I said nervously. I hoped he wouldn't get mad. I didn't want to have a fight, not so soon after we'd made up.

Joshua glanced at his watch. "You've got half an hour to freshen up," he said.

"Maybe I should shower," I said. "I feel kind of sticky."

"I know a better way to freshen up," he said. He put his arms around me.

"I thought you were going to help me unpack."

"First things first."

We sat down on the edge of the bed. It was really huge.

"I guess they expect you to have a lot of company," Joshua said, looking at it.

"I won't, don't worry." I looked at him, frowning. "Josh, half an hour isn't that much time. Do you think we should? It might be sort of rushed."

"It won't be rushed," he said, starting to unbutton my dress. "It'll be nice and slow." He helped me take off my dress and then, while I was pulling off my underpants, he yanked his clothes off and threw them on the floor. I put my dress neatly over a chair. I didn't want it to get wrinkled. When I looked at Joshua, he was sitting on the edge of the bed, his penis sticking straight out, as though it was looking around wondering what was going on.

He pulled me down on his lap and we grabbed at each other and kissed, as though we hadn't done it in years. It's funny. Maybe it was because we hadn't done it for so long, or even the scariness of knowing Joshua shouldn't have been there, but I felt extremely excited right away. Joshua seemed to be, too. He entered me while we were kissing, it just sort of happened. It hurt for a second because of the way we were sitting, but I was so wet, it felt okay a minute later. I was holding him by the shoulders, he had his tongue all the way in my mouth. We did it really fast, in a couple of seconds practically. "Oh God, Rusty," Joshua gasped.

I started to come. "Oh, I love you," I said, clutching him.

Afterward we fell back on the bed in a kind of daze. We looked at each other. Both of us were sweaty and out of breath.

"Well, I guess that was worth two hundred and fifty-eight dollars," Joshua said, smiling.

"What?"

"That's what a round trip to L.A. costs."

"Joshua! Is that all you came out here for?"

"No! Of course not. I mean, it did cross my mind, I have to admit. . . . Are you glad I decided to come out with you?"

I nodded. "Very." I hesitated. "I thought it was really good, didn't you?"

Joshua leaned over and kissed me tenderly on the nose. "It was more than good, Rust. It was an important, thrilling, meaningful experience." Suddenly he got an anguished look. "Have you been doing it with anyone since we . . ."

"No!"

"Are you sure?"

"Of course I'm sure! What do you mean?"

"Would you tell me if you had?"

"Of course I would . . . anyway, how could I? I didn't have a diaphragm." Suddenly I gasped. "Uh oh . . . we didn't use anything."

"Well, one time. I don't think one time usually—"

I leaned my head on his shoulder. "Do you think I'll get pregnant?"

"Not from just one time. . . . Are you going to get another diaphragm?"

"I guess . . . I better go to another doctor, though. I'll feel pretty stupid going back to the same one."

"You could tell her you lost it."

"True." I looked at him. "Did *you* do it with anyone since we—"

He shook his head.

"Would you tell me if you had?"

He was silent a minute. "I don't know," he said.

"Joshua!" I felt awful.

"Well, Rust, if I told you, you'd just get all upset, wouldn't you?"

"Of course."

"So what would be the point of telling you?"

"Joshua, did you or didn't you?" I stared at him.

"I didn't."

I turned away. "But if you had, you wouldn't tell me anyway," I said angrily, "so that's like saying you did!"

"Rust, listen . . . I didn't do it, okay? That's the truth."

"But you tried?"

"No, I didn't try either."

"Because you didn't meet anyone who . . ."

"I wasn't *looking* to meet anyone. I was just lying around mournfully thinking about you."

I sighed. "I want to believe you."

"It's true . . . I felt I'd acted like a dope and I was afraid you'd never speak to me again."

"What if I hadn't?"

He frowned. "If you'd never spoken to me again?"

"Yeah."

"I'd have felt really awful."

"But would you have gone off and done it with someone, then?"

"Eventually, sure."

"Well, by eventually do you mean two weeks or two years or what?"

"Something in between," Joshua said. He looked at me. "Rust, come on."

"I feel so awful."

"Did you think I'd take a permanent vow of celibacy if you rejected me?"

I tried to smile. "Yes."

He kissed me. "And were you going to do the same?"

I shrugged my shoulders.

He laughed. "Great! What a double standard!"

I put my head on his shoulder. "I love you and I couldn't *stand* it if you did it with anyone else. I couldn't bear it."

"I couldn't stand it if *you* did it with anyone else either."

"But you said I was bad at it," I said, remembering our fight.

"No." He frowned. "When did I say that?"

"When we had the fight. You said in this really sarcastic way something like, 'Sure, I just see you for sex.' "

"Rust, look, I was really upset . . . I was just trying to get at you. I said a lot of stupid things."

"*Do* you think I'm bad at it?"

"Of course I don't . . ." He kissed my cheek. "I think you have a great natural gift."

"Do you really?"

"Uh huh."

"More than at acting?"

He hesitated. "I think you're wonderful at both, okay?"

We were silent a minute.

"I thought it was so good before," I said hesitantly.

He squeezed my hand. "Yeah, you seemed really turned on."

"Weren't you?"

"Sure . . . well, I always am when I'm with you. I'm in a state of perpetual horniness."

Just then the phone rang. It was Kelly Neff. "Tatiana, I hate to rush you, but we really should get moving. Can you come right down?"

"Oh sure." It was past two! I leaped up, raced into the bathroom, washed really quickly and put on my dress. I looked at Joshua who was still sprawled out on the bed, naked. "Josh, what do you want to do? I have to go right down."

"I haven't finished unpacking for you," he said.

I went over and kissed him. "Do I look freshened up enough?"

"Like a daisy."

"When's your plane?"

"I'll make it . . ."

I looked at him longingly. "I wish I could fly back with you. Should I?"

"No, look, they've got it all set up. You'll have fun."

"No, I won't."

"Well, don't have too much fun," he said.

"I'll think of you all the time, every second."

Down in the lobby Kelly Neff smiled when she saw me. "I hope you had time to rest a little, Tatiana," she said. "I'm sorry it had to be so rushed."

"Oh, no, it was fine," I said. "There was plenty of time."

Chapter Nineteen

The first interview was a talk show. Felix was on it with me.

"How *was* it working with Tatiana?" the host asked. "Did you two develop a working rapport?"

Felix grinned at me. "Definitely . . . wouldn't you say, Rusty?"

I tried to be serious. "Well, Felix had done much more acting than me, so he helped me a lot with how I should say my lines."

"You'd never done any cinematic work, though, had you, Felix?" asked the host. His name was Myron Downs.

"I've been in four movies," Felix said. "I was a cowboy in *The Electric Horseman,* a freaky teenager in *Foxes,* and I ended up on the cutting-room floor in *Fame.*"

"Do you contemplate working together in the future?"

"Well, I'll probably be playing Laertes in *Hamlet* this summer," Felix said. "Shakespeare in the Park."

"Shakespeare's quite a change of pace after *Domestic Arrangements,* isn't it?"

"I might be in Shakespeare, too," I said. "My father's directing *The Tempest* and he wants me to be Ariel."

Myron smiled. "That'll be an interesting experience for you,

Rusty, won't it? Being directed by your father? Do you think that will work out?"

"Yes," I said. "I guess I'm a little scared about doing Shakespeare, though."

"What do you think, Felix? Do you think Rusty can handle Ariel?"

"Rusty can handle anything," Felix said.

Afterward I said, "Felix, it makes me nervous when you do that."

"Do what?"

"Kid around that way."

"Sweetie, otherwise I'd go bonkers. . . . They keep asking the same questions."

"I know."

"And I hate TV. . . ."

"Do you? *I* don't."

"You're gorgeous . . . gorgeous people are fine on TV."

I looked at him. Felix is thin with blue eyes and blond hair. "I think you're handsome," I said, sincerely.

"Let's face it, I'm not Burt Reynolds."

"Ugh! You're a *million* times better looking than him."

"Bless you."

"You know who you look like in a way?" I said, regarding him closely. "That person that was in *Gone with the Wind*."

Felix looked surprised. "Clark Gable?"

"No, the other one . . . the one she was in love with."

"Leslie Howard? The limp sensitive type? Well, thanks, sweetie."

"He wasn't limp!" I think Felix has an inferiority complex.

"So, when's our next debacle?" he said to Kelly.

"Dinner . . . it's an interview with the local press."

"I don't know if I have anything more to say," I said, worried.

"You don't have to say anything more," Kelly said. "You were just fine."

"But can I just say the same things over and over?"

"Look," Felix said, "if *they* can't think of anything but the same questions to ask us over and over, why should we think up new answers?"

"The point is," Kelly said, "they haven't heard those answers before so it's new to them. You just say whatever makes you feel comfortable."

I frowned. "I don't want to sound stupid."

"You don't . . . believe me, Tatiana. I've seen actresses with lots more experience than you get all frozen and uptight and do terribly."

Even thinking about that made me nervous. "Would that make the picture do badly . . . if I acted like that?"

"No. . . . Look, there's no direct correlation. But if the public likes you as a personality, it gives us that much more to work with."

I kept thinking how Joshua would hate that, how he would think I was selling myself or something. I wondered where he was now, if he was on the plane already, flying home. My underpants were wet. I guess some of the sperm or whatever take a while to come out of you. I hoped I didn't smell funny or anything.

"Don't worry about a thing," Kelly said. "Listen, I'll pick up those sandwiches now. Just stay put."

Felix looked at me. "Where does she think we'll go?"

I smiled. "I don't know. She's really nice, isn't she?"

"Yeah, well, they have this strange experiment they perform out here. They take Barbie dolls and wave a magic wand over them and lo and behold they become waitresses, publicity girls . . ."

I giggled. "That's mean."

"Did you see? Her joints are still a little stiff."

"Felix? Does it bother you, all the questions and stuff?"

"You mean, am I nervous? Sure . . . but it's all part of the game. If you don't learn to hit the ball back over the net, no one's going to ask you to play anymore."

"Yeah." I never thought of it that way. I hesitated. "How is it with Marvin?"

"Don't ask, kid."

"Okay."

"No, what can I say? Marvin is just . . . Marvin is not rising to this particular occasion, to put it mildly. He's jealous as a hornet and just as nasty."

"*I* had a terrible fight with my boyfriend," I said, hoping that might make him feel better.

Felix sighed understandingly. "Did you make it up, or are you still—"

I looked at him. "Well . . ." I told him how Joshua had flown out with me and how we'd done it in the half hour I was supposed to be resting.

Felix looked at me appraisingly. "You look well rested," he said.

"Don't tell her, okay?" I said nervously.

"Not a word. . . . So, he spent three hundred dollars just to—"

"Two fifty-eight . . . but it wasn't just for that." I blushed. "He said it was worth it."

Felix laughed. "I bet it was."

"What's this?" Kelly said, coming back with our sandwiches and seeing Felix laughing. She does look a little like a Barbie doll, now that I think of it.

I opened my sandwich. Felix smiled at me.

"Oh, Tatiana," Kelly said. "I wondered if you'd mind . . . since nothing special is scheduled for this afternoon, I thought I'd take you around to our beauty shop and they might work on your hair a little."

"Work on it?"

"Well, you have such lovely hair, dear, just magnificent, but it's a little . . . I thought if we had it styled just a bit . . ."

"Not cut!"

"Oh no, we'd never cut it . . . that would spoil that look. But maybe just a touch of makeup."

"How about me?" Felix said, pretending to sulk. "Aren't I going to get the star treatment?"

"We decided you were perfect as you are, Felix," Kelly said crisply.

Felix shrugged. "What can I say? So, see you both at six?"

"Make it five thirty, could you?"

Kelly took me to this very small, quiet place where a man washed my hair in a special avocado shampoo, which he said was good for redheads. He said he would just trim a hundredth of an inch. Then he wanted to braid it into lots of thin braids like Bo Derek. I looked at Kelly. "I think that might look kind of weird," I said.

"Listen, try it," she said. "What can you lose? You can always let it loose if it looks lousy. You can trust Pierre. He wouldn't suggest it if he didn't think it was right for you."

I was feeling a little sleepy, so I closed my eyes while he braided my hair. When I opened them, I couldn't believe it. I had around nine million braids all over my head, each one knotted and fastened with a little wooden thing at the end. I looked horrible!

"Sensational!" Pierre said. "Will you *look* at the difference?"

"It really is lovely," Kelly said, smiling at me. "Don't you love it, Tatiana? It's a whole new you."

Frankly, I liked the old me a lot better, but I didn't want to hurt their feelings. "Well, it's interesting," I said, faintly. "But I—"

"It's sophisticated, but young . . . a little polish, a little insouciance . . ."

I'm so glad this show won't be seen in the East. Joshua would vomit if he saw me like this. "I'm not sure I want to keep it this way," I said to Kelly when we got out.

"Well, let's just see how it goes over tonight," she said. "It's going to photograph just beautifully. That's why I always take people to Pierre. He has a wonderful sense of what photographs well."

I went back to my room to lie down before dinner. It was really uncomfortable with all those braids. Every time I moved, they'd flop from side to side and the little wooden things would konk against me.

I wore this Greek dress Mom got for me a year ago on a trip. It's white cotton and I think over there it's a wedding dress, though it doesn't come to the ground. It laces up the front, but it looks ladylike. Mom calls it a "first communion dress."

"Jesus God, what did they *do* to you?" Felix said when he saw me.

"Now, Felix, *stop*," Kelly said. "We're trying out a new look on Tatiana, and everyone who's seen her thinks she looks enchanting."

"Tatiana would look enchanting with her head shaved," Felix said, "but—"

"It's just for tonight," I said miserably. I already wished I hadn't let them do it.

We had our dinner and then over dessert all these photographers and reporters came over and began taking photos of us and asking us questions. One of them asked if my hair was a new look. "Is this a way of saying you think you're a 'ten,' Ms. Engelberg?" one man asked.

I shook my head.

"What number would you give to yourself, then?"

I hesitated. "I don't think people are numbers," I said.

He smiled. "You don't like the idea of women being graded by men? It seems sexist, is that it?"

I nodded, though I hadn't been thinking of that exactly.

"Is the women's movement important to you, Ms. Engelberg?" a woman reporter asked.

"Yes," I said, "it is. . . . It's important to my mother and sister, too."

"In what way?"

I cleared my throat. "Well, my sister wants to be the first Jewish woman president so she wants everybody not to be prejudiced or they won't vote for her."

"I'm going to vote for Tatiana as the first woman president," Felix said.

"You think she could do it?" another reporter asked.

"Tatiana can do anything," Felix said. "She scares me at times."

"Do *you* agree with that?" the reporter asked. "*Can* you do anything, Tatiana?"

"No!" I said. "There are millions of things I can't do!"

"Like what?"

I thought. "I'm not sure I can act that well . . . yet."

"Tell me, Ms. Engelberg," an older man asked, "do you think acting in *Domestic Arrangements* came easily to you because you were essentially playing yourself?"

I shook my head. The braids flopped back and forth.

They were all looking at me. "Could you expand on that a little?" he said.

"I *wasn't* playing myself," I said intensely. "People keep saying that, but it's not true. I'm not like Samantha at *all*."

"Could you tell us in what way you're not?"

"Well, like she didn't have any girl friends that she talked to about things. It was like she just had him—" I pointed to Felix.

"Whereas for you friendships with girls are important?"

"Yeah."

"So you can talk about boys and clothes and makeup and that kind of thing?"

"Well, sort of."

"How about *you*, Mr. Propper?" another reporter asked. "Were you acting yourself?"

"A little," Felix said. "I was kind of shy and awkward at that age, like Warren. But I'm afraid I never had anyone like Tatiana to cheer me up."

"Do you wish you had?"

He smiled. "How can you ask?"

"How did you find acting with Ms. Engelberg? The two of you seemed to have a great deal of rapport going, even in the scenes where you . . . where there wasn't that much verbal communication."

"Getting along with Tatiana," Felix said, "wasn't very difficult. She's a lovely, warm person."

"Would *you* give Tatiana a ten?"

Felix hesitated. "I'm afraid I feel that ranking women or people in general lacks class. But, if pressed, definitely."

It went on like that, more really dumb questions. I wonder why it's like that. When you think of all the interesting things they could ask you, but never do. They asked me for the millionth time how it was doing a nude scene.

"It was okay," I said warily. "I just got sort of cold because we had to keep shooting it over and over."

"But you didn't feel any moral compunctions about it? Some actresses feel that unless the male members of the cast are willing to display their bodies as well, they won't."

I never thought of that. "Well, but he did," I said, looking at Felix. "He just had underpants on in one scene, too."

Everyone laughed. I felt funny. I didn't see what was so funny about that.

"What lies ahead for you, Tatiana?" one reporter asked. "What roles would you like to be playing in the next few years?"

I thought a minute. "Well, I guess I'd like to act someone really different from me in every way . . . like a soldier or someone who's crazy or something like that."

"Are you thinking of any particular script?"

"No, but I thought since women are going to be drafted, maybe I could be someone who, like, fights in a war."

"You think that's a good idea, then? Women in combat?"

"Yeah."

The reporter smiled at me. "I think the U.S. may have a secret weapon in you, Ms. Engelberg. With someone like you on the front lines, the army shouldn't have any trouble with recruiting."

"Thank you," I said.

Everybody laughed again. I looked at Felix, puzzled. He smiled in a nice way and reached over and squeezed my hand.

Finally they let us actually eat our dessert. It was ice cream, but mine had melted practically into soup.

"Was I okay?" I asked Felix.

"Honey, you were lovely . . . but, Jesus, where do they *find* those guys?"

I finished my ice cream. "I didn't understand why they laughed. *I* didn't think I said anything that funny."

Felix was silent a minute. "People have a peculiar sense of humor out here."

In a way, doing the one week of publicity was like being in summer camp. I felt like I got to know Felix really well just because I didn't have anyone else to talk to that much. By the end of the week I felt like we were really good friends, much more than when we made the movie even. He's a funny person. Sometimes he'd say things and I couldn't tell how he meant it. He says that's because he has a dry wit. My drama teacher, Mr. Poleman, is like that too. Anyway, it was good having Felix to do most of the interviews with me because it did get tiring, smiling all the time and having to act poised and relaxed, whether you felt tired or not, and pretending to find the same dumb questions interesting even when you'd answered them a thousand times.

"I wish *I* could answer your questions and *you* could answer my questions," I said after we'd done our fifth or sixth show.

"Hey, how about that?" Felix said. "I'll be Tatiana and you be Felix."

"How do you feel about doing nude scenes, Tatiana?" I asked. "Did it give you any problems?"

Felix smiled and raised his eyebrows. "Honey, when you have a body like mine, why not show it? Spread a little pleasure around."

"I suppose you and Mr. Propper were really, er, um . . . intimate after filming this great picture?"

"Intimate isn't the word . . . We were, like—hey we're on the air aren't we?"

"Oh, you can be perfectly frank."

From then on we always called each other in private by each other's name. Felix called me Felix and I called him Tatiana. "I love it," he said. "Why didn't my parents give *me* a pretty name? Why didn't *my* father teach Shakespeare at Yale? How'd you like to go through life as Felix?"

"I wouldn't mind," I said, "if I was a boy."

"To be a real Felix you have to be five feet tall and have a mustache and play the oboe," Felix said.

"It's true," I said. "You do look more like a Warren, like the guy in the movie. You could grow a mustache."

"I could learn to play the oboe . . . but I'll never be five feet tall."

"I don't think *I* look like a Tatiana," I said. "I mean, I think a Tatiana should look like Vanessa Redgrave—tall and willowy with platinum blond hair, imperious, sort of regal."

"Right, I get what you mean, Felix. Maybe *you* should learn to play the oboe."

"I do already."

"Terrific. And I'm a platinum blonde . . . almost."

"Is it natural?"

"Almost."

One thing happened that bothered me, though. It was at the end of the week. I called Joshua's house and their housekeeper answered. She's a very nice black woman named Beryl, who's about sixty years old. "Oh, Joshua's not here now, hon," she said.

"Well, when will he be back?" I said.

"He's gone away for the weekend," she said.

"Where did he go?"

"Can you hold a minute? Let's see . . . He went to a place called Andover."

"Oh," I said. Pam.

"He has a friend there. That's what he said anyhow."

"Yeah." I felt really depressed. "Okay, well, thanks."

After I hung up, I sat there feeling bad. First of all, Joshua told his parents he was going to Andover when he was really flying out to California with me. So who knows if he really went there or not. Maybe he just uses that as an excuse since he knows Pam will back him up. But if he didn't really go there, where *did* he go and how come he didn't even tell me? I spoke to him two days ago and he didn't say anything about visiting Pam. Then I started worrying maybe he really did go to visit Pam. I know I should trust Joshua, and I do, sort of. I mean, I think he really does love me and all that. That's not the kind of thing you would lie about. But the thing is, Pam really does like him a lot. He's shown me some of the poems she sends him and I once read a letter she wrote where she said what good comments he made on her work and how sensitive and perceptive he was. "I really miss the talks we used to have," she wrote. "Somehow, letters aren't quite the same thing." What also bothered me was she didn't even mention me! I wonder if she even knows I exist. Maybe she thinks he hasn't slept with anyone since her. Joshua says they're just friends, but that can mean anything. Mom says she and Simon are just friends and Daddy says he and Abigail are just friends. The point is, he should have told me he was going away. Or written me, or left a message with Beryl. That just wasn't a nice, considerate thing to do.

I guess I seemed sort of depressed when Felix and I did this TV show in the afternoon because afterward he said, "What's up, hon? You seemed a little quiet."

"Nothing special," I said. "I guess I'm getting tired. I wish I could just go home right now."

"I know what you mean," he said. "Well, go back and nap . . . that always helps."

"Okay . . . should I come by and get you at five thirty?" We were supposed to go somewhere that night, too.

"Sure . . . that'd be good."

But when I went back to my room, I couldn't fall asleep, even though I lay there for over an hour in the dark with my eyes closed. I just kept worrying about everything. Finally I decided to get up. I took a shower and got dressed. I hate having to wear fancy things all the time and looking all done up. I wish I could just put on jeans and not wear makeup, like at school. I undid all those braids and for the first day or so my hair looked really frizzy and wild, almost as bad as the braids. So I washed it and now it looks pretty much the way it did before. Tomorrow I have to go meet those men who are doing *Lolita*. They said I should come after lunch. Kelly said there wasn't anything set up for then.

Chapter Twenty

I knocked lightly on Felix's door. There wasn't any answer. I knocked again. "Tatiana?"

"It's open," he muttered.

I opened the door slowly. Felix was lying in bed with a washcloth on his forehead. "Hey, are you okay?" I asked, going over.

"Oh, Felix," he murmured.

"What? What's wrong?"

"I am sick as a dog."

"What is it?"

"A migraine. . . . Hon, listen, could you do me a huge, huge favor?"

"Sure."

"Take this washcloth and soak it in ice cold water, wring it it out and bring it back and put it on my forehead?"

I did that. "Do you want me to, like, go away?"

"Well, I guess you have to, don't you? What time is it?"

I looked at his clock. "Almost six . . . oh, I don't want to do another show!"

"Maybe we should both say we're sick," he said.

"You really *are* sick."

"I just took this pill, which my doctor claims is some new medical wonder drug which'll have me dancing down the aisles in half an hour."

"What should *I* do?" I asked him.

"Say *you're* sick."

"Won't they be mad?"

"Listen, they've squeezed us dry. We've done our thing."

"You don't think it's, like, an immoral thing to do?"

"Sweetie, if that's the most immoral thing you'll ever do—"

"Do you have her number?"

"On the desk."

I called Kelly and said I was feeling really lousy. "It must be some kind of virus," I said, trying to sound limp and exhausted.

"You poor thing," Kelly said. "I've heard something like that is going around."

"I'm really sorry about tonight," I said.

"Oh, not to worry . . . Felix'll carry the fort. Maybe I'd better call him and check."

"Okay." I hung up. "She's going to call you," I started saying just as the phone rang.

"Sweetie?" Felix said. "Listen, I have terrible news for you. I am literally at death's door. She is? Goodness, no, I had no idea. No, I'm afraid this is just a plain garden-variety migraine. Oh sure. No, tomorrow I'll be righter than a trivet. Thanks, take care."

After he hung up, Felix winked at me. "We did it, kid." He threw the washcloth on the floor.

"Tatiana! I thought you had a migraine."

"You want to know something? I am feeling sen-*sa*-tional! That fool doctor knew what he was talking about."

I frowned. "Don't you feel guilty? After they went to all that trouble."

He sat up. "You want to know something? I must have a criminal mentality. I don't have even the smallest *twinge* of guilt. You know what I think we should do, Felix?"

"What, Tatiana?"

"I think we should call room service and order something fantastic. I know what I'm going to order . . . a turkey sandwich on white toast and a coffee frosted. That's my favorite meal. I'm so cheap! What's wrong with Marvin? Where's he going to find a witty, charming friend whose favorite meal costs less than five dollars?"

"Where is he?" I said.

"Do you want to hear a long and mournful story?"

"Sure."

"Well, Marvin—you met Marvin, didn't you?"

"Yeah, sure, on the set."

"Okay, well, Marvin . . . where shall I start? Marvin is Jewish, and his father was, like, a very big deal intellectually. Graduated Harvard at twelve, got his doctorate in Romance Languages at thirteen—"

"Really?"

"Really . . . wrote huge weighty tomes, one of which won the National Book Award. Heavy stuff. Breakfast conversation was the death of Freud. That was small talk."

"What was his mother like?"

"The standard obsessive. 'I don't ask for anything, dear. Just grow up to be a genius, marry a college grad with money and have two point five darling kids I can show pictures of to my friends.' Anyway, when Marvin was eighteen, his father killed himself. Really messy—a bullet through the head—and so the poor kid had nine million hangups in *addition* to the ones he'd have had being gay and a Jew. I mean, those are, like, the *least* of his problems. He's supposed to be a genius, do great things. And he's one of these pleasers, you know? He wants to please Mommy, he wants to please me. He worries if the elevator man doesn't smile at him! He makes *me* look like the healthiest, most normal person that ever walked the face of the earth."

"You do seem normal," I said. "Aren't you?"

"Me? Felix, bite your tongue. Listen, before we continue with the plight of Marvin, how about room service? What'll it be? Champagne? Caviar? They're paying so—"

"I do like champagne," I said. "Is that awful?"

"It's terrible . . . Felix, I'm never speaking to you again. And what with? Name your favorite."

I thought. "Do you think they'd have lox and cream cheese on a toasted bagel?"

"But of course! You're as cheap as I am, kid." He called

room service and ordered everything: a split of champagne, Nova Scotia salmon, the works. "Lox would've been okay," I said.

"Honey! Lox is for peasants. We're movie stars, remember? You're Carole Lombard, I'm Clark Gable. We're celebrating."

"We are?" I giggled. "What are we celebrating?"

"We'll think of something. Wait, the night is young." He sat up and turned on the light near the bed. "So where were we?"

"That Marvin worries about a lot of things," I prompted him.

"Okay . . . so just to leap ahead, Marvin meets me. Now to you I might seem totally off the wall, but compared to the people Marvin was with, I am a calm, steady influence, a wonderful listener. He'd come home and pour out all his angst, I'd sit there, offer sage advice, witty rejoinders . . . it was perfect, till this thing. . . . Do you know where he is right now?"

I shook my head.

"At the University of Vermont, and with who? With this evil, rotten, petty man named Louis-Henri Bizzel."

I frowned. "What's so evil about him?"

Felix sighed. "He's not evil. Did I say evil? Look, here's what he is. Here's the story. When Marvin was in college, this guy was the head of the Romance Languages department and Marvin was a French major, because his mother once spent her junior year in Paris and it was the sexiest year of her life—*before* she met Marvin's father, need I add. So, to make a long story short, Louis, who's about fifty-five and the classic silver-templed 'Come into my study for some sherry' type, seduces more-meshugenah Marvin who doesn't know up from down. It was just a *pure* father-figure thing, I mean classic, a textbook case. This man wrote books on Mallarmé, Baudelaire; he *was* Marvin's father —depressed, enigmatic . . . Marvin was just a *total* catatonic when he was with him, stuttered, overawed . . . and then with me he was, like, blooming! He looked better, he gained some weight, he was beginning to feel good about himself and then, suddenly, he called up Louis who said, 'Why don't you come up for the weekend?' And . . . that was a month ago."

"That's awful," I said.

"It isn't just selfishness on my part," Felix said. "Of course it's partly that, I miss him, but Louis is bad for him, he becomes a *nonentity* when he's with Louis."

"*I'm* worried about Pam," I said.

"Who is Pam?" Just then there was a knock at the door. A man brought in a tray with our food. Felix opened the champagne. They'd brought two glasses so he poured some for both of us. He said he'd have the frosted for dessert. "To love," he said. "Wherever it may be found."

I clinked glasses with him.

"What does Pam have that you don't?" Felix said. "I can't imagine."

"She writes poetry," I said, biting into the bagel. It was really yummy. "She's . . . sensitive and they talk about intellectual things."

"How about the sex part?"

"Well, they did it once . . . so they could do it again."

"But I thought you and what's-his-name made it up."

"Joshua. *I* thought so," I said. "But I guess you never know."

Felix shook his head. "That's for sure. Now who would believe this? Here we are—two beautiful, talented young people sitting alone, rejected, mournful . . ."

"We're not alone," I pointed out. "We're together."

"Right." Felix started on the second half of his sandwich. "Hey, mine is great . . . how's yours?"

"Want a bite?" When he shook his head, I took another swallow of champagne. I was beginning to feel really good and cheerful. "Have you ever done it with girls?" I asked. I hoped that wasn't too personal a question.

Felix smiled. "Yes, Felix, I *have* done it with girls," he said.

"How was it? Was it awful?"

"No." He looked thoughtful. "I'd say it ranged from pleasant to excruciating."

"But pleasant was the best?"

"Pleasant was the best . . . and it was pleasant only, let's say, twenty percent of the time."

"Huh . . . but with Marvin it's really good?"

Felix sighed. "It's not just that sex is good with Marvin. Everything is good. Talking is good. Not talking is good."

Felix is so nice! I wish I had a brother like him, someone

I could tell anything to, who'd listen and be sympathetic. I lay back on the bed. "I feel dizzy and funny . . . but good."

"Me too." He lay down next to me. I leaned over and kissed him on the cheek. "What was that for?"

"Because you're so nice . . . and I guess I'm a little drunk."

He reached out and touched my hair. "Thank God, you took those braid things out . . . your hair is so beautiful. How could you let them do that to it?"

"Don't ask me. 'Pierre wouldn't suggest it if he didn't think it was right for you.' "

He frowned. "My best friend in fourth grade had hair this color. He died of leukemia when he was eleven. I always feel sad when I see red hair. It makes me think of him."

"What was his name?"

"Thor . . . Thor McGuire."

We lay there quietly. "I wish I had a brother like you," I said. "Someone I could tell everything to."

"You have a sister, don't you?"

"Yeah, but it's not the same . . . she's so jealous and competitive. Every time something good happens to me, she gets really mean."

"I have a sister," Felix said, "but she's not at all like you. . . . She makes Kelly Neff look like Simone de Beauvoir. You know? Four tow-headed kids, a white frame house. When she reads, it's *Family Circle,* or novels she gets off the rack at the IGA: *Love's Wildest Flame.*"

"How does she feel about Marvin?"

He laughed. "Felix! If Harriet knew about Marvin she would faint away dead."

"Gosh . . ."

"To her, Anita Bryant is one of the patron saints. She wrote her a *fan* letter."

"Families are weird." It was funny. Lying there next to Felix I really began feeling attracted to him, even though I know he's gay. I suppose it's just that he's so nice and really handsome, too.

"Hey!" He smiled. "Why are you staring at me?"

"I guess because I feel attracted to you . . . I'm sorry."

"Sweetie, don't be sorry. I'm flattered."

"Do you feel attracted to *me?*"

He touched my hair. "I think you're one of the most beautiful creatures I've ever seen," he said wistfully.

"Would you like me to take my clothes off?"

"Uh, let's see . . . sure, why not? But Felix, the thing is, I—"

"We don't have to do anything," I said. "Joshua and Marvin wouldn't like it."

"Oh, the hell with Joshua and Marvin!" Felix said. He took his clothes off, too.

Maybe this is hard to believe, but we didn't fuck. Do you believe that? We really didn't. We just lay in each other's arms and kissed and talked and kind of stroked each other. And it was really, really nice. After a while I started getting sleepy and Felix pulled the cover up over me. Then he turned out the lights and I fell asleep. I slept much better that night than I did the whole time I was in California. When I slept in my own hotel room, I used to wake up in the middle of the night, at two, or three, and feel funny lying there all alone. But this time I slept straight through till eight, when Felix's alarm went off. I sat up with a start. Felix was already up and showering. I waited till he was done and then I showered too.

"I have this audition today," I told him when we were both dressed.

"You'll knock 'em dead, kid," Felix said.

"I can't sing."

"They'll dub it . . . that's no problem."

"I should've read the book."

"You read the script, didn't you?"

"Yeah."

"So . . . no problem. I'll see you tonight?" He kissed me. "Thanks for keeping me company last night."

"It was nice." I smiled at him. "You know, I was feeling really shitty yesterday, and now I don't at all. I mean, what Joshua does is his business. Why should *I* worry?"

"Right . . . and if Marvin just wants to be miserable with Louis the Forgettable, that's his shtick."

We grinned at each other. Who were we kidding?

Chapter Twenty-one

There were two men who met me for the audition, the producer and the director; Jim Something and Greg Something. Jim was extremely handsome and tall with a blond mustache. He looked a little like Donald Sutherland. He had on a denim shirt and faded jeans. Greg was little with wild curly black hair and kind of squinty eyes. First we talked some in their office. It was a really gigantic room with big tall plants and a couch and a desk and some comfortable chairs, almost like a living room.

"Well, I think we ought to say," Jim said, "that we're both really delighted you're willing to consider the part of Lolita. We personally think you'd do a smash-up job."

"But the thing is," I said, "I saw the movie. You know, the *other* movie with Sue Lyons? And she was blond so I don't know if I look right."

"It's interesting," Jim said. "Most people seem to have that misconception . . . but, in fact, in the book, Nabokov says specifically that Lo has light gray eyes and auburn hair."

"I didn't read the book," I confessed. "My father thinks it's a really good book, though. He said it's a classic. He doesn't think it's dirty."

"Do you?" Jim said. Greg just sat there and stared at me really intently.

229

"Um, think it's dirty? Well, it's sort of strange."

"In what way?"

"Well, I mean the girl . . . liking someone so old."

"He's in his late thirties."

I felt bad. They were probably that old and I guess you shouldn't call people old. "But she was thirteen."

"Yes," Jim said. "But that age difference isn't so unusual these days, is it? Twenty-five years."

"It isn't?"

"Well, one certainly hears all the time of men who run off with women who are twenty or thirty years younger than them."

I swallowed. "I guess I don't know anyone like that."

"It seems strange to you that a girl that age would like someone old enough to be her father?"

"Yeah . . . well, the thing is, I guess most girls sort of like boys more their own age."

Jim and Greg smiled at each other. "Do you, Tatiana?" Jim said.

"My boyfriend's sixteen."

"Uh huh . . . is he . . . you really like each other a lot?"

I nodded.

They were silent a moment.

"Well, Tatiana, the scene we wanted you to read first is the one where Humbert has just picked Lolita up at camp, after her mother's death. She doesn't know her mother has died yet. Do you remember that scene?"

I nodded.

"They go, as you may remember, to a motel and she, in effect, seduces *him*. He's rather surprised at the extent of her experience. He had thought he would be the one to introduce her to . . . the pleasures of the flesh, as it were."

I just sat there, listening.

"Now, one thing . . . you say you saw the movie. You may recall it was made in the sixties when there was considerably less frankness about many things than is the case today. We feel we want to capture more of the actual spirit of the book . . . and that will mean a much greater amount of frankness, nudity and so forth. . . . How does that strike you?"

I bit my lip. "I guess it's okay," I said. "If it's intrinsic to the story."

"In this case we definitely feel it is." He looked at me carefully. "Have you, uh, grown a lot in the past year, Tatiana?"

"I think I'm five-three," I said.

"Well, I meant . . . now let's see, how shall I put this? You know, Lolita is supposed to be . . . she—"

"You don't want someone with really huge breasts," I said, to help them out. "You want her to look young, kind of."

He looked both embarrassed and relieved. "Right."

"I don't think mine are that huge . . . but maybe they'll get bigger. Mom doesn't think so. She's sort of flat-chested and she said she thinks I won't get that big. I don't know."

He nodded. "Well, I just thought I'd . . . that isn't a primary consideration, but it does happen at times that you hire an actress for a part and by the time you've turned around she's gained fifty pounds or grown half a foot. . . . You don't have a weight problem, do you, hon?"

I shook my head.

I read the scene in the motel. Jim read the part of Humbert. I think it went all right. Lolita is sort of a tough person. I imagine her like Angela Crashaw, this girl in my class at Hunter who says things like, "Lay off," or "Oh, go take a powder." Shellie can't stand her.

In the middle of the scene I said, "Could I . . . um . . . ask you a question?"

"Sure, fire away."

"Is she supposed to like him?"

He was silent a moment. "Well, yes, I'd say . . . the point is, *he* clearly is madly and insanely in love with her, and she . . . well, feels flattered, for one, at his adoration, and—"

"I guess I don't exactly see *why* he's so insanely in love with her," I said. "I mean, she doesn't act that nice to him."

"True. . . . Well, partly of course, he has this . . . fascination with young girls."

"Maybe he should've gone to a psychiatrist," I suggested.

Jim smiled. "Maybe . . . but then there wouldn't be any novel, would there?"

"I don't know. There could be a scene where he goes to a psychiatrist."

I read that scene a couple of times, and then they wanted me to read this other scene where Humbert tells Lolita her mother is dead and she runs off and then comes back to him because she has nowhere else to go. I'm really good at crying. I don't know why. I can just cry like that! It isn't even hard for me. I just did that scene once.

"That was really lovely, Tatiana," Greg said. That was practically the first time he'd said anything. "That's a very . . . complicated scene. You seemed to really get into it."

"Well, she seems sort of nicer in that scene," I said. "Missing her mother and everything. . . . I mean, I'd feel really awful if something like that happened to my mother, so I can imagine how she feels."

"You like to identify with the character you're playing?"

"Yes."

"Okay . . . well, now, you know this is a musical, and, of course, we *can* dub it . . . but do you think you could sing us something? Just to give us a rough idea of what we'd have to work with?"

"Sure." I'd decided to sing this Beatles song called "She's Leaving Home" because I learned it at camp. I did a duet with Sara Winship. "There are two parts, though," I said. "Could one of you sing the other part?"

They looked at each other. "We're awful," Jim said. "We can't sing to save ourselves."

"That's all right," I said. "Just say the words, okay?"

I'm a fair singer. I mean, I can carry a tune and my voice is pretty strong, but it doesn't have that much "lustre" to it. I'm saying that not to be modest, but because the singing teacher at camp said so. Sara's voice had a lot of lustre. This is how the song goes. The parts in parentheses are the parts Greg sang. That's supposed to be her parents talking.

Wednesday morning at five o'clock
As the day begins
Silently closing her bedroom door
Leaving the note that she hoped would say more

She goes downstairs to the kitchen
Clutching her handkerchief
Quietly turning the back door key
Stepping outside she is free.

She (We gave her most of our lives)
Is leaving (Sacrificed most of our lives)
Home (We gave her everything money could buy)
She's leaving home after living alone for so many years.
(Bye bye)

Father snores as his wife
Gets into her dressing gown
Picks up the letter that's lying there
Standing alone at the top of the stairs
She breaks down and cries to her husband,
"Daddy, our baby's gone.
Why would she treat us so thoughtlessly?
How could she do this to me?"

She (We never thought of ourselves)
Is leaving (Never a thought for ourselves)
Home (We struggled hard all our lives to get by)
She's leaving home after living alone for so many years.
(Bye bye)

Friday morning at nine o'clock
She is far away
Waiting to keep the appointment she made
Meeting a man from the motor trade.

She (What did we do that was wrong)
Is having (We didn't know it was wrong)
Fun (Fun is the one thing that money can't buy)
Something inside that was always denied for so many years.
(Bye bye)

She's leaving home—Bye bye.

"Nice," Jim said thoughtfully when I was done. "Your voice
has a very nice, plaintive quality . . . don't you think, Greg?"

"Perfect," Greg said. "Did you ever study voice?"

I shook my head.

"I think with a little coaching . . ." Jim said. "It's not like on the stage where you really have to project. We can do a lot with sound equipment to build it up. Well! The next thing may sound a little funny, but do you play tennis, Tatiana?"

"Sort of."

"I wondered if you'd mind going out with us and hitting a few with Greg here . . . who's a real hotshot."

"I'm not that good," I said, alarmed. I couldn't remember a scene where she played tennis. "Is that in the movie?"

"Yes, it's toward the end. Humbert is watching her play. . . . Don't worry about not being good. Lo isn't supposed to be a star athlete, no little Chris Evert. Just play the way you would normally."

We drove to this club. They rented me something to wear, a white tennis dress with a halter top. One awkward thing was I didn't have a bra, but I didn't know if you could get one at the club. I like to wear a bra when I play tennis because otherwise my breasts jiggle around and it's uncomfortable.

"Try these two rackets," the man behind the counter said. "I think they'd both do nicely."

I picked the Billie Jean King one. I hoped that might make me play well since she's such a good player.

What made me feel so bad was that if I'd known I was going to have to play tennis, I could have practiced with Deel or Daddy. They both play sometimes. Deel is quite good. She almost made the tennis team.

I was surprised Greg was the one to play with me. Jim looked more like the tennis type, being tall and blond, but Deel says height isn't that important. Actually, Greg was good. He was very quick and he hit everything back. "How about a set?" he said after about five minutes.

"I can't serve that well."

"Tatiana, remember, we're not testing your tennis."

"You're not?" I know they said that, but why play tennis with me if they don't care how I play? That doesn't make sense. I played just terribly. My serve is so weak; it isn't really a serve even. See, the problem is, I know you're supposed to throw the ball up really high and then smash down on it, but I'm always afraid if I throw it up too high, I won't be able to keep track of it. So, I just kind of toss it up a few inches. Then it's too close to me to really swing at it so I quickly whap it before it hits the ground. Deel says I look like someone swatting a mosquito. Sometimes it doesn't even go over the net, and even when it does, it's so soft a lot of people can just murder it. You know how usually people stand back at the back line to receive a serve, especially a first one? Well, with me, they stand right up in the middle of the court!

I could tell Greg wasn't trying that hard to put the ball away. However I'd hit it, he'd just hit it back, right at me, the way Daddy does when we're volleying. He won anyway because I double faulted millions of times. I felt just awful. Here I'd done so well on the acting part and wrecked it just because I'm so bad at tennis! And my breasts kept jiggling, and Jim was watching me like a hawk through the whole thing. It was really humiliating. Finally after one set, Greg said, "I think I've had it . . . how about you, Tatiana?"

"Me too." I knew my face was probably all pink the way it gets when I'm out of breath. "I'm sorry," I said. "I should have practiced more, but I didn't know I'd have to play tennis as part of the audition."

"Honey, listen," Jim said. "Your game is perfect."

"What?"

"Promise me you won't take a single lesson."

"Not even on my serve?"

"I *love* your serve! Where did you learn to do it that way?"

"I didn't . . . I mean, that's not the right way." I guess he doesn't play tennis much, or he'd know that.

"And the way you kick up your left leg after you hit a backhand," Greg said. "Is that your idea?"

"It isn't an idea so much," I said. "It's more like a nervous habit."

As we walked back to the club house, I said, "Usually I wear a bra . . . I mean, for tennis." I just thought they ought to know that with a bra I'd feel more comfortable.

"Why?" Jim asked.

"Well, it's just more comfortable. If you play without a bra, you jiggle around."

"Well." He smiled at me. "You jiggle beautifully."

I felt uneasy. "But in a movie that wouldn't be good," I said. "Would it?"

"It would be perfect. Does it make you uncomfortable?"

I thought of how Mom said men always like to look at women's breasts and you shouldn't mind. "Sort of," I admitted.

"If you're a movie star, you're going to be the object of a lot of men's fantasies," he said. "That's what movies are. Suppliers of fantasies for the masses."

"They are?" I didn't know that.

"Anyway," Jim went on, "it's not that different from life. In life you must be used to men ogling you and—"

I shook my head. "No, I'm not. They never do."

He smiled again. "They must, Tatiana."

"I don't think so," I blurted out. The whole conversation was making me feel awful. I wondered if that's what Jim had been doing while I was playing tennis, ogling me. And I didn't even know it. I just thought he wanted to see how I played tennis.

"Tatiana?" Jim said.

I looked up, startled. I guess I was in sort of a daze. "Uh huh?"

"You look . . . worried about something."

I took a deep breath. "Was that what you were doing before, ogling me?" I asked.

"I was trying to look at you through the eyes of the typical American male," Jim said.

"Horny, dumb, and five-foot-nine," Greg muttered.

"But you didn't even care about my tennis? You just wanted to see me jiggle around?"

"You know, it's an interesting metaphysical question," Greg said. "Which would one prefer to be—the ogler or the oglee?"

"Is that a word?" I said. "Oglee?"

"It ought to be if it isn't," Jim said. He reached over and squeezed my shoulder. "You were perfect, honey. You don't have a thing to worry about. Let's go get a drink, shall we?"

The drink they bought me was wonderful. It was made of all kinds of fresh fruit and soda. They asked me how I thought the publicity had gone and I told them how I was getting tired, having to answer all those dumb questions again and again.

"Well, that's the life of a star," Jim said.

"I know," I said. "That's why I'm not sure I want to be one." I told them how I really wanted to be a doctor.

"I wanted to be a veterinarian when I was your age," Greg said.

"You did?" Jim said. "The dog and cat kind?"

"The 'All Things Bright and Beautiful' kind . . . horses and cows."

Jim laughed. "Well, I was going to import rugs from Iraq and be a pimp in a harem."

"You missed your calling, James," Greg said.

"I know it's a lot of work going through medical school," I said, scooping up the strawberries at the bottom of the glass. "But I don't mind. My boyfriend is going to make movies, direct them."

"What kind?" Greg asked.

I hesitated. "More sort of serious movies . . . like Ingmar Bergman, you know, like with a philosophy of life?"

"Those are the kind I like best," Greg said.

They drove me back to the hotel. It was nearly dinner time. "We've really enjoyed this," Jim said.

They said they'd call my agent to discuss the terms.

While I was getting ready for dinner, I kept thinking of that word: oglee. It sounds so much like ugly, even though in a way it means the opposite, if it is a real word. I'll ask Deel, she'll know. She always knows things like that. I don't think I want to be an oglee. I don't care *what* Mom says. I don't like it when men look at me that way, like I was a thing. It's different if Joshua looks at me that way because he loves me. I guess I felt bad because it seemed they cared just as much or maybe more about seeing how my breasts jiggled than if I had a good singing voice or if I could act. If I'm going to be an actress, then how I act should be the main thing, shouldn't it?

That night was the last night before I went back to New York. Kelly Neff took Felix and me out to dinner at a fancy restaurant. She said she was glad we were both feeling better and that we had both been "terrific sports" about the whole thing.

"How did your audition go, Tatiana?" she asked.

"Okay," I said hesitantly. I'd ordered melon for an appetizer and they brought me this huge slab of honeydew, like a quarter of a melon, practically.

I told them how awful I'd felt when they were watching me play tennis without my bra. "It was like all they cared about was, you know, sort of evaluating my body."

"Did they make you undress?" Felix asked.

I shook my head. "But it was like that . . ."

"Well, look, they've got to sell tickets," he said.

I stared at him. "What do you mean?"

"Sweetie, tits and ass sell tickets. What can you do about it? That's the world."

I almost choked on my melon. "How about acting?" I squeaked.

"Acting sells one ticket per hundred thousand people . . . in a good year."

"Felix, I think you're a little cynical," Kelly Neff said crisply. She turned to me. "Didn't they ask you to act at all, Tatiana?"

"A little bit."

"There are millions of teenage girls with lovely figures," she said to Felix. "But Tatiana has something extra."

"Am I denying that? It's just what they're buying and what she's selling may not be the same thing."

Out here everything seems to be buying and selling, ogling and jiggling. I feel safer at home. Maybe this is more the real world, but I guess I'm not used to it. I like the world of Mom and Daddy and school. At least there I know where I stand.

In a way it seems like I was away much more than just a week. I think it's always like that when you travel. I'm glad I went. I didn't enjoy it exactly, in the way you'd enjoy something if you were with friends, but I think I did a good job.

I stopped at the newspaper stand to get some magazines to look at on the plane. I was standing there, looking to see what I hadn't read, when I almost fainted. There I was on the cover of *People!* It was this big close-up of me, mostly my face, though you could see I was wearing the fox coat. Across the top it said: *The Girl with the Silver Eyes.* I looked around nervously. I was scared someone might recognize me. They had about fifty copies of the magazine, all piled on top. Right while I was standing there, a woman came and picked one up and bought it! I didn't know what to do. I didn't know if it would look funny if I bought it, but I didn't think I could stand not reading the article. I wonder why Mom and Daddy didn't mention it. Maybe they didn't know. Maybe they wanted to surprise me. Finally, I picked up one copy and then I got *Us* and put it on top of *People* and I put a Marathon bar on top of that. The man behind the counter didn't seem to notice.

Chapter Twenty-two

I had about twenty minutes before it was time to board the plane so I sat down and opened it up to the article. I was scared, my hands were shaking and I kept getting two pages stuck together. This is what it said:

The New York critics have lost their hearts to her, co-star Felix Propper thinks she "can do anything; it's almost scary," Twentieth Century Fox is beside themselves at the prospect of her appearing in their new $9-million-budgeted musical, "Lo," based on Vladimir Nabokov's 1958 controversial novel, "Lolita." But fame, thus far, seems to have left Rusty (née Tatiana) Engelberg, 14, totally unchanged. "I'm not even sure if I want to be an actress," says Rusty, nicknamed for her mane of radiant red hair which has critics running to their dictionaries for appropriate adjectives. "I might want to be a doctor—you know, that kind that delivers babies."

Rusty grew up with show business very much in her blood. Her mother, stunning six-foot Amanda Tobias, gained renown in the 60s as the girl in the zebra-skin suit who purred infectiously on TV screens about an underarm deodorant. Kentucky-born Amanda, 39, a stalwart of CBS's "The Way

We Are Now," claims to have no difficulty accepting her younger daughter's sudden catapult into fame. "Rusty deserves everything that's happened to her," she says, beaming proudly at her nubile offspring. "She has enormous natural grace, talent. She did things in "Domestic Arrangements" that I couldn't do now, God help her."

"But Daddy wasn't sure I ought to be in the movie," Rusty confides. "He wasn't sure it was serious enough . . . and he wasn't that happy about the scene . . . you know, the one with the hair dryer." Daddy is director Lionel Engelberg, 50, Emmy-award winner for his unrelenting portrait of a cancer victim, "Death Rites," former professor of Drama at Yale (where he met Amanda, who enrolled in his class and wrote up an interview with him for the school paper; his childless marriage to the former Dora Cartwright was "crumbling"), and onetime theater critic for the prestigious literary quarterly, *The Hudson Review*. "It's important to all of us that Tatiana not be exploited in any way," he insists. "She has a natural talent that I'd like to see nurtured and tended to." Plans are afoot for Rusty to appear as Ariel in a summer production of "The Tempest" at The Long Wharf. Will being directed by her father faze the young star? "I think it'll be fun," Rusty confides. "Daddy's going to coach me on the poetry part."

The only member of the family ("We're just a typical New York family," says Amanda) who seems to take a somewhat jaundiced view of Rusty's stardom is older sister Cordelia, a third-year student at Riverdale. "Let's face it," says Cordelia, named, as was her sister, after a literary heroine, " 'Domestic Arrangements' isn't exactly 'Hamlet.' " Cordelia, who wants to be the first Jewish woman president, says she found her sister's semi-nude scene "gross." "I wish she'd acted under another name so people wouldn't know it was my sister."

What appears to have caused the most controversy about Rusty's first starring role is not just the R rating or even *Time* magazine's accusation of the film as being "soft-core porn dressed up as radical-chic satire." It is an unusual combination of physical delicacy and sensuality that Rusty projects. She is, in the eyes of many parents, their daughter, caught somewhere between paper dolls and the pill. "She's the heroine of the 'Glass Menagerie' crossed with Candy," says Charles O'Hara, the director of the film. "Rusty has a tentativeness, a softness that I hoped would eradicate any aura of sleaziness in a very complicated, demanding role. Samantha is a catalyst. Everyone in the family reacts to her out of their own frustrations and desires. Yet, she, in her true and compelling innocence, is, in a sense, untouched."

Whether that innocence can be preserved as Rusty moves on into the upper-middle-class New York world of teenage sex and drugs, as well as the Hollywood scene, is a question that concerns many people. One of them is clearly Rusty's erstwhile boyfriend and would-be film director, Joshua Lasker. Joshua, 16, son of prominent divorce attorney Patrick Lasker, is evidently dismayed at what is happening to his former girl friend. "He thinks she's going to be spoiled," one of his school friends reports. "I guess she dumped him for some older guy. He's really taken it hard." Rusty and Joshua met in the spring of 1980 when he took some color photographs of her in a Japanese kimono for a school photography contest. The photos, showing a more demure side of the then thirteen-year-old actress, were reproduced in the school newspaper. "He said he had some of her in the nude," a friend reports, "but I guess he isn't showing them to anybody." *Playboy?*

Rusty is generally close-mouthed about the relationship, admitting only that she now considers herself "too young for sex." Characterizing their relationship as "fairly intense," she admits that the diaphragm her parents purchased for her was never actually used. "But I definitely believe people my age can be in love," she insists. Her father is more wary. "This is a difficult time for girls Tatiana's age," he says. "Peer pressure forces them into relationships they aren't emotionally prepared to handle." Citing statistics that only 20% of teenage girls are having orgasms, Engelberg deplores what he calls "premature sexual activity which robs young people of the real joys of childhood and adolescence." Cordelia, who is currently dating Joshua Lasker's older brother, lute-maker Neil, a bearded high school drop-out, says her father's statistics are far from accurate.

Rusty herself seems unperturbed by any possible negative effects "Domestic Arrangements" might have on her peers. Characterizing her own parents' marriage as "extremely happy," she seems secure in her own world and admits that the elegant 3-story dollhouse her father built for her when she was a child is still used in idle moments. "I don't think the movie was dirty, not at all. I wasn't even naked and my hair covered me practically altogether."

The possibility that people will confuse her with the character she plays disturbs Rusty. "We're *totally* different people," she vehemently asserts. Her best friend at school, Sheila Montgomery, agrees. "Rusty's not the type who'd flirt with someone's boyfriend or try to steal him away. She's a completely straightforward, open person." "If anything," adds Amanda Engelberg, "Rusty is *too* naive for her age. That wide-eyed 'I'll tell you anything you want to know' bit is no act. She's never had any reason not to trust people. I hope she never will."

It's precisely that quality of wide-eyed innocence which producers Gregory Sampson and James Liss hope to capitalize on in their "Lolita" remake, which should go before the cameras this summer. "Lo is supposed to be a pre-adolescent," Sampson states. "On the verge of blooming. We're not looking for a typical 80s teenager who's done it all and is jaded at sixteen. We want someone with a certain poignancy, a wet-behind-the-ears look. We think Tatiana will be perfect."

Rusty is less confident. "I'm not blond like Lolita is supposed to be," she says, with a worried frown. "And I can't really sing that well." When it's pointed out that her voice could be dubbed, Rusty looks apprehensive. "Wouldn't that be cheating?" she wonders. As for the book itself, although she hasn't read it, Rusty has some doubts about that, too. "I guess it's hard to imagine someone my age actually, well, liking someone that old." She looks pensive. Then with a shy glance at her father who is in the kitchen fixing supper, she adds, "Could you not put that in about being old? I don't want to hurt anyone's feelings."

I was so intent on reading the article, I didn't even notice that people were boarding the plane already. Then I happened to look up and rushed to get on line. Columbia was flying me back first class again, which means you get these really comfortable seats that are almost like couches. I had a seat near the window. I was glad. I didn't feel like talking to anyone.

I felt so weird! Being on the cover, especially. Mike Nadler and Trudy never said they were thinking of putting me on the cover. They called back a couple of times after the interview to check some facts, but they never said anything about that. They made me sound so dumb and awful! It's odd. They didn't misquote me or anything, but it just came out differently the way they put it. And saying I never used my diaphragm! I guess Daddy'll be glad about that. I wonder what made them think I never used it. It's true I never said I *did* and I told them about throwing it out, but I'd had it almost a month before I did that.

And how did they find out about Joshua? Deel swore to me she wouldn't tell! And interviewing his friends and all. Did he really tell someone I "dumped" him for another older guy? I don't think Joshua would've said that. He might have said he was scared I was going to, or something. And how could he have told people about those nude photos! How awful! Maybe I better burn them when I get home. What if *Playboy* really wants to use them? That really would be gross.

But I'm glad in a way that I'd broken up with Joshua when the article was written. He would just hate it if they'd come around and tried to interview him . . . or maybe they did. But wouldn't he have told me? Oh, I hope Mom and Daddy think it's okay. Mom should like it. They called her "stunning." And they gave all those quotes from Daddy. He really does believe all those things. I don't think it was such a bad article. I only wish they hadn't put me on the cover. In fact, when the stewardess came to bring me dinner—I wasn't really that hungry—she did a kind of double take and said, "Aren't you Rusty Engelberg?"

I nodded.

She called one of the other stewardesses over and said, "I told you it was her."

The other one, who was tall with long, straight brown hair, said, "Why, honey, you're as cute as can be! Just like your photo. You must be so proud!"

"I didn't even know about it till today," I said. I tried to speak quietly because the man sitting next to me was listening.

"They didn't even tell you? Well, goodness, how about that?"

I was glad when they had to move on to serve other people their dinner. The man next to me was about Daddy's age. He said he hadn't seen *Domestic Arrangements*, but he'd heard about it. "My stepdaughter loved it," he said.

"I wish they hadn't put me on the cover of *People*," I said. I decided to eat just the fruit salad.

"Why? Isn't that good exposure for your career?"

"I don't want a career that much," I said. "Not that kind. . . . I just want to be a doctor."

"Then you'll be one," he said. "All it takes is a strong mind. Don't let anyone tell you what to do. You decide for yourself."

"Does that seem dumb to you?" I asked. "Not taking advantage of something like this?" I told him how I wasn't sure I even wanted to be in *Lolita*.

"My dear, the only dumb thing in life is doing things because other people expect it of you. I didn't find that out till I was forty-five. You do what *you* want."

"Well," I said, munching on the cottage cheese. "I'm going to try."

Mom, Daddy and Deel all met me at the airport. I hugged them. "Did you see *People?*" I said.

"Oh, you saw it already," Deel said. "We wanted to surprise you."

"I bought it out there. Did you know it was going to be on the cover?"

"Not till the day before yesterday," Mom said.

"Did you like it?" I asked anxiously. "Did you think it came out okay?"

Daddy had a funny look on his face.

"You really said all those things," I reminded him.

"I thought they did a marvelous job," Mom exclaimed. "I loved it."

"How come they said you never used your diaphragm?" Deel said. "Did you tell them that?"

"Uh uh."

Deel touched her chest and declaimed, " 'I'm too young for sex . . . but I believe in love.' "

"I thought Tatiana handled that part of the interview very well," Daddy said.

"Sure . . . she just lied through her teeth, that's all."

"I *do* believe in love," I said.

"Well, if you're too young for sex, how come you're doing it?" Deel countered.

"Cordelia, it's perfectly natural to have ambivalent feelings," Daddy said. "I think it's very courageous of Tat to acknowledge that."

"Sure, just like she plays with her dollhouse all the time," Deel said.

"I didn't tell them I played with it *all* the time," I said. "I said I still played with it sometimes."

"They made you sound like some kind of baby," Deel said contemptuously. "Wide-eyed innocence, my ass."

"Daddy, will you make her stop?" I wailed.

"Cordelia, Tati has just returned from a long hard week. The idea was to take her out to a nice restaurant and relax. Can you get into the spirit of that or do you want to go home?"

"I'm in the spirit," Deel grunted.

But somehow the "spirit of it" wasn't that great. We went to this quite fancy place called Café des Artistes, which is on the West Side. The waiter said, "And what will you have, Rusty?" I mean, can you imagine? Someone I don't even *know*, that I never even *met*, just a waiter, calling me by my nickname!

"Is this going to happen all the time?" I asked.

"Well, it may . . ." Daddy said.

"Why don't they *ask* you at least if you want to be on the cover?" I said suddenly. "Lots of people would probably want to. Why do they have to pick on me?"

"Mike said the editor just fell in love with the photos Trudy took," Mom said. "They'd scheduled someone else, but he said he couldn't resist it."

When I fell asleep that night, I had a terrible nightmare. I dreamt I had this stuff on my skin like rust and they couldn't figure out how to get rid of it. Joshua didn't want to see me, I was all covered with scales like a lizard, and when I looked in the mirror I was all orange. They wanted to give me away to a zoo! I woke up in the middle of the night all drenched in sweat, like I had a fever. I looked in the mirror. I wasn't all orange. I was the same as usual.

But in school it was awful. The boys kept teasing me all day long. Even some of the teachers commented on it, or made remarks. But the worst was just walking down the street or going into a store. People would say "Hi" to me like they knew me. The first couple of times I thought it was people I really did know, but it never was. "Hey, Rusty, is your boyfriend going to sell those photos to *Playboy?*" some boy yelled. "Tell him I'd like to see them."

One little boy, around eight, came up to me at the bus stop and said, "I love you," and then walked away! When I walked into the Pizza Place with Shellie, the woman behind the counter, Flo, said, "Hey there, Lolita! How goes it?"

"Her name's Rusty," Shellie snapped. "And leave her alone."

Flo came over and said she was sorry, she hadn't meant to be rude, she was just so proud that she knew me. "I told all my friends," she said in this really excited way. "They couldn't believe it. I said, 'She comes in here almost every day. She gets the same thing every day. A slice, orange soda. She's just a quiet, sweet little girl,' I told them. Not spoiled at all. Just as pretty as her picture. Prettier, I said. 'You should *see* that hair,' I said. 'You wouldn't believe it.'"

When I walked out of the store, I put the hood of my coat up and zipped it tight so my hair wouldn't show. I never wear it that way, but I felt like I couldn't stand it if one more person recognized me. "Shellie, listen," I said. "Would you do something for me . . . it's going to sound really weird."

"What?" Shellie said.

I told her my plan. I'd been thinking about it all day actually, off and on. "I want to cut my hair," I said in a whisper, "and dye it blond."

"What?" Shellie looked horrified.

The reason I picked Shellie to tell wasn't just that I can trust her, but she cuts her sister's hair. Her mother got this book on how to do it and she's really good. "I'm going to do it," I said, "whether you help me or not."

"What *for?*"

"I hate everybody recognizing me!" I said fiercely. "I just *hate* it."

"How much do you want to cut off?" she asked anxiously.

"All of it!"

"You mean, you'll be bald, like that lady in *Star Trek?*"

"No! I just mean short . . . like Georgia Witt." She's a girl in our math class who has hair in a kind of gamin style with bangs. "Like your sister."

"So, why dye it too?" Shellie asked. "You're going to look like a completely different person."

"I know," I said. "That's the whole idea."

Shellie sighed. "Well, I'll help you if you really think you want to . . . but think it over real well, okay?"

"Okay . . . I thought we could do it Friday night . . . at your house," I said. I know Shellie's mother and stepfather go to the movies every Friday night.

"I just can't imagine you blond," Shellie said, looking at me carefully. "How about that movie? You said they told you red hair was perfect."

"I don't think I want to be in the movie," I said.

"Even for a hundred thousand dollars?" Shellie looked amazed.

"Yeah . . . I mean, what's money? Big deal."

"Think of all the stuff you could buy!"

"I know . . . but I just . . . I just don't feel like it."

Shellie reached over and squeezed my hand. "I understand," she said.

When I got home, I felt a little better. I don't think anyone will recognize me on the street with short blond hair. And it's only four more days. I can just wear my hood up all the time till then. While I was sitting in my room thinking about it, wondering how I'd look as a blonde, Joshua called.

"Where were you?" I said. I'd almost forgotten I was mad at him with all the stuff about the cover.

"I was at Andover, visiting Pam. Didn't Beryl tell you? I told her to. I left a message."

"But you said that when you flew out with me . . . I thought maybe that was just something you made up."

"No, I was up there."

"What for? You didn't even mention it on the plane."

"She called me all of a sudden, really depressed. She just broke up with someone and she was feeling really lousy. The funny thing was, the day after I got up there, they made it up."

"Who was he?" I said, relieved. "Was he nice?"

"It's a she, actually . . . Maria Lopez, some Argentinian girl."

"I didn't know Pam was gay!"

"Neither did she . . . I don't know this proves she is. They just kind of fell for each other."

"Weird."

"They're coming into the city this weekend. Do you want to see them with me? I told Pam we might all get together."

"Sure . . . does she know about me?"

"Of course. I guess she's a little worried that I'll be critical of their relationship, but I don't care. I mean, look, if it makes her happy, why should I—"

I thought of Felix. "Lots of very nice people are gay," I said. "It's just a matter of taste."

"*You* haven't fallen for some girl, have you?" he said.

"Joshua, come on . . ."

"Just checking. Hey, I missed you. The plane ride back was really dull."

"I missed you a lot too."

We talked some more. I told him how I felt about the cover. I didn't tell him about what I was planning to do with my hair.

"How come you told people you took nude photos of me?" I said.

"I told one person," Joshua said. "It just shows you can't trust anybody."

"Did you tell them I dumped you for an older man?"

"Look, Rust, there was this one guy I used to talk to . . . I guess I told him I was afraid. I never said you actually did it."

"I think Daddy was pleased they said I never used my diaphragm."

"Did you get a new one yet?"

"Take it easy! I will."

"By Saturday?"

"Joshua . . . come on. I thought we were supposed to have so much in common besides sex."

"We do . . . that doesn't mean sex doesn't count."

"True."

"Did any Hollywood types come on to you out there?"

"I was just there a week!"

"It only takes a couple of minutes."

"You have a lot of faith in me, don't you?"

"I'm sorry, Rust."

"How do I know what you and Pam were doing that night before she made up with her friend."

"We were reading her poetry."

"Sure."

He laughed. "She's off men . . . she thinks they're coarse and insensitive."

"Even you?"

"She thinks I'm the best of the lot, but still not to be compared . . ."

I decided to believe him. He sounded sincere. Anyway, since I had that night with Felix, even though nothing happened exactly, my conscience wasn't totally clear.

Chapter Twenty-three

After school Wednesday I went to the drugstore near us, Mandel's, and looked at hair dyes. I didn't want to end up a real platinum blonde, since that would look odd with my coloring. I ended up buying this dye that Mom uses, called Apricot Haze. Her real hair color is brown, and this makes it turn out blondish red. That way people will really think we're related when in fact it won't be the real color for either of us. Also, Mom does it herself at home, so I know how it works. Basically, you put on these rubber gloves and pour it on your hair. Then you wait about half an hour or maybe less and wash it out. I think I'll have Shellie do the washing out part.

What I feel worst about is cutting my hair. I've had long hair all my life, all except the first two years of my life when I was practically bald. I look sort of like a boy in my baby pictures. Then it suddenly began to grow in really fast and by the time I was in kindergarten, I had a whole lot of it. Mom used to braid it or put it in bunches with colored ribbons to match whatever I was wearing. I love long hair. I like the way it feels when it hangs down my back. I love washing it and drying it. In the winter it even keeps you warm, like wearing a scarf, and in the summer I like putting it up, which makes me look elegant and older. Joshua will feel terrible about my cutting it. But I don't care. It'll be worth it.

Shellie learned this odd way of cutting hair. What you do is gather all the hair into a ponytail. Then you just cut the ponytail off with a big strong kitchen scissors. For some reason that makes it fall in a nice way. So much hair came off! It all just lay there in heaps on the floor. Shellie looked at it in dismay. "It's like that O. Henry story we read," she said sadly.

"But I'm doing it for me," I said. I looked at myself in the mirror. My head looked so big and my eyes looked gigantic.

"Listen," Shellie said. "I want to fix it a little. You need bangs or something and curls on the side . . . otherwise it looks too . . . flat."

I sat very still while she trimmed it with these other scissors she has. She has one that's for thinning and shaping. She did it really carefully and slowly and when it was done, it looked like a real haircut, the kind you'd get at a store. One reason I didn't want to go to a beauty shop, though, was because I was afraid I might change my mind.

We gathered all the hair up and put it in three large Ziploc bags.

"Don't tell anyone I did it, okay?" she said. "Because your parents might kill me."

"Don't worry," I said. We'd agreed that I would get up early on Saturday and go home before Shellie's parents could see me so they wouldn't know either.

We did the dyeing part in the bathroom. I sat on Shellie's desk chair and leaned back in the sink while she poured this stuff on my hair. It really smelled bad, I guess because of the bleach. "Does your mother really use this?" Shellie said. "It doesn't look like her color."

"It changes once you wash it out and dry it," I said. I began getting scared. This was probably the worst thing I've ever done. "Joshua probably won't ever want to see me again," I said mournfully.

"Come on," Shellie said. "He doesn't like you for your hair." But she didn't sound that positive.

She washed the dye stuff out a couple of times. You have

to make sure to get it all out. My back was getting really stiff. Then I dried it with her blow dryer. But it was funny. With short hair it only takes around one second to dry it. I guess that'll give me a lot of extra time that I didn't have before. Then Shellie brushed it around a little. We both stood in front of the mirror, looking at me.

"You certainly look different," Shellie said.

I did. I really looked like a completely different person. The color was okay. It wasn't exactly like Mom's. It was more red, but it was a lot lighter than my hair usually is.

"One good thing," Shellie said, "is it *kind* of matches with your eyebrows and eyelashes."

"It does?"

"Sort of . . . I think it's cute, kind of. It's just hard for me to get used to."

"Me too. It's not that I look bad, I just look like someone else."

"You know who you look like?"

"Who?"

"Susanna Karpinsky."

"Yeah, I know what you mean." Susanna Karpinsky is this petite blond girl who's studied ballet since she was born practically.

"I mean, you look prettier, but you look like you might be a dancer or something."

I shook my head. "It feels so light. It's such a weird feeling." I sighed.

Shellie began fixing up the bathroom. "Maybe you'll develop a whole new personality to go with it," she said.

"I hope not."

But lying in bed, I began to worry. Maybe it was a rash, dumb thing to do. Maybe if I'd waited a little, people would've forgotten. I was afraid I might have another bad dream, but I didn't. I slept really well. I usually do at Shellie's house.

We set the alarm for six o'clock. It was really nice of Shellie to get up that early with me because she likes to sleep late on weekends. I tied a green scarf around my head and we went into the kitchen to have breakfast. All of a sudden, while we were standing there, waiting for the toast to pop up, Shellie's little sister, Zoe, came in. "Hi," she said cheerfully. She looked at me. "How come you have that weird scarf on?" she said.

"It's a new style," Shellie snapped.

"It is?"

After she left, Shellie and I began giggling. "God, wait till my parents see me," I said. "I wish I didn't have to go home."

"They'll get used to it," Shellie said encouragingly.

"Oh, Shell!"

"Are you sorry you did it?"

I frowned. "No, not exactly . . . just nervous."

"Call me later, okay?"

"Definitely."

When I got home, Deel was up. She was in the living room, practicing her lute. "Hi," she said. Then she looked up. "God, what happened to you?"

I still had the scarf on. I came into the living room and took it off.

Deel's mouth fell open. "What? What'd you *do*? Are you crazy?"

"Ssh . . . I just wanted a change."

"What happened to all your hair?"

I showed her the Ziploc bags.

"Seriously, why'd you do it? You look like Mom!"

"I didn't want people to recognize me," I said. "People were coming up to me on the street and pointing and saying things. It was awful!"

Deel kept staring at me. "Boy, Mom and Daddy're going to have a cow," she said with some satisfaction.

"Does it look really ugly?" I said, looking in the hall mirror.

"Oh, come on . . . you'd never look ugly no matter what you did. I don't mind the style so much . . . but why'd you change the color too?"

I sighed. "I don't know."

I went in my room and went back to sleep till noon. It seemed like the safest thing to do. When I woke up, I heard Deel and Daddy talking in the kitchen. "She felt tired," I heard Deel say. "She's sleeping."

"No, I'm up," I called out.

Daddy opened the door to my room. When he looked at me, it was as though I had come home with one arm and one leg. "Darling, what *happened* to you?"

"I cut my hair," I said.

He rushed over to the bed. "But . . . the color! What happened?" He acted like I'd been in an accident.

"I wanted a change," I said, looking down. "I wanted to look different."

"But sweetheart, you should have consulted us. Did you . . . tell anyone? Does Amanda know?"

"I didn't *want* to tell anyone," I said, "because I knew you'd stop me."

"It's just such a drastic thing to do." He looked around in bewilderment.

"I don't think it's so bad," Deel said. I could tell she was really enjoying the whole thing. "You have to kind of get used to it."

Daddy touched my hair. "When did you do it?"

"Yesterday."

We all sat there in silence. It was sort of as though I'd just been expelled from school. Daddy didn't even seem mad, more just stunned and sad. He kept looking at me as though he thought it was a bad dream and he might wake up from it if he tried hard enough. Then Mom peeked in. She let out a whoop.

"Tat! How darling! I *love* it!" She rushed over. "When did you do it?"

"Yesterday," I said softly. "Do you really like it?"

"I think it's sensational. What a difference!"

"But she had such beautiful hair," Daddy said plaintively.

"But it was too much," Mom said briskly. "It overwhelmed her. All you saw was *hair*. Tat has such a delicate build. It was like half girl and three-quarters hair. Now you can really see her face."

I smiled. Well, at least someone liked it. "I just did it because I was sick of people coming up to me on the street, you know, because of the cover."

"But that would've passed," Daddy said. "That was just a temporary thing."

"Well, whatever the reason, I think it's a hundred percent

improvement," Mom said. "Who did it for you, hon? It's a marvelous cut."

"I can't tell," I said.

"I'm so glad you went to someone good," Mom said, inspecting me from all angles. "Some of those guys just butcher you, even the most expensive ones. This is a good, sensible cut . . . I love the little pieces on the side."

"But the color!" Daddy said.

"It's my color," Mom said wryly.

"Yes, but I'm used to it on you," Daddy said. "And Tat's hair was such an unusual color."

"True," Mom said. "Well, dyes grow out quickly, a month or two. No, I agree, fourteen *is* a little young for monkeying with color, hon, though it's lovely in a way."

"What will Sampson and Liss say?" Daddy said. "They called Helen saying how Tat's coloring was so perfect for Lolita."

"Daddy, I'm not sure I want to be in *Lolita*," I said.

"You don't?" Mom and Daddy said in unison.

I looked down. "I don't want to ever act again."

"Darling," Mom came over and took my hand. "This is all just . . . temporary. It's always hard getting used to in the beginning. But, believe me, it passes. Next month they'll have a new superstar and you'll be totally forgotten."

"That's not true," Daddy said indignantly. "She won't be forgotten that easily."

"I don't mean forgotten in that sense," Mom said. "I just mean in that sense of everyone gawking. Did you save your hair, sweetie?"

I showed her the bags full of it.

Daddy went over, unlocked one bag, and ran his hands through it. "It's so soft," he said mournfully. "Feel it."

Mom put her head to one side. "It'll grow . . . but I think it was definitely time for a change. She'd worn her hair that way since she was four!"

When Daddy had left, she said, "Hon, don't mind him . . . Lionel just clings to the status quo like a mad beast. He can't abide change in any way, shape, or form. He wants you preserved, forever, just as you were at six. This style really suits your face. Look at what it does to your eyes! You can really see your face for the first time in *years*."

"I'm afraid Joshua will hate it too."

"Look, hon, men are just . . . they're like that. They like things one way, but one has to go forward. You're your own person. You're old enough to make decisions on your own. And if you don't like the color, we can dye it back tomorrow."

"We can?"

"Sure . . . the point is, it'll grow in in a month anyway, but if you'd rather, we'll just buy a bottle of dye and do it ourselves. I do it every month."

"I know," I said.

She looked closely at my hair. "See, the thing is, they didn't do a really first-rate dye job. The cut is super, but they didn't shade it in right. It's a little too harsh, I think."

I was supposed to meet Joshua, Pam, and Maria at twelve at the Museum of Modern Art. I put my hood up, even though it wasn't that cold. Joshua was waiting outside, near the man who sells chestnuts. He hugged me. "Hi," he said.

He didn't even notice my hair. Of course most of it was under the hood. "Josh?"

"Yeah?"

"I have to tell you something," I said slowly.

"What?" He looked suddenly anxious, like he thought I was going to say I didn't want to see him anymore.

"I did something really stupid." I looked at him pleadingly. "There was a reason for it, though. Should I tell you the thing I did first, or the reason?"

"The thing you did."

I untied the strings of my hood. "There," I said, letting him see.

"Your hair?" He looked bewildered.

"It was awful," I said. "Everywhere I went, since the *People* cover, people kept staring at me and pointing and saying things. . . . I couldn't *stand* it!"

Joshua's face had such a mixture of expressions it was hard to tell what he was feeling.

"Say something!" I said desperately.

"Well, I'm relieved in a way," he said. "I thought—well—I thought it was something different."

"I know what you thought."

"What did I think?"

"You thought I fucked with Woody Allen or something."

"Or something." Joshua grinned. He looked at me. "It's not so bad," he said. "You look nice . . . just different. You look like a ballet dancer."

"That's what Shellie said."

He touched my head. "You must weigh about ten pounds less."

"Mom says we can dye it back to the same color if I want . . . should I?"

"Yeah . . . you're not the blond type, somehow," he said.

"In what way?"

"Well, blondes are usually more . . . giddy and light-hearted."

"Aren't I giddy and lighthearted?" I said, worried.

"Sure," Joshua said. "I didn't mean it in a bad way."

"So, you're not mad?" I said. "You still feel the same way about me?"

"Yes," Joshua said. "You arouse the same calm, brotherly, protective feelings that you always have."

"I thought I aroused wild, lustful feelings."

"Oh, from time to time," he said, moving closer. "Just occasionally. . . . Speaking of which, did you get a new, you know what?"

"They should have a pill for men," I said, kissing him.

"They're working on it," he said, "but till then . . ." He turned. "Oh, hi, Pam, hi, Maria . . . this is Rusty."

"Hi, Rusty," Pam said. "I'm really glad to meet you."

They were a funny couple. Pam was tall and thin with straight brownish blond hair. She had a really big nose, but it kind of went with her face. It was what you'd call an "aristocratic nose," sort of like a tapir at the zoo. Maria was short with a mop of black curls and big round black eyes. She was wearing a bright poncho striped in lots of bright colors.

We walked around together. Pam and Maria held hands,

so we did too. It felt good to be with Joshua again. I feel like at least he's the same and so I'm the same when I'm with him and the rest of it doesn't seem to matter so much one way or the other. We went into the cafeteria for a snack afterward.

"Hey, listen, I thought of an ending for 'Now-times,'" Pam said.

"It's great," Maria said. She seemed sort of quiet. Pam was very intense and talked fast. "Read it, Sookie." For some reason she called Pam "Sookie."

Pam said to me, "This is a poem I've been working on for ages . . . since I was eleven, practically. And this magazine said they liked it, but they weren't sure about the ending. But even before they said that I'd thought something was wrong with the ending and I'd changed it."

"I liked the ending," Joshua said. He was still holding my hand, under the table.

This was the poem. Pam read it in a quite loud voice. I saw some people sitting near us look our way and listen.

now-times for people with now-dreams

slightly
over to the right
a little to the left

you can bottle perfection
and it will sell
all you have to do
is mark down the price

then again
maybe it won't

you can talk faster and still
say less than we do
or you can talk slower
and say more

either way
we're saying the same things

sometimes love is another
anecdote for what happens
between things

over here a little more
that's right
but no—wait—over a little more
there, that's perfect

perfection is a stepping-stone
to imperfection

dreams are stepping-stones
to realities

spilling coffee on the newspaper
and putting on your shoes too fast
is another way of saying
slow down

is another way of saying good-bye
there, it's perfect now
you've got it
don't move it

or we'll have to start over again.

I guess I can't imagine ever writing a poem. Even if someone put a gun to my head and said: Write a poem or I'll shoot
you, I just couldn't. "That's really beautiful," I said when she
was done.

"Do you like it?" Pam looked pleased. "What do *you* think,
Josh?"

"Well, I liked it the other way," he said judiciously. "But
this is good too."

I didn't feel so jealous, having actually met Pam. Not just
that she was gay, but I got the feeling she and Joshua liked each
other more in a brother-sister way.

"You going to be in another movie?" Maria asked me. She
talked with a little bit of a Spanish accent.

"I don't know," I said. "I don't think so."

They all, including Joshua, looked at me in surprise.

"The thing is, it really disrupts your life," I said. "I didn't realize that so much with the first one. You have to travel and miss school and everyone looks at you differently. It's just . . . I don't know if I like it."

"My mother," Maria said, "she is an actress . . . on the stage, you know? She says it eats up her life, that the theater is like a cannibal, it eats you up alive."

"Well, writing is like that," Pam said, "if you mean it takes a lot of time and energy."

"But with acting you are giving *yourself*," Maria said, intensely. "Your body, your person."

"That's right," I said, relieved she understood. "It's like that. It's you."

"I could never do it," Pam said. "I once had two lines in a school play and I muffed both of them."

"I could never write a poem," I said shyly.

"Me neither," Maria said. "I have no artistic talent. My mother doesn't understand. She says it's as though I was born without a soul."

"She sounds like a bitch," Pam said, reaching over and taking a forkful of her pie.

After they left, Joshua and I walked hand in hand to Fifth Avenue.

"Josh?"

"Yeah?"

"I'm not positive I really understood Pam's poem."

"Well, poems are . . . What didn't you understand?"

"I didn't understand that part about perfection is a stepping-stone to imperfection and—"

" 'Dreams are stepping-stones to realities'?" he quoted. "Well, I think it means that you can't want things to be perfect, even though you do, in a way. You have to accept the ragged edges of things because things are always changing. Even if they were perfect, one second later they'd be different . . . like you."

I frowned. "What do you mean, like me?"

"Well, I mean, like our relationship. I want it to be just

a certain way. I want to control you, and I can't . . . and it makes me mad. It's frustrating because you have all kinds of feelings and ideas that are you, not me. I have to learn to accept that."

"I didn't know that," I said. "I didn't know you wanted to control me."

"Sure . . . I want to put you in a cage and be the only one with the key."

"I don't want to do that with you," I said.

"You don't have a thing about controlling people," he said. "You just flow with things more."

"I don't know," I said. I never thought of that.

"Pam is like me," he said. "She wants order, she wants perfection. She gets angry when people don't do what she wants."

"She's nice, though. She reminds me of Deel in a way."

"Yeah."

I hesitated. "I don't mind that you slept with her," I said, then added, "that much."

"Well, it wasn't one of the great sensual experiences of all time," Joshua said, smiling down at me.

"You mean, like with Marjorie?"

Joshua laughed. "Oh, Marjorie! Marjorie was just pretending I was a horse."

We had to use condoms that night, but I promised Joshua I'd go back to the doctor next week and get a new diaphragm. I think it's not just that it feels nicer for him. I think it's that my getting it shows him I care about doing it with him, something like that. But it was good, even with the condom. It just seems like since that time in California it's been different. I remembered what Felix said about Marvin. "It's not just that sex is good. Everything is good. Talking is good, not talking is good."

"It sounds like you got pretty friendly with him," Joshua said, "if he told you all those personal things." We were lying in his father's den.

"Why shouldn't he have? You tell Pam personal things."

"Yeah, but . . . I didn't realize you were that close to him."

"It was just—out there I didn't know anyone, and Felix is easy to talk to. He's gay, so you don't have anything to worry about."

"Who's worried?" Joshua said. After a minute he said, "Is he gay or bisexual?"

"I guess you'd have to call him bisexual," I said.

"Why would I have to?"

"Because he's done it with girls."

"How do you know?"

"He told me!"

Joshua narrowed his eyes. "Did he try to do it with you?"

I hesitated just a second. "No."

"Why didn't you answer right away?"

I sighed. "Joshua, come *on!* He has a lover. His name's Marvin and they really love each other."

"Was Marvin out in L.A.?"

"No."

"Gays don't have any sense of fidelity," Joshua said, his lips tight. "They just do it with anyone who appeals to them physically."

"You're really prejudiced, you know that?" I said. "They're just as faithful to each other as we are!"

"What does *that* mean?"

"Just what I said . . . they love each other and, well, sometimes they have fights, but—"

"Shit," Joshua said. "Felix was at that party after the screening, right?"

"I introduced him to you!"

"He was that thin, blond one?"

"Joshua, you *saw* him in the movie. He was Warren."

"The one you were fucking with?"

"In the movie!"

"Life imitates art."

"What does *that* mean?"

"People who act lovers end up falling in love."

I just looked at him. "You're really an idiot."

"And he's really handsome," Joshua said morosely.

"He's not that handsome," I said. "He's sort of the limp, sensitive type . . . like Leslie Howard."

"That's your type. You love Leslie Howard."

"I don't *love* Leslie Howard." I felt really mad. "And I don't *love* Felix. He's just a nice, friendly, understanding person."

"As opposed to me, I guess. I'm just a mean, unfriendly, not-understanding person."

"I didn't say 'as opposed to you'! You're always picking fights! You're doing just what you said. You're trying to control me. Stop it!"

Joshua looked taken aback. "Yeah, I guess I was," he said quietly.

"You have to trust me," I said intensely.

"Okay."

"I mean, really . . . not just say it."

"Okay, I will."

I put my hand on his shoulder. "I trust *you*," I said. "Even though maybe I shouldn't, but I just decided I'm going to, and I do."

Joshua pulled me close to him. "You look so pretty with your hair short."

"I thought you liked it the other way better."

"I like it both ways." He began kissing my neck. "Stop being so pretty, Rust."

Chapter Twenty-four

I had a talk with Daddy the next morning. Mom had dyed my hair back more the color it was to begin with. "I think I'm getting used to it," he said, looking at me. "I'll be nice for Ariel . . . delicate."

"Anyway, in six months it'll grow in," I said. "If I want it to."

"True," Daddy said. "A lot can happen in six months."

I wasn't sure what he meant by that. Maybe he's still hoping I'll stop seeing Joshua so much or stop fucking. I don't know. "Daddy?"

"What, darling?"

"The thing is, remember what you said about how girls my age don't get orgasms and how that shows they shouldn't be having sex because it's all due to peer pressure—?"

"Well," Daddy started to say. "I didn't mean—"

"Well, the thing is, I do now, I started to . . ."

"You—" He looked bewildered.

"I thought it would make you feel better."

"In what way?"

"Well, you said . . . Now you know I'm doing it for myself."

Daddy didn't say anything. He gave a deep sigh. "It's not a matter of orgasms, Tat."

"It isn't? I thought you said it was." I felt mixed up.

"No, that's one . . . factor, of course, but . . . my real point was that girls your age are influenced by a number of things, the media, what their friends are doing, movies. . . . It makes it hard to do something just for its own sake."

"Don't you believe Joshua and me are in love?"

He looked cautious. "I believe you . . . think you are."

I felt angry. "We *are!*"

"Thinking something doesn't make it so."

"We don't just *think* it!" My cheeks were flaming. "We *do* love each other. It's *not* just sex. We love *lots* of things about each other. We love each other just as much as you and Mom do!"

Daddy was silent. We just looked at each other.

"What I feel is this," Daddy said carefully. "Teenage boys have a very strong sex drive. That's been documented many, many times. Due to that, they may try to drag their girl friends along with them, as it were, and the girl friends may go along . . . just to be nice."

"But I'm not like that, Daddy," I said. "I don't do it just to be nice."

"You're sure?"

"Anyway, that's just a prejudice!" I said, flushing. "Teenage girls like sex just as much as boys do."

He smiled helplessly.

"They do, Daddy. You just have all these prejudices from the time you were that age. Things are totally different now. Anyway, Mom says *she* was interested when she was my age."

He sighed. "Amanda is . . ."

"What?"

"No, look, I have one foot in my mouth already . . . I better quit while I'm ahead. It's just that I have a certain nostalgia for what one might euphemistically call the good old days."

"But Mom says they *weren't* good old days. She says girls were really miserable then because if they did it people wouldn't marry them and they had to pretend they wanted to wait for their one true love when they were just horny. She says it was

all hypocritical and made people do awful things, like marry
people they didn't even *like!*"

"Oh, darling," Daddy said.

I smiled. "What?"

"I just want you to be happy."

"I *am* happy, Daddy."

"You know, celibacy isn't such a bad thing. There are
times when sex is important and times when it's perfectly fine
and natural to abstain."

"Sure," I said. "If I didn't have Joshua, I wouldn't be doing
it with just *anyone.*"

We went into the kitchen. Daddy poured himself some
coffee. I got out a bowl of blueberries and began eating some.
I realized I hadn't even had breakfast. I had the feeling we'd
reached a sort of stalemate, that we hadn't convinced each other,
but didn't feel like going on.

"Tat?" Daddy said. "I wondered—have you given any more
thought to *Lolita?* I spoke to Helen again today. They're evidently really wild about your doing it. She said they'd up their
price to two hundred thousand."

"Do you think I should do it?" I said. I hate arguing with
Daddy. I wanted us to be on good terms again. "Do you want
me to?"

"Well, I think it's quite an opportunity. They're very well
thought of, the script is marvelous . . . I think you could learn a
lot."

"Wouldn't I have to leave school?"

"You can make that up. Possibly Amanda can stay out
there with you during the filming."

"But she wouldn't want to leave her show," I pointed out.

"I think she might . . . for something like this."

"But, Daddy, I got such a slimy feeling when they were
interviewing me. . . . I don't think they care about my acting at
all. They were just watching me jiggle around."

"I can't believe that's all they wanted to see you do."

"I just felt awful," I said despairingly. It made me feel
terrible that Daddy didn't understand. "I'll be ogled by millions
of people. I'll be an oglee."

Daddy looked at me. "A what?"

"It's a word for someone that people stare at a lot in a kind
of awful way."

"I never heard of it. Interesting. I wonder what the deriva-
tion is."

"Will you be mad at me if I turn it down?" I said.

"I want you to do what will make you happy, and you're
the best judge of that."

"Do you really think I am?" I asked. "You don't act like
you do . . . about everything."

"Well, I think you can be very stubborn at times. . . . Tat,
I just want to help you with these decisions. I've seen so much
more of the world than you have. I—"

"I don't think I want to do it," I said.

"That's a considered opinion?"

I nodded.

He sighed. "Well, I won't call Helen now. Let's wait a
week or so. That'll give you a bit more time to think it over."

"Okay." I put the blueberries away. I was afraid I'd eat all
of them if I didn't. "Daddy? You know I've been looking at *The
Tempest* and . . . do you really think I can do it? It looks so
hard, speaking in poetry like that."

"You can do it, Tat. I'm sure of it."

"Will you help me, though?"

He softened. "Of course. Nothing would give me greater
pleasure."

"How was Mom in it? Was she good?"

Daddy looked thoughtful. "Yes, Amanda was good . . . she
had a kind of coltish quality, like Peter Pan. It's a pity really . . ."

"What?"

"Well, just that she never continued, that she got so caught
up with . . . all this other nonsense."

"Do you think it's nonsense?" I said, knowing how much
Mom would hate that description.

"Between you and me," Daddy said. "Yes."

It wasn't so bad about my hair at school as I'd dreaded. I
didn't get teased half as much as I had about being in the movie
and being on the cover of *People*. And I'm glad I did it. Now
I can walk down the street and not so many people recognize
me. A few times someone has come up to me and said, "Aren't

you . . ." and I just said "No" and walked away. I wonder if most people will think I'm crazy if I turn down *Lolita*, throwing away a chance to earn two hundred thousand dollars. But what would I do with all that money anyway? Daddy'd just make me save it. I just don't think I'm the type for Lolita. She didn't sound like such a nice person to me. Mom says she loves playing people that in real life she'd absolutely hate. She regards that as a challenge, to try and understand them, to get under their skin. Maybe that shows I'm not cut out to be an actress, I don't know.

———————

Tuesday afternoon something really strange happened.

I came home from school the usual time after Shellie and I had gone for pizza. I walked into our apartment. It was quiet so I figured no one was there. Then I walked in toward the kitchen. When I was just at the entrance to the dining room—the kitchen is about ten feet away—I saw this: Mom and Simon were standing there with their arms around each other. They weren't kissing or anything. They were just standing like that, perfectly still, like they were statues. I stayed perfectly still too. I didn't know what to do! My room is through the kitchen. I thought I might turn around and go outside again, but I was sure if I moved, they'd hear me. Finally Simon opened his eyes and saw me. Then Mom opened *her* eyes. But they didn't pull apart and rush around, trying to make it look like they were really just scrambling eggs and happened to bump into each other. Mom just smiled at me and said in a regular way, "Hi, Tat."

"Hi," I said cheerfully, relieved in a crazy way that the moment was over.

"Would you like a little tea, hon?" Mom said as I came into the kitchen. She and Simon had moved apart but in a natural way. "We're just having some."

"Okay," I said, "the mint kind."

"I think we may be out of it," Mom said. "Si, could you look? It ought to be behind that cannister there."

"I hear you're deciding about *Lolita*," Simon said, handing Mom the tea.

"Yes," I said.

"I always thought it was kind of a dumb story," Simon said.

"Dumb?" Mom said. "In what way?"

"I don't know." Simon pulled on his mustache. "Men like that who go after young kids seem kind of gross to me."

Mom laughed. "Gross!"

He smiled. "Okay . . . just unappealing, somehow."

"I think so too," I said. "Anyway, I can't even sing."

"They can dub it, sweetie," Mom said. "They often do. . . . Audrey Hepburn couldn't sing for *My Fair Lady*."

"That's cheating," Simon said, taking some brownies out of the refrigerator.

"What a nest of moralists I live among!" Mom smiled. "Cheating?"

"I know what he means," I said. "It's not *real* somehow."

"Either you sing or you don't," Simon said. "If you don't, you don't act in musicals."

I was glad Simon understood. We went into the living room and had our tea. I feel relaxed with Simon, despite the thing with Mom. Maybe it's that I can't take it seriously. I can't imagine Mom actually being in love with someone six years younger than her. I can't imagine her loving anyone but Daddy when it comes right down to it. But the way they were standing there together was so . . . intimate in a way. So quiet. I looked at Simon while he drank his tea. He's never married, not even once. He told me once he lived with someone, but they broke up.

After we had tea, Simon got up to leave. Mom went with him to the door. I was sitting so I couldn't see them, but I heard him say, "Call me, darling, okay?" Darling! Mom murmured something I couldn't hear. Then she walked back into the living room. She was wearing black jeans and a shirt with a big design of a parrot on it in black and white. "So," she said, looking at me. She had a funny embarrassed expression.

I reached for another cookie, just to have something to do.

"Tat, I'm in love with Simon," Mom said. "And he's in love with me . . ."

"Oh," I said. I know that was a dumb thing to say, but I couldn't think of anything else. After a second I added, "Does Daddy know?"

Mom frowned. "I don't think so . . . do you?"

I shook my head.

Mom smiled at me. "You know, I'm glad you came in when you did today, Tat, I really am. I'd been thinking for such a long time about how to tell you, but I couldn't, I couldn't quite work up the courage."

"How come?"

"I was so scared you'd be mad at me and I couldn't stand that." She looked at me with a kind of pleading expression.

"Be mad at you?" I would never have thought of being mad at Mom for that.

"I wanted to love Daddy forever," Mom said, sort of sadly. "I really did. I thought I would. I just—this happened."

"So, are you and Daddy going to get divorced?"

"I don't know. I want to *marry* Simon, I want to *live* with him, I want to *be* with him, not just in snatches of time, but together, having tea together, all that. I'm not good at arrangements, at little adulterous things. It's not my style, somehow. I know it's hideous to say, but I love being married. I guess it's never prevented me from doing things I wanted to do. I never got stuck in that victimy thing so many women do . . . but I feel *so* shitty about Lionel."

I thought about Daddy. "Well," I started to say, but Mom interrupted.

"If only I could find the perfect person for him! I've even thought of putting an ad in the *New York Review of Books*. You know, in those personal columns they have? 'Soon to be ex-wife searches for female companion for spouse. Interviews between two and five'! I know *just* what Lionel needs."

"What?" I was sort of curious.

"Well, he needs someone . . . lively, peppy, pretty, bright, not intellectual necessarily—"

"I thought you said he liked intellectual women."

"No, not really . . . you know who'd be perfect for him, actually? Andrea Markson. She's getting her doctorate in theater at Columbia but she used to act. She's little and kind of perky . . . do you remember her, Tat?"

"Is she blond and wears really bright colors?"

"Right, and hats! She looks *fantastic* in hats. The only trouble is she's seeing someone now and I think it's serious. . . .

Poor Lionel. I just don't want him to suffer. It's not *his* fault. He can't help his personality, and it isn't even that his personality is *bad*. It's just that he's . . . oh, and I'm so afraid he'll take it personally, first Dora, then me. He'll think there's something wrong with him, and there isn't, not at all. I just know he'd make someone deliriously happy if she only—"

"Mom?"

"Yeah?"

"I don't think you have to worry about Daddy." I told her about Abigail.

Mom listened in fascination. When I was done her face lit up. "Abigail! How sweet. It's perfect! It's *better* than Andrea Markson. It's perfect beyond *belief*. Young enough to fall for all the usual stuff, to be impressed, doting, in his field—they'll have something to talk about. Oh, what a relief! My God, Tat, I can't tell you." She came over and hugged me. Her cheeks were bright pink.

"She has Kerim, though," I said.

"Kerim?"

"Her little boy . . . he's just six."

"Six! Oh dear. Poor Lionel."

"You said he always wanted a son."

"True, but my goodness, at fifty . . . living with a six-year-old? Is he terribly quiet and bookish?"

"Not really."

"Still . . . no matter. I mean it's perfect, really. They'll manage. They just need a big apartment and help. Oh, I *pray* she'll marry him. Lionel is so tediously monogamous." She looked thoughtful. "Maybe I should call her up. I could give him a fantastic recommendation. He's a pretty good cook, limited, but good. His omelets are great. He's a decent father, don't you think, sweetie?"

"Sure."

Mom looked wistful. "He's a darling, really. She's lucky to get him. Good men are hard to find."

I ate another cookie. I was just eating cookies mostly out of nervousness, but they were also really good cookies from William Greenberg. "If Daddy's such a darling, why do you want to divorce him?"

Mom reached for a cookie too. "Tat, I just fell madly and *crazily* in love with Simon. I mean, it happens, even at thirty-nine. Lionel is just so . . . serious. He doesn't have a sense of fun, really. And I think fun is important." She looked grave. "I think fun is just about the single most important thing in life, when you come down to it. What do *you* think, sweetie? Will you like Simon as a stepfather?"

"Sure, he seems nice."

"He *adores* you and Deel. He says you're the brightest, most terrific kids he's ever *seen*."

"Deel'll feel bad because of Daddy."

"I know! Poor Deel! But she likes Simon. He's such a darling, really. He's just irresistible."

"Did you like him right from the beginning?"

Mom gulped down the rest of her tea. "Horribly, and he liked me. But the thing is, sweetie, when you're married, you, well, you try *not* to be attracted to people because, well, if you are, this is what happens! We really both fought it off for *ages*. We just used to go to the movies together and not even *touch!* It was just indescribably frustrating."

"And then what happened?"

"Well, then, you know, one day you feel—what the hell! I mean, you only live once and all that. And then you think: Well, it'll just be a one-night stand, we'll get it out of our system and before you even know where you *are*, whammo! You're totally, *wildly*, in love."

I hesitated. "That's how I feel about Joshua," I said shyly.

Mom beamed. "I know . . . Isn't it a nice feeling?"

"Yes," I said. "It really is."

Chapter Twenty-five

Mom decided to have Simon tell Deel. I guess she chickened out. I don't blame her. Simon and Deel went out one Saturday afternoon to a play and then they had dinner. The next morning I asked her how it had gone.

"You know about it, huh?" she said.

I nodded. I told her about walking in on them the week before.

"What's weird," Deel said, "is that he actually wants to *marry* her."

"Why is that so weird?" I said.

"Mom?"

"You're just prejudiced against her. She's really pretty and nice."

"Listen, I don't care . . . let them do what they want."

"Do you still want to live with Daddy?"

Deel looked horrified. "With some little six-year-old kid rampaging around the house? You've got to be kidding!"

"How did you know about Abigail?" I was really surprised.

"What do you mean, how did I know? They've been at it for years."

"What?"

Deel grinned. "Sure . . . you could tell a mile away."

"Tell what?"

"That she had a mad crush on him and—"

"But, how could you tell Daddy liked her?"

"Oh, Daddy's pretty transparent in an opaque kind of way," Deel said.

Deel is so smart. I remember how one of her teachers once wrote in a report that she was "terrifyingly perceptive." Imagine figuring all that out! "Do you think she made that dirty phone call?" I said, suddenly remembering.

"I don't know. It doesn't seem like something she'd do, exactly."

Daddy was coming back that night from a trip. Mom had said she wanted that time to talk to him. "Poor Daddy," I said. "He's the last to know."

"Oh, he probably knows," Deel said. "He's not so dumb."

"How could he?" I said. "You mean they've been pretending all along?"

"Pretending what?"

"Pretending to be happily married when they weren't."

"They weren't pretending anything . . . they *were* happy, more or less. They just happened to fall in love with other people."

I guess what I can't get over is how blasé Deel sounds. Maybe being in love with Neil has made the whole thing less important to her. "I might actually live with Neil," she said. "He's thinking of buying a loft with this friend in Soho."

"Mom and Daddy'll kill you!" I exclaimed.

"What do you mean? They'll be delighted. She'll want to be alone to cuddle up with Simon and Daddy'll be getting it all together with Abigail. They don't need us."

That made me feel awful. "We're still their children."

"I'm not a child," Deel said haughtily. "And neither are you."

"Well, I still want to live with them."

"With which of them?"

I thought a minute. "Maybe I could live part time with both."

Deel looked thoughtful. "Listen, let me give you one piece

of advice. Take weekends with Mom and weekdays with Daddy."

"Why?"

"If you take weekends with Daddy, you'll be stuck baby-sitting for Kerim."

"Yeah, I guess you're right."

"Simon said Mom's keeping the apartment."

"Well, since it's a co-op . . ."

"That'll be good," Deel said. "I can keep all my junk here."

I stayed over with Shellie that night since Mom had said she wanted to be alone with Daddy. Shellie was understanding and good. Of course, her parents have been divorced and remarried for ages so it doesn't seem so strange to her. "Yours stuck it out pretty long," she said, impressed. "A lot longer than most."

"I think they were happy," I said. "I think they really loved each other."

"Probably they did," Shellie said. "They usually do in the beginning."

When Deel and I got home Sunday night, everything looked just the same as usual. Daddy was in the living room, listening to music. But for some weird reason when I saw him, I burst into tears.

"Darling," he said hugging me. "Don't . . . it's going to be fine. Don't worry."

He said all this stuff about how he and Mom had stayed together because they loved Deel and me so much and wanted us to have a happy home, but now that we were older, it just didn't seem possible anymore.

"Will you live way down in the Village?" I said.

"Definitely not," he said. "We'll look for something right around here."

There were so many things I felt like asking him, like whether he and Abigail had liked each other a long time, like Deel said, but I didn't know if I should. "Did Abigail send you that valentine, Daddy, the one I thought was addressed to me?"

He smiled. "Yes."

"Did she make the dirty phone call, too?"

"No," Daddy said. "I don't know who that was. It will remain one of life's many unsolved mysteries."

I know this is awful, but I feel a little bit jealous of Daddy having another child, even if it is a boy. "Are you going to have more children?" I said.

Daddy sighed. "I think Kerim is going to be enough for me, at my age," he said.

"I'll help you with him," I said. "I think he's cute."

"That's nice of you, Tat." He beamed at me affectionately.

"Daddy, what if Mom hadn't fallen in love with Simon and wanted to marry him? What would you have done?"

"I wanted us to stay together," he said. "For you and Cordelia. I wanted you to have a solid base, something that would be there always."

"But what about Abigail?"

He reddened. "What do you mean?"

"What would you have done about her? I mean, aren't you in love with her?"

"Well, people work these things out," Daddy said, tapping his fingertips together. "There are many ways—"

"No, what I mean is, wouldn't you have felt funny? Being in love with one person and being married to another person?"

Daddy sighed. "Darling, all of this is much more complicated than it seems. People start out in marriage naturally expecting that, well, they'll be in love forever, but inevitably—"

"Inevitably?"

"Maybe not inevitably, but often something happens and . . . well, one can't just walk out like that. There are children, there's a home. People fall in and out of love all the time. But it's irresponsible to use that as an excuse to dissolve a marriage."

"Do you think Mom is being irresponsible?"

He hesitated. "I didn't say that."

But I could tell that's what he thought.

Poor Mom and Daddy! I feel so sorry for them. I remember how Deel and I used to worry about how they'd manage once we were both out of the house and in college. It's true, they have jobs and interests and things like that, but it does seem like they spend an awful lot of time worrying about us and planning things around us. We were terribly afraid they'd both go moping forlornly around the house, totally at loose ends, like those people Deel read about in *Passages*. Now at least *that* won't happen.

I hope they know what they're doing, though. I hope they'll be happy. It's funny. All these years they kept giving me advice about what to do and I took it because I thought they knew everything about everything. Now I'm not so sure. I don't *blame* either of them. I wouldn't have liked it if they'd stayed together just for me and Deel, being in love with other people. I don't care *what* Daddy says, that sounds awful to me. Well, I know one thing. When I grow up, I'm going to do it differently. I'm not going to marry until I find someone I know I can love forever. Even if that means waiting till I'm forty or never marrying at all! And if I have children, I'm going to be completely honest with them about everything. I won't pretend to give advice, if I don't know what I'm doing myself. I won't put on a false front.

When I got home from school the next day, I found Mom in the bedroom, just staring out the window. It's rare for Mom to just sit. She's a very active kind of person. When I came in, she jumped. "Oh, hi, Tat."

Ever since they said they were getting divorced, I have the feeling that Mom and Daddy have been avoiding each other. At least, they're hardly ever both at home together. I went over and sat down beside her. I kissed her on the tip of her nose. "Are you okay?"

"Sure." She smiled, but it was a sad smile. "I just hope I'm doing the right thing. Do you think I am, sweetie? Tell me honestly."

"You mean about Simon?"

She nodded.

"Sure, I mean, if you love him . . ."

"But, his being younger—"

"I don't think age matters . . . anyway, I think Daddy's wrong."

"About what?"

"Well, he says you should have stayed together even if you loved other people. But that sounds awful to me."

"I couldn't live like that," Mom said. "Maybe men can, more easily. . . . What else did Lionel say?"

"Oh, stuff about sex, like he always does."

Mom laughed. "What stuff?"

"I just think he wishes Joshua and me would stop fucking. He kept talking about how great celibacy is."

"Sweetie, you know, I wish you wouldn't use the word fuck quite so often."

"Why not?"

"Well, it's . . . fuck is like sauerkraut. It's such an *ugly-*sounding word."

"*I* don't think so."

"Maybe it's a euphemism, but making love sounds more romantic to me."

"But nobody says that anymore, Mom, nobody my age."

"I know." She looked wistful. "Fuck sounds so bare boneish, like two animals humping each other. Sometimes I worry that your generation is missing out on the romance of things."

I don't think we're missing out, not at all. I didn't want to say it because I didn't want to hurt Mom's feelings, but I think my generation is a lot better than hers and Daddy's. I think we're more honest about things. I know what she means about fuck, though. I used to think it wasn't such a pretty word either. But lots of words aren't and you still have to use them. Screw isn't that much better. It sounds like something a carpenter would do. And Daddy always said 'having sex' reminded him of ordering something in a restaurant.

Joshua was good when I told him about Mom and Daddy getting divorced. I thought he might make some snotty remarks about "I told you so" but he didn't. "It sounds pretty civilized, compared to some," was all he said.

"Yeah." I thought of Henrietta Combine, whose father kicked her mother out of the house after she tried to hit him on the head with a frying pan and how they had to live with her grandparents in New Rochelle for seven months. And Jane Weston, whose father ran off with someone who had three children of her own and then he and that woman, who supposedly wasn't even that nice or pretty or *anything*, had twins. I guess I'm pretty lucky.

"Simon seems like a good guy," Joshua said.

"Do you think it matters that he's seven years younger than Mom?"

"Matters in what way?"

"In any way?"

"If it doesn't matter to them, why should it matter to anyone else?"

"True." Joshua is like Deel in some ways—sort of detached about things. "You were wrong about Daddy," I said.

"I thought I was right."

"No! You said he was having an affair with his secretary. Abigail's not a secretary."

"Well, secretary, film editor—same difference."

"What do you mean same difference?"

"It's the same thing. Just one rung up. It's the same idea."

"Joshua! It's *completely* different. Abigail isn't some dumb blond secretary who just likes to fuck with married men."

"The Secretaries Union'll get after you for that statement," Joshua said.

"The Film Editors Union'll get after *you*," I said.

He hugged me.

"I hope they'll be happy," I said. "That's all."

"Oh, they probably will," Joshua said. "For a while."

"Why only for a while?"

"Everything's for a while . . . life is for a while. No, it's just sex is harder when you're that age. Everything's harder. Not like for us. For us it's easy. We just look at each other and . . . boing!" He staggered, as though he'd been hit on the head.

"Why do you always tease me?"

"I don't know. You're just a very teasable person and a very—" He started sliding his hands under my shirt, up to my breasts.

"Josh, I don't think I feel in the mood for doing it tonight, is that okay?"

He looked hurt. "How come?"

"I don't know. I just don't feel like it. And I thought, you know, you'd rather I only did it if I was really in the mood."

"You always seemed to be in the mood before."

"I wasn't . . . I just figured I sort of had to, that you'd be mad if I didn't." I know this is odd, but before, when I never used to come when we did it, I figured one time was more or less the same as any other. But now that it's gotten really good,

I like the idea of it being special, not just always doing it every time we see each other.

Josh was still scowling. "Is this some kind of power play?"

"No! What do you mean?"

"No sex unless you do what I want, that kind of thing?"

"No, not at all." I tried to explain how I felt about my parents putting pressure on me in different ways, like wanting me to be in *Lolita* or Daddy wanting me to break up with Joshua.

"But it's different with your parents," Joshua said.

"Yeah, but it's the same issue, don't you see, Josh? Wanting to please everybody and ending up doing things I know are wrong for me."

He grinned. "Sex isn't wrong for you. It's right. What could be more right?"

I went up close to him. "I love doing it with you," I said softly. "More than I ever did before. Don't you believe me?"

"Sure, Rust." His voice got husky. "Of course I believe you."

"I don't want you to watch me on the 'Today Show,' okay?"

"Okay, but why not? Are you going to tell lurid stories about what a fantastic lover I am?"

"No! I'll just feel funny if I know you're watching."

"I never watch the 'Today Show,'" Joshua said. "All those dumb celebrities shooting their mouths off. Big deal. Anyway, I have one right here and I can just turn her on whenever I want."

"You can *not* turn me on whenever you want!"

He grinned. "Sure, I can. Where's that knob?" He pretended to find one in the middle of my back. "Okay, here it goes. Instant color, sound . . ."

They picked me up for the "Today Show" in a limousine. Paula Myers, someone from publicity, went with me. I thought of what Felix had said about the Barbie-doll syndrome. She looked a lot like Kelly Neff, but she had a bigger nose. "It's a pity about Felix," she said.

Felix was going to be on the show with me, but he had to

go to the hospital to have his appendix out. "Yeah." I was starting to feel a little nervous, the fact that it would be just me.

"Carter Fenwick is a darling," Paula said. "Don't worry."

"I'm not," I said.

Actually, Carter Fenwick looks a lot like our social-studies
teacher, Mr. Belinsky. That made me feel more relaxed, like I
already knew him.

When the cameras were on, he stepped up close to me and
peered into my face. "I'm not trying to be rude," he said. "But
I'm trying to see if your eyes really *are* silver, Rusty. *May* I
call you Rusty? I know the public at large knows you as
Tatiana, which is certainly a beautiful name. Which do you
prefer?"

"Rusty, I guess."

"What color would *you* say your eyes are, Rusty? They
look slightly blue to me, but they do have a silvery cast to them
at a certain angle."

"I think they're gray," I said. "But it depends on what I
wear."

"Well, we'll let TV audiences decide for themselves, but I
would say today they're blue. That must be interesting—waking
up with different color eyes each day . . . and your hair, Rusty.
I seem to recall from *Domestic Arrangements* that you were, if
not *all* hair . . . there was certainly a lot more of it than appears
to be the case now. That wasn't a wig, was it?"

I shook my head. "I cut it."

"For any special reason?"

I hesitated. "Well, I'm going to be in *The Tempest* this
summer, my father's directing it, I'm going to be Ariel, and I
thought I'd look more like a fairy, a spirit, with short hair."

"That's quite a change of pace from *Domestic Arrangements*. . . . Do you think you can handle Shakespeare? I'm sure
you can. I just ask because I would think it would present
altogether different acting challenges."

"My father said he'd help me with the poetry part."

"Have you learned any of it so far?"

"A little."

"How about reciting something for us?"

"I could recite this song, if you want . . . I've been practicing it with my sister. She plays the lute."

"That would be lovely, Rusty. . . . I'm afraid I don't have a lute handy myself." He called off stage. "Anyone with a lute out there? I guess not. Well, you'll just have to make do without a lute."

Luckily I'd been practicing the song a lot and it's pretty short. This is how it goes:

Full fathom deep thy father lies
Of his bones are coral made.
Those are pearls that were his eyes,
Nothing of him that doth fade
But doth suffer a sea-change
Into something rich and strange.
Sea nymphs hourly ring his knell:
Hark, now I hear them—ding dong bell.

At one point my voice cracked a little, but I thought it went okay. "That was beautiful," Carter Fenwick said. "Thank you very much, Rusty. I see you have a very lovely singing voice in addition to your many other accomplishments. And I imagine that will stand you in good stead in your first musical role, Lolita, which I understand will be going before the cameras this summer."

"Only I'm not going to be in it," I said.

He looked surprised. "That must be a recent decision."

I nodded. Actually, I'd just decided right then. It just came to me that I don't want to do it. And I know now that I know just as much what's right for me as Mom and Daddy do, maybe more. "I thought about it a lot, though," I said.

"What made you decide to turn it down?"

"Well, I don't want to be a star. It takes all your time and energy. I want to finish school. Maybe I'll act a little in between, but that's all."

"That sounds like a very sensible decision," he said. "But it must be very hard, turning down offers like that, which I assume would make you a very rich young lady."

"My father would've made me save the money," I said.

He smiled. "Fathers are like that, aren't they? Spoiling all the fun. . . . Now just to divert for a moment, I imagine most of our viewers have seen *Domestic Arrangements* by now, and I wondered if you could tell us a little about how you came to be in the movie. I understand you hadn't taken acting lessons and don't go to any special school that emphasizes performing arts?"

"Well, Daddy knew Charlie, the director? And Charlie said he especially wanted someone who *hadn't* acted before. And he liked my hair. I don't know. I guess I wasn't that nervous for the audition because I never thought I'd get it. . . . I was really surprised when I did."

"I think many people were extremely impressed by your capacity to hold the audience's attention. You're on screen almost all the time, even if you're not always speaking."

I nodded.

"Your mother's an actress, isn't she, Rusty? Did she give you any tips in that area?"

"She said to always think of something the character might be thinking of . . . not to just start thinking things *you* would think of. . . . I tried to do that, but sometimes I'd forget."

"It certainly wasn't noticeable. You mean sometimes you'd be thinking, 'I wonder what we're having for dinner tonight?' when you were supposed to be concentrating on seducing your stepfather, that kind of thing?"

I nodded.

"What did you think of Samantha, Rusty? Did you like her?"

"No, not that much . . . I mean, if I met her in real life, I don't think we'd be friends."

"Why is that?"

"She's not that friendly to girls. She seemed more like she cared a lot about what boys thought of her."

"Don't *your* friends care about that?"

"Sort of . . . but that's not *all* they care about. They care about other things too."

"Such as?"

"Such as school or hobbies, what they want to do when they grow up, their parents, stuff like that."

"What are you going to be when *you* grow up, Rusty?"

"A doctor," I said firmly. "I'm going to deliver babies."

"That takes a long time, a lot of training."

"I don't mind," I said. "I'm prepared for that."

"I suppose one way in which your own background is very different from Samantha's," he said, "is that her life was concerned with coping with the complications of stepparents, stepsiblings . . . whereas you, from what I've read, come from a very stable home."

I hesitated. "Sort of."

"You don't?" He looked really surprised.

"Well, my parents are getting divorced. They just decided to."

"Oh. I'm sorry to hear that."

"That's okay," I said. "They're in love with other people so no one's upset or anything."

"I see."

"They still love each other, but they fell in love with other people."

Carter Fenwick looked at me as though he couldn't think of what to say. "That happens in the best of families, I guess," he said.

"Yes," I said. "It does."